Spies and Intrigues

Gabriel Samara, Peacemaker
Mr. Billingham, the Marquis, and Madelon

E. Phillips Oppenheim

Leete's Island Books
New Haven, Connecticut

Gabriel Samara, Peacemaker

Mr. Billingham, the Marquis and Madelon

GABRIEL SAMARA, PEACEMAKER

BOOK ONE

CHAPTER I

MISS SADIE LOYES, the manageress of the Hotel Weltmore Typewriting and Secretarial Bureau, set down the receiver of the telephone which had its place upon her desk and looked thoughtfully around at the eleven young ladies who comprised her present staff. She stood there, an angular, untidy-looking person, tapping a pencil against her teeth, unconscious arbitress, not only of the fate of two very interesting people, but also of the fate of a great nation. Portentous events depended upon her decision. A man's life in this teeming city of New York was a small enough matter of itself. The life of this prospective client of hers, however, waiting now in his suite on the eleventh floor for the help which he had summoned, was hung about with destiny. Meanwhile, Miss Sadie Loyes continued to tap her teeth with the pencil and reflect. Which should it be? The nearest and apparently the most industrious?

Her eyes rested disparagingly upon Miss Bella Fox's golden-brown coiffure. These were dressy days in New York and style was all very well in its way, but there was no mistaking the abbreviations of the young lady's costume — very low from the throat downwards and displaying a length of limb which, although perhaps sanctioned by fashion, paid no excessive tribute to modesty. Miss Fox's jewellery, too, was a little in evidence and there were rumours about dinners at the Ritz! On the whole perhaps it would be better to keep this particular young lady back for one of these western millionaires. Dorothy Dickson might do: a young woman of far more modest appearance, but a little careless with her shorthand. Possibly it was as well not to risk her on an important assignment. Then there was Florence White — expert enough, but a little mysterious in her private life, and the recipient of too many boxes of candy and offerings of roses from her clients to inspire her employer with thorough confidence as to her commercial ability. Then the pencil stopped. Miss Borans! Nothing whatever against her; efficient, self-contained, reserved alike in dress and demeanour, but with an air of breeding which none of these others possessed. Absolutely an obvious choice!

"Miss Borans," the manageress called out, in a shrill tone, "just step this way, please."

The young lady addressed rose with composure, pushed her chair back into its place, and approached her employer. Space was limited in the Hotel Weltmore and the Typewriting and Secretarial Bureau was really a railed-off portion of the lounge on the first floor reserved for "Ladies Only."

"I guess you'd better slip up to number eleven hundred and eighty," Miss Loyes directed. "I'll send a machine and the rest of the stuff right along — gentleman there in a hurry — his secretary caught the fever while he was in Washington. Samara, his name is — the Good Lord knows where he got it!"

The girl seemed to stiffen.

"Samara, the Russian envoy?" she asked.

"You've got it, honey. Speaks with an English accent, though, you could cut with a knife."

"I would rather not work for Gabriel Samara," the girl declared.

It took a great deal to surprise Miss Sadie Loyes, but this newest recruit to her secretarial staff had certainly succeeded.

"How?" she exclaimed. "What's that?"

Miss Borans had not in the least the appearance of a young woman of mercurial or changeable temperament. Nevertheless, she seemed already to be repenting her rather rash pronouncement.

"I beg your pardon, Miss Loyes," she said. "That was perhaps a foolish speech of mine. Number eleven hundred and eighty, you said. I will go there at once."

"Say, do you know anything of this Mr. Samara?" the manageress enquired.

"Nothing personally," was the prompt reply.

"You haven't worked for him before? He hasn't tried to be familiar with you or anything of that sort?"

"Certainly not."

"Then what's the idea, eh?"

Miss Borans hesitated.

"I am of Russian descent," she confided. "One has prejudices. It was foolish."

Miss Sadie Loyes had had a great deal of experience of the younger members of her sex, and she studied her employee for a minute thoughtfully. Miss Catherine Borans conformed to no type with which she was familiar. She was a young woman of medium height, slim and with the promise of a perfect body beneath the almost Quaker-like simplicity of her gown. She was rather full-faced, with a broad forehead, dark silky eyelashes and clear brown eyes. Her features were distinguished by reason of their clean-cut clarity, her mouth was perfectly shaped although her lips were a little full. Her expression was not to be reckoned with, for during the few weeks she had been employed at the Bureau she had wrapped herself in a mantle of impenetrable reserve.

"I guessed you were a foreigner," Miss Sadie Loyes remarked finally. "Well, anyways, this Mr. Samara is a great guy over there, isn't he? The New York Press, at any rate, seems to be giving him an almighty boom."

Miss Sadie Loyes had spent a busy life in narrow ways and, leaving out England, France and Germany, "over there" represented for her the rest of Europe.

"In his way I have no doubt that he is a great man," Miss Borans acknowledged coldly. "I was foolish to have any feeling in the matter."

She passed on with her notebook in her hand, a noticeable figure in the bustling promenades of the hotel, both from the quiet distinction of her appearance and her utter indifference to the cosmopolitan throngs through which she passed. She took her place in the crowded elevator, ascended to the eleventh floor, received a pleasant nod from the young lady seated on guard at the corner of the corridor, and touched the bell of number eleven hundred and eighty.

"Mr. Samara's right there now," the latter observed from behind her desk. "I guess he's needing help badly, too. They're talking of having to take his secretary away to the hospital. Stomach trouble, I guess. These foreigners eat different to us."

The door in front of them was suddenly opened. Miss Borans was confronted by a somewhat alarming looking personage; a man of over six feet in height and broad in proportion, florid, blue-eyed and of truculent appearance. Not even the studious sombreness of his attire could bring him into line with any recognised types of domestic servitor. He stared at this visitor without speaking.

"I have come from the Typewriting Bureau downstairs to do some work for Mr. Samara," she announced.

Typists, especially of this order, were unknown quantities in the world where Ivan Rortz had spent most of his days, but he stood aside and ushered her through the little hall to the sitting room beyond. It was of the ordinary hotel type, but flooded with light, overheated, and, as it seemed to her in those first few seconds, almost overcrowded with flowers. Everywhere they flaunted their elegance against the uncouth decorations of the room; a queer contrast of exotic beauty and pretentious ugliness. A man swung round from a writing desk to look at her,—a man who she knew at once must be Samara.

His study of her was superficial and incurious. She, on the other hand, brought all her powers of observation to bear upon the man whom it was her daily lesson to learn to hate. The illustrated Press of many countries had made his features in a sense familiar—yet, in a further sense, they had never done him justice. She saw a man of well over middle height, broad-shouldered yet with a tendency to stoop. His face was as hard as granite, cruel, perhaps, and as expressionless as her own, yet redeemed by a mouth which had wonderful possibilities of tenderness and humour. His hair was black and short, his eyebrows over-heavy, his clear grey eyes almost unduly penetrating.

"Well?" he exclaimed curtly.

"I am from the Typewriting Bureau," she announced once more.

He nodded.

"Where is your machine?"

"On the way up."

He pointed towards the book she was carrying.

"You write shorthand?"

"Certainly."

"Take down some letters. Sit where you please. I usually walk about. Some I will give you direct on to the typewriter, when it arrives."

She seated herself deliberately at the end of the table, opened her book, and glanced at her pencil to be sure that it was sharpened. Then she waited. He rose to his feet and stood with his back to her, looking out of the window. Presently he swung round, took up a sheaf of letters from the desk, and grunted as he inspected them.

"Rubbishy work," he declared, "but it must be done. Invitations to every sort of a function under the sun. One reply will do for the lot — 'Mr. Gabriel Samara regrets that he is unable to accept the invitation,' etc., etc.," his thick eyebrows almost meeting in a heavy frown. "Got that?"

"Yes," she answered.

He threw a selection of the letters on the table before her, destroying the remainder. Then he made his way back to the desk and loitered there with his hands in his pockets.

"I can't do these until the typewriter arrives," she reminded him.

"Naturally," he replied drily. "I was wondering about the rest of the work. Here is your machine."

There was a knock at the door and a boy arrived with the typewriter, which he set upon the table. Catherine Borans began her task. Presently the telephone bell rang. Samara motioned her to answer it.

"A gentleman from the *New York Hemisphere* would like to see you," she announced.

He shook his head.

"You can answer all applications from journalists in the same manner," he said. "Just tell them that Mr. Samara has nothing to communicate to the Press — with one exception, mind. A Mr. Bromley Pride will ring up from the *New York Comet*. I will accord him an interview. And, whilst we are on this subject, be so good as to inform the young lady outside that I will not have people waiting about in the corridor to waylay me when I come out. My lips are sealed. I have nothing to say to any one."

Miss Borans carried out her instructions faithfully. Then she recommenced her task. Suddenly Samara paused in his restless perambulation of the room and looked at her intently.

"Are you to be trusted, young lady?" he enquired brusquely.

She abandoned her typing for a moment and looked up at him.

"I should say not," she replied.

CHAPTER II

SAMARA was distinctly taken aback. His expression was one of incredulous surprise, mingled with some irritation.

"What do you mean?" he demanded.

"My reply to your question," she explained, "was truthful, though of course relative. I should not, as a matter of fact, care to be trusted with any of your important political correspondence."

"And why not?"

"I prefer not to discuss the matter further."

He smiled with gentle sarcasm.

"May I ask if this self-advertised untrustworthiness is universal amongst the young ladies of the Bureau from which you come?"

She considered for a moment.

"Of course you can send for some one else if you like," she said. "I would not trust any one of them with confidential documents, though. Your private secretary is the person to deal with them."

"But my private secretary," he confided, "is ill. They are talking of taking him to hospital."

She shrugged her shoulders.

"That is unfortunate," she admitted. "Still, you have an Embassy in Washington and a Russian Consul here. Surely they should be able to help you."

"You are without doubt a young lady of resource," he declared with an indulgent smile. "Nevertheless, there are reasons why I do not wish to avail myself of the services of any one having an official connection with my country."

"Then," she advised, "I should write my letters myself."

He stood looking down at her, his hands in his pockets, his thick eyebrows almost meeting in a heavy frown. She felt her heart beating a little more quickly. Notwithstanding her even manner and her very equable poise towards life, she was conscious of something in this man's presence which was akin to fear.

"Your candour," he said, "inspires me with a certain amount of confidence. I hate writing letters. My brain moves so much more quickly than my clumsy fingers, that anything which I put on paper is generally illegible. There is a boat leaving to-night for Cherbourg where I have a special agent waiting. It is necessary that I send an account of my negotiations here. What is to be done?"

"I can only repeat that, if your report has to do with your negotiations with the President, I should write it by hand and hope for the best," she rejoined coolly.

His eyes flashed. For a moment he seemed almost to lose control of himself.

"What in the name of all the Holy Saints of Russia do you know about my negotiations with the President?" he demanded.

"Nothing more than a few million people of the city," she replied. "I am an intelligent student of the daily Press, like most American girls."

He looked at her suspiciously.

"I am not at all sure that you are an American girl," he growled.

"I have lived in New York for twenty-three years," she said meekly. "You may not think it, but I can assure you that has not left me much time to imbibe the instincts of other nationalities."

He sat at the opposite end of the table, staring at her, his hands in his pockets, his expression curiously dominated by the uncertain curve of his lips. For a brief moment she wondered whether he were not laughing at her.

"Are all the young ladies of the Weltmore Typewriting Bureau gifted with such glib tongues?" he enquired.

"By no means," she assured him. "Believe me, I am quite an exception. I think I was sent because I was considered the most serious-minded."

"Heaven help the others!" he muttered. "Now listen. I am going to trust you to a certain extent against your own advice. I shall dictate to you all except the vital part of my communication. A great deal of what you are going to take down I should prefer you to forget. The most private part of all I shall write in my own hand, and God grant that some one at the other end will be able to read it."

Catherine Borans thrust a new sheet of paper into the typewriter and bent over her task. For half an hour or more the man opposite to her dictated. Then he took the sheets which she had typed over to his desk and drew pen and ink towards him.

"You can go on with the other work," he enjoined, commencing to write.

The scratching of his pen ceased almost as she addressed the last of her envelopes. He turned in his chair just as she had risen to her feet.

"Don't go yet," he begged, throwing another pile of letters upon the table. "There are all these to be attended to and it is necessary for some one to be here to answer the telephone. Besides, I have a question to ask you."

"A question?" she repeated doubtfully.

"Yes. I am a stranger in your country and I hope that you will gratify my curiosity. If I had dictated the vital part of this letter to you, wherein lay the fear of your probity? Do you mean that you would have sold its contents to the Press?"

"That would have been a temptation," she confessed, carelessly tapping the keys of her typewriter. "I am a working girl, you know, and am supposed to be well paid at thirty dollars a week. I think that any newspaper in New York would probably give ten thousand dollars for a true account of your conversation with the President and the arrangement at which you arrived. Fancy the clothes I could have bought and the countries I could have visited with ten thousand dollars!"

"Yes," he admitted thoughtfully, "I suppose I was running a certain amount of risk. By the bye, I presume it would have been the Press with whom you would have dealt?"

"With whom else?" she asked.

"There are others," he observed, watching her keenly; "politicians, shall we call them? — who would be curious to know the precise conclusions at which we arrived in Washington yesterday."

"Naturally," she assented.

"Even in Europe," he went on, "this business of secret societies and international espionage is a little on the wane. One nation only continues to use it as her great weapon. In America I never dreamed of coming across anything of the sort. Have I by some chance stumbled upon the unexpected, Miss — I beg your pardon, I have forgotten what you told me your name was."

"I have not told you my name."

"Please repair the omission."

"I do not see the necessity," she objected. "I am the young lady typist from the Hotel Bureau. You have been unfortunate inasmuch as I am the only one in the office likely to be interested in your mission and its results. To-morrow you had better ask for some one else. There are two or three there, perhaps not more trustworthy than I, but who will take down anything you dictate without a glimmer of comprehension. I should recommend Miss Bella Fox."

He shook his head.

"The name is sufficient," he declared. "I should dislike Miss Bella Fox and I could not dictate to her. I shall ask for you. Tell me how to do so."

"My name is Catherine Borans."

"And if I had dictated to you what I have written with my own hand, what would have been the nature of the risk I should have run?"

"I decline," she said, "to answer your question."

The telephone at her elbow rang whilst Samara stood scowling down at her. She turned and took the call. As she listened she frowned slightly.

"Tell me your name again, please?" she asked.

The name was apparently repeated. The girl spoke into the receiver.

"Please wait," she begged. "I will tell Mr. Samara that you are here."

She laid down the receiver and pushed the instrument a little away. Then she turned towards her companion.

"There is a gentleman downstairs who says that his name is 'Bromley Pride' and that he has called from the *New York Comet* to see you."

Samara nodded.

"That is quite in order," he assented. "He can come up. Please tell him so."

She did not at once obey. She was evidently perplexed.

"Since you are so much interested in my affairs," her companion continued, "I will tell you that the President himself, looking upon the paper which I understand Mr. Bromley Pride represents, as his official mouthpiece, has suggested that I confide to him a certain portion of the result of our negotiations."

"Indeed," she murmured.

"Recognising to the full," he went on, with a faint note of sarcasm in his tone, "and thoroughly appreciating that kindly interest, I would yet point out that this is a matter which is already decided. Will you kindly therefore ask Mr. Pride to step up?"

"I would do so," she replied, dropping her voice a little and holding the telephone receiver still farther away, "but, as a matter of fact, he is not there."

"What do you mean?" he demanded.

"I happen to know Mr. Bromley Pride quite well," she explained. "I am also very well acquainted with his voice. The man who is impersonating him downstairs is a stranger!"

CHAPTER III

GABRIEL SAMARA seemed for a moment puzzled and unable to appreciate the significance of his companion's words.

"In any case," he rejoined, "beg whoever is down there to come up. Mr. Pride has probably sent a substitute."

Catherine leaned over the instrument with an expressionless face.

"Is it Mr. Bromley Pride himself speaking?" she asked.

"Yes."

"You are to come up, then."

She laid down the receiver without remark.

"Well?" Samara demanded impatiently.

"The man who is below insists on it that he is Mr. Bromley Pride," she announced.

"And you still don't believe him?"

"I know that he is not," she replied. "I have worked for Mr. Bromley Pride. We are old acquaintances."

"Some journalistic dodge, perhaps," he muttered.

She began gathering together the paraphernalia connected with her machine.

"It is not my business," she continued quietly, "to offer you advice. I am not sure that I am disposed to do so, but as a matter of common sense I must say that I wonder at your admitting to your apartments a man who is visiting you under a false name when you have a document, presumably of some interest to the world, lying there on your desk."

Samara looked at her with wide-open eyes.

"But my dear young lady," he protested, "we are in the very centre of civilization. This is New York!"

"A city of which you are evidently extremely ignorant."

Her attitude suddenly inspired him with disquietude. He began to reflect.

"There are some people, of course," he muttered, "who would give the price of a kingdom to know this before I got home. But surely — here —— "

She interrupted him.

"Mr. Samara," she said quietly, "I have read several biographies of you. In every one of them, the chronicler has observed that, for a diplomatist of world-wide fame, you are possessed of a remarkably unsuspicious nature. I agree with your chroniclers. Good morning."

"Stop!" he begged her.

There was the sound of the bell. It was rung in quite an ordinary manner, but to both of them there seemed something sinister in its drawn-out summons. She looked at him.

"Your servant?"

"He is sitting with my secretary, Andrew Kroupki."

"I will answer the door," she announced.

"And remain, if you please," he insisted.

She turned away, threw open the outside door, and returned a moment later, ushering in a visitor. She made no comment as she stood on one side to let him pass, but both she and Samara himself studied the newcomer curiously. He was a pleasant-looking man, neatly dressed, with an amiable expression, and the shoulders of an athlete. He carried a black portfolio under his arm, which he set down carefully upon the table, close to the typewriter, before proceeding to introduce himself. His voice, when he spoke, was distinctly a home product and free from any foreign accent.

"I am very pleased to meet you, Mr. Samara," he said, as he gripped the latter's hand. "This is an honour I appreciate very highly."

Samara motioned his visitor towards a chair. He was wondering why his dislike had been of such quick conception.

"I must tell you, Mr. Pride," he explained, "that my own desire was to have kept absolutely secret the nature of my negotiations with your Government until I had had an opportunity of setting them before my advisers in Moscow. Your President, however, thought that complete reticence as to my mission would be too much to ask of your Press and that therefore an idea of the arrangement concluded had better be given to a representative journal such as your own."

"Quite so," the visitor murmured. "My paper holds almost an official position here."

"May I ask what post you occupy upon it?" Samara enquired.

"I am a member of the Board of Directors," was the prompt reply. "I am also leader writer on international affairs."

"And your name is Pride?"

"Yes — James D. Bromley Pride. You can speak right out to me. No need to keep a thing back!"

A quiet voice from the other end of the room suddenly intervened. The words themselves seemed harmless enough, but their effect was cataclysmic.

"There is surely some mistake. Mr. Bromley Pride of the *New York Comet* is in Philadelphia."

Samara himself was a little taken aback by the unexpected intervention of his temporary secretary. The expression on his visitor's face was momentarily illuminative.

"Who is this?" he demanded sharply.

"My name is Catherine Borans," was the composed reply. "I belong to the Typewriting Bureau downstairs. I have often worked for Mr. Pride. You are not he."

The pseudo Mr. Pride had regained his presence of mind. He pointed to the card which he had laid upon the table.

"This young woman's interference is impertinent and absurd," he declared. "If I am not Bromley Pride of the *New York Comet*, how is it that I am here at all? I received my instructions from the editor himself this morning."

Samara looked across towards Catherine.

"Telephone the editor of the *New York Comet*," he directed. "Ask him to send some one round to identify this gentleman. I do not wish to be offensive," he went on, turning to his visitor, "but your identity is a matter upon which I must be entirely assured."

The *sang froid* of this caller of disputed personality was amazing. Before Catherine could take off the receiver he stepped quickly towards the telephone and faced them both.

"The young lady has spoken the truth," he confessed. "I am

not Bromley Pride. I am, as a matter of fact, the representative of a rival newspaper. You do not need to be told, Mr. Samara, that here in New York a live journalist will go further than assume another man's name to get hold of a big scoop — and then some! He will risk more even than being thrown down eleven flights of stairs! Is there any price you are inclined to name, sir, for the particulars which you were about to hand on to the *New York Comet?*"

Samara's eyes flashed and his frown was menacing.

"An imposter!" he exclaimed. "I request you to withdraw at once from my apartment."

"And I decline," was the prompt and determined reply. "I may tell you right away that I am prepared to go to any lengths to secure this information from you."

"Indeed," Samara scoffed. "May I ask in what direction you propose to make your effort?"

The visitor stretched out his hand backwards and, from one of the folds of that harmless-looking black portfolio which he had left propped up against the typewriter, he drew out an automatic pistol of particularly sinister appearance. His mask of amiability had gone. There was a malicious gleam in his eyes, a cruel twist to his mouth.

"Gabriel Samara," he announced, "I am no journalist at all. I am, as a matter of fact, in another line of business altogether. It is up to me to discover what arrangements you have come to with the President, and how far such arrangements are going to help you with your plans in Russia. I do not desire to alarm either you or the young lady, but I am going to have the truth."

Samara smiled contemptuously. There was not a flicker of expression in Catherine's face.

"Pray set your mind at ease so far as we are concerned," he begged. "Neither the young lady nor I are in the least alarmed at your braggadocio. As a matter of curiosity," he went on, "supposing I were disposed to submit to this highway robbery, how do you know that I should tell you the truth?"

The intruder pointed to the typewriter and to the written sheets on the desk.

"There is only one task upon which you could be engaged this morning," he said. "I guess those sheets will do for me, anyway."

"And supposing by any remote chance I should refuse to give them to you," Samara persisted, "is it your purpose, may I ask, to assassinate me?"

"To be candid, yes," was the blunt reply. "But for the fear of canonising you in your own country, you would have been assassinated long ago. To-day things are different. Even Russia can spare you. Let the young lady fetch the papers and hand them to me."

"The young lady will do nothing of the sort," Samara declared firmly. "So much of the result of my mission as I propose to make public at present you can read in the *New York Comet* to-morrow. Now, if it is your intention to assassinate me, you had better get on with it."

The gun was slowly raised to a horizontal position. The face of the man behind it was hideously purposeful.

"What you don't realise," he said deliberately, "is that I am in earnest. You are a marked man, Gabriel Samara, less popular in your own country than you were and hated in mine. Sooner or later this would have been your end anyway, but listen — I'm telling you — your time has come now, unless you place those papers on the table in front of you — before I count five. Before I count five, mind, or I shall shoot!"

Samara looked around the room quickly. There was no fear in his face, only the reasonable search of a man who loves life for some means of escape. There was none which he could apprehend. His assailant was between him and the bell, and the breaking of a window on the eleventh floor — even if it attracted any attention in the street — would be unlikely to bring help in time. All the while the young woman behind the typewriter was watching him, with steady eyes and unmoved expression.

"One — two — three — four —— "

"I shouldn't worry," her quiet voice interrupted soothingly. "That gun will not hurt you."

There was a second's stupefaction, then the sound of a harmless click. The silence which followed seemed intolerable, broken though it was in a matter of moments by the piercing shrillness of the whistle which Catherine held to her lips. For the first time

Samara himself was dumbfounded; so was his would-be murderer, who was staring open-mouthed at his useless weapon.

"You see," the young woman who had dominated the situation explained to Samara, "this bungling conspirator — really he ought to take a lesson from one of the novelists — put down his satchel behind the cover of my typewriter, having opened it himself first — to get at his gun easily, I suppose. I saw the glitter, so whilst he was indulging in one of his little bursts of eloquence, I slipped out the cartridge roll."

She held it up. Outside there was the sound of a key in the door.

"I have a smaller gun of the same pattern at home myself, so I understand all about them," she went on equably. "And I hope you don't think I was blowing that whistle for its musical properties. It belongs to the hotel detective. What are you going to say to him, I wonder?"

The door was thrown open and a stalwart, broad-shouldered man entered hastily. He was in plain clothes but the stamp of officialdom was unmistakable.

"I'M BROWN, the hotel detective," the newcomer announced sharply. "What's wrong here?"

The pseudo Mr. Pride shrugged his shoulders resignedly.

"I'm a free-lance journalist," he declared; "got connections with half a dozen New York papers. I wanted Mr. Samara's news and I tried to bluff him into giving it to me."

"A little more than that, I fancy," Samara observed. "There wasn't much bluff about your automatic."

"Are you carrying firearms?" the detective asked.

The man who had called himself Pride handed over his gun.

"I'm through," he confessed. "If I could have bluffed Mr. Samara into giving me a report of his interview in Washington yesterday it would have been worth fifty thousand dollars to me. I failed and I guess it's up to me to take the consequences."

The detective was impressed but noncommittal. He appealed to Samara.

"Is this all there is to it?" he enquired.

Samara shook his head.

"The man threatened to assassinate me and appeared to be in earnest," he replied. "If the young lady there had not withdrawn the cartridges from his automatic pistol, he would probably have done so. I do not believe that he is a journalist at all. It is, I imagine, a political affair."

The detective turned to Catherine. Her deep brown eyes were filled with what appeared to be amazement. She shook her head.

"Mr. Samara was naturally alarmed," she said, "but I do not believe that he was in any actual danger."

The detective looked quickly from one to the other of the three people in the little tableau. Their faces were an interesting study.

Both Samara and his would-be assassin were obviously surprised; the latter, however, quickly concealed his emotion.

"You don't think that he meant business, then?" the detective asked.

"My impression is that he was only bluffing," was the confident reply.

"Then why did you blow that whistle?" her questioner persisted.

"I am rather a nervous person," she confided. "I hated the thought that there might be trouble while I was in the room."

Samara's amazement was genuine and sincere. He came a little farther into the centre of the apartment and stood looking down at Catherine.

"You didn't hear the click, then, when he pulled the trigger of his gun?"

"Did he pull it?" she asked. "Well, after all, it wasn't loaded." He pointed to the roll of cartridges.

"But you admitted yourself that you took those out of his gun."

She smiled enigmatically.

"This has been rather a shock to you, hasn't it?" she said. "I was quite worked up myself. I think we probably took the whole matter too seriously."

The self-styled journalist who, during the last few moments, had been suffering from an amazement equal to Samara's, recovered himself and played up to his cue.

"Of course," he declared, "it is ridiculous to imagine that the whole thing was more than a bluff. I wanted the news and I failed. Well, there you are! Fine or prison, it's all the same to me. I'll pay the price!"

"Have you any charge to offer, sir?" the detective enquired of Samara.

The latter considered the matter under its new aspect.

"If you will undertake," he stipulated, "to keep that man under surveillance until I am out of the country, that will satisfy me. I am convinced, however, that he is a dangerous person and, notwithstanding all that has been said, I am also convinced that he is capable of making a deliberate attempt upon my life. Under the circumstances, however, I can make no charge. If you take my advice, you will enquire into his antecedents and his connection with journalism. You may experience some surprises."

The detective was inclined to be disappointed at this tame conclusion to the affair.

"I guess we'll take you to police headquarters," he decided, turning to Bromley Pride's impersonator. "The clerk can ask you a few questions and we'll have you held. I'll take care of your gun, if you don't mind, and you can hand me over those cartridges, young lady. Will you step across with us to police headquarters, Mr. Samara, and state your case?"

Samara shook his head.

"In the face of the young lady's statements," he observed drily, "I don't think that my evidence is necessary. Do what you will about the man. I have told you the truth about him."

The detective and his charge left the room. As the latter neared the threshold he looked curiously back at Catherine. Her face, however, was inscrutable. The door closed upon them. Samara and his temporary secretary were alone. The former took a cigarette and lit it.

"In the first place, young lady," he began, "will you permit me to thank you for having saved my life? In the second place, unless you wish me to die of curiosity, will you tell me at once why you gave false evidence to the detective and placed me in a rather absurd position?"

Catherine continued her task of collecting her belongings.

"If you have no more work for me," she said, "the office will be expecting me to report. They will charge you for this extra half an hour as it is."

"I engage you for the day," he declared, frowning.

"You must arrange that with Miss Loyes," she replied coldly. "I have an appointment at three o'clock."

He took up the telephone receiver.

"Typewriting Bureau — urgent," he demanded. "Good. Mr. Samara speaking. Can I secure the services of the young lady who is with me now for the rest of the day? Good! Certainly."

He replaced the receiver and turned round with a faint smile of triumph.

"You belong to me for the day," he announced.

Her fingers strayed over the keys of her machine.

"My secretarial accomplishments," she reminded him. "Not my confidence."

Samara had never been more than a casual observer of women, had never studied them intimately, had certainly never appreciated them. Other passions had lain more closely intertwined with his life. He scrutinised Catherine for the first time with a half-reluctant interest, realising the finer qualities of her, the delicate femininity, coupled with an amazing self-reliance. He realised, too, that in the subtlest of all ways she was beautiful.

"Did you know that assassin whose cause you suddenly espoused with such vigour?" he asked a little abruptly.

"I never saw him before in my life," she declared.

"Then in the name of wonder," he begged, "tell me why you chose to sit there and tell deliberate falsehoods for his sake?"

"It happened to amuse me," she observed, smiling. "After all, you have nothing to complain of. I saved your life and subsequently I prevented your taking vengeance upon your would-be murderer. We might call it quits, I think."

Samara was immensely puzzled. He frowned down at her moodily.

"Sheer sentimentality," he muttered. "I hate cutthroats. It's a dirty business shooting at unarmed men."

"He wasn't a pleasant person," she agreed. "I disliked his moustache and the colour of his tie. Shall we decide to forget him? I am at your disposal for the rest of the day. Have you letters to give me?"

He shrugged his shoulders. It was a novelty, this, to find a woman with a will as strong as his own. Then he glanced at his watch.

"I have to go out for half an hour," he announced. "I shall be glad if you will arrange the typewritten sheets I gave you and pin in the pages I wrote by hand in the proper order."

She looked at him in surprise.

"But this is the document all the trouble has been about!" she exclaimed. "I might read it!"

He crossed the room to the desk where he had been writing, collected the sheets and brought them over to her.

"My dear young lady," he said, "you are welcome to read my little contribution — if you can."

She studied the closely written pages with an apparently puzzled air.

"So that is Russian," she remarked.

He nodded. "Looks terrible, doesn't it? Here is my servant back again. Ivan, bring me my coat and hat and watch over this young lady whilst I am away. With Ivan Rortz about the place," he continued, "no one will be likely to disturb you. I shall give orders outside, too, that no visitors are permitted to enter."

She was still gazing at those sheets filled with strange-looking words.

"Very well," she assented, "I will have this all in order by the time you get back."

To all appearance nothing had happened when Samara returned from his visit to a great banking house in Wall Street. He gave his coat and hat to Ivan who was sitting — a grim, silent figure — in the little hall. Then he passed into the inner room where Catherine, having apparently completed her task, was leaning back in her chair, turning over the pages of the document which she had pinned together.

"Well?" he asked with sardonic pleasantry. "Did you make anything of it?"

She laid it down and glanced up at him.

"Naturally," she replied. "I read it."

"But the Russian part?"

"The Russian part, of course. It was the most interesting."

He stared at her. "What do you mean?" he demanded. "You can't read Russian?"

She laughed. "What an accusation!"

For a moment he looked at her. All the time he had been troubled by a sense of vague likeness; not, perhaps, to any particular person, but to a type.

"Surely you told me that you were an American?" he asked.

She shook her head.

"Oh, no," she replied. "I told you that I had lived in America for twenty-three years."

"Then what are you?"

"As much a Russian as you are," she assured him, smiling.

SAMARA, though a great statesman and undoubtedly a great ruler, was a man of unsuspicious temperament and had more than once committed what might have turned out to be diplomatic blunders. He was also, however, at all times a man of action. He locked the door behind him, drew a chair in front of the telephone and sat facing the young lady whom he had engaged to be his secretary for the day.

"I think," he said, "we will have an explanation."

She smiled graciously.

"As I now know exactly the arrangements you have made with the Government of this country," she remarked, "I am perfectly willing to tell you anything you want to know."

"In the first place then," he asked, "are you a spy, and, if you are, in whose interests are you working?"

"I am nothing of the sort," she assured him. "I am in effect exactly what I seem to be. I am a young lady of New York City, of scanty means, earning a living by typewriting and secretarial work."

"But you are Russian?"

"My father and mother were both Russians," she acknowledged. "I recognise it as my country. I have lived here all my life, however."

"We are getting on," he said. "Is Borans your real name?"

"A sufficient portion of it," she answered. "The rest of it is not important."

"Will you explain to me," he went on, "why you first saved my life and then behaved so strangely with regard to my would-be murderer?"

"Now that I have read this document," she said, touching it with her fingers, "I am disposed to explain to you. I am not a spy in any sense of the word but I am a patriotic Russian. I belong to a little circle of Russians living here, who are filled with one idea as regards our country. We have not even the dignity of being a secret society. Every one knows everything about us and every one laughs at us. We look upon you with respect but as a very obstructive person."

"Upon me?" he exclaimed. "And you call yourself a patriot! Don't dare to tell me that you are a Bolshevist!"

"I am not," she replied indignantly. "I am free to confess that you have wiped Russia clean of a great curse. You have done a splendid work but you have not done it our way."

"What, in God's name, are you then?" he asked impatiently. "What party do you represent? I have dragged Russia out of the slough. I have reëstablished her institutions, her economic position. Already she is lifting her head amongst the nations of the world."

"I admit all that freely," she acknowledged. "It is because I realise what Russia owes you that you are alive. I do not wish, however, to tell you any more at present about myself and my political views. I saved your life because I believe that you are still necessary to Russia, but in a certain sense, I and your would-be assassin are alike. We share one great grievance against you. We resent — or perhaps some might say fear — your great scheme of demilitarisation."

Samara laughed a little harshly.

"Really," he said, "I never imagined that life in New York could be so interesting. The atmosphere of this room, however, is getting on my nerves. I have been through all I can stand for one morning. I can hear the click of that wicked-looking pistol even now. Young lady, where are your friends? Why do I not know them? I thought most of the Russians in New York who had aims or views had been to see me."

She shook her head. "Not all," she told him. "There are still a few of us who hold aloof."

"Miss Borans," he invited, "will you please do me the honour of taking lunch with me?"

She rose to her feet with alacrity.

"Not in the hotel," she begged. "It isn't allowed. Anywhere

else with great pleasure. I warn you, though, that my morning's work has given me an absurd appetite."

"I shall be proud to minister to it," he assured her.

They lunched at a secluded table in the balcony of the Ritz Carlton. Gabriel Samara, like many another man whose life is immersed in his work, and who finds himself committed to an unusual action in his everyday routine, was conscious of a curious light-heartedness. He felt as if he were a schoolboy at play. He, Gabriel Samara, taking his companion of a morning to luncheon in a restaurant!

"It intrigues me," she remarked, "to think that notwithstanding all your diplomats here and Mr. Bromley Pride of the *New York Comet* — who, by the way, telephoned to say that he is on his way back from Philadelphia and will see you this afternoon — I am the only person in the world with whom you can discuss the result of your mission to Washington."

"What I shall do with you, I can't imagine," he groaned. "Everything will come out in due course, naturally, but premature disclosure before I get back might do an enormous amount of harm. I have a very strenuous opposition to face, as you may realise."

"You need not be afraid," she assured him. "If you are really going to give me *lobster newburg* I shall keep your secret! I warn you that if I thought that disclosure would aid our own cause, not all the precious stones in your mines could keep me silent, nor all the gold which will soon be flowing into your banks. As it is you are safe."

"That is something to be thankful for, at any rate," he declared. "Miss Borans, treat me with confidence. You interest me. Let us talk frankly. If indeed you are a patriotic Russian, and have studied in any way the history of our times, you will know that I too am one. Wherein does my policy of reconstruction differ from yours? Why don't you approve of demilitarisation? Why should I consent to my country keeping under arms the greatest war machine in Europe to pull the chestnuts out of the fire for another nation?"

"There I agree," she admitted. "There must be no more wars."

"But for my errand here," he continued, "there would have been war within a few years. You cannot keep four million men under arms indefinitely without trouble. If you knew the tension at the present moment, the stream of proposals, the envoys who have been continually sent to me!"

She nodded.

"Don't tell me too much about them," she warned him. "You might find that I am not so much on your side as you think."

"But this demilitarisation," he persisted. "You must approve of that. We have three perfectly trained armies, of a million men each, ready to fight at a moment's notice. Why? You know why, and so do I. Isn't it a sane thing to disband a million according to my arrangements, now that I have been able to obtain a credit in Washington for the reconstruction of the industries for which we can use their labour? Think! In six months' time, not a man of that million will be bearing arms. They will be miners, or on the land, working in factories, on the railways, or road making, just according to their natural bent. Why, it's blood and bone in the country; a million productive toilers instead of a million wastrels!"

"Theoretically I agree," she acknowledged. "It is because I agree that I saved your life."

"Then why did you take his side?" he demanded bluntly.

"Because, although our point of view and ultimate aim are entirely different," she replied, "your would-be assassin stands, in a sense, for the same things that we do."

Samara gave the waiter an order and leaned back in his place.

"Explain," he insisted. "In as few words as possible, please. I am weary of not understanding."

"Why should I explain?" she murmured. "It is all very simple. We grant you that you have lifted Russia out of the slough, but we do not believe that your methods, that your system of government will place her back where she has a right to be."

The light broke in upon him then.

"I see!" he exclaimed. "Who are your friends here? Can I meet them?"

A sudden deepening of the little lines at the corners of her eyes and the twitching of her lips betrayed a genuine amusement.

"What a sensation I should cause if I took you to see them!" she laughingly informed him. "I can see their faces now when I present you! It would be amazing!"

"Risk it," he begged. "Why not? I am proud to look any Russian patriot in the face and tell him who I am."

She was interested.

"Yes, I suppose you do feel like that," she observed, after a moment's pause. "Why shouldn't you? Sometimes I, myself, make almost a hero of you. I'm quite sure that I shall always be proud to think that I have lunched with the great Samara. I shall be grateful, too, for other reasons. Do you find me very greedy?"

"Delightfully so," he admitted. "All healthy people are greedy. The vice of it only creeps in with the lack of self-restraint."

"I suppose," she remarked, "my manners are good, but if you only knew how I longed to see whether he has remembered the olives with the chicken. Hold tight to your chair now, please, and prepare for a shock. I am going to ask you a sickeningly obvious question. Tell me how you like America."

Gabriel Samara looked around him thoughtfully. He answered the spirit which prompted the question rather than the question itself.

"I venerate America," he declared. "Why shouldn't I? In a sense I am the champion of modern democracy. America is a shining light to all other nations, yet I maintain that Russia, with its unified population, has a better chance of reaching the supreme heights."

"I sometimes wonder," she sighed, "whether the true spirit of a republic can flourish in a land which knows such terrible extremes of wealth and poverty?"

"It is a drawback," he agreed. "That is where we in Russia have an advantage. We are framing a new constitution. Our laws are adapted to meet existing circumstances. Communism is dead, but we shall never tolerate the multimillionaire."

"Do you think," she asked, "that Germany will ever let you become really powerful?"

"Not willingly," he replied, "but the monarchical sentiment in Germany is not strong enough yet to upset the government of the country. Germany, of course, will bitterly resent the success of my mission over here, but she will have to get rid of her republic before we need take the war scare seriously."

She looked at him across the table.

"Do you think that the monarchist party in Germany is gaining ground?" she asked.

"I know nothing about German internal affairs," he answered evasively. "I have more than enough to do to keep in touch with the trend of opinion in my own country."

The thread of conversation appeared to be suddenly broken. Samara began to ask questions about the people by whom they were surrounded. The restaurant on this fine spring morning seemed like a great nosegay of brilliant flowers. Three quarters of the guests were women and it was a season of abandonment in colour, with yellow and pink predominating. New York too, no less than Paris, was a city of subtle perfumes, cunningly distilled and exotic. Samara, smoking his cigarette with the air of an epicure, found much to interest him in his environment.

"These people are like Russians in one way," he remarked. "They spend their money."

"I have a German friend here," she confided, "who argues that there is always more extravagance under a republic. His point is that the *bourgeoisie* make money easily and spend it readily. The aristocrat who has to keep up a great appearance is compelled to be the more miserly of the two, apart even from the question of good taste."

"Is this the prelude to a discussion upon the ethics of government?" he suggested, smiling.

"Indeed, no," she replied. "I am not so presumptuous. My principles are matters of instinct with me. I do not argue about them. I accept them."

She helped herself to one of his proffered cigarettes and he paid the bill.

"Quite the monarchical touch," he observed. "If you are postponing your return to your native land, however, until there is a Tzar upon the throne, I am afraid you are doomed to a very long spell of homesickness."

"Who knows?" she exclaimed carelessly. "Revolutions are

rather the fashion just now. I may return to find you in chains and the knout cracking once more."

She had spoken lightly enough, but he chose to take her seriously.

"As a matter of fact," he confided, "there is a certain amount of very disquieting truth in what you say. I have stamped out Bolshevism in Russia forever. The spirit of anarchistic communism, at any rate, is dead, but I honestly believe that, especially amongst the peasantry, there is an unwholesome sort of craving for the burdens of Tzardom."

"That is almost the most interesting thing that you have said," she remarked, as they rose to go. "Thanks very much for my wonderful luncheon. Do you really require my services this afternoon?"

"Without a doubt," he insisted. "I am going on from here to pay a call. At four o'clock I shall be back in my rooms. Let me find you there, if you please."

They were about to part in the hallway of the restaurant, when Mrs. Saxon J. Bossington intervened. She sailed down upon them with the air of taking both into custody; ample, fashionably dressed, a triumph of artificiality, forty — or perhaps fifty — lisping with the ingenuousness of childhood.

"Why, if this isn't our little working girl!" she exclaimed, gripping the none too willing hand of Samara's companion. "Well, well, is this where you young women who earn your livings lunch as a rule? The number of times I've asked you to make one of our little luncheon parties here, Catherine, and you have always told me 'nothing doing in working hours.'"

Catherine presented the appearance of a young person of good breeding, striving to be polite whilst in bodily pain.

"To-day is an exception," she said. "I am lunching with a fellow countryman."

Mrs. Saxon J. Bossington smiled graciously. She had just sufficient discernment, born of her social cravings, to appreciate distinction even when it did not conform to type.

"Present your friend," she suggested.

Catherine, with a deprecating glance at her companion, murmured his name. Samara bowed — a little lower perhaps than was usual in a city where hand-shaking is almost sacramental. He did not seem to notice, however, the pearl-gloved hand so frankly extended.

"You're not Mr. Gabriel Samara, who has come over from Russia to see our President?" she exclaimed breathlessly.

"My name," he replied, "is Gabriel Samara. I know of no other. I have just come from Washington where your President was good enough to receive me."

Mrs. Saxon J. Bossington simply quivered with excitement. It was without a doubt a most thrilling meeting.

"I want to tell you, Mr. Samara, right now," she declared, "that you've met the one woman in New York who has read every line that's been written about you since you landed and who has been just crazy to meet you. This is going to be wonderful. Catherine's bringing you to-night, of course?"

"I beg your pardon," he observed, genuinely perplexed. "I have not the honour —— "

"Catherine? Miss Borans, of course — you will come to-night with her? It's the meeting, you know. Why, it will be great! Prince Nicholas is coming, General Orenburg, Colonel Kirdorff, the dear Grand Duchess — all of them! It's most opportune!"

Samara turned to his companion. He was guilty of a gross breach of manners. He addressed her in Russian.

"What is this woman talking about?" he demanded.

Mrs. Bossington was delighted. She rippled on before Catherine had a chance to reply.

"Such a wonderful language!" she exclaimed. "Sometimes they talk it in conclave and I can assure you, Mr. Samara, it just thrills me. Some people call it harsh. I love it. Don't you think, Catherine dear," she went on, her tone becoming almost wheedling, "that you could persuade Mr. Samara to come a little earlier and dine with us first to-night — just a very small affair — twenty covers or so? Joseph would be tickled to death."

Catherine laid her hand upon the arm of her loquacious acquaintance.

"Mrs. Bossington," she said, "I am afraid you don't quite understand. Mr. Samara is a Russian, of course, and a very distinguished one, but his aims are scarcely the aims of our friends. I do not think we should agree. It never even occurred to me to bring Mr. Samara to the meeting."

Mrs. Bossington was horrified.

"My dear," she cried, "you're crazy! There you are, a dozen of you, all Russians out of a home and out of a country and longing to get back again. Why, here's the man who can help you. Get together and talk it over. I'm only thankful it's my turn to entertain you. I should be the proudest woman in New York to think that Mr. Samara had paid me a visit. If we could only fix up that dinner!"

Gabriel Samara was a little weary. His glance was straying through the windows to the sunlit streets. The close atmosphere of the lounge, the heavy perfumes, the din of conversation were beginning to nauseate him.

"I have a call to make in the hotel, Miss Borans," he reminded her. "If you and Mrs. — Mrs. Bossington, I believe — will excuse me, I will take my leave. The Ambassador from my country is expecting me at half-past two."

His would-be hostess gripped him by the arm.

"Not one step do you move from here," she insisted, "until you have promised to come and see these good people to-night."

"So far as that is concerned," he replied, "I am in Miss Borans' hands. If it is her wish — if they are country people of mine who desire to meet me — I shall be charmed."

Mrs. Saxon J. Bossington had attained her object. She saw some friends to whom it was necessary that she should immediately communicate the fact that she had been discussing Russian politics with Mr. Gabriel Samara. With a little shower of farewells she departed. Catherine glanced up at her companion. There was something of mutual comprehension in their smile.

"It appears to be our fate to spend the evening together," he remarked.

"We shall see," she murmured. "Shall I expect you about four?"

"I shall not be later," he promised.

Samara watched his departing companion as she passed through the little throng of gossiping women on her way to the street. Amongst all this flamboyant elegance, these vivid splashes of colour and elaborate toilettes, there was something almost aloof in her still drabness — her disdain of all those freely displayed arts. Yet, so far as sheer femininity was concerned, Samara felt the spell of her so strongly that not one of the many attractive women by whom he was surrounded, several of whom looked at him with friendly curiosity, seemed in any way comparable to her. He watched her disappear and turned back into the hotel to keep an appointment with the Ambassador of his country, who had followed him from Washington the night before. His eagerness for the approaching discussion, however, had suddenly evaporated.

"I am, after all, a pagan," he muttered, as he stepped into the lift to make his call. "For the moment I had forgotten Russia."

CATHERINE, on her return to Samara's suite at the Hotel Weltmore, found the sofa in the sitting room occupied by a young
man who stared at her with curious eyes as she entered. He was
tall, phenomenally thin and phenomenally sallow. The hollows
in his cheeks were so pronounced that the higher bones themselves seemed almost on the point of pushing their way through
the flesh. His coal-black hair was long and dishevelled, and his
unshaven condition added to the wildness of his appearance.
Catherine, with the instinct of her sex, took note only of his
obvious ill health, and her tone as she addressed him was kindly.

"You must be Andrew Kroupki, Mr. Samara's secretary," she
said, removing the cover from her typewriter. "Mr. Samara
scarcely expected that you would be well enough to get up to-day."

"I cannot lie in bed here," he declared feebly. "I become nervous.
It is terrible to be ill so far from home. There is only Ivan, and
Ivan hates me."

"Why should he do that?" she asked soothingly.

"Because he and I live closest to the chief," was the impatient
reply. "Ivan is jealous. He is very foolish. It is his strength which
protects, and my brains. We are allies but he will not have it so.
Have you been working for the Chief?"

"All the morning," she answered. "I still have a long list of
invitations to decline. He is returning at four o'clock."

"Do you know anything about a despatch for Cherbourg?" he
continued. "My brain was on fire this morning. I could not even
ask."

"The despatch is finished and Mr. Samara took it away with
him," she confided. "Part of it I typed and the more important
part he wrote in by hand."

The young man closed his eyes for a moment.

"It is terrible to be like this," he groaned, "when one is needed."

She rose from her seat and came over to the couch, laid her hand for a moment upon his head and felt his pulse.

"Have you seen a doctor?" she enquired.

"Yes," he answered; "I am taking some medicine. He told me to lie in bed and let my brain rest."

"Would you like a drink? Some iced water?"

He made a little grimace.

"I hate it," he muttered. "In Russia we do not drink water."

She drew a phial of eau de Cologne from her bag, soaked her handkerchief with it and laid it upon his head.

"That is very pleasant," he sighed gratefully.

"I wonder," she suggested, "would you care 'for some tea — tea with lemon, freshly made and clear coloured?"

"Wonderful," he assented eagerly.

She sent for the floor waiter, procured some materials, and busied herself for a few minutes with the equipage which he brought. The young man sipped the beverage when she handed it to him with something approaching ecstasy.

"I have had nothing like this since the fever came," he told her. "What is your name?"

"Catherine Borans."

He looked at her with wide-open eyes. Already there was a gleam of something more than admiration in them.

"Where do you come from?" he asked.

"The Weltmore Typewriting Bureau downstairs," she replied. "Now try to go to sleep for a little time. Do you think that the sound of the typewriter will disturb you? If so, I will write some of these letters by hand. I do not think that Mr. Samara would mind."

He shook his head.

"It will not disturb me," he assured her. "I should like to lie here and watch you work. You are a very wonderful person. Are you an American?"

She smiled.

"You are not to talk any more," she enjoined. "Close your eyes and try to sleep."

"I like to watch you," he murmured.

Catherine was a person unafflicted with self-consciousness, so she continued her work methodically, although every time she looked up she found his eyes upon her.

"More tea," he begged once.

She gave him another cup, and renewed the eau de Cologne on her handkerchief. Presently he closed his eyes. When Samara returned he was sleeping peacefully.

"You didn't tell me that I was to be hospital nurse as well as typist," she remarked, speaking in an undertone.

Samara crossed the room and looked down at the young man.

"You've done very well with him," he said. "His respiration is better, the fever is down. What have you been giving him? Tea? It smells very good. I should like to try it myself."

She made some more and he drank it gratefully. He appeared a little tired; his interview had not been altogether satisfactory.

"You have the Russian touch for tea," he told her. "There is nothing like it in the world. I drink wines and spirits — everything — but tea like this is better than all."

"And better for you," she observed.

"Sometimes its exhilaration is not rapid enough," he said.

The young man stirred in his place. His master's tone was suddenly kind as he turned towards him.

"You are feeling better, Andrew?" he asked in Russian.

"Much better," was the eager reply. "This young lady has been very good to me. Did you find her by accident, sir?"

"By accident," Samara assured him.

"She is intelligent?"

"She is adequate," was the expressionless reply. "I need your help, though, Andrew. Get well quickly."

"I am almost well now," the young man declared, sitting up. "In a few days I shall be able to do anything. It is fortunate for you, master," he went on, still speaking in his own language, "that you hate women."

"I do not hate them," Samara protested. "I simply do not appreciate them."

"You hate them," Andrew repeated emphatically. "Even when you play with them you show it in your manner. It is fortunate for you. This young lady might cause you trouble."

Samara glanced behind uneasily. Catherine was continuing her task with immovable face.

"I am going to take you to your room now, Andrew," he announced. "Your leaving it was against the doctor's orders."

"I am content," the young man assented. "I am very weary, but I feel sleep coming."

They crossed the room together, the young man leaning on Samara's arm. At the door he turned back.

"Thank you very much, miss," he said in English.

"Get well quickly," she enjoined, with a smile.

Samara returned a few minutes later. Catherine leaned back in her chair.

"Thank you for being kind to Andrew," he said.

"He seems delicate," she remarked.

"A little neurotic, and, I am afraid, consumptive," Samara agreed. "He is the son of one of my great friends, the man who first helped me fight against the anarchists. When he died I took the lad to work for me. He is able and devoted, but he has exaggerated ideas of everything. Your kindness has been good for him. He is already asleep."

"He is very devoted to you," she said.

"Almost foolishly so," he admitted. "There are times when I have trouble with him. Tell me now about these friends of yours. I see that I was right in my assumption. You and your companions are amongst those who hope for the impossible things."

"If I may, I will explain," Catherine suggested. "My mother died in this country when I was three years old and left as my patroness the exiled Grand Duchess Alexandrina, Sophia of Kossas. I have been brought up, therefore, indirectly attached to a strange little circle. Would you really like to know about them?"

"Most certainly," he assured her emphatically. "They are Russians."

"Very well, then," she continued. "There are six of them. We live in an apartment house a long way the other side of Central Park. We all share a sitting room for the purposes of economy. Every one is poor, every one is shabby, every one is miserable. Now, if you wish, I shall tell you about them, one by one."

"If you please," he murmured.

"First of all, then, there is Nicholas Imanoff," she began. "He is the nearest living descendant of the last Tzar. He is twenty-five years old, was educated with great difficulty at Harvard, and ekes out an embittered existence selling bonds on commission for a New York stock-broking firm. He calls himself Mr. Ronoff, but every one knows who he is, and I think it very probable that the little business he gets is because he appeals to people's curiosity. He is rather bad-tempered, does not take enough exercise, drinks a little more than is good for him, but is quite capable at times of justifying his descent."

"An admirable sketch," Samara declared. "Proceed, please."

"I will speak of my patroness, the Grand Duchess," Catherine continued. "She is a fair, fat old lady of sixty-eight. She dresses abominably, her walk is almost a waddle, she takes no care of her person, and she earns a few dollars a month by making artificial roses. She calls herself Mrs. Kossas."

"Less interesting," Samara commented. "Proceed."

"There is Boris Kirdorff," she went on. "Sometimes I believe he uses an obsolete title of 'Colonel.' I think that he has more brains than any of the others, and certainly less conscience. He comes from a great family, as I dare say you know. His is a cold, unattractive personality, but he is a born schemer and if ever the others have hopes it is through him they are expressed. He is secretary to a very *bourgeois* card club, but I think the greater part of his small earnings is spent in gambling.

"General Orenburg is a more pleasing personality, but he is older. He is the only one who has any money and that is a very small amount. He puts it into the common stock. He spends his whole day at the libraries, and he has fifteen different schemes for bringing about a monarchist rising in Russia."

"Any other young people?" Samara enquired.

"There is Cyril Volynia Sabaroff of Prem and his sister, Rosa. Cyril is interested in the sale of automobiles. His income varies a great deal, though. Rosa is engaged as reception clerk at a photographer's shop. They are less serious than the rest of us, and, if only they had money, I think they would be content to stay in this country for the remainder of their days. The others of us, as you may have gathered, have only one desire in life, and that is to return to Russia."

"Why not?" Samara observed. "You are all Russians. You have a perfect right to live in your native land."

There was a moment's silence. Catherine was gazing across the top of her typewriter at her companion. Samara was lounging on the other end of the table, his hands in his pockets, a cigar which he had lighted, without remark, between his lips.

"You seem to forget," she said quietly, "that there is such a thing as a decree of banishment against the absentee aristocracy of Russia."

"Rubbish!" he exclaimed. "Out of date! Antediluvian! I'll revoke it the day I get back. You can consider it revoked now. Mind you," he went on, striking the table a mighty blow with his fist, "there is another decree in Russia which will never be suspended. It is my aim to make Russia the freest country in the world, but if I find an anarchist in café, street or public meeting, he is shot within the hour. Against anarchists the law of Russia is as the law against vermin — death; summary, unquestionable! There is no one else calling himself a Russian who is not welcome to take his place amongst the community."

"Will you repeat this to my friends?" she asked and there was very nearly a tremor in her tone.

"Take me to them," he invited.

"I shall call for you at nine o'clock," she promised. "Please let us work now. I feel that I am wasting your time."

It was a dejected, almost a pathetic little crowd gathered round the sparsely laid dinner table in a back apartment of the Amsterdam Avenue Private Hotel. The furniture, the table appointments, the faded carpet upon the floor were all according to type. The prospect from the solitary window was of brick and masonry and a jumble of telegraph wires. Occasionally the room shook with the thunder of an elevated train passing near by. A coloured servant, whose dress seemed to have been put on in scraps, was serving the meal from the sideboard. There were two jugs of water and a carafe of light beer upon the table; in its centre a little vase with a handful of cheap flowers. General Orenburg sat at one end and Alexandrina of Kossas at the other. Conversation was intermittent. They all appeared to be engrossed in their own thoughts.

"Catherine is late to-day," Alexandrina observed.

"Catherine is late but here," the young lady in question remarked, opening the door in time to hear the sound of her own name.

They all looked at her with interest. She seemed somehow or other to represent the vitality of the little circle, which brightened visibly at her coming. Kirdorff, whom nothing in this world escaped, watched her curiously, as she took her place. His was a queer, hawklike face with black eyes and indrawn lips. His hair, thin about the temples and carefully brushed, was unexpectedly light-coloured.

"Catherine has something to tell us," he observed.

"I have something very wonderful to tell you," Catherine confessed, as she pushed aside a bowl of very unappetising soup. "You need not bother about my dinner. I lunched at the Ritz Carlton, and I shall eat a great many of Mrs. Saxon J. Bossington's sandwiches later on. Listen to me, everybody. Of all men in this world, with whom do you think I lunched? It is absurd to ask you to guess. I lunched with Gabriel Samara!"

A thunderbolt through the roof could have scarcely created a greater sensation. There were exclamations in every key. Then, with the passing of that first wave of astonishment, came a fierce and intense interest. Kirdorff leaned across the table, his fists clenched, his eyes protuberant. The Grand Duchess talked to herself in broken sentences. Nicholas Imanoff spoke.

"How came you to meet Samara?" he demanded.

"In the most natural way possible," Catherine explained. "He telephoned to the Bureau for a typist — his secretary has been taken ill. The assignment was given to me. My work pleased him. He invited me to lunch."

"You lunched with that man!" Nicholas muttered.

"There are very few men I wouldn't lunch with at the Ritz Carlton," Catherine rejoined coolly, "but I will tell you this now of Gabriel Samara. He stands for other principles than ours, but he is a man. He is what Cyril Volynia here, when he came back from England, called a 'sportsman.' We met Mrs. Saxon J. Bossington, and she spoke of to-night. Samara asked me who my Russian friends were, and I told him. Then listen to what he said. 'They are Russians. Why do they live in New York? Why do they not go back to Russia?' "

"Samara said that!" Kirdorff intervened.

"Absolutely!" Catherine continued. "I reminded him of the decree of banishment. He scoffed at it. He undertook that it should be revoked. He has told me in plain words that you are all of you free to return to Russia."

There was an almost awed silence. Alexandrina was sobbing quietly into her handkerchief. Kirdorff was drumming upon the table.

"Free to return!" he muttered. "Why not? If one could only breathe there — could live —— "

"Or die," General Orenburg interrupted fervently, "so long as it was in Russia!"

"There is surely a living to be made there as well as here," Cyril Volynia declared. "Perhaps my firm would let me open a branch depot in Moscow."

"Listen," Catherine warned them, "you must make up your minds to this. It is necessary and it may lead to great things. You must meet Samara."

The Grand Duchess left off sobbing. The suggestion was so astounding that the words themselves seemed to convey no definite meaning to her.

"Meet Samara!" Kirdorff reflected. "He will want to know our attitude towards his Government, of course. He will require pledges."

"I have not the faintest idea what he will say to you," Catherine observed. "I can only tell you this. He is a brave man. He is rash. He is broad-minded. He is ingenuous. He does not in the least resemble one's idea of a democratic leader."

Nicholas Imanoff looked across the table. There was a note of covert jealousy in his tone.

"Does he know who you are?" he asked.

"He does not, and I desire that he should not know," she rejoined. "I have spoken of Alexandrina of Kossas as my patroness."

"Tell us this," Kirdorff asked quietly, the instincts of the conspirator already stirring within him. "In the course of your work to-day did you come to any conclusion as to the success or failure of his mission over here? Have you formed any idea as to how far he means to go with this mad scheme of his?"

"We will talk of that later," Catherine replied. "It is better for you to know nothing to-night. What I want you all to remember now is that in half an hour's time we leave here to hold one of our formal meetings under the roof and patronage of Mrs. Saxon J. Bossington."

"You are coming with us, Catherine?" the Grand Duchess demanded.

"I am going back to the hotel to fetch Mr. Samara," was the unexpected rejoinder.

Nicholas half rose to his feet.

"I will escort you," he declared.

Catherine smiled at him coldly.

"You will do nothing of the sort, Nicholas," she said. "If you take my advice, you will remember what I say. So far as Gabriel Samara knows, I am a typist from the Weltmore Secretarial Bureau. It is my wish that he knows no more than this. Kindly remember that."

Kirdorff nodded approvingly.

"Our little sister knows best," he pronounced.

Mrs. Saxon J. Bossington dispensed hospitality in a Fifth Avenue palace, built by a multimillionaire of world-wide fame and purchased by her obedient spouse at the time of the last oil combine. She entertained lavishly and indiscriminately. Society, diplomacy, and even artists were all alike welcome. Her peculiar fancy, however, was acting as hostess to what she was endeavouring to make known in New York as the "Russian Circle."

"My dear Saxon," she explained to her husband, "no one knows who these people are. All we do know is that they are aristocrats. There's the Grand Duchess, of course, and the General, and Colonel Kirdorff — they are the bluest blood in Russia, but those others aren't pulling the wool over my eyes, though they call themselves plain 'Mr.' and 'Mrs.' and 'Miss.' It's my belief there's more of the Royal Family than one in that little crowd. And Saxon — there's Prince Nicholas now, an Imanoff —— "

"What is an 'Imanoff,' anyway?" Mr. Bossington interrupted, giving his coat tails a pull.

"The family name of the Russian Royal Family," his wife declared in a tone of awe.

Mr. Bossington appeared unimpressed.

"Thought they were all wiped out in a cellar or somewheres," he objected.

"All the direct branch were assassinated — murdered," his wife agreed, "in a cellar. The details were too horrible. Some of the others, however, got away, and one or two escaped out of the country. Prince Nicholas is the next heir to the throne of those left alive."

"Well, there isn't going to be any throne," Mr. Bossington

observed. "Russia's doing thundering well under her new Republic. That fellow Samara has set her going again. I had an offer for some oil concessions from his Government to-day, made me through Washington. I shall have to send a man over next week."

Mrs. Bossington deemed that the time had come for her great announcement.

"Saxon," she said, "to-night I want you to be at your best. Gabriel Samara, the greatest man in Russia, is coming here."

"You don't say!" Mr. Bossington exclaimed, properly impressed at last. "Does he know anything about oil, I wonder?"

"You can cut out that stuff," his wife enjoined angrily, with a brief relapse into the verbiage of past years. "What I mean, Saxon, is that I want you to be the perfect gentleman to-night — the broad-minded American host. We may get asked to Russia. Come right along into the library now. They'll be here before we know where we are."

"What I want to know," Mr. Bossington demanded as they crossed the hall, "is how our friends and this man, Samara, are likely to pull together, and where on earth did you come across him?"

A butler in command motioned to a footman, who threw open the door of a magnificent library. It was an apartment which much resembled the interior of a chapel, with vaulted roof, stained-glass windows, and an organ in the far end. There were divans and chairs, a round table at which a score of places were set, and a sideboard, groaning with edibles of every sort, flanked by a long row of gold-foiled bottles. Mrs. Bossington looked around her critically.

"I guess this is cosy enough for them, Saxon," she observed.

"There's plenty of the stuff, anyway," he remarked, with a glance towards the sideboard. "But what I want to know is how did you get hold of this fellow Samara? Those others all seem as if they had stepped out of a dime show, but Samara's the real goods! — as big a man, in his way, as our President!"

"I met him with that little Catherine Borans, the typewriting girl, lunching at the Ritz Carlton," Mrs. Bossington explained. "Of course it's all stuff and nonsense about her being really a working girl. There isn't one of them has a better air than she has. They are close-mouthed and all," she went on, listening for the bell. "I tried to get the old General, the other day, to tell me who she was. He just smiled and shook his head. The Duchess seemed on the point of telling me and then she pulled herself up. 'She is of our order, Mrs. Bossington,' was all I could get her to say."

The door was suddenly thrown open. The little stream of expected guests began to arrive; a curious company in their way, but each with his own peculiar claim to distinction. General Orenburg, who first bent over his hostess' hand, was ponderous and bulky, his shabby dinner clothes carefully brushed, the ends of his black tie a little shiny. Nevertheless he bore himself as a man with a great past should. He was accompanied by Prince Nicholas, whose irritation had departed for the evening, but whose manner was still stiff and abstracted. The Grand Duchess entered the room directly afterwards. She had changed her gown since dinner time and her hair was parted and brushed so smoothly back that it seemed almost like a plastered wig. Cyril Volynia Sabaroff of Perm followed, with his sister Rosa. Behind them came Colonel Kirdorff. They all stood in little groups whilst a footman served coffee and liqueurs. Mrs. Saxon J. Bossington flitted from one to the other, with much to say concerning their expected guest. Her husband listened to the description of a new automobile which some friends of Cyril Sabaroff were soon to put on the market.

"If this isn't too sweet to see you all together!" their hostess exclaimed. "Now I do hope you'll make yourselves comfortable and have your little chat just as though no one were here. There's a table you can sit round and a bite of supper for you later on. I hope you gentlemen will pay a visit to the sideboard whenever you like."

Prince Nicholas detached himself from the others.

"Your hospitality is wonderful, madam," he declared. "We beg that you will not leave us. Colonel Kirdorff has promised to talk to us to-night about the probable result of the Samara type of government and the General has a few remarks to make about these rumours of demilitarisation in Russia."

"Very interesting, I'm sure," Mrs. Bossington murmured, sailing away to greet some fresh arrivals — an elderly professor and his wife.

"Will Samara back out, do you think?" General Orenburg asked his neighbour anxiously.

Kirdorff shook his head.

"If he promised, he will come," he declared confidently. "I have that much faith in him, at any rate. He is not likely to break his word."

The greater part of the little company was now assembled. They were about a dozen outside the circle of Catherine's immediate entourage; all Russians and ardent Monarchists, but of various types and positions in the world. They were barely settled in their places round the table, when the eagerly expected event happened. The door was opened and the butler made his announcement.

"Miss Catherine Borans — Mr. Gabriel Samara!"

The newcomers advanced towards their hostess. They exchanged a few words of salutation whilst Samara bowed low and raised her somewhat pudgy fingers to his lips. Then Catherine led him towards the table.

"Please, all of you," she said, "I have ventured to bring a visitor to see you. We have been very curious about him, very critical, sometimes censorious. After all, though, we must remember that he is a fellow countryman."

There followed a few moments of intense silence. They were all engrossed in their study of this man, the foremost figure of their country; the man who, from their somewhat narrow point of view, stood between them and their desire. Certainly so far as appearance went he was at a disadvantage with none of them. He was well groomed, his evening clothes were impeccable and he possessed to the fullest extent the natural dignity of a man holding a great place in the world.

"Samara! Gabriel Samara," Alexandrina murmured, looking at him through her lorgnettes.

"Samara!" the fair-haired Rosa Sabaroff exclaimed, looking at him with undisguised awe.

"Gabriel Samara!" the General said, under his breath, stiffening insensibly.

The attitude of the little gathering towards their visitor could scarcely be called hospitable. The General and Prince Nicholas both inclined their heads, but did not offer their hands. Samara, however, showed no signs of taking offence. His bow to Alexandrina had been the bow of a courtier. He was himself too interested in his own contemplation of the rest of the party to appreciate their lack of cordiality. Mr. Bossington, as though he judged the moment propitious, introduced himself into the circle.

"Mr. Samara," he said, "glad to meet you, sir. Saxon Bossington, my name — glad to be your host. There's a proposition about oil they were asking me to look into, somewhere north of the Caspian Sea."

Samara smiled.

"You are without doubt, sir, one of the capitalists whom your President mentioned to me," he rejoined politely. "Russia has need of your brains and your money. We think that we can repay all that you have to offer. Our greatest necessity just now is to find employment for a large number of men."

"You are really going to demilitarise then!" Colonel Kirdorff intervened.

Samara, who had been standing a few feet apart, turned once more towards the table.

"You seem to be all my country people," he observed. "Why should I have secrets from you? It is my intention immediately on my return to Russia to demobilise the whole of our Third Army, consisting of about a million men. I should have done so before if I could have been sure of finding employment for them. My mission over here was to arrange something of the sort."

"What about the Germans?" Prince Nicholas demanded bluntly.

Some part of the geniality seemed to depart from Samara's manner. There was a note almost of hauteur in his reply.

"The armies of Russia," he said, "have been trained by and perhaps learned their vocation partly from German officers. Those German officers have been well paid for their labours. For anything else, the army consists of Russian soldiers, bound together for one purpose, and one purpose only — the defence of their country. In my opinion and in the opinion of my counsellors, the necessity for their existence on so large a scale no longer exists."

Samara was still standing. The General rose to his feet and indicated a chair.

"Will you join us, sir?" he invited.

There was a breathless pause — the remainder of the handful of Monarchists sat spellbound. With a grave bow to the General, Samara accepted the invitation. Prince Nicholas was on his left, the Grand Duchess a little lower down.

"This is a strange day," the General continued. "We never thought to welcome amongst us the head of the Russian Republic. I and my friends, Mr. Samara, represent a broken party; yet a party which has yielded everything except hope. We do not desire to begin our acquaintance under the shadow of any false pretence. Prince Nicholas of Imanoff here, we acknowledge as the hereditary ruler of Russia. We cannot recognise any other government."

Samara bowed his head.

"You have every right to your convictions," he admitted. "If I believed that it was for the good of Russia once more to enter upon a period of Tzardom, I should myself immediately accept the monarchical doctrine. But I tell you frankly that I do not believe it. I am a Russian by birth and descent and I think that I have earned the right to call myself a patriot. I have worked — I still work — for my country's good as I see it. That is why, with a clear conscience, I have accepted this invitation to come and visit you."

"Our friend speaks well," the General declared, looking around him. "After all, we must not forget that he has accomplished a great deed. He has freed Russia from the Bolshevists, he has destroyed Soviet rule. If the form of government which he has set up does not wholly appeal to us, it is still a million times better than the one which he has crushed."

"That is common sense," Kirdorff agreed. "Yet it leaves us with this reflection. Bolshevism and Soviet rule were impossibilities. From that hateful extreme we expected the swing of the pendulum back to the conditions of our desire. Samara here has intervened. He has intervened — happily, perhaps, for Russia — but disastrously for us. While he lives our cause will languish."

There was a tense silence. The significance of those words "while he lives" seemed to make itself felt everywhere. Samara looked around with a faint smile upon his lips — a smile about which there was already a shadow of defiance. It was a strange scene: the eager faces of the little crowd gathered round the table, the wonderful room with its great spaces and unexpected flashes of almost barbaric magnificence, the lavish hospitality displayed upon the huge sideboard, Mr. and Mrs. Saxon J. Bossington, almost grotesque in their position of host and hostess, seated in the background, waiting.

"A true accusation," Samara admitted. "But after all I can honestly assure you that I, who know the temper of the country personally better than you can by the offices of correspondents, have seen few indications of a desire on the part of the people to submit themselves once more to the domination of a monarchy. I had no idea until a few hours ago that I was to have the honour of meeting you this evening — you, Prince Nicholas, or you, General, whose name is still remembered in Russia, or you, Colonel, or your Royal Highness. Let me say this to you, if I may. The Bolshevist days and the days of insane hatreds are over. Russia is a free country — as free to you as to me. Why not come back and live in it?"

"Come back!" the General groaned. "My estates —— "

"My mines!" Kirdorff muttered.

"They took from me five hundred thousand English pounds," Alexandrina sighed wearily.

"I will be frank with you all," Samara continued. "There is a new code of laws in Russia to-day. We are prospering to an amazing extent, but we have taken upon our shoulders an immense burden. The Russia of to-day desires to pay the debts of the past. If I alone had power, I would add to those debts the sums and estates of which the Bolshevists deprived you. But in that desire I am almost alone. I spoke of it and my own people listened in silence. But I believe — I believe from the bottom of my heart — that the day will come when Russia will repay you every farthing which you have lost."

"If one could dream of such a thing!" the General faltered.

"My mines are being worked by a Japanese Company," Kirdorff sighed.

"There will be difficulties," Samara admitted, "but we shall overcome them. In the meantime, why live in exile? Russia is your country. Russia is open to you. I am not afraid to invite you all freely and whole-heartedly to return; the sentence of banishment against absentee Monarchists, I promise you shall be revoked. I am not afraid of your influence. If Russia, at any time, should want a monarchy, let her have it. I will buy a villa in the south of France, be myself an exile, and grow roses. I am but the servant of the will of the people."

"Rienzi said that before he climbed over their shoulders into power," Kirdorff reminded him, with a curious flash in his eyes.

"Rienzi was a man of more ambitious temperament than I," Samara retorted. "Besides, his scheme of government in those days was less wide-flung. He was a dreamer as well as an idealist; I am a practical man. I desire what is good for Russia, and it is certainly not for her good that any of those who might be foremost amongst her citizens are living in exile. General, return to Russia and an Army Corps or a post at the War Office is yours. You, Colonel Kirdorff, shall have a division whenever you choose to apply for it. There is not one of you who shall be deprived of the opportunity of doing useful work for your country. Why sit here and weave impossible dreams? Why not attune your patriotism to the music of real labour?"

"What about me?" Nicholas asked eagerly.

Samara reflected for a moment.

"Prince," he confided, "I will be frank with you. We are living too near the shadow of regrettable days. Come if you will and be sure of my protection, so far as it goes. You shall have a commission in the army, but an Imanoff in Russia, even to-day, must take his chance."

Nicholas nodded. Catherine, who had moved round to his side, looked across at Samara.

"Remember this," she insisted. "If the tide of feeling should flow, at any time, towards the reëstablishment of Russia's real ruler, it is upon Nicholas here that the people's choice must fall."

Samara listened indifferently. Perhaps in that hour of his magnificent and superabundant vitality, when his brain was at its zenith, his vision unerring, the idea of any serious rivalry between himself and this pale-faced young man of peevish expression seemed an incredible thing.

"All I can say is," he replied, "that if Prince Nicholas cares to come, he is welcome. Such protection as I can afford him he shall have. If he plots against my Government and his plots are discovered, he will be shot. If, by open election of the people or by vote of the Duma, a monarchy is desired, then I shall never lift a hand against him."

The General stroked his grey imperial. Something of the weariness had gone from his face. Something of the languor, indeed, seemed to have passed from all of them. They had listened to a wonderful message. Samara read their thoughts. He rose to his feet.

"I thank you, General, and all of you for your reception. I fear that in the past you have counted me an enemy. Wipe that out, please. The greatest of possible ties binds us together — our country!"

He bowed low and moved away. Mrs. Bossington arose from her chair and came bustling towards him.

"Now, my dear Mr. Samara," she exclaimed, "I am sure all this talking must have tired you. What it's been about neither Saxon nor I have the slightest idea, for on an occasion like this we make it a rule to keep ourselves to ourselves. One thing, however, I insist upon, you must take a little refreshment before you go."

Samara suffered himself to be piloted by his hostess to the sideboard, ate pâté sandwiches and drank champagne. Presently they were joined by her husband, who was curious about the oil-producing centres of Southern Russia. From the table behind came a drone of subdued but eager voices.

CHAPTER VIII

Miss Sadie Loyes set down the telephone receiver upon the instrument with a little bang. She was obviously annoyed.

"Miss Borans," she announced sharply, "eleven hundred and eighty wants you again. Keep a record of your time."

Catherine rose to her feet and placed the cover on her machine. Miss Loyes watched her with critical eyes.

"Crazy about you, seemingly," she continued. "They're making such a fuss about him in the papers this morning, I thought I'd go up myself for an hour or so. Knows his own mind, anyhow — you or nobody. What kind of work is it?"

"Not work you'd enjoy very much, I think, Miss Loyes," Catherine replied, smiling faintly as she thought of the previous morning, "correspondence and documents and that sort of thing. Yesterday afternoon Mr. Bromley Pride interviewed him for the *New York Comet*. He didn't get much of a story, though."

"These foreigners leave me cold," the manageress declared. "What we Americans make such a fuss about them for I don't know. They just come over here for what they can get. One of the papers this morning said that this Mr. Samara has fixed up a loan with the President of something like two hundred millions. Keep your time card carefully, Miss Borans. There's one thing about these Russians, they aren't mean!"

Catherine descended the stairs into the hall and made leisurely progress towards the lift. On the way the fancy seized her to call in at the florist's shop and buy a single dark red rose which she pulled through the waistband of her dress. The elevator man, who had scarcely noticed her before, watched her disappearing figure with undisguised admiration.

"She sure is some girl, that!" he remarked to one of the messenger boys, as he stepped back into the elevator.

The young lady seated behind the desk at the entrance to

the corridor wished her good morning with a faint air of surprise. She called to her associate at the other end of the place and motioned after Catherine.

"Did you see that pale-faced ninny from the typing room, all dolled out, this morning?" she demanded. "She's got a beau all right. I never noticed that she was so stylish."

It was a very different sitting room which Catherine presently entered. There were half a dozen men present and conversation was a little vehement. At her entrance it subsided. Samara motioned her to a chair at the smaller table and proceeded to dismiss his callers.

"I agree," he said. "It seems cowardly but perhaps you are right. At one o'clock Carloss, and at three o'clock the bank president. Louden can make all the arrangements. He had better bring an automobile here and cable Cherbourg."

They drifted away, one by one. Samara himself escorting them through the little hall to the door. Presently he returned and threw himself into an easy-chair.

"Trouble at home, here, and everywhere," he remarked grimly. "I've got to hurry home."

"About your demilitarisation scheme?" she enquired.

"Half the unrest is owing to German influence," he answered, with a nod. "We've had so many commitments to her in the past that she's grown to look upon these armies as her own. Our people over here are quite right, though. I must get back at once and make a tour through the military district. In the meantime, I am going to cable over a proclamation. Ready?"

"Quite," she answered.

He dictated rapidly for half an hour or more. As soon as he had finished he went to a cupboard in which was an array of bottles, mixed himself a drink and tossed it off. Then he sat in his easy-chair with his hands in his pockets and a frown upon his forehead, while she gathered up the loose pages of her work.

"Tell me," he asked abruptly, "what did your friends think of me last night?"

"They were surprised," she admitted.

"Favourably or unfavourably?"

"On the whole favourably. Your offer to them all has made a great stir in their quiet lives."

"It was a serious one," he declared, rising to his feet and pacing the room. "There is no reason why they shouldn't come back. I have nothing against the Monarchists so long as they accept the situation and desist from plots. The people against whom I wage war to the death are the anarchists. They are a waning force but I have not done with them yet. I am a humane man but I would kill an anarchist as I would a fly, because of the poison they carry with them."

She looked at him thoughtfully, but she made no remark. Presently he stopped in front of her chair.

"Don't you agree with me — I mean about your people?" he demanded. "Don't you think I was right to ask them to come back? They are, after all, Russian citizens."

"I think you were right," she replied, "with one exception."

"One exception?" he repeated.

"Nicholas Imanoff. If you allow him to return, I don't think I should have him in the army. You know what the Russian peasant soldier is. Communism is a meaningless cry to him, although he may shout for it if he is bidden. God and the Tzar are still in his blood."

"You are giving me advice against your own people!" he exclaimed suddenly.

The faintest tinge of colour stole for a moment under the creamy pallor of her cheeks. The same idea had flashed in upon her.

"I am tired of plots and rebellions," she explained. "Changes of government should be worked out by the will of the people. If the people call for a Tzar — well, there is Nicholas. But if he is once in the army, there will be plots. It isn't for our own good. I should like to see the monarchy reëstablished, but I should like to see it reëstablished by orthodox means."

"You tell me that Alexandrina of Kossas is your patroness," he said. "Does that mean that you too are an aristocrat?"

"By inclination," she confessed. "You must remember that it is not only the aristocracy who would support monarchy. I am one of those who consider it the sanest form of government.

Would you like me to do anything with this proclamation?"

He took the sheets from her and glanced them through, made a few alterations in pencil, and laid them down again. Afterwards he resumed his restless perambulation of the room. She leaned back in her chair and waited. Samara was evidently disturbed. Occasionally he muttered to himself. Once he stood for quite five minutes gazing out of the window, down into the windy, sunlit streets.

"I am sailing this afternoon, Miss Borans," he announced, suddenly turning round. "My people are all emphatic and they are right. There is danger here and trouble to face at home."

She did not attempt to conceal her interest.

"I read your interview in the *New York Comet,* this morning," she said, "but after all it told us very little. As the General was saying last night, you are still outside the Pact of Nations. You can demobilise the whole of these first million men and still remain, on paper at any rate, the greatest military power in Europe."

"I could," he assented. "But that is not my intention. I want my Russian people back on the land instead of behind the guns, and I'm going to have them there. That's all I can say. Later on I have a scheme of my own for a citizen army — the only sort of army any country ought to have. Miss Borans, will you go back to Russia with me?"

"Will I do *what?*" she asked, looking at him intently.

"Precisely what I have asked," he persisted. "What relatives have you here?"

"A sort of aunt," she replied, "and a second cousin."

"Good! You work now for the management of this hotel. Work for me instead. I need a secretary like you. If your friends accept my offer, you'll have company over there. You won't clash with Andrew. He has his own line of work."

She shook her head.

"I could not work for you, Mr. Samara," she said.

"Why not?" he demanded roughly. "You are a Russian patriot. So am I."

"Our ideas of patriotism might not be the same," she pointed out. "If there were a movement in favour of the reëstablishment of the monarchy in Russia, for instance, I should join it."

"Join it and welcome," he answered. "I'm not at all sure that you would, though, if you were on the spot. Russia to-day is leaping onward towards prosperity. I can prove that to you. What do you want a monarchy back for? Not for the sake of the Russian people. They'd be no better off. Who are you for, Miss Borans — the people or one particular class?"

"That one particular class is a section of the people," she reminded him.

"An infinitesimal one," he scoffed. "Majorities count. You must work for the good of the greatest number."

"All the same," she said, "I am not disposed to be your secretary."

His face darkened almost into a scowl.

"Don't be absurd!" he protested angrily. "It's a good offer. You can name your own salary in reason. You would be able to live in your native country instead of being an exile."

She shook her head.

"It is an impossibility," she assured him.

He glared at her for a moment furiously. Then, without further reference to it, he abandoned the subject.

"Take down these letters," he directed. "Take copies but be sure you give them to me."

"I am quite ready," she murmured.

He dictated for an hour. When he had finished, he read the letters she handed him with almost meticulous care, signed them and watched her as she placed them in their envelopes. Then he took the copies, looked them through and locked them up in a despatch box.

"How is Mr. Andrew Kroupki this morning?" she enquired.

"Better," he answered shortly. "He will not be able to travel with me, though. It is most annoying."

She glanced at the clock.

"What time does your boat sail?" she asked.

"Eight o'clock," he told her, "but I am going on board at six. It seems that although the police released our friend of yesterday morning, a hint or two of what he was after got about. I'm practically being smuggled out of the country."

"You have appointments at one o'clock and three," she reminded him. "Is there anything more that I can do for you before I leave?"

"There is only one thing you could do for me, and you won't do it," he growled. "I'm not a woman's man and I never learned how to talk to them, but you're the sort of human being it does one good to work with. I believe in you. You could help me."

"There are many others who could do that," she assured him.

"I don't meet them," he answered. "My biographers have written a lot of nonsense about me. Because I have swept clean the roads of life and driven the masses along the appointed way, they talk about my magnetism, my intense sympathy with human beings. It's all rubbish! I have no sympathy. Men and women are mostly puppets to me and life is a chess-board. If I could find some one who would teach me tolerance, some one whom I could trust, for whom I could feel human things, I could accomplish greater deeds than I have ever accomplished yet. There are times when I am frightened of my own materialism. I have thought all my life universally, in composite blocks. The world is becoming like a doll's house to me. I have a fancy that you might be able to change this. Will you come and try?"

Again she shook her head. "It is an impossibility," she repeated.

"That ends it, then!" he pronounced abruptly. "Tell your people to send an account for the typing in to the hotel. The Embassy are arranging to pay my bill after my departure. All the evening papers are announcing that I leave on Saturday. You will perhaps consider what I have told you concerning my movements as confidential."

"I will remember," she promised.

She rose to her feet. He glowered across the room at her.

"Some day," he concluded, "you may see that you've wasted a great opportunity. No woman ever had a greater. You've read of me and my work but you don't know. When I crushed Bolshevism, the heart and soul of Russia began to beat again. The work's only begun. You and your little monarchist plots! Why don't you lift your head and see the greater things? You could help."

"I am very sorry," she sighed, as she turned away.

He heard the door close. Then he crossed the room towards the cupboard. Help in his task from any human being seemed to be the one thing in life always denied him.

THEY were all gone at last. Samara was alone in his capacious stateroom with a single companion — Bromley Pride, the *bona fide* representative of the *New York Comet*. Samara listened to the receding footsteps with a frown. Outside was turmoil. The bugle had just sounded the last call for departing visitors.

"This sort of thing," he declared, "would soon drive me mad."

Bromley Pride smiled tolerantly. He was a largely made, athletic-looking man, clean-shaven and forcible. In New York he was considered to be an authority on Russian affairs.

"I am afraid these last two hours have seemed rather like an anticlimax," he observed. "All the same, I am convinced that precautions were necessary. The Chief of the Police sent for me himself this morning and begged me, if I had any influence with you, to persuade you to leave the country without delay. There are all sorts of rumours about."

"They warned me in Washington," Samara acknowledged gloomily, "and of course there was yesterday's little affair."

"Yesterday's little affair," Bromley Pride repeated with emphasis, "was only the beginning. I honestly believe," he went on, "that the Germans, over here at any rate, look upon the proposed demobilisation of your armies as an act of absolute treachery to them. You don't read the New York papers, I suppose, but the German-owned ones have passionate articles this morning, denouncing your visit here and attacking your whole policy. Whatever one can find to say against the Germans they are not cowards. Five years ago you were a little god in Germany. To-day you have about forty million enemies."

Samara nodded with darkening expression.

"You're right, of course, Pride," he admitted, "but my progress from the Hotel Weltmore to the boat was more like the passage of one of those hated plutocrats of old through the dangerous part of his capital than the departure of one who has brought freedom to a great country from the city which has canonised that particular quality. Twenty plain clothes policemen walking along the customs shed and me in the middle! A sickening sight!"

"If it had been Saturday instead of to-day," Pride observed, "the chances are ten to one you'd have had a bomb in the midst of the lot of you."

There was the sound of cheering, a sense of gliding motion, the screaming and panting of tugs. Samara drew a breath of relief.

"Well, thank God we're off!" he exclaimed. "Can I go on deck now and get a breath of fresh air?"

"Not yet," the other begged. "Two detectives from police headquarters are going through the passenger list with the purser now. As soon as they send me word down 'O. K.' you can do what you like. You must remember that you haven't told me much yet, sir. I'm not only a New York journalist, you know — I'm a friend of Russia."

"My mission was a success," Samara declared. "That's all there it to be said about it. My task lies ahead. Forty years ago, Russia — the best part of Russia — was trying to drill the military spirit into Russian peasants. To-day I have got to knock it out. The Bolshevists were wise people in their generation. They kept a great army going without the slightest difficulty. The soldiers were fed whilst the peasants starved. Who wanted to work on the land, without enough to keep body and soul together, when there was good food and wine and beer in the army? They're an obstinate race, our peasants, you know, Pride. I've got the capital now to make them productive units of the nation, at work in the factories and fields, and to pay them good money. It's quite another matter to make them see that it's for their benefit, though. That is where the difficulty may come in."

"You'll do it in the end," Pride prophesied hopefully. "You've achieved greater impossibilities."

"Yes, I shall do it," Samara assented. "I shall do it, if only they'll let me alone. I shall do it if I can keep intrigue out of the Duma and the Press and the Army. I shall do it if I'm given a fair show."

Pride was gazing out of the porthole at the passing panorama of docks and walls.

"One would pray for you, Samara, if one knew how or to whom. There's a soul in your work — something that reaches out of life — out of the mud of politics and man's ambition. The Jews are the only ones left who really pray. I rather wish you were a Jew, Samara."

"You think that I need faith."

"It isn't that, but you need an inexhaustible stock," was the quiet reply. "You have no one to depend upon but yourself. Russia has not produced a single great statesman yet to stand by your side. You carry on your shoulders a burden so enormous that it makes the hearts of us who watch grow faint. How must it be for yourself?"

Samara was looking into space. They were moving more rapidly now — moving all the time away from New York.

"I am forty-four years old, Pride," he confided. "I came into this fight when I was nineteen. I have never looked back. I have never relaxed or felt fear, but there has been one moment, and that not so long ago, when I almost weakened — if it is weakening to crave for help. I thought I saw something wonderful. It was just the mirage."

There was a knock at the door. A detective entered. He smiled the smile of a man who has accomplished good work.

"Everything 'O. K.' now, sir," he declared. "Mike's got 'em — one from Chicago, one from Washington. They've got the bracelets on and the guns are in Mike's pocket. They had a stateroom nearly opposite to you, too, sir," he added, turning to Samara.

"You think they were really after me?" the latter asked.

The detective laughed confidently.

"They were after some one on board, sir, and they had a plan of your stateroom. Not a paper between them, and scarcely any luggage. One's a Russian — a red-hot Bolshevist still, they say, whom we've had under observation for years. The other's a German. They won't trouble you any more, sir. As for the rest

·of the passengers, I think they're all right. The stewards and the crew, of course, we can't vouch for."

"Should I be running any grave risk," Samara enquired, "if I invited you to visit the smoking room with me?"

The detective accepted the idea with enthusiasm but ventured upon an amendment.

"I'd try that bell, sir, instead," he suggested, "and a word to the steward."

At last came the clanging of a bell which, this time, brought them to a dead stop. Samara watched his visitors depart; Pride, with his cheerful carriage and buoyant air; the two detectives with their quarry; finally the pilot into his little rowboat on the other side. The great semicircle of lights had flashed out through the windy twilight. The freshness of the sea was a marvellous tonic after the spring lassitude of the town and the overheated rooms. Samara strode the deck with a sense of reawakening life in his veins. These croakers had gone. He was his own man again, free to muse upon his great achievement, to revel in the exhilaration of the voyage. Behind him lay New York — and what else? It was an absurdity, but he was heavy-hearted.

The clamorous dinner bugle left him undisturbed. His anticipations of the coming night, the long roll of the ship, the scent of the sea, and the wind upon his face elated him. And then, in the midst of his long, swinging walk, he came to a sudden standstill. A woman was leaning over the rail. He had passed her several times without notice. Now, something in her figure, the poise of her head, startled him with a flood of ridiculous memories. She turned and faced him. For once in his life, he, the man of many words, was speechless.

"You see, I changed my mind," she said, with a quiet smile. "I wish you'd go and see the purser about my stateroom."

They dined together half an hour later at the little table in a secluded corner of the saloon which Samara had bespoken for himself. Catherine was very frank.

"It has been the dream of my life to visit my own country," she confided, "but all the same I had not the faintest idea of accepting your offer. When I got downstairs after leaving you,

I found Kirdorff waiting for me. You may not realise it, but Colonel Kirdorff is a great schemer."

"You are to spy upon me!" he exclaimed.

"I rather think that is the idea," she assented. "You little know what you have brought upon yourself by your candour last night. They are all planning to return — even Nicholas. When I told Kirdorff of your offer, he thought that I should be mad to decline it. You mustn't be angry with them, Mr. Samara. They have lived away from their country a long time. They are getting old and the idea of intrigue stirs them as nothing else in life could. They are not to be ignored but they are scarcely to be feared."

"And you?" he asked. "Are you going to spy upon me?"

"I may," she admitted. "I shall make you no promises. I want to see what you have made of Russia. I want to travel about there and to talk to those people who understand. Maybe you will convert me. If you do not, I shall give you fair warning. In the meantime I hope you will find me plenty of work and pay me enough money to buy some clothes directly we land. These dear friends of mine all hurried me off with little more than a handbag."

"How is it that you are so intimate with all these people?" he enquired. "You are one of them, I suppose?"

"Don't ask me," she begged. "Let me remain a mystery. I am a working girl and I am going to be a very good secretary. Isn't that enough? Tell me, do you live in a palace at Moscow and what will become of me there?"

"I live in a portion of the old palace," he replied. "We call it now Government House. You can have your quarters there, or look after yourself outside, whichever you like. Then you can also have an office in Government Buildings where Andrew does most of his work."

"It sounds delightful!" she declared. "We are impulsive people, you and I! You haven't had any references about me and as for you — well, I know that you are Gabriel Samara and that is all. I don't even know whether you are married."

He smiled.

"I think you do," he said. "In case I am wrong, I will tell you. I am unmarried and I have no women friends. As to references,

I asked none from you; you must place a similar trust in me."
She returned his smile understandingly.

"I think," she confided, "that I have made up my mind to do that."

Catherine went to her stateroom early and Samara, after a brief visit to the smoking room, struggled out on to the rain-splashed deck. They were facing the Atlantic now, with a gale blowing, driving the spray in blinding sheets across the ship. He found a comparatively sheltered place where the thunder of the wind was heard rather than felt, and where he could watch the flecks of foam leap into the dazzling light and pass away into the black gulf beyond. He was on his way back, his mission accomplished; the second part of the great struggle of his life begun. There was never a time when he needed clearer vision, a more detached and concentrated grasp upon the great realities. Courage he had in plenty, even to rashness; his will no one had ever questioned; yet in the midst of his content he was troubled with a queer sense of some indeterminate quality in his thoughts, some disposition to find less than vitally important the great issues of life. His mental balance had been disturbed. Another element had entered into the background of his sensations beside the joy of achievement. He filled his pipe and smoked savagely, staggered down the deck and took a stiff drink at the bar, came out again and crawled even farther towards the bows, until the music of the wind was in his ears like the crack of thunder and the hiss of the sea, as the waves were parted by the mighty bow of the ship, seemed like an unearthly scream. There were stars shining occasionally, shining here and there through a filmy lacing of clouds; a promise of the moon from behind the jagged pieces of black cloud, these latter so low down that it seemed as though the tall mast rising from the top of the sea was almost stabbing into their bosom. Gusts of rain swept into his face. The seamen who passed him were wrapped in oilskins and silent. The singing in his pulses continued, the exhilaration of spirit which he tried in vain to believe came from the knowledge that this journey of his, towards which the eyes of the world had been directed, had met with a success which he alone had prophesied.

And all the time he knew that there was something else, —

another problem to be faced; a personal self creeping into life, demanding, nay, insisting upon recognition. It was all fancy, he told himself, born of the winds and the stars and the romance of travel. He suddenly realised upon what a trifle the whole great machinery of his mind had been engaged.

CHAPTER X

It was not until the middle of the next morning that Gabriel Samara appeared on deck. A long line of semi-somnolent passengers watched him with interest; Catherine, who was sipping some beef tea, looked up expectantly. He did not, however, pause in his promenade, but raised his hat slightly and passed on, his hands thrust into the pockets of his great coat, his underlip a little protruding, a general air of unapproachability about him. If there were not actually newspaper men on board, there were men connected with newspapers and they looked at him wistfully — even followed him at a respectful distance along the deck, seeking an opportunity to venture upon a friendly word. They were, however, doomed to disappointment. Samara, after a restless night, had no desire for the amenities of life. He climbed to the higher deck where few people were disposed to face the wind, and, assured of a certain measure of solitude there, he leaned against the rail, looking down into the steerage. Again as on the previous night, he felt the scrutiny of a little company of white-faced, black-eyed shadows of men, with skulking movements and general air of furtiveness. One of them he watched in particular, with something more than ordinary curiosity. The man looked over his shoulder twice and, although his expression was entirely passive, there was recognition in those stealthy glances. Soon he disappeared behind a ventilator, and Samara, after a few minutes' hesitation, recommenced his promenade. This time, however, it was speedily interrupted. The First Officer, who was descending from the bridge, caught sight of him and waited for his approach at the bottom of the steps.

"Mr. Samara," he said, saluting, "may I have a word with you?"

Samara nodded.

"Certainly."

"We are very pleased and proud, of course, to have you as a

passenger, sir," the officer went on, "but I wish very much you had followed the example of some other over-popular statesmen who travel with us, and done so incognito."

"My friends arranged my passage," Samara explained. "I came on board, as you know, quite unexpectedly."

"Just so," the other assented. "That would have been all right if they had used a little more discretion. The trouble of it is that we have at least a score of your country people in the steerage — red-hot Bolshevists, every one of them — who came out here and haven't been allowed to land. They've been at Ellis Island for some time and now we've orders to take them back to Naples."

"I think I've recognised one or two of them," Samara remarked drily.

"We are taking every precaution," the officer continued. "Not one of them will be allowed to land until after you have left the ship and we have stationed a guard at each of the communicating passages leading from the steerage aft. At the same time they are crafty fellows. I'd have a care if I were you, Mr. Samara, and particularly, I'd lock both my doors at night. Yours is rather an exposed suite."

"I am very much obliged for the warning," Samara said. "I don't think that my attitude towards life is exactly that of a fatalist, but so far as regards these repeated attempts upon my person, I have grown just a little callous, I'm afraid. Or perhaps it is that I have faith."

"It's a fine thing to have," the other observed gravely, "but some of the greatest men in the world have been struck down by the most utter miscreants. We will do our best to take care of you, sir, you may be certain of that."

"I am sure you will," was the slightly more cordial reply.

The morning wore on. Some of the ship's passengers indulged in sports. Down in the steerage a man who called himself a Hungarian, but who had been christened "Simon the Jew," was doing tricks with knives, to the amazement of a little group of spectators. He pinned a piece of paper on the wall and from twenty paces he threw short-bladed, ugly-looking knives into a perfect circle. He threw them into the air and caught them by the handles, three or four at the same time, the sun shining upon the blue steel of their blades. Some of the women turned away. Even the men — and they were used to knives — shivered a little. The man was a magician.

Back on the promenade deck Catherine was conscious of a vague sense of annoyance. Samara had not been near her all the morning. Once or twice, as she passed along the deck, she had seen him sitting in a corner of the smoking room — smoking a pipe and reading. It was not until after the bugle had sounded for luncheon that she met him in the companionway.

"I thought," she said, a little coldly, "that I was supposed to be here as your secretary."

He nodded.

"No work this morning," he declared.

"I had no intention of coming," she continued, "simply for a sea voyage. May I ask whether there will be work to do this afternoon?"

The gruffness passed from his manner. He looked at her abstractedly. She was wearing a long jumper of a distinctive shade of green, a cap of the same colour, and the wind had brought a wholesome touch of pink to her cheeks. Her tone was almost severe but her lips were already framing for a smile.

"There is a despatch," he announced, "which I wish to prepare for forwarding to London. We will begin it at three o'clock, if that suits you."

"It suits me very well indeed," she assured him.

They separated without further speech. A few minutes later, as he sat at his corner table from which the other chair had already been removed, he saw her coming towards him. This time there was a distinct frown upon her face.

"I understand," she said, "that you have told the second steward to give me a place somewhere else."

"I thought it would be more agreeable to you," he replied.

"You were entirely wrong," she confided. "I shall sit with you or take my meals on deck."

He rose at once to his feet and summoned a steward.

"Kindly relay this table," he directed. "Mademoiselle will share it with me."

She seated herself and looked at him severely.

"Why do you desire to dispense with my society after having made use of so much eloquence to obtain it?" she enquired. "I can assure you that I am a very desirable companion. I can be silent. I can be an eager listener—especially if you talk of Russia—or I can talk nonsense. You have only to name your humour, and I can respond to it. But I will not sit with that noisy crowd of fat, curious women and their male belongings."

"You are very welcome here," he conceded, trying to conceal his own satisfaction. "The arrangement I proposed was largely for your sake. I thought that you would like to make acquaintances on board."

She drew herself up and looked at him with a smile, half amused, half haughty.

"Why? Acquaintances?"

His retort was prompt.

"As a young lady typist from the Bureau of the Weltmore Hotel, taking her first ocean trip," he began——

"The trick is to you," she interrupted. "I don't like the sarcasm, though. Are you sure that you still believe in me, Mr. Samara?"

"Ought I to?" he retorted unexpectedly.

"We will waive the question," she decided, after a moment's deliberation.

The second steward came up to pay his respects and to suggest special dishes for dinner that night or luncheon on the morrow. The wine steward followed with news of some old brandy for which Samara had enquired, and his place in turn was taken by the First Officer, who paused for a moment or two on his way out.

"I trust, Mr. Samara," he said, "that you are keeping the matter in mind about which I spoke to you this morning."

"It is scarcely a matter which slips easily from one's memory," was the somewhat grim reply.

"What was he talking about?" Catherine asked, glancing curiously after the retreating figure.

"A gang of Bolshevists on board, being returned to their native country with thanks. They hate me like poison, of course, every one of them."

She looked troubled.

"I am sure I saw some of them," she confided, "when I was looking over into the steerage this morning. Even though they are my own country people, I thought they were horrible."

"There's nothing to fear from such cattle," he said shortly. "You'll have to get used to believing that I am immune from that sort of thing, if you work for me. You have had one dose of it already. As for these fellows, they are no good without organization. They may hate me like poison, but there isn't one of them would have the courage to risk his own life by trying to get rid of me for the sake of his fellows. The Bolshevist hasn't altruism enough for that."

After luncheon they parted for a time, and at three o'clock, preceded by a steward carrying her typewriter, Catherine presented herself in the little sitting room attached to Samara's suite. He was already there, talking to Ivan, or rather the latter was talking and Samara listening. Ivan had apparently worked himself into a state almost of passion. The words came from his lips in a little stream; his fists were clenched. His master pushed him out of the room with a few soothing words.

"Ivan's been down in the steerage," he explained, turning to Catherine with a smile. "Been running amuck with some of the scum there, I expect. He thinks that they'd do me a mischief if they could. So would a hundred thousand more of them, but they don't get the chance."

"I have not quite made up my mind about you yet," she said, as she seated herself at the table. "One thing I am quite sure about, though; I do not wish you to be assassinated whilst I am around, or indeed until I am convinced that your work for Russia is over. So far as you have gone, I look upon you as the greatest Russian benefactor we have ever had. If only you would complete the work!"

"Restore the monarchy?"

"Yes."

"Some day we will argue the matter," he promised. "Now take down the text of my communication to the English Cabinet."

They worked for several hours, Catherine fascinated by the substance of what she wrote, the directness and lucidity with which Samara expressed himself. Sometimes he was at a loss for a word and at her suggestion he supplied her with a Russian one. They drifted now and then into the habit of exchanging remarks in that tongue.

"It seems odd to think that you have never actually been in your own country since you were old enough to remember!" he said abruptly.

"I spent three very strenuous years there, according to my mother," she confided. "My impressions are naturally a little mixed."

He returned to work and dismissed her only when the bugle sounded an hour before dinner. Afterwards he walked outside for a few minutes alone. It was already dusk, quieter than on the previous night but still with a long swell and half a gale blowing on the windward side of the ship. He paced the almost deserted deck once or twice thoughtfully. A whistle sounded from the bridge. Presently the boatswain came up to him and saluted.

"The Captain's compliments, sir, and would you speak to him for a moment in his room?"

Samara followed the man on to the covered deck and into the Captain's quarters. The latter, who had been changing for dinner, came out of his room.

"You will take a cocktail with me, Mr. Samara?" he invited.

"With pleasure."

In a moment there was the sound of the ice clinking in the shaker and the Captain's steward appeared with two frosted glasses full of amber liquid.

"You musn't think us a lot of old women, Mr. Samara," the Captain begged, as he pushed the cigarettes across, "but I tell you frankly that we're rather nervous about you. We've got a rotten steerage on board, and I'm going to ask you not to walk these decks after dusk. If you care to come up on the bridge while the weather is in any way decent and clear, I shall be delighted. Plenty of exercise there, and all the wind you could want in the world."

Samara smiled faintly.

"I have to stick it out in Moscow, you know, and a good many other places which I visit in my own country," he reminded his companion.

"Precisely," the Captain agreed, "but permit me to point out a very vital difference. In your own country, for one man who would raise his hand against you there are a million to whom you are something like a god, and any would-be assassin would have to face the fact that he would probably be torn to pieces in a matter of seconds. On board this ship it is a very different matter. My First Officer tells me that we've got a score or more of the worst of your country people on board, who honestly believe in an ignorant way that they've got a grudge against you. It excites them to think that you are so near. They feel that they have a chance of getting at you they wouldn't have on land. I'm one of your great admirers, Mr. Samara, but there's a selfish side to this, too. I should hate anything to happen on my ship."

"I'll take every care," Samara promised. "Give me a cocktail like that now and then, and I'd almost promise to hide in my stateroom!"

The Captain smiled as he divided the remainder.

"It will take a load off our minds if you'll promise to be careful," he said. "We watch those fellows day and night, but they're as slippery as eels. Even now my boatswain tells me there's one of them he can't account for."

"Have they any firearms?"

"Not now. We've taken seven revolvers away from them — not a bad haul for less than a score. In one respect they are not as bad as the Dagos — they haven't all a knife up their sleeves."

Samara was escorted back to his quarters by the boatswain. Ivan, who was busy brushing his clothes, was still disturbed and anxious.

"I do not like this ship," he declared, as he shook out his master's coat. "There are evil men upon it."

"Turn on my bath, Ivan. Even evil men without arms in their hands can do no more than think evil thoughts," his master reminded him. "What in hell's name is that?"

There was a strange fugitive glimpse of a white face pressed against the large, square window which took the place of a porthole; a face which slowly appeared from underneath the frosted lower part and came into sight gradually — a mass of black matted hair, sunken eyes, sunken cheeks, an expression scarcely human. Samara sprang forward, but Ivan held him back with all his giant strength. He pushed his master on one side and hastened to the door.

"It is for me, this, Master," he cried.

He was out on the deck in an instant. Samara snatched up a pistol from the drawer of his writing desk and followed him. There was not a creature in sight. He looked up and down. Ivan crept underneath the boats. The place appeared to be deserted. Samara, with a shrug of his shoulders, returned to his stateroom. Ivan stood still on the deck; a giant figure, his long hair blowing about in the wind, the muscles of his arm taut, rage in his heart.

CATHERINE had just finished a morning's work, which even she found severe. She leaned back in her chair with a little sigh of exhaustion. Her fingers were stiff, her arms numb, there was a slight dizziness at the back of her head. Outside, too, as though to tantalize her the more, the wind had gone down and the great liner was ploughing its level way through a blue sea as smooth as a carpet and bespangled with sunlight. Samara, with the inspiration of his last few sentences still in his brain, was like a man removed altogether from the world. He, too, was looking through that wide-flung porthole but with the air of one who seeks something beyond the swelling sea and the narrow boundaries of the blue horizon. Catherine, watching him with curious eyes, forgot for a moment her fatigue. He had indeed the air of a prophet. There was no follower of the cause which lay next to her own heart like this, she reflected sorrowfully. With a momentary pang she thought of Nicholas and that little circle back in New York, even now making their plans. The recollection failed altogether to exhilarate her.

The sound of the luncheon bugle brought their feet back to the ground. Samara turned swiftly around. For the first time that morning, as it seemed to Catherine, he looked at her as though she were a human being.

"You are tired," he exclaimed, — "of course you are tired! I have worked you for three hours without a pause. Ivan!"

The man appeared, silently for all his bulk, and without a moment's delay. His master gave him a rapid order in Russian.

"If I am tired, it is a pleasure to feel so," she assured him. "I feel mentally as you men feel physically when you return from a long day's hunting. Only, if you will give me an hour's rest after luncheon, I shall sleep in the sunshine."

"I shall not work again to-day," he declared. "I've got rid of much that was in my mind. These thoughts collect in their little cells. One must bring them into shape or sometimes they slip away."

Ivan returned with two glasses full of frosted liquid on a tray. Catherine took one gratefully. Samara tossed his off at a draught.

"Come out into the sunshine for ten minutes before lunch," he invited.

She finished her *apéritif* and followed him gratefully enough on to the deck. They walked up and down once or twice. Then Catherine sank into her steamer chair and, after a moment's hesitation, he seated himself by her side.

"One scarcely needs exercise," she murmured. "The sun and this air are so wonderful and the decks are crowded. Besides, I hate walking. Tell me, Mr. Samara, if you will, — you write openly enough of the second stage in your great struggle for the regeneration of Russia. What is it?"

"Can't you imagine?" he answered, a little gloomily. "The escape from our obligations, written and unwritten, to Germany."

"Germany!"

She repeated the word. The full understanding of his announcement evaded her.

"Don't you see," he pointed out, "in the early days of Bolshevist Government, Germany obtained almost a strangle hold upon Russia. The best of her industries were seized upon and worked by Germans. These profiteers made piles of money, but instead of investing it to develop Russia's resources, they kept it for themselves, to spend in their own country when they had sucked the thing dry. German capital was used freely enough but not for Russia's ultimate good. The fortunes made went abroad. Russian resources, Russian cheap labour, were merely the cat's-paw of German capitalists. The same thing in a different manner applied to our armies. It is quite true that German officers and German efficiency have made us a military power far in advance of our requirements, but for what purpose were those armies to be used, do you suppose? Not for Russia's benefit. That is why —— "

It was precisely at that moment that an incredible and amazing thing happened — seen first, to Samara's preservation, by Catherine. Scarcely fifteen feet from them was hung a boat, covered by a tight canvas covering. There was hardly a breath of wind and yet Catherine's attention had been attracted by the inexplicable movement of one of the knotted ends of rope which tied it down; an end which disappeared underneath the canvas as though drawn there by invisible fingers. There was a sudden gap in the folds of the canvas itself, and swiftly following, black tragedy, pregnant with fate; the instantaneous reappearance of that horrible face first seen by Samara through the window of his cabin and now more than ever like some diabolical jack-in-the-box, the top part of a body, collarless, clad in a grey flannel shirt only, a long skinny arm, gripping in its yellow fingers something that gleamed like silver in the sunlight.

It was an affair of seconds. Catherine never knew the instinct which prompted her. She caught hold of Samara by the neck and dragged his face against hers. Even as she did so something flashed across those fifteen feet of space like a silver thunderbolt; something that hissed in the air and buried itself in the woodwork where Samara's head had been — buried itself almost to the hilt, and stayed there quivering. There were people walking both ways. They paused in amazement. Samara felt the fiery grip of Catherine's fingers released. He sprang to his feet, just as the misshapen little figure leaped out from the gap in the boat, jumped on to the deck and turned towards the steerage. Samara, large and loose-limbed though he was, was no less nimble. One long leap — and the man was in his grasp. It was like a rat in the grip of a well-conditioned sporting dog. Afterwards, it seemed to Catherine, sitting there numbed and motionless, that these things could scarcely have happened. A matter of seconds saw the beginning and end of an episode which might have changed the world's history. Samara, shaking with a great anger, held his miserable captive high over his head, shouted one word to him — a Russian word, harsh and uncouth it sounded — strode to the rail, held him for a moment poised, in full sight of half a hundred shivering and paralysed passengers, and flung him out into the sunlight, far away from the ship's side, into the soft blue bosom of the sea. Even people who had not seen, heard the splash and ran to the side of the boat. Samara leaned with the others over the rails. He became suddenly a spectator. Behind him, embedded three inches deep in the woodwork, the knife was still quivering, the sunshine reflected from it like gleams of lightning.

Pandemonium followed, but pandemonium through which ran a thread of order. There was the clanging of the gong from the Captain's bridge, the sudden shock of reversed engines, a boat in the sea almost before people realised its lowering — a boat which seemed to be left far behind as the liner drifted on with her own momentum. A hundred glasses watched it. A hoarse murmur ran all down the line of anxious passengers. Samara felt a hand, as cold as ice, clutch his. Catherine was standing by his side.

"Have they picked him up?" she asked.

He nodded.

"These fellows have the lives of cats," he observed resignedly. "I quite thought that I had broken his neck when I threw him over."

A little crowd had gathered round the sinister-looking knife; others watched the return of the boat with the half-drowned man. In the background people gazed with awe and wonder at Samara — a man who had escaped death by a miracle, and the taking of life by a second one. He was momentarily engaged in tying a handkerchief round his right hand from which a few drops of blood were falling.

"The fellow tried to bite me when I got hold of his neck," he explained. "I shall go and see the doctor. Any one who touches this carrion needs disinfectants."

People made way for him right and left. The sight of that amazing retaliation of his had imbued him with a grotesque, yet heroic air. It was like a deed from a book of the Sagas. Then into that blazing atmosphere of tragedy there intervened a readjusting note. With puffed-out cheeks and earnest manner a pallid young man produced from a shining bugle the call for luncheon. Untoward and unexpected events are coldly looked upon on board ship. Routine and discipline are paramount. When Samara returned from the doctor's room with his hand neatly bandaged, he found most of the passengers, including Catherine, already seated at luncheon.

THE knife thrower brooded, so far as his narrow mind allowed him, in irons, for the remainder of the voyage, without even the solace of a word from his cowed companions. Samara, with Catherine always at hand to help, worked for several hours each morning, preparing a detailed report of his proceedings in New York. The other passengers loafed and idled and flirted their time away, very much in the usual fashion. Three uneventful days brought peace of mind to the Captain and to the First Officer.

"Am I a good secretary?" Catherine asked one evening at the completion of a long day's work.

"The best I ever had," he admitted promptly. "All the same, I am not so sure after all that we shall be able to work together for very long."

Her eyebrows were slightly raised.

"It should not be for you to say that," she protested. "If I am useful here, why should not I be equally so in Moscow? Andrew Kroupki, you tell me, will not be able to leave New York for more than a month."

"That is true."

"There is some one else in Moscow, perhaps?" she persisted.

"There is no one else," he assured her. "I have never had a woman secretary."

"Some one in your household would object to my presence?"

He frowned irritably.

"There is no woman whatever in my household," he said, "except an old housekeeper who was my nurse when I was a boy. It is not that. The bald truth is that you are not the sort of secretary for a man like myself."

"Because of our political lack of sympathy?" she asked. "I can't help being a Monarchist, but as against that you have done

Russia a magnificent service by freeing her from Bolshevism. I could never forget that."

"It is not a matter of politics at all," he confessed. "Can't you realise that I dislike having women around me as women? I prefer to keep an unbiassed mind. Women belong to the arts and graces of life. They have no place in our serious moments and enterprises."

She looked at him with gentle pity.

"Dear Mr. Samara," she said, "it is terrible to hear a man of intelligence like yourself talk such absolute nonsense. You are looking out on life with one eye shut."

"No great man was ever cumbered with womenkind," he declared. "Those who were, fell."

"If you quote Mark Antony and Napoleon to me I shall shriek," she threatened. "I wish we were entirely of the same way of thinking in other matters. I would soon convert you as to this."

"You should accept my obduracy as a compliment," he said. "If association with you had not its effect upon me I should automatically forget your sex."

"I should never let you," she assured him.

They were promenading the deck together. It was during the hour before dinner and they climbed to the boat deck and walked on the windward side to avoid the crowd. Here they were almost alone.

"My mind this afternoon," Catherine confided, "has, in intervals of work, been engrossed by thoughts of my own future. When do we reach Monte Carlo?"

"Next Thursday," he replied.

"How long do we stay there?" she enquired.

"At least a week," he answered. "One of my ministers is coming from Moscow to meet me, and there will be an emissary from a foreign country waiting for me."

"And after that?"

"We shall go to Moscow via Naples and Budapest. So far as you are concerned, when we arrive there, you will naturally be your own mistress. I hope, however, that you will continue to help me, at any rate until Andrew returns. I do not like to speak of money in connection with such services as you have rendered me, but I shall of course see that financially you are unembarrassed."

"Thank you," she said. "In any case I quite intend to come to Moscow with you."

He was silent, for a cause which, had she known it, would have flattered her.

"When you asked me to come with you and I, by the way, refused," she continued, "I knew nothing about Monte Carlo. I took it for granted that I should be taken direct to Moscow."

"You are disappointed?"

"Not I," she laughed. "What girl in the world would be disappointed at the chance of seeing Monte Carlo for the first time in her life! All the same, I am looking forward very much indeed to returning to my own country. Thanks to you, my friends are coming. The Grand Duchess has offered me a home, and I have no doubt that Nicholas would give me a post as his secretary if I asked him. Tzars have to have secretaries, I suppose."

"Nicholas Imanoff will never be Tzar," he told her grimly. "I haven't saved Russia from the Bolshevists to hand it back to one of his breed."

"Really," she murmured. "Well, Nicholas quite thinks he is going to be. He'd look rather wonderful, wouldn't he, in white uniform and a crown?"

"For an exceedingly sensible young woman you talk a lot of nonsense," he said.

"When I'm in the mood," she confided, "no one can stop me. Still, if you don't press me to remain with you after we get to Moscow, I shall always believe that it is because you are afraid of me."

"You will be quite right," he confessed. "I am already."

She laughed softly and turned to the Captain whom they had just encountered.

"Such a confession, Captain!" she exclaimed. "Mr. Samara here, who fears no cutthroat, laughs at bullets, and despises bombs, is afraid of poor me."

"I do not wonder," was the prompt reply. "It is his peace of mind which is in danger."

"It may be that," she reflected. "It is at any rate a flattering thought."

"What are we to do with your Russian lunatic?" the Captain enquired, turning to Samara.

The latter shrugged his shoulders.

"What do I care? Keep him in irons until I have left the ship, and then, whatever you will. You'd much better have left him where I sent him."

The Captain smiled.

"Sometimes," he admitted, "I think that the ways of a few hundred years ago were the better."

He passed on and Samara and his companion continued their walk.

"I have quite made up my mind as to my future," Catherine declared. "I wish to come to Moscow with you, to find apartments in the city pending the arrival of my friends, and to continue my work as your secretary — your junior secretary, of course — until that unfortunate young man in New York recovers. I am deeply interested in your outlook. I think there are certain aspects of the life and evolution of my country which you understand better than any living person. Don't send me away from you, please, Mr. Samara. Remember that you are entirely responsible for my coming."

"Why the devil shouldn't I?" he demanded with sudden harshness. "You'll leave me as soon as you've learnt all you want to learn. You haven't come at all in the spirit in which I appealed to you to come. You patronise my outlook. In your heart you despise it."

She contrived to keep by his side without loss of dignity, although he had turned abruptly around and was making for the steps.

"You are very severe all of a sudden," she complained. "Where are you off to in this tremendous haste?"

"To the smoking room to drink cocktails," he growled. "Beware of me at dinner time. I may have a few home truths to tell you."

"I shall come with you," she declared. "I need sustenance myself. I wish I did not look so strong. Then you would perhaps be more sympathetic. And as regards those cocktails you are a very fraudulent person. Nothing that you ever drink makes the slightest difference to you."

He laughed hardly.

"You are quite right," he admitted. "It doesn't. Still there are times when I like the fire in my veins, even when it leads nowhere. Come if you wish to, by all means."

They sat at a corner table in the smoking room, the object, as usual, of a great deal of attention, although few people at any time ventured upon more than a respectful salute. When she had finished her *apéritif,* Catherine rose.

"Go and change now, please," she begged. "I feel that our conversation at dinner time may be interesting, and I don't want you to sit here and drink more cocktails and be half an hour late."

He rose to his feet but only to let her pass. For a few minutes after she had gone, he remained silent. To the bartender, who paused before him in expectation of a further order, he only shook his head. He told himself that a certain minor crisis in his life was arising, and that he must meet it with a cool brain. He had been conscious of its near approach ever since he had found it more easy to remember the cling of Catherine's arm around his neck than the hiss of the knife with its sickening little stab, from which she had saved him. Even now there was a strange and unfamiliar sensation of pleasure as he recalled the clasp of her fingers, the touch of her cheek against his. Folly for any man. Lunacy for him!

Yet, at its very outset the spontaneity of their dinner conversation was ruined by an untoward and ugly episode. The second steward bore down upon them almost as soon as they had taken their places, whilst Samara was still stroking the green-eyed black cat who came to his chair every evening. He was carrying a silver tureen which he set down upon the table.

"Our under-chef," he confided, "has sent you some Russian Bortsch soup, with some cream sauce. He was in service once with a Russian family at Nice and learnt something of their cooking."

"Very good, if it is really Bortsch," Catherine remarked. "Am I to have a little?"

The steward smiled reassuringly.

"The chef has prepared plenty, madam," he said, as he served it. "I was specially to recommend the sauce."

Samara poured some of the latter a little absently into his plate and held it toward the cat.

"You'll never get rid of him if you give him cream, sir," the man observed, as he turned away.

Samara held out his hand towards Catherine, who was about to commence her dinner.

"Wait," he insisted, "just one moment."

She saw the horror creep into his face and leaned over. The cat lay on its side. Already its eyes were half closed and its limbs were stiffening. The second steward, who had been talking at a table close at hand, came hurrying back.

"Why, what's wrong with the cat, sir?" he exclaimed. "Seems as though he was going to have a fit."

"It is your chef's specially prepared dish that is the matter with the cat," Samara said drily. "You had better take the rest of it to the doctor."

The man's face was white with horror.

"Just a moment, sir," he begged. "I've got to get down to the kitchens first. I wonder whether you'd mind coming with me?"

Samara rose and followed him. Two of the stewards carried out the cat. The chief steward himself came and removed the dishes from the table. There was a babel of conversation. No one knew exactly what had happened.

There was a certain drama in the little scene below, although Samara himself was chiefly conscious of a sense of bitter anger. The under-chef, in his soiled white clothes and white cap, stood with folded arms, leaning against the wall in the doctor's little consulting room. The doctor was present, also the chief steward and the Captain. The latter wasted little time upon the matter.

"Look here," he said to the young man, "you declare that there was nothing harmful in the soup or the sauce you sent up for Mr. Samara."

"It was made as I have always made it," was the sullen reply. "As for the cat, he has fits. It was that and nothing else."

"Very well," the Captain continued. "There is the sauce upon the table. Doctor, I dare say you can find a wineglass. You shall drink a wineglassful and we will believe you."

Something of the chef's bravado left him. He watched the sauce poured into a medicine glass which the doctor held out towards him. He took it into his hands and hesitated for a moment. Then he dashed it on to the floor.

"I will not drink it," he declared. "You cannot force me to."

The Captain nodded to a sailor who had been waiting outside. "Put him in irons at once," he ordered.

The man made a sudden spring for the door, but the chief steward caught him by the collar and swung him round. He stood shivering, helpless, but with a look of hate in his eyes. He glared at Samara and the desire to kill was mingled with the hate.

"I may fail and others may fail," he cried, "but some day, some one will succeed!"

Samara's anger seemed to have passed. He looked at his would-be assassin curiously.

"You are a Russian?" he asked.

"Yes," was the sullen reply.

"Why should you try to kill me — you and these others you speak of? I have worked hard for Russia."

The man spat upon the floor.

"You have worked hard for yourself," he snarled. "You are an autocrat, worse than any Tzar who ever ruled at Peterhof. You're a tyrant, an enemy of Soviet Government. That is why we hate you. You stand for the personal; I, and all real Russian patriots, for the Republic!"

They led him away. There was a look almost of sadness in Samara's eyes as he turned to leave the cabin. The man was obviously one of an ignorant band of anarchists, ill-educated, filled with poisonous doctrines. Yet a gleam of truth sometimes flashed out from unexpected places.

CHAPTER XIII

CATHERINE, a morning or so later, leaned over the white rail of the boat deck and watched the blue fires playing about the wires overhead.

"These Marconi people must bless you, Mr. Samara," she observed.

"I think they are more disposed to curse me," he answered. "They've had very little rest for the last twenty-four hours."

She looked at him meditatively. He was, without a doubt, notwithstanding a certain uncouthness and an ungraceful stoop of his broad shoulders, a fine figure of a man. The touch of sunburn acquired during the last few days became him. She approved of the few grey hairs by his ears, the inflexible mouth, his eyes so full of colour.

"I never thought I should like a man with blue eyes," she said irrelevantly.

"Do you like me?" he asked.

She laughed ironically.

"What a question! Why else should I be here, putting myself, as one of these dear old ladies said the other morning, 'in a most difficult position — private secretary to, and travelling alone with, an unmarried man'? They don't know what a tower of strength you are, do they?"

"I hope," he answered gruffly, "that they have sense enough to realise that I have something else to think about these days besides playing the gallant."

She glanced upwards again at those blue fires which seemed ceaseless.

"One loses one's sense of proportion out here at sea," she ruminated. "I am inclined sometimes to forget that you are a very important person. This sort of thing reminds me," she added, pointing to the wires overhead. "How many messages have you received to-day?"

"I have not counted," he answered. "The last one from England is the most important. For the first time I am inclined to regret that this is not a Southampton boat. I think that I must go to London."

"Delightful!" she murmured. "I can't believe that it compares with New York, but I should like to see it."

"You probably will, then," he assured her. "The Prime Minister has invited me to visit him before I return to Moscow."

"If I were Andrew Kroupki," she remarked suggestively, "you would perhaps go a little further and tell me just what he wants to discuss with you."

"There is no reason why you should not know," he observed, after a moment's hesitation. "Your own common sense can very likely visualise the situation. Naturally what I am doing is of immense interest to England. For the last fifteen years the Russian armies have been the greatest menace to peace in Europe. I have realised that myself, although I have been powerless to act. The rumoured demobilisation of even a portion of them is an event of the utmost importance to England and France."

"I quite understand that," Catherine declared, "but tell me, are any of those messages from Berlin?"

A smile parted his lips, a smile which she was beginning to look for and appreciate. It was like the grin of a boy who sees mischief ahead. He pointed to the blue fires which were still snapping away above them.

"Hell!" he confided. "Hell and every kind of fury!"

"What fun!" she murmured. "When do we face the storm?"

"The first breath of it in Monte Carlo," he replied. "Von Hartsen is meeting me there, and I don't think he's exactly carrying the olive branch."

A messenger from the Marconi office brought Samara still another despatch. He tore open the envelope and read it carefully.

"From the War Office at Moscow," he remarked. "They're deluged with enquiries from Berlin. I must send them a short reply."

He strolled away and climbed the steps into the Marconi room. Catherine descended to the lower deck and made her way to her chair. She had scarcely seated herself before she became aware of a new neighbour on her left-hand side — a middle-aged man with dark beard and moustaches, wearing tortoise-shell rimmed spectacles and a travelling cap with long flaps. At her approach, he laid down the book he had been reading and glanced cautiously around.

"I have been looking for an opportunity of a word with you, Miss Borans," he said, speaking with a thick guttural accent. "It is very difficult to find you alone."

"Who are you and what do you want?" she asked coldly.

"My name is Lorenzheim," he told her. "Karl Lorenzheim. I am a friend. Look at this, please."

He handed her a crumpled-up visiting card of Kirdorff's. On the back was a line scrawled in pencil:

"Lorenzheim is a friend. You can treat him with confidence."

"So you know Colonel Kirdorff," she remarked.

"I am a member of the Club of which he is secretary," her new acquaintance confided. "He is a Russian and I am a German, but we are friends. We see things the same way. We are all friends. He desired me to make myself known to you when a safe opportunity occurred."

"You are very mysterious," she observed. "What do you mean by a 'safe opportunity'?"

"When Mr. Samara is not around," was the significant reply.

She twisted the card which he had given her in her fingers and returned it to him.

"Mr. Samara is on the upper deck attending to some Marconigrams," she said. "He will be back directly."

"Marconigrams, eh!" Mr. Lorenzheim repeated. "You see them — what?"

"I know what some of them are about," she assented.

He smiled.

"You are very cautious," he declared. "I do not blame you but you can trust me. Mr. Samara," he went on, "is a very great man, but he is a great man for his own people — not for yours or mine."

"I know nothing about his relations with your country," she said. "So far as regards my own friends he has treated them with great generosity."

"Generosity!" Mr. Lorenzheim scoffed. "What is this you say? Generosity, indeed! There is Nicholas Imanoff, who should to-day be ruler of Russia, selling bonds in New York. Who rules the country in his stead? Samara! Oh, you all say he's a great man because he drove out the Bolshevists. I tell you that the Bolshevists committed suicide with their follies and excesses. If Samara had not dealt them their death blow, Russia would have reverted to a monarchy fifteen years ago."

"That may be," she replied. "I still say that Samara has acted generously in summoning my friends back to Russia."

Mr. Lorenzheim took off his spectacles and polished them.

"We must not quarrel, you and I," he said tolerantly. "You call it 'generosity.' I call it 'folly.' Never mind! I have been looking for you to ask you a question. What you tell me is as though you told it to Kirdorff himself. We want to know whether Samara has any idea of tampering with the Second Army, and whether his messages from Moscow have spoken of any disaffection amongst the soldiers themselves."

Catherine moved a little uneasily in her chair. She was suddenly conscious of a sense of immense repugnance to this intruder, to his message and all its suggestions. It was with almost a feeling of horror that she realised how entirely it was taken for granted that she was occupying her present position under false pretences, that she was in reality a spy upon the man for whom she was supposed to be working. Her tone when she spoke lacked all enthusiasm.

"There is nothing definite at present which I can impart to you," she declared.

He turned and looked at her through his bespectacled eyes.

"You do not doubt my credentials?" he asked. "Kirdorff has known me for many years."

"It has not occurred to me to doubt anything that you have said," she replied. "I am not used, however, to have my new occupation taken so much for granted."

"Occupation?" he repeated mystified.

"As a spy."

He shrugged his shoulders.

"Those who toil for great causes," he said, "must stoop sometimes to displeasing methods. Pardon if I return to my book. We speak again together. Mr. Samara approaches."

Samara carried more despatches in his hand. He paused in front of Catherine's chair.

"Come and walk with me," he invited a little abruptly. "I have something to say to you."

She rose at once and he led the way to a sheltered corner aft where there were usually some empty chairs. He ensconced her in one and remained himself standing beside her.

"We shall land in three days," he announced. "It is essential that after my meeting with Von Hartsen I should go at once to Moscow, or remain in Monte Carlo for a few days. There is, however, this invitation from the Prime Minister of England to be dealt with. Will you undertake a commission there for me?"

They were nearing the Straits and she looked thoughtfully out across the sea to the bare rocky coast of North Africa. Samara watched her with impatience.

"I wonder whether you realise," she said at last, "that it is less than a fortnight since I came to your rooms from the Hotel Weltmore Typewriting Bureau to work for you?"

"Twenty-seven hours less than a fortnight," he assented. "What of it?"

"You have already entrusted me with a great many of your secrets," she reminded him, "and the little you know of me is not altogether, from your point of view, a recommendation. I belong, in fact, to a political party opposed to your views and your system of Government. Don't you think that you are placing a little too much trust in me?"

"I do not," he answered, "or I should not ask you to undertake this mission to London. You are a patriot and even though your sympathies are still engrossed in a romantic but hopelessly out-of-date cause, you admit that I have done a great work for Russia. Why should I not trust you? When I find you embroiled in a monarchist plot it will be time enough for me to send you to a fortress."

"Will you ever have the heart to do that?" she whispered, looking at him with a provocative gleam in her eyes.

"Heart!" he repeated gruffly. "I have no heart. If you betrayed my confidence, I should see that you had what you deserved."

"Nevertheless," she persisted, with a return to her more serious manner, "I think you are disposed to put too much trust in me."

He looked down at her with the momentary irritation of an elder towards a child.

"Neither a guarantee of secrecy," he declared, "nor absolute immunity from theft can ever be purchased or built up with bolts and bars. Trust, considered and calculated trust, is safety. To know where to bestow it is, I admit, a form of genius. If I seem to you flamboyantly trustful, it is your judgment that is wrong. I believe in your sense of honour and my own instinct. Kindly let that end the discussion."

That night they were anchored in the Bay of Gibraltar, in the shadow of the great Rock ablaze with its thousand pin-pricks of fire. Samara was summoned from the dinner table to receive a call from the Governor who had come aboard in his launch, and Catherine leaned for some time over the side of the ship, watching the little boats below with their wares of fruit and flowers and tinselly merchandise. Presently room was made at the foot of the gangway for the Governor's launch, and he and Samara stood for a moment or two at the top of the steps talking. Then the former took his leave and soon after Samara found his way to her side.

"Come on the upper deck," he invited. "These people below are so noisy."

She obeyed at once. They sat on one of the fixed seats with their back to the Fortress and as far removed as possible from the hubbub of the extemporised market. She asked him a question about the Governor.

"A pleasant man and very friendly," he told her. "Naturally, as an old soldier, he was interested in the demobilisation of our armies. He was very anxious for me to go and spend the night at Government House."

"Why didn't you?" she asked idly.

He made some casual answer, but his sudden realisation of the truth was a shock to him. A celebrated French traveller was staying there whom he was anxious to meet, and an English writer whose works had interested him, yet the desire not to leave the ship was paramount. He frowned as he looked meditatively across the Bay to the lights of Algeciras.

"I shall go to London if you wish me to," she announced abruptly.

"I imagined you would," he replied. "Your mission, of course, will be more personal than official, but at the same time I shall entrust you with a message to the Prime Minister which I do not care to send through our own representatives there. We have three days more to talk of that, though."

"I wish it were longer," she confessed.

"You do not regret having come, then?" he asked.

"I have never regretted it for an instant," she assured him. "All the same, to me this voyage seems to grow in unreality every day. I can't really believe that I have left New York behind, that we are here in European waters and that I am working day by day with you. It doesn't seem part of my life—like something detached, something which might have happened but didn't."

She turned to catch a glimpse of an expression in his face which startled her. There had been moments lately when she had been almost terrified of him.

"It has been an unusual experience for me," he admitted. "I have never worked with a woman before."

She suddenly laughed. His way of alluding to their association appealed to her sense of humour as she thought of the long nights they had sat on deck, with the rushing of the wind around, the leaning stars and the long golden pathway to the moon; of their long talks and their long silences. More than once, tragedy, passing by, had lifted them out of the world of commonplace things and forced them into a position of more than ordinary intimacy. Was it his sense of honour, of guardianship, she wondered, which had kept him always so aloof, or was it that she herself made no appeal to him? She had remained all the time perfectly natural, had made no effort at any artificial reserve. Vaguely she found herself somewhat resenting his attitude. Many of the men on board had, in their own way, directly or indirectly, done their best to intimate the fact that they found her attractive. Samara had never once even looked at her as though he recognised the desirability which made other men hang around her chair and seek her company. An irresistible longing to evoke a more personal note in him assailed her.

"You find it as easy to work with me as with a man?" she asked.

"I have never noticed the difference," he answered calmly. "You are very efficient."

Her lips relaxed and she smiled at him.

"I am a great deal nicer to look at than your other secretary," she said reflectively. "I do you more credit, too."

"In what way?"

"Poor Andrew Kroupki," she murmured. "He looks half-starved and very miserable. I, on the other hand, look well fed and content. No one would suspect you of ill-treating me."

"One does not choose a secretary for her personal appearance," he remarked.

"Some men do, I am afraid," she replied.

He looked at her and she was not quite so sure of herself. In the darkness his face seemed more dominant than ever, his mouth almost cruel in its strength. Only his eyes were a little disturbing.

"You don't imagine that that sort of thing would appeal to me?" he asked scornfully.

"I wonder what does appeal to you," she sighed. "Evidently I don't."

"How do you know that?" he demanded.

She shrugged her shoulders.

"How does a woman generally know?" she retorted.

She had an indefinable sense of disaster — or triumph. She suddenly felt the clasp of his arm around her waist, the touch of his fingers upon her hair and cheek. She had not before doubted her ability to meet any situation which might arise, but in this moment of trial she failed utterly and helplessly. She was suddenly weak in all her limbs. She made not the slightest resistance to a thing which had never yet happened to her, which she had never, for a moment, contemplated. His eyes seemed like fires, but softer — softer every moment. The cruel lines of his mouth, too, seemed to have relaxed. His lips touched hers firmly yet softly, lingered there whilst passion grew. She was almost swooning in his arms.

He released her quite gently yet with a certain abruptness. He rose to his feet and stood looking down at her, massive, unemotional, yet with some subtle air of the conqueror. She returned his gaze, helpless, her hands gripping the back of the seat. A corner of the moon showing from behind a jagged mass of cloud faintly illuminated her face. Her lips were still quivering. It was not for her to know that a new light in her eyes had suddenly made her more beautiful than ever before.

"Mr. Samara!" she gasped.

"I am sorry," he answered, "but I am also glad!"

She heard his receding footsteps along the deck, saw him knock at the door of the Captain's quarters, enter and disappear. Below there was still the subdued hubbub of the hucksters. In a more distant boat a swarthy Spanish woman was singing a love song to the music of a guitar.

CHAPTER XIV

An Englishman seated upon a divan in one of the lofty rooms of the Salons Privés nudged the arm of his companion, newly arrived from England. He was by way of being showman and had been pointing out the notabilities of the place.

"Do you see the fair young man moving round the table on the left?" he asked.

"Good-looking fellow with a scar on his face? Yes. Who is he?"

"In his way a very interesting person," was the earnest reply. "That is Prince Frederick of Wehrenzollern. They say that he is the most popular young man in Germany."

"I was reading about him only last week," the other observed. "One of the papers was saying that he had modelled himself entirely upon our present King when he was the same age — goes in for all sorts of sports and is always doing something thoroughly democratic."

"If Germany is ever foolish enough to discard her republic, there goes the future Kaiser," his companion announced.

The young man in question made a very slow progress through the rooms. He apparently met friends at every moment, with most of whom he stopped to talk, and although he seemed scarcely in the place for the purpose of gambling, he occasionally risked a twenty-franc piece at the tables. Presently he passed out of the ken of his two observers, and, having completed a tour of the rooms, as though in unsuccessful search of some one, collected his hat and cane in the cloakroom and strolled out. He was greeted everywhere with a great deal of attention, and he was obviously exceedingly careful to return all salutations. As soon as he was alone, however, a somewhat supercilious smile took the place of his apparent bonhomie, and he yawned once or twice on his way to the Sporting Club. Here he was again received with great consideration, and made his way up the stairs into the smaller roulette rooms. An elderly man of exceedingly aristocratic appearance moved eagerly towards him from one of the little groups. Prince Frederick welcomed him with a sigh of relief.

"I have been looking everywhere for you, General," he declared. "Come and tell me the news."

They moved off towards the bar.

"There is no news," the older man replied. "He has not yet arrived."

Prince Frederick seemed disappointed.

"I thought the boat was due in yesterday," he observed.

"It was due," the General assented, "but it has been delayed by bad weather. I am expecting to hear at any moment that it is in the bay."

The two sat in a corner of the bar. In his own country the Prince always drank beer. Here, he called for a mixed vermouth. They spoke for a little time upon incidents connected with his journey. It seemed that he had only reached Monte Carlo that afternoon.

"It is a relief," the General declared with a little sigh, "to be in a place like this, my dear Frederick, where you and I can meet and talk openly. Even though I was your tutor, people whisper in Berlin if we are seen much together, especially since I became a member of the Government. You have been as busy as usual, I suppose?"

Prince Frederick yawned.

"Last week," he confided, "I opened two flower shows, unveiled a statue, opened a tennis tournament and played in it myself, took the chair at the Flying Club dinner, and joined in the parade, opened a new fencing academy and fenced the first bout and attended two commercial banquets. Not so bad, considering that I had to show up at the bank each day. Lucky no one knows how little work I really do there."

"It is not necessary for you to do any at all," the General reminded him. "The directors are all our friends and members of our party."

"All the same," the young man declared, sipping his vermouth, "it is a grind. That dear English relative of mine in whose footsteps I am supposed to be treading, only had to pose as a democrat in sentiment — not to transform himself into a bank clerk. I hate the atmosphere of these places. The camp and the barracks are my home."

His mentor smiled tolerantly.

"You must remember, my dear Frederick," he said, "that until our day comes it is as well for you to keep your military instincts as far as possible in the background. The *bourgeoisie* would be shaking their heads and likening you to your respected great-grandfather if you gave them the opportunity. That side of it will come later. All that I pray is that I may live to see it."

"All good Germans must pray for that," the Prince agreed, lighting a cigarette. "We have become giants of commerce during the last twenty years simply because we are a great people and bound to succeed in anything we undertake — but at heart we are a military nation."

The General looked at his pupil and smiled fondly.

"It is in the blood," he murmured.

"Tell me the latest news of this man Samara," the latter demanded a little abruptly.

The General frowned.

"It is very hard to speak of the matter coolly," he declared. "We Germans made Russia a military nation. We trained their men, we made their guns and flying machines, we taught and equipped them from conscript to general. We constructed a mighty engine of destruction ready for our use when the time came. It suited the old régime. The soldier was the only man who could be sure of regular food and comfortable living, and every one wanted to be in the army. Now, under the new order, everything is changed. Industrially and agriculturally Russia is forging ahead, and now, without warning to anybody, Samara calmly announces to the world that he desires to reduce his army to the proportions suggested by the League of Nations and insists that he needs the soldiers for industrial developments. His representative in Moscow told Baron Gusman plainly a few days ago that the Russian Government no longer recognised any military understanding with Germany."

"What about our own Cabinet?" the Prince asked eagerly. "How do they take the matter?"

"Their attitude," the General replied, "is, so far as it goes, satisfactory. I am here as a special envoy, instructed to formally protest against any further demobilisation of the Russian armies, to remind Samara of our previous agreements, and to demand an explanation of his present policy. Except for a handful of socialists, the motion in favour of my mission was carried unanimously."

"They say Samara is a great autocrat," Prince Frederick reflected. "Supposing he takes high ground?"

His companion was silent. He glanced around the room and, although they were in a retired spot, he dropped his voice.

"Then he may bring the day of fulfillment nearer," he said. "Samara's hold upon the people is as yet unproved and propaganda amongst the army has already begun."

A young man who had been standing upon the threshold, as though in search of some one, suddenly recognised the General and advanced. He bowed respectfully to Prince Frederick and handed a despatch to the former.

"A wireless from the American boat, sir," he announced. "She is in sight and expects to land her passengers within the hour."

The General tore open the envelope and read its contents.

"Samara will see me at six o'clock to-night at the Hôtel de Paris," he announced, with satisfaction. "Excellent!"

"Then, by dinner time to-night," the Prince began slowly ——

"By dinner time to-night," the General interrupted, "I shall know what is at the back of Samara's mind. If he means to play us false — well, it will mean a complete reversal of our present foreign policy. It may lead to even greater changes than that."

A very beautiful and world-famous young woman looked in at the door and, recognising Prince Frederick, smiled at him. He rose at once to his feet.

"I go to play baccarat with Mademoiselle," he announced. "We have an arrangement."

His mentor in chief laid a hand upon his shoulder.

"Amuse yourself," he said tolerantly, "but remember — these little escapades are as well kept secret. There are gossips amongst our newspaper men and the Princess Freda is exacting in some matters."

The young man smiled.

"Even my sainted prototype," he remarked, as he turned away, "had a weakness for beautiful ladies."

General von Hartsen played roulette for a time, took a stroll along the front, watching the great American steamer which had just arrived, and finally presented himself at the Hôtel de Paris at the appointed hour. Samara was engaged in the task of sorting his letters with Catherine's help. He received his visitor at once, however, shook hands with him and motioned him to a seat.

"Is this a visit of courtesy, General," he demanded, "or am I to consider it, in any sense of the word, official?"

"Friendly, if you please, sir," was the slightly formal reply, "but also official. I am the bearer of representations from the Government in whose labours I have the honour to share, to the Chairman of the Council of the Russian Republic."

Samara shrugged his shoulders and turned away from the letters. He had the air of one preparing to receive battle.

"In that case, General," he begged, "pray proceed. I am entirely at your service."

The latter glanced courteously but questioningly towards Catherine.

"The young lady," he began ——

"Let me present you," Samara interrupted. "General von Hartsen — Miss Borans, my secretary."

The General bowed low but his expression was still a puzzled one. His eyes remained fixed upon Catherine.

"Miss Borans," he repeated, "you will pardon me, I am sure, but I am under the impression that we must have met before."

"I think not," Catherine replied, shaking her head slightly.

"Unless you have ever been a visitor to the United States, it is improbable," Samara intervened. "Miss Borans has lived there all her life."

"In that case I am doubtless deceived by a likeness," the General confessed. "You will forgive my adding, Mr. Samara, that our present conference must be a private one."

"I have no secrets from my secretary," Samara insisted. "Miss

Borans is discretion itself. She would in any case handle any report of our interview which I might have to submit to my Council."

Von Hartsen bowed.

"Very well, sir," he said, "I will proceed. I am directed by the ministers of the German Republic to ask you for full particulars concerning this proposed demobilisation of a portion of your armies and further to enquire what change of policy such a step is meant to indicate. I think I need not be more explicit."

"Not the slightest need of it," Samara acquiesced. "Pray sit down. Smoke a cigar if you will, and I'll tell you all about it. I'll tell you just what my plans and hopes are for the future of Russia and incidentally, at the risk of shocking you, you shall learn my exact views as to the establishment of what I term mercenary armies."

The General's face grew a shade sterner. He put back the cigar which he had been in the act of clipping and folded his arms.

"I am at your service, sir," he announced.

THE General listened with more or less patience to all that was in Samara's mind, and found the situation a great deal worse than he had expected. Towards the conclusion of their interview he became very angry indeed.

"I consider that the course of action which you propose, Mr. Samara, is entirely at variance with your obligations towards my country," he announced.

"I recognise no obligations towards your country," was the brusque reply. "I have from the first warned you that it was my intention at the earliest opportunity to rid myself of the great armies which my misguided predecessors, aided by you, have brought into being. To have done so would have been my first action on coming into power if it had been possible to have found the men employment. I have now made arrangements which will enable me to put half a million men on the land and half a million into industrial pursuits. Demobilisation of the Third Army will commence the day I return to Moscow."

"And what about the First and Second?" the General demanded.

"I shall follow suit with the Second almost at once," Samara answered. "I look upon a trained army as an incentive to militarism, and I don't intend to maintain one. Since you are here I may as well inform you that my Government will issue a proclamation before the end of next month, requiring all officers of German nationality to resign their commissions and leave the country. A certain bonus will be allotted to them but that will be a matter of adjustment."

General von Hartsen found self-control an exceedingly difficult matter.

"You recognise, I trust, Mr. Samara," he said, "that such a proceeding will be considered by my Government as an unfriendly act?"

"I'm not afraid that you'll go to war about it, if that is what you mean," was the prompt retort. "You won't waste your resources on us whilst England and France are upon the face of the earth. And to be perfectly frank with you, General, if it was ever in your mind to use any part of the Russian army for any German military enterprise, I can assure you that the idea was hopeless from the first. I do not intend that during my tenure of office the blood of a single Russian peasant shall be shed upon the battle field. There was too much of that in nineteen-fifteen and sixteen."

"You're more of a pacifist than I ever believed possible for a man of vigorous action, Mr. Samara," the General sneered.

"That may easily be so," Samara assented. "I'm a pacifist at any rate so far as this, that I do not intend to support a standing army. Every Russian citizen, as he grows up, will be taught how to fight in his country's defence if ever it should become necessary. Beyond that — nothing."

Von Hartsen rose to his feet.

"You realise, Mr. Samara, I suppose," he said, "that even at home you will have to face something like a cataclysm. Your men do not wish for demobilisation."

"They will wish for it fast enough when they see what I can offer them," was the confident reply. "America has lent me enough money to provide for a million of them, and Great Britain has asked me to explain my needs so far as regards the others. I am sending an envoy there to-morrow."

The General bowed coldly to Catherine and to Samara without extending his hand.

"I shall report the issue of our conversation to my Government, Mr. Samara," he announced. "They will probably make further representations to you."

He took his leave. Samara, with his hands in his pockets, walked to the window and stood looking out at the great front of the Casino and at the gardens below, whistling softly to himself.

"Well," he remarked presently, "it's a stupid game. German diplomacy is always so obvious. As though any one couldn't see that our armies were meant to be the cat's-paw to snatch out of the fire the chestnuts of revenge. Russia will never fight in my day except in self-defence."

"You might have civil war," Catherine reminded him calmly.

Samara swung round on his heel.

"Civil war," he growled. "About as much chance of it as the end of the world. The whole fault of the Russian as a politician is that he's too indifferent. That's why the Bolshevists were able to keep going as long as they did. The Russian wants peace and to go on as he is going. It is the aim of my life to see that he gets his wish. Miss Borans, listen to me for a moment, please."

"I am listening," she assured him.

"I hear from the Chief of the Police that enquiries are being made in Moscow for suitable accommodation for pretty well the whole of your Royalist friends. Well, I told them that they should be welcome back to Russia and they are welcome, but I want it to be clearly understood that they must live and behave as ordinary citizens. They must recognise and observe the law and the government of the country."

Catherine inclined her head.

"That seems reasonable," she admitted.

"I do not imagine for a moment that they are foolish enough to entertain the idea of anything in the nature of a definite conspiracy," Samara continued, "but if they did attempt anything of the sort, I should be quite powerless to help them. You will drop them a hint perhaps."

"I will certainly do so if I think it necessary," she promised.

They parted a little stiffly, Samara to interview an emissary from Moscow, Catherine to spend a delightful hour wandering about the gardens and Terrace of the little principality. She returned about eight o'clock, dined alone in the spacious salon attached to Samara's suite, and was standing at the window gazing rather longingly at the curving arc of lights along the Terrace when Samara himself suddenly entered the room.

"You?" she exclaimed. "I thought you were dining with your man from Moscow."

"I have dined with him," Samara answered. "I have sent him back home to-night. General von Hartsen's attitude does not disturb me in the least but it is necessary to prepare them at the War Office."

"And you?" she enquired.

"I have other affairs to attend to here and shall await your return from London. You will leave to-morrow morning, or rather midday."

"Do you wish to work now?" she asked.

"Don't be absurd," he scoffed. "Who ever works the first night in Monte Carlo? I wish to take you to the Casino and to the Club, but you must be differently dressed."

"Indeed," she murmured with a smile. "Well, you didn't give me much chance to bring clothes along, did you?"

"You must be able to do something," he insisted impatiently.

"As a matter of fact," she confided, "I have bought a little black frock this evening whilst I was wandering about. It is very simple and I don't know that it has come yet."

"Go and put it on," he directed, "and meet me here in half an hour's time."

She moved towards the door but on the threshold she looked back at him reflectively.

"I am not at all sure," she declared, "that I wish to go out with you."

He returned her gaze without moving a muscle.

"Because I kissed you and haven't apologised?" he asked.

She laughed softly.

"Not quite that," she admitted.

"What then?" he demanded.

Her eyes mocked him inscrutably.

"What an *ingénu* you are when you leave your own world for a minute," she said, disappearing through the door.

An hour later they were seated side by side on a divan in the Sporting Club. People were standing three and four deep around the tables and play was for the moment impossible. Catherine, serenely beautiful, and with her intense curiosity concealed by the force of habit, was entirely content. Samara was moodily interested.

"But who are these people?" she asked him. "I've never seen such jewels even at the opera at New York. And the men — here at last is a new type."

Her companion smiled.

"I am a poor showman," he admitted. "I have been here twice before in my life, but even I recognise some faces. There is Prince Artelberg, the Austrian Premier, the man who has very nearly made a country of Austria again."

"But the lady with him, in blue silk?"

"One seldom recognises the ladies," Samara answered drily. "The two men passing by are English. The nearer one is in the British Embassy at Moscow. The tall man with the grey beard and the small order is the King of Gothland. Alas, I am recognised! He is coming to speak to me."

The King detached himself from a small group of friends and crossed the room towards Samara, who had risen to his feet.

"A most amazing meeting!" the former exclaimed, holding out his hand. "You are on your way home from America, I presume?"

"I landed this evening, your Majesty," Samara replied.

"You will accept my heartiest congratulations on the success of your mission," the King begged. "But what about my cousins? What will they have to say to your altruistic efforts?"

Samara shook his head.

"One can but hope," he said, "that they will appreciate the advance of the inevitable."

The King smiled.

"I fancy that you will find General von Hartsen rather a handful," he remarked. "He has been here waiting for you for days, fuming like a madman most of the time. Present the young lady, if you please."

"With your Majesty's permission," Samara replied. "Miss Catherine Borans, my temporary secretary — the King of Gothland. Miss Borans has been good enough to replace Andrew Kroupki, who was taken ill in New York."

The King bowed and held out his hand.

"To be secretary to Mr. Samara," he said, "is to stand behind the curtains of the diplomatic world. I congratulate you, Miss Borans."

"I find the work exceedingly interesting, your Majesty," she observed.

The King looked at her curiously.

"You are American?" he enquired.

"I have lived there most of my life," she answered.

"It is curious," he continued. "You have a family likeness to some friends of mine. You stay here for long, Mr. Samara?"

"Perhaps four days, sir," was the reluctant reply.

"I am at the Hôtel de Londres," the King announced. "If you have the leisure, please sign your name in my book."

He bowed to Catherine, nodded to Samara and passed on. The two resumed their seats.

"I am quite sure," the former said demurely, "that Miss Loyes would have come up to your room herself if she had realised that it might mean a trip to Europe and an introduction to a King."

"There is worse to come," Samara muttered, glancing apprehensively at two approaching figures. "I thought this fellow, at any rate, was never going to speak to me again."

General von Hartsen clicked his heels, bowed and held out his hand.

"Mr. Samara," he said, "my young friend here desires the advantage of a personal acquaintance with you. Will you pardon my taking this opportunity? Prince Frederick of Wehrenzollern — Mr. Samara."

Samara studied the young man with interest as he shook hands. The latter smiled frankly.

"My name may convey to such a world-famed democrat as you, sir," he observed, "unpleasant reminiscences. I have resumed my title, it is true, but I am a German citizen and a faithful subject of the Republic. I work in a bank. The General tells me that you have just arrived from New York."

"This afternoon," Samara assented.

"You will do me the honour, perhaps," Prince Frederick continued, "of presenting me to the young lady."

Samara acquiesced without comment.

"Prince Frederick of Wehrenzollern — Miss Borans of New York."

"Is it possible that you are an American, mademoiselle?" the young prince murmured as he bowed low over her hand.

"I have lived there all my life," Catherine assured him.

"And this is your first visit to Monte Carlo?"

"My first visit to Europe."

"It is amazing," he murmured. "You stay for some time here, I hope?"

Catherine was imbibing the atmosphere of diplomacy.

"It is uncertain," she replied.

"You will permit me, perhaps," he ventured, with another bow, "to show you the rooms? Mr. Samara will not object?" he added, turning to the latter.

"By all means."

The two young people strolled off together, without waiting for Samara's somewhat surprised acceptance of the situation. General von Hartsen watched them critically.

"Magnificent!" he exclaimed. "The blue-blooded aristocracy of the east and the red-blooded aristocracy of the west. Mademoiselle is doubtless the daughter of one of these great American millionaires."

"Mademoiselle's income, so far as I know," Samara replied drily, "is thirty dollars a week, the salary I pay her. She happens to be my secretary. I should perhaps have mentioned the fact."

"What the hell's this?" Samara demanded, as he entered the salon on the following morning and found a cardboard box the size of a washing basket on the table.

"Roses," Catherine replied, raising her head from the interior which she had been examining. "The most wonderful I have ever seen in my life. For me, too! And from a prince! I'm glad I came to Europe!"

"A prince who is also a bank clerk!" Samara scoffed. "Believe me, the world has finished with princes."

"This one was very pleasant," Catherine confided. "He invited me to spend the greater part of to-day with him."

"You told him you were going to London, of course?" Samara asked quickly.

"I certainly did not. Ought I to have done so? I rather thought that was between you and me."

Samara nodded his approval.

"They wouldn't suspect you of being a real envoy," he observed. "That is one reason why I am sending you. Still, there is no need to run unnecessary risks. You have had your coffee?"

"An hour ago," she answered, "and packed my things, and walked on the Terrace."

"With your princeling?"

She shook her head.

"He was invisible," she sighed. "Of course it may have been that he didn't know that I was going to be there. He spoke of a party at the Carlton last night, wherever that may be. Perhaps he was late."

"Perhaps he was," Samara agreed.

"It seems a little unfortunate," she murmured, as she poured out the coffee, "that I am leaving Monte Carlo so soon. I was.

never so great a success at the Hotel Weltmore in New York. On my first day here, a king has told me that I reminded him of some friends of his, and a prince has invited me to luncheon and sent me roses."

"Just as well you're leaving," Samara growled. "Your head would soon be turned."

"I am very well balanced," she assured him.

"How about your memory?" he asked. "I hope your flirtatious successes haven't driven the serious matters out of your head altogether."

"Absolutely," she confessed. "What am I going to London for? I am sure I don't know."

"In that case you had better stay behind," he suggested gruffly. She laughed in derision.

"My dear master," she said, "there isn't a word or a point of the whole thing that isn't in my brain. As an envoy I'm going to be the greatest success of modern times. I shall be irresistibly logical, delicately persuasive. What sort of a man is the British Prime Minister, please?"

"A married man with a large family and serious views," Samara warned her, "and as for politics he is as sincere a democrat as I am."

"I won't expound my little hobbies about government then," she promised. "What a pity you aren't coming with me."

"If I could make the journey," he replied coldly, "there would be no need for you to go."

"I hope you won't get into trouble here while I'm away," she sighed. "It really is a most attractive place."

"There is seldom any trouble here except of one's own making," was the somewhat curt rejoinder. "Monte Carlo is a sort of sanctuary for all the criminals of the world. They meet here and exchange notes, but they look upon it as a sort of neutral ground. To attempt evil against a man in Monte Carlo is almost a breach of etiquette."

He accompanied her presently to the railway station. Her bag had been sent on and they walked through the gardens, bathed in sunshine, along the Terrace and waited a few moments for the lift. Catherine, humming softly to herself from sheer despair at her companion's silence, was looking amazingly beautiful. It was as though all the youth of her nature had responded to the entrancing change in the conditions of her life. In her neat travelling dress, with a great bunch of the roses in her hand and her almost lizard-like absorption of the glinting sunshine, she seemed to have imbibed with it the joyous spirit of her surroundings and the passing hour. The drabness of cities and of cramped labour were things utterly discarded. She was a young princess of the coming day; eager yet gracious. Samara, on the contrary, was not altogether at his best. His clothes, as was often the case, needed brushing, his hair and chin needed the services of a barber. There was a streak of red in his eyes, too, and a shadow underneath them, as though the night had gone ill with him. Catherine, as the lift rattled up, paused in her humming and looked at him critically.

"Were you late last night?" she enquired.

"Moderately. I had a great many despatches to read."

"You had no bad news from Moscow?"

He shook his head.

"None at all. Politically everything seems to be reasonably quiet. It is from outside all the disturbance will come for some time. Our own people have scarcely realised yet the change which has come into their lives."

They were alone in the lift. She drew a little nearer to him.

"You are afraid of Germany, perhaps?"

He brushed aside the suggestion scornfully with a wave of his hand.

"I am afraid of no one," he answered. "A certain clique of statesmen in Germany will be furious and will start an agitation against us. I doubt whether they will do any good. As I have already warned you, they will watch London closely. That is why I prefer to send you there in this manner, without letters or documents, rather than to make you the bearer of any written proposition."

"You are placing a great trust in me," she reflected, as they watched the approach of the train.

"There is no success in life possible for any one who has not learned to trust," he declared.

The train came thundering in. Catherine's seat was found without difficulty. Samara stood in the corridor for a moment, looking in at her.

"You are a strange person," she said, holding out her hand, "rather a bully and terribly unreasonable sometimes, but I shall be glad to see you again. Promise me that I may come back here, that you will not send word for me to go direct to Moscow or anything of that sort."

He smiled.

"A statesman is always at the mercy of circumstances," he reminded her, "but the Duma is not summoned to meet until the week after next and my arrival in Moscow before then would be premature. I think you may take it that I shall be here, awaiting your return on Saturday night."

He backed away at the last urgent call and stood on the platform whilst the train rolled out. There was nothing to be seen of Catherine, and he gazed carelessly into the passing windows. Suddenly he gave a start. A young man who had boarded the train at the last moment was leaning breathlessly down from the platform of his car, waving his hand to a friend. As he recognised them, Samara's frown grew blacker. An entirely new and unwelcome sensation sent him back to the hotel with a curse upon his lips.

Catherine was by no means a secretive person, but she had received a letter that morning of which she had said nothing to Samara. As soon as the train had started she took it from her handbag, spread it out and reread it, a smile of amusement upon her lips. It was dated from the Hôtel de Paris on the preceding night:

MADEMOISELLE!

The roses which I shall send you to-morrow as soon as the shops are opened bring too tardy a message. I cannot rest to-night without sending you a line to beg for your gracious permission to see you at the earliest possible opportunity, to assure you that since the moment we met, only a few hours ago, every other thought has been driven from my mind, every other woman's face into which I have ever looked has become a blank. Please believe in my sincerity as I believe in you. There is no one so adorable in the world!

Forgive my presumption! It comes from a heart overfull! I count the minutes until I shall see you again!

FREDERICK.

The smile deepened. Catherine laughed softly to herself. She tore the letter into small pieces, held her hand out of the window and let them go fluttering by. Then, whilst her handbag was open she looked at herself in the little mirror, handled her powder puff lightly for a moment, closed the bag and leaned back in her place. For a time she watched with interest the unfamiliar landscape. Presently, however, she yawned, closed her eyes and dozed. She was awakened by the soft opening of the door of her compartment. She sat up and recognised the intruder with amazement.

"Prince Frederick!" she exclaimed.

He held out his hand.

"Please not," he begged earnestly. "Even if you are angry with me let it be 'Frederick.' I am not — not exactly supposed to be here."

"I should think not," she agreed with decision. "Why are you?"

He closed the door and with some diffidence took the seat opposite to hers.

"For the reason, mademoiselle," he confessed, "that I tried to express in my letter."

"But this is absurd," she protested. "I am going to England."

"I know it," he answered. "So am I."

She looked at him for a moment steadfastly. Then she glanced out of the window.

"You did not mention your intention yesterday," she said.

"I had no idea of it myself," he assured her.

"Do you wish me to understand that I am in any way connected with your journey?" she asked.

"I beg of you not to be angry, mademoiselle," he rejoined almost humbly. "You are the sole cause of it."

"Then, if you will allow me to tell you so," she said deliberately, "I think that you are mad."

"I think so myself," he acknowledged. "I thought so all night. I have thought so every moment since we first met. But it is, after all, a glorious madness."

She looked at him again steadily. He was a personable young man, dressed in grey tweeds cut after the English fashion, with shiny brown shoes of the shade she liked, fine linen and a well-chosen tie. His features were good, if a little over-reminiscent of an unpopular ancestry. There was weakness in his face but nothing much that was bad. So far as it was possible for any one to judge, he seemed to be in earnest.

"Would it cure you," she enquired, "if I told you that this madness of which you speak is not in the least reciprocated?"

"That would be too much to hope for," he admitted. "I am content to wait. I have not had a chance to speak to you seriously."

"Seriously? How on earth could you be more serious?" she demanded.

He hesitated. He had sufficient tact to be aware that he was on delicate ground. Young American ladies, he knew, were used to a great deal of freedom, and this one had doubtless been a little spoiled. It was scarcely a case for rushing tactics.

"Mademoiselle," he said, "the idea of my devotion is a new one to you. You have not accustomed yourself to it. Will you remember at least that we do not meet as strangers? I may claim the privileges of a travelling companion?"

"I suppose there is nothing to prevent your doing that," she acquiesced, "but I might point out that the remaining three seats in this compartment have been engaged in my name."

"I shall leave according to your instructions, mademoiselle," he promised. "The whole of the corresponding compartment next door is mine."

Catherine began to laugh to herself. He watched her questioningly.

"You see it is my first visit to Europe," she explained. "I had no idea that such things as this really happened."

"Far more wonderful things than this happen," he assured her earnestly. "Your American men, mademoiselle — pardon me, but they have no sentiment. They would not throw convention to the winds as I have done — abandoned all my engagements to follow the person whom I adore on the merest chance of a kindly word, to the one city in the world which I detest."

"I'm not so sure," she reflected. "Some of these American young men are fairly rapid."

He shook his head.

"They are not capable of sentiment so intense," he declared.

"The one I am engaged to is quite headstrong when he is roused," Catherine remarked.

Prince Frederick glanced at her with a flash in his blue eyes which made him seem almost like a man.

"Engaged! You engaged!" he cried. "That is nothing."

"My young man thinks that it's a great deal," she observed. "He very much disliked my coming to Europe. He's on his way over here now."

"Who is he? What is he?" Prince Frederick demanded. "I must know all about him."

"He is called Nicholas," she confided, "and he is — well, he's very much what you are."

"A banker!" her companion exclaimed. "But that is only a blind. I have taken a position in commerce so as to establish myself as a German citizen."

"You have other ideas?" she asked him curiously.

He pulled himself up.

"That is of no account," he replied. "When does this young man arrive? You're not going to England to meet him?"

"I don't even know what boat he is on," she declared.

The blue-liveried steward paused for a moment at the door with his customary announcement.

"*Le déjeuner est servi, madame et monsieur.*"

Prince Frederick rose to his feet.

"You will at least do me the great honour of lunching with me, mademoiselle?" he begged.

"I think I may go so far without indiscretion," she assented.

CHAPTER XVII

CATHERINE's first impressions of England were delightful ones. She sat in the very comfortable armchair of a well-hung Pullman and looked out upon a patchwork country of tender greens, of woods bottomed with bluebells, of spinneys and railway banks yellow with primroses, and orchards in which pink, waxy blossoms were already beginning to form. She was far too interested to notice the almost savage gloom of the young man who sat in the opposite chair.

"Mademoiselle Catherine," he exclaimed at last.

She turned reluctantly away from the sun-bathed panorama of fertile country.

"My name is 'Miss Borans,'" she told him. "I do not appreciate the use of my christian name."

"You are brutal," he declared.

She looked at him without kindness, scarcely even with friendliness.

"You are a very absurd and spoilt young man," she said. "You seem to fancy yourself aggrieved because I am not able to reciprocate in any way your very ridiculous feeling for me. You have no common sense. It is rather I who should be aggrieved. I did not encourage you to follow me. For the small services you have rendered me upon the train and the boat, I am much obliged, but I should have preferred being without them. If you wish to remain on terms of friendship or acquaintance with me, please abandon that expression and talk like a reasonable human being."

His face showed no signs of lightening. He seemed indeed thoroughly dejected and miserable.

"Why are you so cruel?" he begged. "Why can you not be just a little kinder? What is there about me repugnant?"

"You're not in the least repugnant to me," she assured him. "You simply do not interest me very much, and so far as my affections are concerned, they are engaged elsewhere."

He watched the flying landscape for a moment, as though he hated the speed it indicated. For the hundredth time he tried to find courage.

"I've always heard that you American girls are so practical," he said. "Why should you remain the secretary of a man like Samara? I am very rich, mademoiselle. I am very fond of travel. It is not my intention to marry for years. Reasons which I cannot confide to you forbid it. There are secondary titles belonging to some of my estates. I always thought that sort of thing appealed to Americans," he mumbled as a gleam in her eyes almost froze the words upon his lips.

"They tell me that you have reëstablished duelling in Germany. Is it true?" she asked.

"It is true," he admitted.

"I have a friend in America," she went on, "who is on his way over here now, who is supposed to be a very expert swordsman. I fancy that I failed to grasp your meaning just now. We are perhaps a little out of sympathy. I propose to read."

She buried herself in an illustrated paper. Her companion rose to his feet, kicked a footstool out of his way, and with scowling face retreated into the smoking car. He ordered a drink and threw himself into a vacant chair.

"A little American typist!" he muttered. "A typist from the Hotel Weltmore!"

He struck the table with his fist. The few people in the car looked up in surprise. He only scowled.

"I want that drink," he shouted to the steward.

At Victoria Catherine smiled at him quite pleasantly, but she had already engaged a porter. As she was stepping into the taxicab, however, to which he insisted upon escorting her, she vouchsafed a few disconcerting words of farewell.

"You can tell your little friend," she said, "or General von Hartsen's friend, that I am very much obliged for the careful way he handled my belongings when he searched my bag, and you can also congratulate him upon his amazing stealthiness when he entered my compartment last night and went through my luggage. I should like to know where he got his master key from."

"I do not know what you are talking about," the young man exclaimed.

"That is possibly true," she admitted. "At the same time, the fact remains that I hate spies. You can also tell him this, that for the whole of the sixty seconds he was in my compartment, he was on the brink of eternity. I had a small revolver pointed at him through the bars of my bedstead and I am not sufficiently used to firearms for my finger to be absolutely steady upon the trigger, especially when one is travelling at fifty miles an hour."

"If what you have suggested has really happened," Prince Frederick declared eagerly, "I promise you —— "

"You need promise me nothing," she interrupted. "I suppose if I undertake a political mission I must risk the consequences. I am only surprised that people think this sort of thing worth while nowadays. But let me tell you this," she concluded, leaning out of the taxicab window, "when the door first opened last night and I saw the covered light of the torch, I thought that it was you, and if I hadn't realised that it wasn't the second I did — well, I was too close to have missed. Good-bye!"

"A damned little American typist!" Prince Frederick muttered once more under his breath as the taxicab rolled off.

Catherine drove to a small hotel in a quiet but fashionable neighbourhood where she found a room reserved and a letter awaiting her, the latter a formidable-looking document, in a large square envelope, with a coat of arms on the back. She tore it open and read:

Downing Street,
    April 21st.
DEAR MADAM:

The Prime Minister desires me to say that he has heard from Mr. Samara of your presence in London and, should you wish for an interview with him, he will be at liberty at five o'clock this afternoon, or at eleven o'clock to-morrow morning.

He asks me in the meantime to suggest that if by any chance

the nature of your mission, if any, should have been mentioned and you should be approached by representatives of the Press, it would be as well for you to preserve the strictest secrecy as to any communications you may have to make.

Faithfully yours, dear madam,

FRANK S. PEACOCK,

Private Secretary.

Catherine glanced at the clock, summoned a maid and ordered a bath. In an hour's time she descended into the small lounge of the hotel. She was accosted immediately by a page boy carrying an enormous bunch of flowers.

"I am taking these up to your room, madam," he announced. "The gentleman who left them is over there."

Prince Frederick stepped eagerly forward. He was immaculately dressed in town clothes and he carried a silk hat and cane in his hand. His expression was anxious and woebegone. He had decided to change his tactics.

"I have ventured to call," he said, "to beg for your forgiveness in case you should have misunderstood anything I said this afternoon."

"Very well," she conceded after a moment's silence, "I am willing to believe that it was, as you suggest, a misunderstanding."

"You are alone here," he went on eagerly. "You do not know London. I, on the other hand, am well acquainted with it. Permit me the great honour of offering you dinner and escorting you to a theatre. I assure you that I will say nothing which could possibly offend, or even embarrass you."

Catherine hesitated. She was, after all, as fond of a good dinner and a theatre as any girl of her age, and her hotel, though highly respectable, had a museum-like appearance. The young man saw her hesitation and hastened to pursue his advantage.

"Madame Ronet is singing at the opera," he announced, "or there are two good musical comedies. If you would not mind dining early we could have supper afterwards, and perhaps dance if you care about it. I shall promise to be nothing but your attentive and most respectful cavalier."

"Very well then," she assented graciously. "If you will find out from the hotel people at what time I have returned from the visit I am about to pay, I will be ready in an hour after that."

She passed on with a gracious little nod and entered the taxi which the hall porter had called for her.

"Where to, madam?" the man asked.

"To the Houses of Parliament," she directed at random.

The man started off. At the corner of the street she put her head out of the window.

"Number ten Downing Street, please," she told him.

CHAPTER XVIII

A VERY alert and polite young secretary, who had met Catherine in the hall, took her at once into the presence of his Chief, Mr. Phillip Rossiter, erstwhile Foreign Minister, and now Premier of England. Mr. Rossiter was a middle-aged man of quiet introspective manner. He welcomed his visitor with easy cordiality, and if he felt any surprise at her appearance he effectually concealed it.

"My friend Samara has already written to me the circumstances to which I owe the pleasure of this visit," he said, as he settled himself comfortably in an easy-chair opposite to hers. "Andrew Kroupki would have come, of course, but for his unfortunate illness. A very brilliant young man, that. I met him when I visited Moscow three years ago."

"Mr. Kroupki would have come no doubt with wider discretion," Catherine remarked. "I am sure you understand that I am here only as a messenger."

"Quite so," the other murmured. "All great men have their hobbies and aversions, and Samara's particular aversion has always been documents and diplomatic correspondence. We have come to an excellent understanding many times through an interchange of visits. I hope Mr. Samara has told you to talk to me quite frankly. I know all about his visit to America — in fact, I am not at all sure that I did not put the idea into his head."

"Mr. Samara has told me certain things," Catherine acknowledged. "He has given me a certain insight into the arrangements he has made and why he has made them. Then he has gone on to tell me that whatever I know I may tell you. So you see I shall reply quite openly to any questions you ask me concerning his success in America. But I must warn you to start with that

I am a newcomer, a stranger to all matters of diplomacy. I know nothing, even, of Mr. Samara's Government. Considering that I have been working for him assiduously during the last three weeks, it is amazing how little I know of him."

The Premier smiled. The subject of Samara was one which always interested him.

"Your Chief is one of the remarkable men of this generation," he declared. "Fifteen years ago Bolshevism seemed to have its fangs deep into the very heart of Russia. It didn't seem possible for any one to prevail against it. Samara has worked miracles. To-day Russia is, if not entirely herself again, well on the way towards reconstruction. Financially, industrially and economically she is making gigantic strides. Samara is daring, but he has the right ideas. Russia will be one of the great powers again long before his work is at an end. Personally — I have told Samara this myself — I see but one danger, and that is his tendency towards idealism. It is a great thing to mount the ladder, but one should set one's feet upon the rungs with care."

Catherine looked at her host intently.

"You don't believe in this demobilisation scheme?" she asked quickly.

"Theoretically, I think it wonderful," he answered. "Tell me — I think I know, but still tell me — the Washington visit was a success?"

"Absolutely," she assured him. "Mr. Samara granted certain concessions and he has arranged for a loan of two hundred million dollars. The whole of the Third Army will be demobilised within six months and employment will be found for every soldier."

"Have you any idea as to the feeling amongst the militarists?" he enquired.

"So far as the Third Army is concerned, the men are perfectly willing to submit to disbandment," she replied. "The officers are mostly German and they resent it. Still, Mr. Samara is very much in earnest. They will have to go, as the works are established, the mines opened and the machinery being shipped."

The Premier looked at his visitor with interest.

"You seem to have a very sound grasp of this subject, considering your recent connection with it," he said. "Are you an American, might I ask?"

She smiled.

"I was born in Russia," she admitted. "I have lived in America, however, all my life. It is my knowledge of Russian, of course, which has given me the opportunity to be of so much use to Mr. Samara."

He continued to study her with curiosity.

"Your people were amongst the refugees?"

"Yes."

The Premier turned to some papers by his side. Something in Catherine's tone told him that, so far as she was concerned, that subject was at an end.

"What have you to say to me, Miss Borans?" he asked succinctly.

"Mr. Samara desires me to present this subject for your consideration," she said. "England was a heavy loser at the time of the Russian *débâcle*. There are many works and industries still languishing which were started with English capital and upon which he considers England still has a claim. It is his wish to demobilise as well as the Third also the whole of the Second Army. He therefore needs — it is Russia's greatest need to-day — a further development of her resources. He asks if you will appoint a committee of business men, preferably those connected with the various enterprises in which English shareholders have lost money, and send them over to treat with him in Moscow."

"To what end?" Mr. Rossiter enquired.

"To arrange with them," she continued, "for further considerable advances which will enable many of the industries and works which have been closed down to be reopened. Mr. Samara does not pretend that he will be able to pay in full those debts incurred in the days of the monarchy and ignored — in fact, repudiated altogether — by the Bolshevists. He considers, however, that some sort of a fund —— "

"A sinking fund," Mr. Rossiter suggested.

"That is the term he used," Catherine acquiesced, — "could be established, so that in time a portion of the old debt could be repaid to English creditors by means of the renewal of the particular industries in which their money had been lost. They would, of course, in the meantime, be making the profits to which they were entitled on the new business."

"I see," the Premier murmured. "I gather from the nature of these suggestions that there is very little unemployment in Russia."

"Scarcely any," she assured him. "Nearly every industry is flourishing. All that the farmers need is more machinery and more workers. Mr. Samara has pointed out to me that the trouble in the demobilisation of these armies is that quite half of the men are not attracted by the idea of working upon the land. That is why it is so necessary to provide them with other means of earning a livelihood."

"I quite understand," Mr. Rossiter said. "Did your Chief suggest any particular enterprises connected with previous British undertakings?"

She drew a paper from her handbag.

"Here is the list, sir," she pointed out, "of industries brought to a standstill during the Bolshevist epoch, all of them launched in the first instance with British capital, which Mr. Samara thinks might be reconstituted. It is the only document I have brought with me."

Mr. Rossiter adjusted his eyeglass and read down the list. Then he rose to his feet and consulted for some time with his secretary, who was writing at the farther end of the room. Presently he returned to his place.

"I cannot, of course, give you a definite reply, Miss Borans," he said. "But my impression is that there would not be the slightest difficulty in launching this scheme and finding the capital required. When do you return to Russia?"

"I am leaving here on Friday morning, sir," she told him, "to rejoin Mr. Samara at Monte Carlo."

"Between now and then," Mr. Rossiter promised her, "you shall have the names of the committee I suggest and approximately the amount which the Government will be likely to vote by way of a subsidy. I have now a question to ask you, the reply to which may not be in your scale of information. What military force does your Chief intend to retain under arms?"

"I know nothing definite," Catherine replied, "but I believe that it is Mr. Samara's idea to do away with the whole of the military establishment of Russia."

Mr. Rossiter fingered his penholder.

"Your Chief," he remarked, "does not believe in war."

"Not against Russia, at any rate," she assented. "He considers that Russia is geographically impregnable. Apart from that, he considers that the folly of warfare has been proved. I have heard him say that the campaign of nineteen-fourteen-nineteen-twenty was more disastrous to the allies who won it than to the German Empire who lost it."

"Perfectly sound," Mr. Rossiter agreed. "The trouble of it is we have all learnt something since then. I don't mind telling you this," he went on. "If the Germans had been victorious, they would have found means of making England and France pay. They would never have been gulled by this higher economic doctrine and gone without their booty. To-day if there were war and Germany won, I have not the faintest doubt that she would know how to extract every penny of what she considered due to her and get full advantage of her victory."

"I do not understand economics," Catherine confessed. "I only know that Mr. Samara does not fear anything of the sort."

The Premier was silent for several moments. When he spoke again he seemed almost to be talking to himself.

"Samara is right up to a certain point," he declared. "The German Republic is not out for war. The Germans know very well that the first breath of it would bring them internal division. To us, who watch such things closely, however, there are very dangerous symptoms in German politics. We should not be surprised any day to hear of a monarchical plot."

"But Germany is so prosperous under present conditions," she murmured.

"Precisely," the other rejoined. "But there is nothing breeds discontent quicker than undue prosperity. You must remember, too, that the racial and fundamental temperament of a nation can never be changed. Russia, France and Germany, all three of them, have the instinct amongst their peasants and *bourgeoisie* for monarchical government. So far as France and Russia are concerned, at any rate, I think that they are right. The Frenchman is too easily swayed. So long as he believes he is a part of the government, he is all the time tearing his hair and changing his mind. That sort of person always makes a loyal and submissive subject. The Russian peasant is in the same position for a different reason. He doesn't want his liberty. He doesn't want to be made to think for himself. He wants to be taken care of. He, too, wants to be ruled. Germany, I must admit, I am not so sure about. The German martial instinct seems to me to be the one great thing which might call back a Kaiser."

"Who would he be?" Catherine asked curiously.

"Without a doubt, Prince Frederick of Wehrenzollern," was the prompt reply. "He is the youngest son of the late Crown Prince and by far the most popular — reminds one rather of our own King, when he was young — a sportsman, a ladies' man, a democrat and a ruler. I don't know much about Prince Frederick, of course, although he manages to keep himself pretty well in the limelight, but I do believe that he is nursing the monarchy — playing to the people all the time."

"Am I to tell Mr. Samara from you that you think he had better leave that First Army alone?" she asked bluntly.

Mr. Rossiter took a cigarette from a box by his side and tapped it thoughtfully.

"My advice to your very distinguished Chief would be to watch internal Germany," he said. "I quite agree with him that the German Republic is not bellicose. On the other hand, a German monarchy would at once seek to justify its existence by a war. Samara knows as much about this, though, as I do. Let him deal with the Third and Second Armies as he will. I think I can safely promise him that the commission I send over to Moscow will be able to start industries which will absorb the whole of the surplus labour."

Catherine rose to her feet. The Prime Minister followed suit.

"I am happy to have had the pleasure of receiving you, Miss Borans," he declared. "Tell Mr. Samara from me that I greatly approve of his new diplomatic methods. You propose to remain in London, I understand, until Friday. Is there any way in which we can be of service to you?"

"None whatever, thank you," she replied frankly. "I have never been in London before. I shall very much enjoy doing a little exploring on my own account."

"I sympathise with you entirely," Mr. Rossiter concluded. "We will show you our greatest kindness — kindness in this instance, because it is a real deprivation — by leaving you alone. Present my compliments to your Chief and don't forget that one word of warning — watch for a monarchist plot in Berlin. I do not need to tell him to protect himself in Moscow. Peacock, show Miss Borans to her car."

CHAPTER XIX

CATHERINE, with the major part of her mission successfully ac-complished, devoted herself, with an abandon which at times amazed her companion, to the spending of a thoroughly frivolous evening. They dined exceedingly well at Maridge's, saw the last two acts of a popular musical comedy and went on to a select and fashionable club restaurant, where dancing was already in full swing. During the whole of the evening, Prince Frederick's behaviour was entirely correct. He had adopted the attitude of the wistful but silent lover. He devoted himself entirely to telling his companion the names of the various notabilities by whom they were surrounded and relating anecdotes about some of them. With regard to himself he spoke scarcely at all and he did not ask her a single question concerning her mission to London. On the three or four occasions when he was greeted or addressed by acquaintances his manner was genial and full of bonhomie. Catherine watched him with amusement.

"You seem to have a good many acquaintances over here," she remarked.

"I was at Eton for two terms and Oxford for a year," he re-minded her. "I have made it my business to understand some-thing of English life and English people."

"With what object?" she asked him point-blank.

His smile for a moment seemed almost sinister.

"We disinherited ones of the world," he answered, "have to keep friends with everybody. Unless I am strictly incognito I keep away from the Court, of course. I was known over here as Frederick von Burhl, the name under which I started my commercial career in Berlin after leaving school. That is eight years ago, however, and to-day the prejudices against the aristoc-racy have declined."

"Do you believe," she enquired, "that imperialism is dead in Germany?"

He raised his eyebrows slightly.

"Is that a question which I could possibly answer?" he protested. "Especially to the confidential secretary of one of the world's great democrats."

She laughed.

"Please don't think that I have designs upon your secrets if you have any," she begged. "I asked merely for curiosity. There was an article in one of the reviews I read on the steamer in which it spoke of a reawakening of the monarchical impulse in Russia, Germany and even France."

"The writer was, I should think, well-informed," Prince Frederick answered cautiously. "I believe the impulse is there. That is why Samara shows so much more than appears on the surface in setting himself to destroy the militarism of his country. A standing army is always on the monarchical side."

Catherine's attention was suddenly diverted by an amazing occurrence. She, like most others in the room, was watching the entrance of two people who were being received with every mark of distinction. One was a very beautiful woman, wearing a Russian headdress and amazing jewellery. The young man with her, to Catherine's bewilderment, was Nicholas.

Catherine laid her hand on her companion's coat sleeve.

"Please tell me who these are?" she whispered.

Prince Frederick leaned forward. The woman seemed to be watching for a sign from him. His expression remained stony.

"That is Adèle Fédorleys, the ballet dancer," he confided. "She is half a Pole and half a Russian. Her companion I do not know."

"I do," Catherine exclaimed in delight, as she watched the blank amazement in Nicholas' face change to pale fury. "He is quite a friend of mine."

"A Russian himself, by the look of him," Prince Frederick observed. "Tell me," he went on curiously, turning towards his companion, "how is it that you, who describe yourself as an American typist engaged by Mr. Samara from the Weltmore Hotel Secretarial Bureau, are acquainted with a young man in this country who is in a position to know and entertain Madame Fédor-leys?"

"A quaint coincidence," she admitted. "Almost as quaint as the fact that you two should be in the same room. That is the young man I spoke of —— "

She broke off suddenly. Nicholas, having escorted his companion to their table, was crossing the room towards them.

"He is much bigger than I," Prince Frederick whispered. "I am terrified!"

"You are safe — here," she laughed. "I may have to smuggle you out the back way when you leave."

The young man who had come to a standstill before the table certainly presented a somewhat formidable appearance. He seemed to have grown in stature and importance since he had left New York. The pastiness of his complexion was gone — replaced by a touch of becoming sunburn. His burly shoulders, closely cropped hair and a certain heaviness of feature suggested, in an indeterminate sort of way, the professional pugilist, an impression, however, which was modified by the keenness of his blue eyes, the levelness of his eyebrows and a certain breadth of forehead. He bowed very low and raised Catherine's fingers to his lips. Then he spoke to her hurriedly in Russian, his voice thick with anger.

"What is this? How is it that I find you here in London, alone with this young man? Samara is in Monte Carlo. I have news of him."

"Contain yourself, my dear Nicholas," she answered in the same language. "I am here on an errand for Mr. Samara, and my companion is an acquaintance whom you will be glad to know."

There was nothing in Nicholas' face to indicate any prospective pleasure. His expression was indeed forbidding in the extreme. Catherine turned to her escort and spoke in English.

"This," she said, "is a most extraordinary meeting. The strangest part of it, perhaps, is that you two should never have met and that it should be left to an insignificant person like myself to make you acquainted. Which takes precedence, I wonder? Such things are a mystery to me in my station of life, so I must take my chance. This is Prince Frederick of Wehrenzollern, better known in this country as Frederick von Burhl — Prince Nicholas Imanoff, whom I knew in New York as Mr. Ronoff."

Prince Frederick had risen to his feet. The two young men, after a moment or two of blank surprise, looked at each other with very natural curiosity. Then Nicholas extended his hand.

"I should have recognised you by your pictures," he said.

"And I you by your likeness to your House," was the courteous reply. "I understood that you had settled down in New York."

"There is only one country in which I shall ever settle down," Nicholas answered with some dignity. "I am on my way to visit it now."

"You are allowed to enter Russia!" Frederick exclaimed.

"At Samara's invitation. It is humiliating but it is still a generous action. A great friend of my House, Kirdorff of Riga, is with me in London. My aunt, the Grand Duchess, and various others of my friends and relatives are following me by the French route."

"This is wonderful news," Frederick remarked. "Samara is a brave man, though. It seems to me that he has chosen a curious time to give you permission to return. I should like very much to talk to you, Nicholas. You will pass through Germany on your way to Russia. I should like you to meet some friends of mine."

"You have already, I see, met one of mine," Nicholas observed.

"I have met in Monte Carlo this young lady, calling herself Miss Borans, the private secretary of the Russian President," Frederick replied eagerly. "Her story is that she came from a typists' office in New York."

Catherine shrugged her shoulders. A faint smile flitted across her lips.

"After all, it does not perhaps matter very much," she observed. "You had better present me, Nicholas."

The latter turned to Frederick.

"You have the honour," he said, "to have made the acquaintance of the Princess Catherine of Russia, hereditary Grand Duchess of Urulsk. The Princess, I may add, is my fiancée."

"I was," Catherine murmured sweetly, "but that young lady over there will take a great deal of explanation. I have lived so long in America that I have imbibed the *bourgeois* view as to proceedings of this sort."

An angry light flashed for a moment in Nicholas' eyes.

"The young lady is a fellow countrywoman and a great patriot," he said. "You remind me of my duty as host. I will return."

He bowed and turned away. Catherine watched him with a smile. The whole episode had appealed to her immensely. It was the young American woman who leaned back in her seat and laughed.

"Some shock for poor Nicholas!" she exclaimed.

"And for me!" Frederick groaned.

"I have been an idiot," Frederick declared bitterly, towards the close of the evening.

Catherine smiled with amused tolerance.

"I do not think that you are to be blamed," she conceded. "Why should you not believe what you are told? Besides, it is quite true that I am a typist. Not one of us out there had any money. Nicholas himself was selling bonds for a Wall Street stockbroker, and Alexandrina earned a few dollars making artificial roses. My engagement by Mr. Samara and my coming to Europe were entirely matters of chance."

"It is true," he demanded, "that you are betrothed to Nicholas?"

"It is perfectly true," she acknowledged, "only I am not at all sure that I shall marry him."

"You must not," was the low reply. "You must marry me."

She turned to answer him with a jest and was amazed at his expression. He was very pale and his eyes seemed to have sunken. The hand which clutched his wineglass was shaking.

"I have thought of nobody else since the first moment I saw you," he went on. "You have driven everything else from my mind. I followed you here to London blindly. I never dared hope that this might be possible. Now I realise that it is. It does not matter about money. I have plenty and who knows, there may be a great future for us."

She listened for a moment to the music, gazing a little absently across the room. She had the air of looking through the walls into space. For a moment, indeed, her thoughts had strayed to the city of her dreams as it had been pictured to her, with its gilded roofs, its palaces and its hovels side by side.

"There is a chance of that, too, for Nicholas," she murmured.

"His chance is nothing to mine," Frederick insisted harshly. "For me the ground has been prepared, year by year and month by month. We have machinery at work. The time is close at hand. For Nicholas there are nothing but dreams. We have no Samara in Germany."

She rose to her feet.

"You are too much in earnest," she whispered. "People are watching you. I believe they guess that you have proposed to me. It is most embarrassing. I insist upon dancing."

His hand as he touched her fingers was cold. No trace of colour returned to his cheeks, even after the exercise.

"Are you not feeling well?" Catherine enquired, as they sat down.

"You can cure me with a word," he answered passionately. "Listen. Give me hope and I will return to Berlin to-morrow. I will send you a welcome from those who count. I will give you proof of what is to come."

"Is it possible that you are really in earnest?" she asked.

"In deadly earnest," he groaned.

Her real nationality suddenly asserted itself. There was a vein of cruelty in her race and it sprang into being. She leaned back in her place and laughed.

CHAPTER XX

CATHERINE, after she had descended from the train at Monte Carlo, lingered for a moment upon the platform, dazzled by the sunshine. She had left London in a mantle of grey, Paris in a rain and wind storm, and now, after a long night in a *salon-lit,* she seemed to have stepped out into a new world of enchantment. The sea and sky seemed bluer than ever, the houses whiter and cleaner, the great stucco-like Casino more of a joke, resembling rather a child's toy dragged from its play-box than a serious abode of drama, an arena for the most sordid of men's passions. And to add to it all, as she leaned back in her little victoria, the music from the distant orchestra at the Café de Paris came with real sweetness through the scented air. She sat forward and watched the people eagerly as she crossed the square. There was the same atmosphere about them all, a geniality and sense of relaxation which after many years of New York was strangely attractive to her. No one was in a hurry; every one appeared to enjoy not having to be in a hurry. There was plenty of time for the amenities of life.

It was a busy hour at the hotel, but each member of the staff seemed to find leisure to welcome her back after her brief absence. A reception clerk persisted in conducting her upstairs; the lift-boy's smile and bow made her feel that she had come home.

"Mr. Samara is walking on the Terrace with some friends, madam," the clerk announced. "I think that he scarcely expected you until to-morrow."

Catherine nodded.

"I meant to stay in Paris for a day," she explained. "I changed my mind. The weather was intolerable."

"Mademoiselle was wise," the man declared, with a farewell bow. "Yesterday we had rain but to-day, as Mademoiselle sees, it is perfect."

Catherine unfastened her coat and glanced around the room before going to her own apartment. She noticed with tolerant disapproval that it was untidy — a little pile of discarded envelopes upon the table, cigar ash upon the mantelpiece. Suddenly, however, the tolerance faded from her face. On the table was a woman's glove. An odour which she hated became more insistent, — an odour of scented cigarettes. There were some crushed flowers, too, upon the table. She rang the bell and pointed out the state of the room to the chambermaid. The woman smiled as she apologised.

"Monsieur was late last night," she explained. "And he only rose an hour ago. I did not wish to disturb him. I will now do all that is necessary."

Catherine went thoughtfully to her room, changed her clothes, bathed and rested for a time. She was conscious of a curious sense of disappointment and depression for which she could in no way account. She knew perfectly well that the private life of Gabriel Samara was outside her ken. Save for that wild moment on the steamer when he had kissed her — a moment alluded to only once since — not one of his actions towards her or any one else had indicated the slightest interest in her sex. When she had left she was quite sure that he had not a woman acquaintance in the place. And now everything betokened at least the beginning of an intrigue on his part. After all, he was a Russian, a genius, a person of passion and temperament. There was nothing so strange about it, even from the point of view of her strict bringing-up. Samara, as she told herself, lying on her bed with her hands clasped behind her head, was not of her world. Already she was beginning to realise the great forces which must eventually draw them apart, the grim possibility that her association with him, her knowledge of his affairs, might before long become the measure of her usefulness to her own people, its betrayal the sacrifice she might have to offer to her own future. Was he perhaps in some respects different to her preconceived ideas? He was an idealist without a doubt. His two books on Russia written before his political prominence, every line of which she had read, were supreme evidence of it. But of his private life she knew very little. There was only her own observation and instinct to guide her. In the foreground of the picture of him which had somehow grown up in her mind, that long glove, the crushed flowers, and the scented cigarette tips were like an ugly blur.

When Samara returned from his walk, he found Catherine seated at her typewriter finishing the copying of some reports on which she had been engaged before she had left. The room had been put in order and swept, the windows were wide open. On the table, however, the glove still remained and the little ash-tray of cigarette ends. He banged the door behind him, came over to her side and shook her hand.

"Congratulations, my wonderful emissary," he declared, with one of his rare smiles. "I defied all diplomatic usage and you have justified me. An hour ago I received a cable with the names of the commission. They start on Thursday week."

"I am glad," she said.

He stood away from her for a moment, looking over her head out of the window.

"Everything is now in trim," he continued. "We leave here on Wednesday. The Duma is summoned for the following Tuesday. I shall announce to the representatives my intentions with regard to the army, issue an authorised edict the following day and commence demobilisation the next week. Your adopted country-people are prompt in their payments. We have already ten millions of American dollars in the Treasury and Argoff, my Minister for Home Affairs, is collecting a staff to open three of the Southern Silver Mines."

"You have no fear, then," she enquired, "but that the Duma will agree with your policy?"

He laughed softly.

"Wait until you have lived a year in Russia," he said, "and you will not ask that question. The Russian of to-day means well enough but he has little mind. The Bolshevists have crushed that. All that he asks is to be led."

"So that you are, in point of fact, almost a dictator," she remarked.

"So much the better for Russia if I am," he answered shortly. "No one knows better what is good for her. No," he went on, "all the opposition will come from outside, and who cares? They think I don't realise it. Idiots!"

She glanced at him questioningly. He walked to the mantelpiece deliberately, struck a match there and lit a cigarette.

"They think I don't know what was at the back of their minds, those others who rattle their war sabres so foolishly!" he exclaimed. "Russian armies, poor patient Russian peasants, trained so zealously and carefully, not for their country's defence but to play the mercenary on foreign soil, to be pushed to the front in dangerous places, that German soldiers might be spared! They are furious here. Von Hartsen scarcely leaves me. He has tried everything — argument, menace, bribes."

He ceased his restless perambulations and came back to her side. His eyes fell upon the glove and the little ash-tray of cigarette tips. He scowled at them for a moment.

"The evidences of my profligacy," he remarked.

"I had noticed them," Catherine acknowledged. "I am rather sorry that she smokes scented cigarettes."

"Foul things," he assented. "Still, I suppose women must have their whims."

She recommenced her typing. He stopped her with an impatient protest.

"Don't do that," he exclaimed. "It's time for lunch. We'll go out somewhere. Get your hat."

"The persuasiveness of your invitation," she murmured, "almost carries me off my feet."

"Don't be sarcastic," he replied. "I want to talk to you."

"What about?"

He pointed to the glove.

"About that."

Catherine knew that she was losing an opportunity but nevertheless she yielded. She should have laughed at the idea that the presence of the glove might in any way interest her. She did nothing of the sort. She went meekly to her room, put on her most becoming hat and walked by Samara's side across the square.

"So you want to know about the glove, eh?" he demanded.

She looked around at the people sipping their *apéritifs* under the umbrella-tented tables and listened for a moment to the music.

"Does it need an explanation?" she asked. "I suppose you're very much like other men and the atmosphere of this place is a little relaxing."

"Why don't you find it so then?" he demanded. "Nothing seems to change you. From whom did you inherit your magnificent imperturbability?"

She smiled. Her own moment had arrived.

"How you misjudge me!" she sighed. "As a matter of fact, I have been behaving rather badly myself."

"That young princeling," he muttered furiously. "I saw him on the train."

She nodded.

"He came all the way to England entirely on my account," she confided. "Not only that but I supped alone with him at Maridge's in London."

"A nice sort of diplomatic envoy you are," he scoffed. "Did you take him with you to Downing Street?"

"Don't be absurd," she replied. "I devoted to him only my moments of frivolity."

Samara remained for a few moments in a moody silence. They had reached the end of the Arcade and were promptly ushered to a table on the glass-enclosed balcony of the famous restaurant. Catherine took off her gloves, looked out at the sea, listened to a violinist in the street below. Notwithstanding a slight feeling of depression she felt very kindly towards the world.

"The glove belonged to Olga Kansky, première danseuse in the Russian Ballet here," her companion confessed abruptly.

Catherine smiled.

"A Russian!" she exclaimed. "Naturally she had to pay her respects."

"She came for nothing of the sort," he declared brusquely. "She had supper with me here. I invited her to my sitting room afterwards."

There was a slight change in Catherine's manner. Her tone became almost haughty. She looked at her vis-à-vis with slightly upraised eyebrows.

"There are some situations," she reminded him coldly, "which do not require explanation."

"This one does," he retorted. "Especially to you, as you are in a measure responsible for what happened."

"Surely my own sins," she began ——

"In plain words," he interrupted, "I found that I was thinking a great deal too much about you. I don't want to think too much about any woman, especially one of your type. I have my own theories about the place for women in the world. I meant to carry them out. That is why I invited Olga Kansky to supper."

"And did you—carry them out?" she asked breathlessly.

"No."

"Why not?"

"A ridiculous attack of sentimentality," he confessed. "Just memory—a windy night, the boom of the sea, a moment of accursed opportunity. I wanted to kiss Olga Kansky—I couldn't."

Catherine laughed, without changing a muscle of her face— laughed inwardly, conscious of an unreasonable joy.

"You kissed me quite nicely," she reflected demurely.

"That was the madness of a moment," he declared. "It will not happen again."

"I wonder," she speculated.

"You need not. I am no woman worshipper, but I know how to tabulate them. You suit me as a secretary. You don't fit elsewhere. That's the end of that! Olga Kansky leaves for Nice to-morrow. Tell me about the Prime Minister."

Their conversation drifted away from the personal note. As they lingered over their coffee, however, she brought it back.

"You are rather a fraud, you know," she said.

"How?" he asked suspiciously.

"You allot women their place in life—a very inferior place —and when you meet any one who deserves something better you pretend not to recognise the fact. You know very well that I was not made to be any one's plaything. Why am I not worthy to be a companion?"

He watched his glass filled with old brandy—held it out for a double portion—then he selected the strongest cigar he could find. Before lighting it he leaned across the table.

"I find you companionable," he admitted. "I treat you as a companion. If I needed a plaything, I should look elsewhere."

"In plain words," she observed, "when you seek recreation you walk in the garden where only exotics grow, like Olga Kansky."

"I hate allegories," he growled. "In plain words, I intend neither to marry nor to give any woman that place in my life which might be the equivalent of marriage."

Catherine was looking out of the window. The train from Paris had just arrived. The busses were beginning to rumble up the hill. A young man passed, seated in a little carriage. Catherine smiled. She had recognised Prince Frederick.

"My fate," she murmured, motioning downwards. "I really believe he has followed me back again. I adore perseverance and, after all, I suppose even a Kaiserin gets some fun out of life!"

The conclusion of luncheon brought a pleasant surprise to Catherine. At the end of the Arcade a powerful motor car was standing, into which Samara ushered her.

"You have seen nothing of this country," he said. "I have a fancy to take you to a spot of my own discovery."

"This makes me very happy," Catherine acknowledged, with a grateful smile. "Like every one else in my adopted country, I am a born tourist."

They turned a little towards Mentone, mounted to the clouds and paused for a moment at the summit of a parapeted road. Catherine looked downwards at the panorama below with amazed delight; Samara, with unassumed indifference.

"It is wonderful," he admitted, with a note almost of tolerance in his tone. "Here and there in wilder countries nature has distorted landscape into even more majestic outlines, but here comes the touch of humanity to interpose a strange element. It is man with his craving for luxury, not his desire for the beautiful, who has dotted these hills with villas, planted exotic gardens and brought his yachts through the storm into the harbour there. Marvellous, of course, beautiful in its way, but with the slur of paganism everywhere, the note of theatricality, from the gingerbread structure of the temple of men's greed to the lights and shadows which play beneath the clouds on the mountains be-

hind. Perhaps you don't see it as I do. Why should you? Now
I shall take you to the place I love."

"Sometimes I wonder," she said thoughtfully, as they went on
their way, "whether I am not more of a pagan than you. You
keep your real self so well hidden. Those gardens, for instance, to
which you pointed a little scornfully. I worship their masses of
colour and forget the twenty gardeners who toiled to produce the
effect. And against that blue sea even the Casino itself appeals
to me — perhaps to my sense of humour more than anything else,
but it pleases me."

He looked at her with an unusually kind smile.

"There is the difference of a whole cycle of humanity between
us," he reminded her, his voice growing a little sad as he proceeded. "You are younger even than your years — you have lived
behind the high fences. I am older than mine, because life came
to me in strong doses before I had time to make up my mind
how to deal with it."

They descended to the sea level, passed through Nice with its
amazing, flamboyant loveliness, through the old, mysterious, disreputable, picturesque town of Cagnes, and turned to the right
along a narrower road which wound its way into the bosom of
softer hills than those which towered down upon Monte Carlo.
Here were vineyards, and many small homesteads, planted around
with olive trees, each with their strip of meadow and arable land,
and a sheltered corner in which grew a little clump of orange
and sometimes lemon trees. The soil became redder, the grass
greener. To Catherine it seemed that there was a gentler quality
in the air, something more languorous than the keen atmosphere
of the rockbound principality. Then the car drew up at a bend in
the road a few kilometers above a quaint, tumble-down stone
village. Samara alighted.

"Just a yard or two this way," he invited.

She followed him along a short cypress grove, scrambled up a
knoll fragrant with the perfume of late mimosas, and uttered a
little cry of delight. A short distance away was an old white stone
house, half villa, half château, with close-drawn green shutters
and a familiar tower at either end. It faced due south and one side

was covered with wisteria and drooping magenta Buginvillaea. Such garden as there had been had run riot, but there was still a wealth of roses growing promiscuously with the olive trees and the mimosas right up to the edge of the vineyard which stretched towards the valley. Inland, a range of fertile hills with many small villages clustered in their clefts, rose to the skies, and beyond towered the pale outline of the snow-capped Italian Alps. A vista of meadowland and vineyard, of small homesteads and picturesque groups of farm buildings, stretched down to the old town of Cagnes itself, standing upon its pedestal of rock, unreal almost in the grey perfection of its rugged outline. And beyond, the great foreground of the Mediterranean, blue and placid. Something different from the ordinary light of admiration crept into Catherine's eyes as they wandered over the old house and lingered lovingly upon the tangled masses of flowers.

"I did not understand you a few minutes ago," she confessed. "I do now. I think that this is more beautiful than anything I have seen."

He smiled.

"I am not sure," he confided, "that there is not poison in this atmosphere. I came here by accident, with a fever of fighting in my blood, scheme after scheme forming in my brain — for Russia, for the world — and before I had been here half an hour I felt something of the spell of the lotus-eaters numbing my brain. I found myself speculating — wondering whether it was all worth while, how far one must travel through the toil of life before rest came. It was because this place spelt rest for me — spelt it differently, spelt it without ignominy, spelt it with beauty instead of sloth. Peace, after all, is the end of all of us."

She was more moved than she had believed possible.

"It seems so strange to hear you talk like that," she murmured. "You, Samara, the man of action, the ruler of a nation, with a great fight looming up before you."

"Have I ever told you?" he asked — "I forget. I believe in God. This might be his compensation for failure."

She was too bewildered to speak, but curiously conscious of an utterly untranslatable emotion. He turned away after a farewell glance around.

"And so," he went on, as he led her back to the car, "I did perhaps the strangest thing I have ever done in life. I found this place for sale and I bought it. I signed the papers this morning. We walk down my own avenue, and I will give you," he concluded, stooping and picking a rose from a bush which had clambered halfway up an olive tree, "the first rose from my garden."

CHAPTER XXI

On the afternoon of the day fixed for their departure Samara was wandering aimlessly around and Catherine was screwing up her typewriter in the sitting room, when the floor waiter knocked at the door and announced a visitor. General von Hartsen, who had followed close behind the waiter, entered and bowed stiffly.

"Come to bid me a last farewell, General?" Samara asked.

"You will excuse me, sir, but my visit is not to you," was the unexpected reply. "Pending an official response to the queries which I have placed before your Government, I have nothing more to say."

"Not to me?" Samara repeated. "To what, then, do I owe the honour of this visit?"

"My visit is to Mademoiselle," the General announced.

Catherine looked up from her work a little unwillingly.

"To me?"

Von Hartsen bowed once more.

"If Mr. Samara permits," he continued, "I shall be glad of five minutes' conversation."

"What sublime effrontery!" Samara exclaimed. "Do you want to suborn my secretary before my face?"

"My visit is not political," the General confided, "but I confess that it would give me greater satisfaction to pursue it in your absence."

Samara was in an evil mood. The trivial business of preparing for departure had irritated him and he had other causes for self-dissatisfaction. He turned on his heel and, without a word, marched through the connecting door into his bedroom.

"Mr. Samara is not in a very good temper," Von Hartsen observed. "He would perhaps be in a worse one if he knew the object of my visit."

"Won't you sit down?" Catherine invited.

The General shook his head. He moved, however, to the farther end of the room, and stood upon the hearth-rug. One could almost hear the clank of his sabre as he walked. Without uniform he seemed somehow an unreal figure.

"Mademoiselle," he said, "I am an ambassador."

"The Prince?" Catherine asked calmly.

"Precisely."

Catherine continued her task of opening the drawers and collecting her oddments of stationery.

"You won't mind my doing this whilst you talk, will you?" she begged. "Our train leaves at three o'clock."

"It is part of the object of my visit," the General pointed out, "to persuade you not to take that train."

"But I must," she replied. "All our arrangements are made. We are going straight to Moscow."

"I am in hopes that if you give a favourable hearing to my mission," the General persisted, "you will not go to Russia at all."

"A plot?" she enquired.

"Scarcely that," he protested. "On behalf of my ward, Prince Frederick of Wehrenzollern, I have the honour to ask for your hand in marriage."

Catherine shut her despatch box with a click.

"You know all about me, then," she said coolly.

"Prince Frederick has confided in me," the General confessed. "I should like to point out to you that my young ward is making you this proposal entirely from reasons of sentiment. He is, if I may say so, very greatly attracted. Since your first coming here, he, whom I have always found so docile, has been entirely unmanageable. It was the wish of his friends that he should marry Princess Freda of Bavaria. Up till now he has been acquiescent. Last night, extravagant though his language was, he convinced me that the scheme had better be abandoned."

"Is she anything like her pictures?" Catherine asked.

"The Princess is personable," was the somewhat brusque reply.

"She doesn't look it," Catherine declared. "I should have said that she was fat."

"It is to be admitted," the General acknowledged, "that she has not Your Highness' claims to good looks."

Catherine frowned angrily and glanced towards the door through which Samara had disappeared.

"Please do not address me in such a way again," she requested. "My name is Catherine Borans and I am a typist whom Mr. Samara has brought home from New York. I prefer for the present to remain as such. As for Prince Frederick's offer, I beg leave to decline it."

"To decline it?" the General exclaimed in amazement.

"Precisely. Life in Berlin as the wife of a banker would not amuse me."

The General looked quickly round the room as though to be sure that there was no possibility of their being overheard.

"Mademoiselle," he said, dropping his voice a little, "there are great things afoot in Europe. It is not Prince Frederick's destiny to remain forever a banker of Berlin. There is no man in this world with such a future!"

Catherine shook her head doubtfully.

"I do not think that you will ever be able to restore the monarchy in Germany," she declared.

Von Hartsen smiled a smile of supreme confidence.

"Mademoiselle," he confided, "it is as good as done."

"You dazzle me," Catherine observed, with irony so faint that her visitor was unable to detect it. "Kaiserin of Germany! It is hard to refuse."

"It is impossible to refuse," the General persisted.

"Nevertheless —— "

He stopped her.

"Let me complete my mission," he begged. "For the first time Russia and Europe generally has been made aware of the existence of Prince Nicholas of Imanoff. That young man has never apparently visited his native country. He is unknown to the people — unregarded. Prince Frederick, on the other hand, has been brought up in his own country. He is a democrat, seemingly, and one of the most popular young men in Germany."

"You are trying to point out to me, I suppose," Catherine said, "that whereas Prince Frederick has every chance of becoming Kaiser of Germany, Prince Nicholas has no chance whatever of becoming Tzar of Russia."

"That is the truth," Von Hartsen insisted. "Prince Nicholas has no hold upon the affections of his people and except in the army there is no royalist following in Russia. The only chance Prince Nicholas would have would be if he remained friends with Frederick. In the future, who could tell what might happen?"

Catherine smiled.

"Subtly put, General," she acknowledged, "but I am afraid that I can do no more than repeat my first answer."

"Mademoiselle!" he exclaimed.

"You see," Catherine continued, "notwithstanding the Russian blood in my veins, I was brought up and educated in America. I have earned my own living there. I have caught something of the spirit of the country. I should not dream for a moment of marrying any man for whom I had not affection. Prince Frederick has inspired me with no such sentiment."

The General looked at her steadfastly.

"It is strange," he muttered, "to hear one of your race speak in such a fashion."

"Times change, General," she reminded him. "To-day the pomp of life appeals less; the desire for decorous living appeals more. I am a Royalist by instinct and conviction, but I should never share even a throne with a man whom I did not love."

"This Nicholas," the General began ——

The typewriter and despatch box were there, but Miss Catherine Borans had vanished from the face of the earth. It was the Princess who corrected her visitor.

"General," she pronounced, "the interview is at an end. I hope that next time I meet Prince Frederick this matter will have been forgotten."

Samara came out from his room, wearing his travelling coat and carrying his hat.

"Still here, General?" he said. "You'll have to excuse us. The omnibus is waiting below."

A gleam of malice shone in the General's face. He realised Samara's ignorance.

"I thank you for your consideration, Mr. Samara," he said. "I need not detain either of you any longer. I am sorry to tell you that my errand was in vain."

"What errand?" Samara demanded.

"I am here on behalf of Prince Frederick of Wehrenzollern," the General explained. "I was the bearer of a proposal of marriage which I regret to say that Her Highness has declined."

"Her Highness?" Samara repeated. "What the devil do you mean?"

Von Hartsen's expression of surprise was excellently simulated.

"It is incredible," he exclaimed, "that you have not discovered the identity of this young lady! I have the honour, then, to present you to the Princess Catherine Helena Zygoff, Grand Duchess of Urulsk, Countess of Borans, and hereditary ruler of the lands of Utoff."

Samara stood perfectly still. His eyes were fixed upon Catherine's face. She smiled at him very pleasantly.

"Rather too bad of the General to give me away like this," she complained. "I hope you don't mind."

"One accepts the inevitable," he answered coldly.

"Her Highness has just refused the hand of Prince Frederick of Wehrenzollern," the General continued. "It would be interesting to learn her future plans."

Catherine picked up her despatch box and laid her fingers lightly upon Samara's arm.

"My dear General," she said, "I must congratulate you on your acquaintance with my titles, which you have remembered more or less correctly, but I am also Miss Catherine Borans from the Weltmore Typewriting Bureau, temporary secretary to Mr. Samara. I think," she went on, looking up at her companion, "we ought to hurry, or we shall miss the train."

"You mean that you are coming with me?" Samara demanded.

"Coming?" she repeated. "Of course I am. We mustn't forget to send them up for the typewriter. Good-bye, General."

Von Hartsen gazed across at her fiercely.

"So you are a renegade," he muttered.

Once again he sank into insignificance at her parting glance.

"I have been brought up in a country," she replied, "where a girl learns to think and act for herself and men do not insult women!"

CHAPTER XXII

NICHOLAS, with his guide and counsellor, Boris Kirdorff, stood upon the balcony of an apartment on the third floor of Berlin's premier hotel and gazed downwards at the swaying crowds. In the distance a flag was flying from the roof of the Reichstag building. There was a general air of holiday-making. Nicholas, who was a little bored, yawned.

"Do you know," he asked, "why Von Hartsen was so anxious for us to stay over for the day?"

"I have an idea," his companion admitted. "I am not sure. That is his knock, however. He will probably explain."

He stepped back into the room and met the General who had just been ushered in. The three men stood together upon the balcony, the newcomer in the middle. The pavements below were crowded. Policemen of decidedly military appearance were riding back and forth. Occasionally a car passed down the middle of the guarded way, greeted now and then with a faint murmur of applause.

"You would like to understand, perhaps," Von Hartsen said, "why I have persuaded you to remain here till to-morrow morning's boat to Moscow. Well, I will tell you. I will tell you because there is something which I wish to point out to you which is in a sense an allegory to all of us. To-day, as you may know, is the opening of the Reichstag."

Kirdorff nodded.

"So much as that we know," he admitted. "To follow your politics, however, seems almost impossible. You appear to have seven parties struggling all against the other, of whom the socialists, who were once the strongest, have become the weakest. How can you form a coherent government with such a muddle?"

Von Hartsen smiled.

"You asked a sage question," he said. "Many of the shrewdest men in Germany are asking the same. The parties will not coalesce. Only one unification is possible."

"And that?" Nicholas asked.

"Wait," was the prompt rejoinder. "Now listen. Here is the automobile of Herr Mayer, the leader of the socialist party, once the most popular man in Germany. See to-day how the people greet him."

The car rolled by, the man who was its solitary occupant — elderly, grey and worn — looking neither to the right nor to the left, seated with folded arms as one who faces an ordeal. Here and there was a faint murmur of applause; here and there distinct hisses. Of enthusiasm there was none at all.

"There passes a grave danger," Von Hartsen declared. "Twenty-five years ago, during the aftermath of the Great War, the socialists came rapidly to the front in the country. They reached the zenith of their power in nineteen-thirty. Since then their influence has steadily declined. To-day they are a forgotten force. Watch again. Here comes the automobile of the President. He is fairly popular. Is there a single real shout of welcome? Watch the people's faces. Who amongst them cares whether that man comes or goes?"

The car proceeded on its way. Many hats were lifted to its occupant, but, although there was all the time an undertone of applause, again there was no enthusiasm. These were the involuntary marks of respect paid by a law-abiding nation to its ruler. A dozen other cars passed by, containing deputies from various political parties. Some were greeted in silence; some with a few courteous salutations; one or two with a little hum of interest. Then Von Hartsen leaned forward.

"The Prime Minister of Germany," he announced. "The leader of our Government. He rides to his doom — his political doom, that is to say."

Again hats were raised here and there, but a stony silence prevailed. Then came a new type of deputy — a general wearing his uniform, seated upright in his car, with his fingers resting as though by accident upon his sword.

"The Baron von Elderman!" Von Hartsen exclaimed. "Listen! Watch the people!"

A little forest of heads were uncovered and hats waved. This time there was a real hoarse murmur of applause. More than once the General saluted in response to the greetings.

"The Baron," Von Hartsen explained, "is Commander in Chief of the German armies. He is also deputy and leader of the monarchist party — so far as we permit it to be known that there is a monarchist party. Does it seem strange to you that republican Germany should find applause for him that it denies to all others?"

"Republican Germany is a misnomer," Kirdorff declared. "The soul of Germany has never been with the Republic."

"You speak well," was the other's solemn admission.

A few more cars passed, attracting varying degrees of notice. Then, from the distance came a volume of welcoming voices, swelling into a roar of enthusiasm. At last the people were moved. Down the middle of the avenue came a single open motor car, in which was seated a young man in uniform, alone.

"Frederick!" Nicholas exclaimed. "What does he do here?"

Von Hartsen smiled.

"He was elected a deputy only a few weeks ago," he explained. "He is coming to take his seat."

"But in uniform!" Nicholas muttered. "I thought that was prohibited."

"He is wearing only the uniform of a Cadet Corps," the General pointed out. "Strictly speaking, it is against the law. We risk it. Listen to the people! What do you think that means?"

The applause was almost deafening; coming nearer and nearer like an inbreaking wave. Kirdorff's pallid face had become set and rigid. There was a streak of colour in Nicholas' cheeks. The car passed like a flash below and went on its way. Every moment or so the young man inside raised his right hand to the salute.

"For you," Kirdorff declared, "it can mean but one thing. It means the return of the great days. If Berlin can speak like that, what of the rest of Prussia?"

Von Hartsen smiled as he turned away from the window.

"It is finished," he announced. "We shall find wine in the further room. It was to see what you have seen that I begged you to stay over. What is coming in Germany," he went on earnestly, "can come also in Russia. We are willing to help, but, like every one else in the world, we have our price. A glass of wine with you, gentlemen. Afterwards I myself must go to the Reichstag."

They passed into an inner room where refreshments were handed around. When the glasses were filled, Von Hartsen briefly dismissed the waiters.

"Listen," he began, as soon as they were alone, "I do not promise that I myself can do for you, Nicholas Imanoff, what I have done for Frederick, but I can put you in the way of doing it for yourself. The seeds are already sown. To-day in your First and Second Armies there is an active monarchist propaganda going on hour by hour. Samara knows it well enough — hence his hurried return from America. It is not altruism alone which has influenced him in this great scheme of demilitarisation. It is because he knows that if ever the monarchy is restored to Russia it will be through the army. You have permission to return, Prince Nicholas?"

"Absolutely," the young man assented. "We all have — even Orenburg."

"It is a brave step of Samara's; I think a foolish one. Since you have the chance, however, show yourself openly everywhere. Ask Samara's permission to join the army. The whole machinery of propaganda is there. There is no reason why Russia should not revert to the only logical form of government within a year from to-day."

"You spoke of a price for your aid," Kirdorff reminded him.

"Naturally. Germany is suffering from peace. She needs war. We need your First and Second Armies before Samara can disband them."

Nicholas frowned.

"How can one of my race," he asked, "draw his sword against France?"

"It might happen," Von Hartsen replied, "that, if you were not prepared to do so, you might have no sword to draw. But consider — the France of to-day has nothing in common with the France who was once your great ally. She is avaricious to a degree. Ascend the throne, reëstablish imperial rule in Russia, and, before a month has passed, France will claim from you countless milliards, the whole debt of your country to her. The alliance, now that Austria has passed away, has ceased to exist. Discard it! Germany and Russia are natural and inevitable allies. Make up your mind to it!"

A cannon sounded from somewhere in the neighbourhood. Von Hartsen finished his wine hastily.

"This is a great day for Germany," he concluded. "I must be there to see Prince Frederick take his seat. Deputy to-day; what he pleases by this time next year! Listen to me now and remember my words. The people will be ruled. No democrat has ever learned the art of kingship. Republics have made laws. They have never governed. It is the will of the people which is calling Frederick back to the throne of his ancestors."

He hurried off, leaving behind him a queer sense of excitement. Kirdorff's eyes were glittering. Nicholas seemed transformed.

"The will of the people!" he repeated ecstatically. "We, too, shall hear that call, Kirdorff! From Berlin to Odensk is not so far!"

BOOK TWO

CHAPTER I

CATHERINE paused for a moment in her task, listened, rose to her feet and moved towards the window. She was in a plain official-looking apartment, separated by a glass partition from many others upon the same floor. She might really have been working in the American office of some great mercantile undertaking. She was, as a matter of fact, on the top storey of a building in a Square of Moscow, given over to the Foreign Department of the Russian Government and entitled Government Buildings. It was exactly fourteen months since she had arrived in Moscow from Monte Carlo.

Down in the Square a great crowd of people had gathered and through them marched, still in fours but without any attempt at military discipline, a long line of men in ordinary civilian clothes. Here and there the spectators raised their hats; now and then came a wave of applause. As they passed the house at the corner of the Square, which was Samara's official residence, many of the marchers paused and looked upwards with something which was equivalent to a salute.

Andrew Kroupki, on his way to his office, saw Catherine standing by the window, hesitated for a moment, then entered and crossed the room towards her. He had recovered from his illness but he had still the air of an invalid; tall and thin, with sunken cheeks, a mass of black hair — a typical visionary. She greeted him with a little nod.

"What does it mean, Andrew?" she asked.

Before he could reply, Bromley Pride had joined them, his keen, clean-shaven face alight with interest, restless as ever, swinging his tortoise-shell spectacles in his hand, apologising for his cigar and pointing out of the window in the same moment.

"Pride knows more about it all than I do," Andrew declared. "At any rate he is more up to date. I have been in Warsaw for three weeks — three dreary weeks," he added, dropping his voice a little and glancing appealingly at Catherine.

"Is it really so long?" she observed indifferently. "Well, that accounts for my having got a little behind the times. I have had your work to do as well as my own."

"I know all about these fellows," Pride declared, moving closer to Catherine's side and pointing downwards. "They are the last of Russia's Third Army. Yesterday they came up from barracks, marched over to the other side of the city, left their uniforms, were provided with civilian clothes, and now they are on their way to their jobs, wherever they may be. The last of a million men, Miss Borans! A wonderful piece of administration!"

Catherine, standing between the two men, watched the crowds with interest. There was a brief silence whilst they listened to the tumult of mingled shouting and cheering.

"It's a fine view, this," Pride continued. "It works in with the stuff I am writing. Do you know, Miss Borans, they sent me over here to see whether Samara could put this thing through — and he's done it! There isn't a statesman in our country or in Europe either could have tackled the proposition. It isn't much more than a year since he issued the first notice and came over to New York to borrow the money, and since then he's just taken a million men from shiftless and unproductive idleness and got 'em all working like bees in a hive. If that isn't a triumph I'd like to meet one. I'm going to shake hands with President Samara to-night and tell him what I think of it."

"Are you going to the banquet?" Catherine enquired.

"I should say so!" was the emphatic reply. "I wouldn't miss it for anything. I've heard most of our own great speakers and a good many of the Englishmen, but Samara has them beaten to a frazzle. I guess he'll tell us to-night a few things that all Europe's waiting to hear."

"And perhaps he will not," Andrew Kroupki observed drily. "My master tells the world too much. He lays the cards too easily upon the table. It is magnificent but sometimes it is not diplomacy."

"Please go, both of you," Catherine enjoined, turning reluctantly away from the window and moving towards her desk. "I have the French President's speech in the Chamber last night to translate for Mr. Samara and he wants it before this evening."

"Make me a copy," Pride begged. "I've only seen extracts and my French is ghastly."

"You journalists are much too lazy," she declared. "You'll get it all in English to-morrow."

"To-morrow's no good to me," Pride persisted. "Slip another carbon in your machine, Miss Borans. It won't take you any longer. I'll wait till you've finished and we'll have a little dinner."

Catherine shook her head.

"Impossible," she regretted. "You forget that I am now officially recognised as Andrew's assistant in the position of private secretary to Mr. Samara. I couldn't possibly be seen dining with an American journalist who is reputed to give pearl necklaces, motor cars or millions for news."

"Bunkum!" he scoffed. "You've got another date."

"That may be," Catherine sighed gently. "I am much sought after. I'll make you a copy of the speech, Mr. Pride, but you mustn't take it as a precedent. Andrew, please come in and see me before you go. I shall want you to take these notes to Mr. Samara."

Andrew made no direct reply beyond a little bow. The two men left the room together and paused for a moment in the main avenue of the floor. The journalist gazed around with an exclamation of admiration.

"This is certainly a live place!" he pronounced. "Might be a stock operator's paradise in Chicago. What's the kiosk at the far end with the open roof and the funnel?"

"Office to receive and decode private wireless," Andrew explained. "They are in direct communication with the Intelligence Department on the floor below."

Pride gripped his companion by the arm tightly.

"Look here, young man," he said, "I expect you're wise to what I want to know. I've got to get my cable off in half an hour. Those Englishmen aren't over here again for nothing. I want to give them an idea on the other side as to whether the

President is going to speak about the Second Army to-night."

"You should have asked Miss Borans," Andrew replied. "She is preparing his notes."

"I might as well have asked the sphinx," the other retorted impatiently. "That's the worst of a woman. She doesn't think — she obeys. It can't matter a cent to any one whether I am in a position to say that the President is going to talk about it or that he isn't — but you can't get that young lady to understand."

"You've tried her then?"

Pride shrugged his shoulders.

"I did just mention it this afternoon," he admitted. "Nothing doing!"

"Nor with me," Andrew observed shortly. "The Chief!" he exclaimed, in an altered tone. "If he speaks to you, you can ask him for yourself."

The main door of the hall had been suddenly thrown open by Ivan Rortz, admitting Samara. Pride stood to attention respectfully, hoping for a salutation, but Samara passed every one with absolutely unseeing eyes. At the far end of the broad passage was a heavy oaken door. This, too, Ivan, hurrying by his master, opened and Samara disappeared into his private room. The American looked a little disconcerted.

"No luck!" he grumbled. "I'll have to wait until to-night. For the greatest democrat in the world," he went on ruefully, "Samara is a perfect wonder at keeping us all just where he wants us."

"The Chief does everything his own way and it is a good way," Andrew declared. "He would never be able to stir a yard if he allowed every one to speak to him whenever he chose. Any one from any country in the world may obtain an audience with him in due course, but no one may speak to him or even recognise him without permission. That is the only way he is able to move about amongst us without trouble or hindrance. You'll excuse me, Mr. Pride. I've some work which I must hurry on. I did not know that the Chief was expected here to-day."

There came a sudden flash in his eyes and he remained a moment where he was, looking through the glass partition into Catherine's office. He saw her answer the telephone, replace the instrument, pick up a notebook, and move towards the door. He watched her pass along the passage until she reached the door of the room which Samara had entered. Ivan, who was standing outside on guard, admitted her without question. All the time the American was studying his companion.

"Say, Mr. Kroupki," he observed, "I sometimes wonder whether you ever regret that month's illness of yours in New York."

It was a purposeful stroke, designed to bring about trouble of a certain sort. The young man's dark eyes were black pools of anger now, his lips quivered. Nevertheless he spoke in a subdued tone.

"It had to happen," he muttered. "It will not last."

Without farewell Andrew Kroupki swung abruptly round and disappeared into his office. Pride stood for a moment looking after him. Then he, too, turned away and opened a door, over which was printed in white letters:

SALON No. 11

For Accredited Representatives of the Foreign Press

"A tough job to get a pull here!" he soliloquised, throwing himself into a comfortable chair and lighting a cigar. "I've offered to immortalise Samara or marry the girl. There seems to be only Andrew left. What about Andrew, I wonder?"

Pride smoked steadily on, his eyes fixed upon the ceiling. He was face to face with the eternal problem of his profession. His own instinct had scented trouble and brought him to Moscow. He was perfectly convinced that there would be news enough and to spare before many months had passed, but news which was shared with rivals was to Bromley Pride no news at all. Catherine was hopeless, and Samara divulged only what he wished known. Complete failure was a condition, the possibility of which he never admitted. There was still Andrew — Andrew, impervious to bribes, impeccable at heart, but plunged suddenly into a maelstrom of passion!

"Crazy about the girl and madly jealous of her at the same time," he reflected. "Something should come of the combination!"

SAMARA, that afternoon, was for some reason excited. He showed it in the manner peculiar to him; his cheeks were a little paler, his eyes seemed clearer and filled with sombre fire. He sat upright in his high-backed chair, his fingers drumming upon the table in front of him. He did not even light a cigarette, generally his first action when he called at Government Buildings after leaving the Duma. The box stood by his side unnoticed. All the time his fingers tapped the table and his eyes asked Catherine questions.

She had paused upon the threshold after Ivan had closed the door behind her. Then she advanced a little farther into the room. Finally she stood almost by his side, her hand resting upon the back of a chair.

"You sent for me," she reminded him.

"Yes," he answered. "Sit down."

She resented his tone, as she frequently did, but in his present mood, obedience from others seemed to become automatic and inevitable. She sat down and, after a moment or two spent in turning over the pages of her notebook, looked up enquiringly.

"Tell me about your people over here!" he demanded.

"My people!" she murmured.

"Yes," he went on impatiently. "The Grand Duchess Alexandrina Sophia of Kossas, your much-to-be-esteemed aunt, and Kirdorff the Moscovite, the self-elected champion of the young man who has left off selling bonds in New York, and General Orenburg, the patriarch, and those two others — the young man who was trying to make an honest living selling automobiles, and his sister. They are all here, aren't they?"

"They are all here now," she admitted. "You yourself gave them permission to return. Nicholas came first and the others have followed him in relays."

"Where did they get the money from?"

"Count Sabaroff — I might, perhaps, call him Cyril, as he is my cousin — is doing exceedingly well selling Ford cars," she announced. "His sister has started a milliner's shop."

Samara laughed shortly — not altogether pleasantly.

"A touch of western democracy come to my capital," he observed. "And the others?"

"Well," she hesitated, "I am not quite sure that I feel free to discuss their financial position, even with you."

"Don't be foolish," he protested. "They have become citizens of my republic. I have the right to know all I choose about them — I and my ministers. There is curiosity in certain quarters as to their means of livelihood."

Catherine smiled at him. She was silent for a moment, thinking that she rather liked his appearance when he was inclined to be angry; his mouth, hard and dominant, his eyes, with all their kindness veiled, keen and insistent, his tone the tone of a ruler.

"I think I shall tell you," she decided. "It may put you in a better humour. They are being financed by Mrs. Saxon J. Bossington."

"What the devil do you mean?" he demanded.

"Well, it does sound rather extraordinary, doesn't it?" she continued. "Almost like the plot of a musical comedy. There was a wonderful Englishman who lived many years ago — Gilbert, his name was — who would certainly have jumped at the idea. Nevertheless it is true. Mrs. Bossington is one of those Western Americans, rapidly becoming extinct, to whom a title is as the hallmark of divinity. She advanced the money for every one to come back to Moscow and settle down here."

"On the chance, I suppose," he suggested swiftly, "that some day or other they might, under more beneficent legislation, regain their estates and be in a position to reward in courtly fashion their generous benefactor."

"Rather high-flown," Catherine remarked, with a smile, "but still I have no doubt that it is a very fair analysis of what is in the back of Mrs. Bossington's mind. So far as I am concerned, I am glad that Andrew Kroupki's illness gave me an opportunity of getting here without such aid. I strongly disapprove of the manner in which some of them — Nicholas Imanoff in particular — draw upon the Bossington exchequer."

Samara stretched out his hand, took a cigarette from the box and lit it. It was, for him, a good sign.

"Listen," he said. "I am one of those men who like to move down the highway of life alone, but I am always open to the advice of my counsellors, who speak to me freely whensoever they choose. Only this afternoon one of my ministers, just as I was leaving the Duma, called me into his room. He wished to consult me upon no less a matter than you."

"That meddlesome policeman, I am sure," Catherine sighed. "He dislikes me immensely. I had to take him over some reports for you only last week, and he seemed shocked to think that I should have been trusted to type them."

"General Trotsk is no fool," Samara pronounced. "He pointed out to me that having succeeded in crushing Communism, there was yet one other danger — less a danger of to-day, I believe, than a danger in years to come — of which we must take account. There is no recognised imperialistic party at present but I've a shrewd idea that there's one in embryo. Trotsk goes farther than that. He believes that the party is already in existence, working chiefly in the great cities and amongst the army, and assisted by German agents. Incidentally he asked me frankly whether I thought I was wise in having for my trusted secretary a young woman who was in close association with the Imperial family of Russia."

"I think I do the work very well," she said. "Did you explain that you took me from the Weltmore Typewriting Agency?"

"I did. Trotsk suspects that there was a design in your being sent to me."

"Then Ivor Trotsk is wrong," Catherine declared firmly. "I was chosen entirely by accident and, to be quite candid, I at first refused to come. If you think," she went on, "that my family associations, of which you know more than any one, render me unfit to be your secretary, send me away. Andrew Kroupki would be very glad so far as the work is concerned."

"What do you mean by 'so far as the work is concerned'?" Samara demanded.

She deliberated for a moment.

"I begin to think," she confessed, "that notwithstanding your stony attitude towards me, I must be quite attractive to a number of male human beings. Andrew is very deeply in love with me. I foresee that I shall have great difficulty with him."

"Better tell him the truth about your identity," Samara advised drily. "That will cure him."

She shook her head.

"I am not at all sure that I wish him to be cured," she observed. "Every well-brought-up girl expects to have at least one man in love with her. Did you send for me, Mr. Samara, merely to tell me of Ivor Trotsk's suspicions, or is there any work I can do for you?"

"I wish to call upon your aunt," Samara announced. "My car is at the door. Show me the way, if you please, to where she is living."

Catherine was a little startled.

"My aunt will be honoured," she said. "Do I understand that you expect me to accompany you?"

"Yes," was the curt reply.

"Whilst I put my hat on," she suggested, "I wonder whether you would care to see Bromley Pride for a moment. He is aching for a word with you."

"He can come in for three minutes," Samara assented. "Do not keep me longer. Tell Ivan as you go out that he can be admitted."

Catherine left the room a little thoughtfully. She knocked at the glass panelling of the office where Pride was sitting. He came out at once, his cigar in his hand.

"I've earned that pearl necklace or whatever it was you hinted at," she told him. "The Chief will see you for exactly three minutes. Don't keep him any longer. We're going out motoring together."

Pride laid down his cigar and moved eagerly away.

"Say, I'm awfully obliged, Miss Borans," he declared. "See you later."

He hurried off to the audience chamber. Catherine moved towards the telephone.

"What do you want, Pride?" Samara asked, as the journalist entered. "Sit down, unless you can talk quicker standing. You can stay for exactly three minutes."

"Standing, please," was the prompt reply. "I've been looking into the streets. I saw the last of a million soldiers go their way. What about the others?"

"Read the report of the Peace Conference, Wednesday week," Samara suggested. "I am going to London to attend it."

"I want to know beforehand," the journalist rejoined eagerly. "My paper likes definite forecasts. I see those two Englishmen are over here again — Lord Edward Fields and Edgar Hammond. It's their third visit. I guess there's something doing this time. Can't you put me wise, Samara, just a few hours before the others? We want to be in the know — not to make absolute statements, but to prophesy — and then be right."

"Excellent from the point of view of your paper," Samara observed drily. "It doesn't happen to suit me. I can tell you nothing."

"Not a hint?" Pride persisted.

"Not a hint. Understand from me now, please, that I have come to the conclusion that it would not be to the interests of the Russian Republic for word of our projected plans to become public property until I give the signal. That's final!"

Pride sighed.

"Nothing else for me?" he asked a little wistfully.

"My God, man, what do you want!" Samara demanded. "Here you are, most favoured of all correspondents in the world. You have seen to-day the passing of that first million. Can't you write about that? Isn't that dramatic enough for you? A million fire-eating monsters dissolved into thin air; a million sturdy, self-respecting Russian peasants bending over their toil, earning food and dwelling and clothes and savings for their womenkind and children! Feet on the earth, head to the skies — men, not puppets any longer! Go and write about it. Finished! Please tell Miss Borans to wait in her office until I fetch her."

Samara waved his visitor away. He never shook hands; seldom indulged in the ordinary amenities which passed between men. He spoke for a moment on the telephone, frowned and laid down the instrument. Then he took up his hat and gloves, left his office and, followed by Ivan, walked rapidly down the broad central passage. Catherine was waiting for him on the threshold of her own apartment. He motioned her to step back, entered and closed the door behind him.

"To whom have you been telephoning?" he demanded.

She looked at him for a moment with immovable face. Then she smiled faintly.

"To my aunt," she replied.

"Why?"

"To tell her to be sure and see that there were hot cakes for tea," she confided.

"You think that I believe that?" he exclaimed.

"Why not? It happens to be the truth," she assured him.

Samara's manner to older women possessed a charm of which he seldom, in his general intercourse with the other sex, gave any indication. His bow to the Grand Duchess was the bow of a courtier; his few words of welcome were admirably spoken. For the first ten minutes no serious subject was mooted. It was Alexandrina herself who introduced another note. She was suddenly deeply and intensely in earnest.

"Mr. Samara," she said, "I should like you to know that in making possible this return to my own country, you have given an elderly woman the greatest happiness life could offer. I recognise the generosity of it. I wish to pay my tribute to it. It is not an easy thing for me to say to you, but I do say it—I thank you."

Samara bowed gravely.

"Duchess," he pronounced, "it is one of the theories of my life that every man and every woman, too, lives more naturally and to the best account in their native land."

He paused for a moment, but was obviously about to continue, when Colonel Kirdorff was announced, and immediately afterwards General Orenburg. They both welcomed Samara respectfully but perhaps with some measure of constraint. A few minutes later the latter rose to take his leave.

"My visit," he explained, turning a little towards the newcomers, "was intended to be one of courtesy to Her Highness. Since I have been fortunate enough to find you, Colonel Kirdorff, and you, General Orenburg, here together, let me make this further use of it. I want to say that I am happy to welcome you back to Russia, and I am glad if I have been able to make your coming possible. So long as you all pursue the lives of Russian citizens — you, General, and you, Colonel, in the army, and Your Highness as a Russian lady of society — you will, I am sure, find no one venture to interfere with you. But I rule, not for myself, but for my people, and I tell you frankly that my espionage system is good. If I wished, I could not exclude you from its activities. I desire, therefore, to give you this warning. If by any chance any one of you should be discovered plotting against the State, the fact that I brought you here would count for nothing. If you enter into any conspiracy of any sort you will be discovered and no representations to me would be of the slightest avail. I did not put you on your parole when I asked you back. I did not do so purposely. I ask you even now for no promises. Live as you think well and shape your futures as you choose, but even though mine has the name of being a humane Government, it has no mercy upon those who plot against it."

There was a moment's silence. No one seemed anxious to reply. Samara, looking round at their expressionless faces, found his mind wandering off to trifles. He realised that the room was small and overheated and the atmosphere heavy with the perfume of musk. Alexandrina was wearing an unbecoming gown but some wonderful old jewellery. The two men had changed since the New York days. Kirdorff stood differently upon his feet, looked differently out of his eyes. The General seemed years younger. As Samara watched them, he was conscious that there was a mutual and silent understanding between them all from which he was excluded. He glanced swiftly at Catherine. She, too, was in it. She was of them — belonged to them. He was a fool to hope even for her fidelity! In the end it was Alexandrina who spoke. There was a slight stiffness in her manner.

"One might conspire in New York," she remarked ——

"In the salon of Mrs. Bossington, perhaps," he scoffed. "Your conspiracies there would very surely end in dreams, but to-day —

listen — there is a line which reaches even from this room, Madame la Duchesse, to the Headquarters of the Second Army at Odensk. I think if I were you I would snap the line."

Again there was a tense silence in the little room. The two men stood like graven images. Alexandrina had picked up a paper fan and was wielding it mechanically. Even Catherine seemed for a moment to have lost her *savoir faire*. With a curt little gesture of farewell, Samara took his leave.

CHAPTER III

BROMLEY PRIDE and Andrew Kroupki dined together that evening in the Savoy Grill Room — not the Savoy of the Strand, but the Savoy of a certain street leading off one of the newly developed boulevards in Moscow. It was a meal which distinctly lacked all the characteristics of a festival. No two personalities in all the city could have been so ill-attuned. Andrew was neurotic, almost neurasthenic; distracted at the same time by his passion for Catherine and his insane jealousy of her. Bromley Pride, full of vigorous common sense, sane, healthy and indefatigable in his profession, saw life as a confirmed materialist, desired only the possible things, and had scant sympathy with the emotional wear and tear to which his companion continually subjected himself. Nevertheless they ate and drank together and made conversation up to a certain point like any other two men brought together in the daily affairs of life.

"One of the by-laws for which I suppose your President is responsible," Pride remarked, tapping the menu which was printed in Russian.

Andrew glanced at it and nodded.

"A reasonable edict," he declared. "Any one who chooses may print his wine list or menu in French, but it must also be printed in Russian. Why not? We are in Moscow. We like French food, we like French wines, but we want to take them as Russians, not as French people. A nation may be adaptive and appreciative, but must not be coalescent."

"I guess you're right," Pride admitted. "Russia's a well-governed country to-day — a country with a definite identity. During the last ten years you have broken loose from the greatest danger any nation ever experienced. You have shaken off German thraldom and German influence."

"Without warfare too," Andrew added eagerly. "By just, discriminating legislation. The man who makes money in Russia, out of Russian industries or Russian mineral wealth, must spend his money here or face a different scale of taxation. We have had enough of foreigners tapping our supplies of wealth, drawing off the profits and flitting to some other country."

"Does it ever occur to you," Pride remarked, "that you are gradually making an enemy of Germany?"

"Better that," his companion retorted hotly, "than to be her tame monkey, ready to pull the chestnuts out of the fire when she gave the word. That is what we were under the Communists. Five years more of their government and the Germans would have marched our armies from Russia to the French frontier and not a soul could have stopped them."

"And now," Pride observed, "it seems that you will very soon have no armies to march anywhere."

"Why should we need armies?" Andrew demanded. "Invasion of our country is no longer to be feared. The Peace Conference has tied most of the nations of the world hand and foot. Germany, through her own cunning, remains outside, but what would it profit her to cross our frontiers? Where would she strike, at what, and with what object? The frontiers of France have been a brazen defiance to Germany for fifty years. All her coal fields, her manufacturing towns, her wine-growing districts, are there, like Naboth's vineyard — a stone's throw across the frontier for jealous eyes to gaze upon. We have nothing like that to offer the invader. A military establishment for us is a farce."

"I heard Samara speak at Geneva," Pride remarked drily.

His companion was unmoved.

"I plagiarize, I know," he admitted. "Why not? Who can repeat the words of a greater man?"

The restaurant was crowded; noisy with a babel of talk, blue-hung with cigarette smoke. In the distance a small orchestra was drowned by the volume of conversation. Most of the people were Russian; here and there a few Germans, an occasional Englishman, a few Americans. Newcomers were still arriving. Pride was immensely interested in the passing of two very distinguished-looking young people — a short, dark young man and a young woman, a little taller, dressed in black, with a black picture hat and ermine wrap, a very graceful carriage, blue eyes with a roving tendency, and beautifully marked eyebrows.

"Amazing!" the journalist murmured. "I knew that young man in New York — he was trying to sell Ford motor cars. And the girl — why, she was in a Fifth Avenue milliner's! What on earth has brought them to Moscow?"

Andrew smiled.

"They are part of the great comedy," he declared. "They own names as long as this menu. They are aristocrats of the Russia which has passed away. Yet you are quite right. The young man learnt the automobile trade in New York and the girl, as you say, was a milliner's assistant. One must live! — even the children of those who escaped from Russia with nothing but their lives."

"What I can't catch on to," Pride confessed, "is what has brought them back to Russia? How do they live?"

"They are back here at Samara's express invitation," Andrew explained. "A whole nest of Monarchists! The President has revoked all edicts of banishment except against anarchists. He maintains that every Russian is entitled to live in his own country and air his own opinions."

"I guess he's right," the other acknowledged. "They'll do no harm and there are not madmen enough left in the world to preach Tzardom here."

Andrew Kroupki shrugged his shoulders. He drained half the contents of his glass before he answered.

"How can one reckon on anything?" he demanded. "Two generations of education have scarcely altered the Russian peasant. He is still the same simple, faithful human being; seeking for something in the world or heaven to lean against — a Tzar or a God or anything he can believe in. He isn't dangerous like the German mob because you can't appeal to his intellect. You can appeal only to his instinct and I am not so sure as I should like to be that his instinct for Tzardom is dead. There are many people, even members of the Cabinet, who think that Samara is doing a rash thing in interfering with the armies."

"Precisely why?" Pride asked.

"For fear he should disturb some smouldering bonfires of royalist sentiment," Andrew answered, enlighteningly.

Pride was inclined to be disputatious.

"A cause," he declared, "needs sinews; money, brains, enthusiasm. Who is there in the world who possesses these things likely to devote them to the overthrow of such a man as Samara or to placing the country once more under its old yoke? There's no real danger."

Andrew threw some money on the table and rose abruptly.

"Let us go to the Club, or a music hall, or somewhere," he proposed. "The atmosphere of this place is stifling."

They left the restaurant and passed along the broad thoroughfare thronged with human beings, hung with sky signs, a marvel of pulsating life. It was a warm evening and the open-air cafés were crowded. From the wide-flung doors, as the two men sauntered along, they heard the sound of music, occasionally the sharp pattering feet of the professional dancers. Music halls and cinemas invited their patronage. In the more dignified streets through which they presently made their way, most of the larger theatres were situated, every one of which seemed able to display the warning notice — "House Full." Pride paused at the corner and looked back. A new sky sign, which was one of the wonders of the world, was flashing hieroglyphics upon the clouds.

"I have just finished reading a book on Moscow during the third year of the Communist rule," he confided. "What a transformation! Your Samara is a great man, Andrew Kroupki!"

"He is one of the world's greatest rulers," was the reverent reply. "No one else could have drained the poison out of the country as he has done and then filled her with new and vigorous life."

They stopped in front of the façade of a theatre. Automobiles were still setting down late arrivals. Pride glanced at the playbill.

"A French comedy," he remarked, "of the type of Edmond About. They sent me a box this morning. Shall we see it?"

Andrew Kroupki had been seeking for an excuse to break away from his companion, but before he could find one, Pride had led the way in. A young man dressed with such precision as to amount almost to foppishness was finishing a cigarette in the vestibule. He touched Andrew on the arm as he passed.

"I am forgotten, then?" he asked. "We were at college together, Andrew Kroupki. We attended the same lectures afterwards."

"Ivor Molsky!" the latter exclaimed. "I remember you quite well. But I heard ——"

He stopped short. The young man smiled. He was rather a saturnine-looking person with an uncertain gleam in his eyes, and a restlessness of manner at variance with his immaculate appearance.

"Well, well," he interrupted, "never mind what you heard. I am not so bad, Andrew. I have often thought about you and our talks. You serve a great master."

"None greater on earth," was the fervent response.

His friend smiled with an air of tolerance.

"Gabriel Samara is a genius," he acknowledged, "but he is like the others. He is bound hand and foot, and the handkerchief is across his eyes. He has the will to go forward but the way into the light has not been shown him."

An attendant broke in upon their conversation and ushered Andrew and his companion to a small box in the second tier, next to the one presently occupied by Molsky. The theatre was unusually full and the performance was just beginning. Andrew drew his chair behind the curtains and sat a little gloomily in the background. Pride, on the other hand, leaned over the ledge and surveyed the house with interest. Nearly every one was in evening dress. It was an audience distinguished not only for its apparent opulence but for other and more pleasing qualities. Men and women were the study of Pride's life. He realised without effort to what class of the community these people belonged.

"My God!" he exclaimed, in an undertone to Andrew. "Your Russia is incredible! Marvellous! All over the world, even in Spain, to-day, the money seems to have got into the wrong hands. You find the wrong people spending it. This is the only country which seems to be holding the balance and to be holding it without a court or aristocracy. These women with their pearls, and these men in their very correct evening clothes, they are not of the *bourgeoisie* as we used to understand the word. They are intellectuals."

Andrew showed a momentary flicker of interest.

"It is the Chief," he said. "Our tabulated taxes are a model for the world. Inherited wealth is taxed first, commercial next, brains last of all. That accounts for what you see. Even in England forty years ago they made ghastly blunders — taxed the brain worker and the artist equally with the war profiteer. Nothing of that here. Hence this audience of which you approve."

The play proceeded; clever and well received. During the interval Andrew touched his companion on the arm.

"My prince of journalists," he murmured, a little satirically, "you have studied this audience so carefully and yet you have failed to notice the most interesting people here — the most interesting to you at any rate, with your journalistic instinct."

"I confess it," Pride acknowledged. "I don't recognize a soul."

"In the box exactly opposite," his companion pointed out, — "the man with the grey moustache and the clean-shaven man. It is — don't you recognise them? You must — one is Lord Edward Fields and the other is Edgar Hammond, the man who they say will be the next British Chancellor of the Exchequer. They are members of the English Commission over to settle finally the terms of this second British loan — if it comes off."

Pride scrutinised the two men closely through the opera glasses, which he procured from an attendant. He sighed as he laid them down.

"If they had belonged to any other nationality in the world," he said, "I'd have gone across and trusted to my luck to get a word with them. A Britisher on official business I simply daren't face. Have they seen Samara yet?"

"Only unofficially," Andrew replied. "They meet the Cabinet to-morrow, and the Council in the afternoon."

"The Council is 'Samara,'" Pride remarked drily.

"And why not?" was the prompt retort. "There is no brain in the world like Samara's! no ruler like him. What does he want with a dozen inferiors, putting in their spoke? The best thing you can say of the Russian Cabinet is that it recognises a pedagogue."

The curtain went up once more and the play was resumed to the interest and amusement of its audience, all unconscious of the drama to come. It was towards the end of the second act, in the middle of a tense scene between the principal actor and actress, that the amazing thing happened. From the very next box to that occupied by Pride and his companion, a man suddenly leaned out. His knee seemed to be upon the ledge of the box, his arm thrown back almost, as Pride said afterwards, with the action of an American baseball pitcher. His shrill cry rang through the house.

"To hell with the foreign capitalists!"

Something black, about the size of an orange, travelled in an arc across the auditorium. The two men watched it with fascinated eyes. It seemed to them that the Englishmen had plenty of time to spring from their places. They remained seated, however, utterly unconscious of their peril. A shout rang through the building.

"A bomb! Beware!"

The missile appeared to pass a little above the box at which it was aimed. As it struck the wainscotting there was a flash which seemed to shoot from the floor to the ceiling of the theatre, a roar and trembling of the earth, the hiss of splintering wood, the dull crash of chairs and woodwork scattered in every direction. Pride sprang to his feet. Both men realised at the same moment that the bomb had been thrown from the next box. They dashed out. The box itself was empty but, coming towards them, evidently headed towards flight, was Molsky, the man who had been its occupant and their neighbour.

The change in his appearance was astonishing. The sallowness of his face had turned to a distinct shade of yellow, his abundant black hair was no longer smooth, but seemed to have been caught by a tornado, his cynical lips had parted; nothing remained of the almost meticulous precision of his toilet. As he came towards them, running with long, uneven footsteps, they could catch the glint of his yellow teeth, almost like fangs, the wild, destroying lust of his expression, filled, too, with a certain joy of the turmoil and roar of his work of destruction. On their right was an open window from which there was only a short drop on to the leads. It was obvious that he was making for it.

Pride stood directly in his way. The man screamed something, lowered his head a little but too late. The American in his younger days had played halfback at Harvard. He was not a man to be passed. The fugitive seemed to realise the fact.

"Let me go!" he shrieked. "This is not for you."

Then he met the impact of Pride's fist and went down like a log. In a moment they were all upon him — attendants, police, and even members of the audience. It was simply a heap of passionate, furious humanity, with little to be seen of the man underneath but a thin stream of blood across the corridor. In the box opposite one Englishman lay dead and another apparently dying.

"It is a pity," Andrew Kroupki confessed, as the two men left the theatre half an hour later. "An event like this is nothing more nor less than a hideous anachronism. It will put us back amongst the nations a score of years."

"I shouldn't say that," Pride remonstrated. "The man was a fanatic. They exist in every community."

The younger man shook his head slowly.

"We were students together," he declared, "and afterwards Molsky became a professor at our premier university. No one could ever fathom what his political principles were. He hated all forms of what he called 'unauthorised rule' and he wrote some very clever criticisms of Samara and his attitude towards Communism. Yet the Chief would never have him touched. He called him his most intelligent critic — read everything he wrote, would have argued with him if he could."

"A man of education," Pride murmured. "It seems incredible!"

"There is no man in the world," Andrew Kroupki pronounced deliberately, "so brilliant in his way, so well-read and so amazingly subtle as the modern anarchist. He derived his first nourishment from the brutalism of Lenin and Trotsky, was suckled on Marx, and completed his education — God knows where!"

"What will be his end?"

"Simple enough," was the somewhat terrible reply. "The Chief has an enactment that any man found even handling a bomb is hung after a drum-head trial. If there is anything left of Molsky, he will be hung before eight o'clock to-morrow morning."

ANDREW KROUPKI'S words were in a sense prophetic. Molsky was hung at dawn on the following morning, and a few days later a hundred thousand Russians watched with bared heads the passing of the English statesman's funeral. Edgar Hammond was in hospital and some hopes of his recovery had been held out. The echoes of Samara's passionate denunciation, both of the crime and of the hideous code of thought from which it sprang, had reverberated not only through the country but through Europe. The simple end of his peroration was always remembered:

"If you wish to kill senselessly," he cried, "kill me. I walk the streets of Moscow day by day unprotected and unarmed. I stand for the things of which the man you have slain was only one link in the chain — I stand for the things themselves. Kill me and do not shame the oldest of the Russian virtues — hospitality!"

That night Samara walked unattended, save by Ivan, from the Duma to Government Buildings, and from Government Buildings to the presidential abode at the corner of the Square. If any would-be avenger of Molsky's shameful death had sought for his opportunity it was certainly freely offered to him. Samara, however, was unmolested. Nevertheless Ivan groaned as the postern gate leading into the courtyard of his master's home swung to after them. They had walked in leisurely fashion but the sweat stood out in dark beads upon his forehead.

"It was folly, that, Master!" he exclaimed. "On an ordinary day, yes, but to-day, with Molsky's body still dangling from the gibbet, there might be madmen abroad."

Samara paused to light one of his cigarettes.

"I expected it, Ivan," he acknowledged simply. "Yet what can one do? When strangers are slain by our people one must face what may come. Bring me a brandy and mineral water into the library. I am beginning to be a coward."

His old housekeeper, imported from the south of Russia, a quaint survival of mediævalism, in her black woollen gown, strange headdress and dialectic speech, met him in the hall.

"There is a woman, Master, who waits for you," she announced.

Samara's language, for a moment, though incomprehensible, was violent. The woman listened without change of countenance.

"This woman would not be denied," she continued. "The Master will understand when he sees her. I tried to send her away but it was not possible."

Samara handed his coat and hat to Ivan and walked with slow footsteps across the marble hallway into the great library which was his official audience chamber. As he recognised the woman who rose to meet him he gave a little exclamation of surprise. There were others who might have been there; he had never dreamed of this visit from Catherine.

"I was at the Duma," she announced brusquely. "I heard your speech. There was something which I felt I must say to you."

"Pray be seated," he begged. "This is the first time you have honoured my humble abode. You must drink from my samovar and smoke one of my cigarettes."

She was still in her working clothes; a little tired, apparently a little dispirited. She accepted the easy-chair he wheeled up for her, drank her tea and lit a cigarette.

"I should not be here without orders, of course," she admitted, a little abruptly. "It's a terrible breach of etiquette, I know, but sometimes I have no chance of speaking to you for days together, and they tell me that you are going to London."

"London!" he repeated bitterly. "London will probably have nothing to do with me after last night. They will say what is the good of trying to help a country who cannot deal with her own madmen?"

"England is not like that," she answered gently. "She certainly is not to be intimidated. They will grant the loan."

"What brought you here?" he demanded. "You must have had a reason for coming. You must have had something definite to say."

"Naturally," she assented. "I had a definite object in coming to you. I wish to give up my work."

"To leave me?"

"Yes."

There was a brief silence — a silence not of indifference, but tense in its way, and pregnant with much hidden emotion. These two might almost have been duellists pausing to measure each other's strength — Samara, grim, almost forbidding-looking, with the drawing together of his heavy eyebrows, an effective figure in his great oak chair, with a background of dimly seen tapestried walls; Catherine, more beautiful than ever in her absolute listlessness. Her skin was clear, bordering upon fragility. Her eyes were large and soft, even if a little weary. The simplicity of her gown detracted nothing from the charm of her lithe figure. There was a certain abandon in her attitude of fatigue, full of attraction from its almost animal-like naturalness. She sat in a gentle pool of shaded light, a subdued glimmer which brought out the flecks of gold in her hair, slightly disarranged after her long day's work. Into her expression, as she met his steadfast gaze, there crept something of the light of battle.

"It was to be expected," he admitted slowly. "Your interests lie elsewhere. You wish to leave at once?"

"I draw my pay weekly," she said. "You are entitled to a week's notice. Accept it, if you please."

"That is done," he assented.

"I will now tell you," she went on, "why I choose to go. You have apparently lost your faith in me. You have conceived suspicions of my friends. It is possible that these are justified. I am only partially in their confidence."

She paused. He watched her steadily.

"Finish," he insisted. "There is more, I suppose."

"To-morrow," she continued, "you have ordered Andrew to come here for the day and send his machine. He is a bad typist, a worse stenographer and he hates all form of dictation. His work has lain along different lines."

"Proceed, please," Samara invited.

"Andrew's duties," she pointed out, "have always been to act as your representative at committee meetings of the Duma. He is a sort of go-between with you and your ministers. He is the one person who enjoys your complete confidence. I do not complain, but when I came with you from New York it was as your confidential secretary. I have become your typist. Now that there is important work to be done even that is taken from me. I resign."

"You will throw in your lot with your family?" he asked with a sneer. "You will exist on the bounty of Mrs. Saxon J. Bossington?"

Her eyes flashed angrily.

"That is ungenerous," she exclaimed. "I consider the position of my aunt and some of her entourage as undignified in the extreme. It is ungenerous of you, however, to remind me of it."

"Perhaps so," he admitted. "As a matter of fact, I am angry. I do not wish to lose you."

"You are very gracious," she murmured.

Ivan entered, after ponderous knocking and asked his master a question. Samara nodded.

"I dine here," he declared. "Have dinner served for two, in an hour's time."

"For two?" she repeated questioningly.

"You will dine with me," he said curtly. "It shall be either our farewell or — a celebration."

"A celebration of what?"

"Of a better understanding," he answered, with a faint softening of those lines at the corners of his mouth.

She lazily removed her hat and smoothed out her hair.

"I shall dine with you as I am," she announced. "I am untidy and my head aches. This mechanical work depresses and fatigues me. I should like to go home and put on a pretty frock, but I have not the energy."

He seemed suddenly changed; infinitely more human, responsive to her altered attitude.

"As you sit there — or should I say, recline? — it seems to me that no change in your appearance could be for the better," he assured her.

She glanced at him in half-pleased surprise.

"A compliment!" she exclaimed.

He shook his head.

"A compliment implies a certain deviation from the truth," he observed. "I meant what I said. Now I will deal with your complaint and offer you an explanation. I have an important document to draw up to-morrow. I was proposing to take only Andrew into my confidence for one reason, and one reason only. Trotsk and some others suspect you of imperialistic sympathies. I, alone, know the truth about you. You are day by day subject to the influence and persuasions of your family. I do not consider it fair upon you yourself that you should be in possession of information which they would give their souls to acquire, especially —— "

She took advantage of his pause.

"It is for what comes after that 'especially' that I wait," she told him.

"Especially," he concluded, "as you have not yet declared yourself as between me and Nicholas Imanoff."

"I realise your problem," she admitted. "I am glad that you have been frank about it."

"Perhaps you have a pronouncement to make," he suggested.

"I wish I had," she replied. "I can at least be truthful. All my life I have prayed for the return of Tzardom to this country. That I suppose is in my blood. I have looked upon you with respect because you delivered Russia from the yoke of the Bolshevists, because you have evolved at least a sane form of republicanism, but I have looked upon you at the same time as a stumblingblock in our way."

"Your candour," he declared, "is most attractive. Pray continue."

"I am trying to let you into the back of my mind," she went on thoughtfully. "I am a daughter of Tzardom and a belief in monarchical government is in my blood, but I am also a daughter of Russia. Every spare minute since I returned here I have devoted to studying your system of government, seeking justification for it. I am not clever; I often wish I were. I have not even a knowledge of history to guide me. Of one thing, however, I am still convinced, — that there is exceedingly little difference between a beneficent Tzardom and the Government of to-day."

"Absurd!" he scoffed. "The present Government of Russia is the most democratic in the world."

"And the most autocratic," she retorted coolly. "It is you who rule Russia."

"By the mandate of the people," he reminded her.

"Nothing of the sort," she objected. "The people elected a republican government. You travelled the country for a year. You hypnotised them. They voted according to your decree. What has your Cabinet or even your Inner Council to do with the Government of Russia? Nothing! You are an autocrat more supreme than any Tzar who ever lived."

"I make no comment on what you say. Whither does it lead?"

"To this," she replied. "If Russia is to be ruled by one man, why not a Tzar? The Royalists have learnt their lesson. An Imanoff has more right upon the throne than you."

"Nicholas Imanoff," he jeered. "You would put him in my place!"

She was a little disconcerted, but she did her best to conceal the fact.

"Nicholas would never assume such powers as you have done," she replied. "He would govern through his ministers. If you remained a patriotic Russian you would probably be one of them."

"I am cheaper than a Tzar," he pointed out. "I do not cost the State even a modest million a year, nor do I —— "

He broke off in his speech. His housekeeper was standing upon the threshold, gazing expectantly towards Catherine.

"My housekeeper will show you where to rearrange your hair, if you really think that it needs it," he said courteously. "With your permission, I will not change my clothes. Shall we meet here in twenty minutes? You shall tell me then whether I can qualify as a bartender when the Royalists have driven me out of Russia!"

She made a little grimace over her shoulder as she left the room; a quaintly human touch which seemed to lessen at once the strain of their relations. He stood with his fingers upon the bell, listening to her departing footsteps.

The simplicity of Samara's life was typified in the dinner which was presently served. The house itself was an old palace of the Grand Duke Nicholas, sacked by the Bolshevists in nineteen-seventeen, occupied by Lenin for some time during his stay in Moscow, and finally transformed into the official dwelling house of the Chairman of the Council, sometimes called President of the Russian Republic. Little remained of its former splendour, ex-

cept its architectural proportions and the tapestry-covered walls
of the room in which they sat. Dinner was served at one end of a
long mahogany table, the greater part of which remained uncovered. The only illumination in the room was that afforded by
wax candles. Ivan waited behind his master's chair, and a single
manservant was the other attendant. The dinner itself was plain
but excellent; the champagne exceptional in age and quality.

"I am free to confess that I am no longer tired," Catherine observed, as she sipped her wine. "It is wonderful that you should
have been alone. One fancies you always doing something official
at night."

"There was a banquet to the Englishmen," he told her. "That
had to be cancelled, of course."

He turned and gave Ivan a few rapid orders. The cloth disappeared as though by magic. Coffee, fruit and liqueurs alone
were left upon the table. Even Ivan presently withdrew. Catherine
was conscious of a little thrill — she scarcely knew whether of
excitement or apprehension — when she realised, not only that
they were alone, but that they were alone with certain things yet
to be said.

"So you want to leave me, Catherine Borans," he remarked.

He had pushed his chair around and crossed his legs, so that
they were almost side by side. The chairs themselves were relics
of ancient magnificence, with huge black oak backs and up-
holstered in worn rose-coloured damask. Looking at him as he
bent forward to light his cigarette Catherine felt herself compelled to half-reluctant admiration. The wine which he had drunk
freely had brought little more than a faint flush of colour to his
cheeks; his eyes were bright and full of clean fire; his mouth, as
usual, incomprehensible. She found herself wondering what it
would look like if ever he should by chance speak tenderly.

"It is better that I leave you," she said, "since I no longer
possess your full confidence."

"Are you worthy of my full confidence?" he asked, quickly.

"So far I have never abused it," she answered.

"For that very reason," he admitted, "I owe you frankness.
You shall continue to have it. If you had studied history and
philosophy of government, you would understand the truth of

what I am going to tell you. All the beneficent legislation of the world is effected by moderate government, but a government, even though it brings a country from the slough of despond to the fields of paradise, cannot exist for ever. The desire for change in an electorate is an inevitable and ineradicable instinct. Before many years are gone by I and my Government will disappear. To which extreme will Russia swing? Back to communism-cum-anarchy, or in the other direction towards a monarchy? There is a fear of both. That is why I, who theoretically hate all such things, keep up a wonderful secret service. I watch the anarchists and I watch your friends. Your friends, here at my invitation, are already conspiring. Both of the men to whom I gave posts in the army are already at work with royalist propaganda. Both of these are your relatives. For whom are you, Catherine Borans—for them or for me?"

"I am a Monarchist," she said proudly, "but it does not follow that I should betray your trust."

"The work which I have summoned Andrew Kroupki to do with me to-morrow," he went on, "concerns the future of Russia's two remaining armies, deals with the matter of the new conscriptions, and would be full of the most amazing interest to your relatives. They would read my proclamations before they were issued and be prepared with contra-propaganda. They would also learn the means I am taking to prevent serious trouble. You still wish to do the work?"

"If I am to remain your secretary," she answered with a certain unaccustomed doggedness.

"You will be here at nine o'clock to-morrow morning, then," he directed. "You will take a taxicab first to Government Buildings and collect your machine, both code books, and instruct Peter Tranchard, the head of the private printing department, to be prepared for important work during the afternoon. You will be engaged here for the whole of the day. May I take it now that your notice is withdrawn?"

"If you wish," she answered a little wistfully. "But are you sure you still desire to keep me? Other people, if they knew who I was, would feel the same as General Trotsk. You would be considered very indiscreet to have a secretary with such connections."

He poured himself out some liqueur brandy and held the glass between his hands for a moment.

"Indiscreet," he repeated. "Yes, there is indiscretion in keeping you near me, Catherine Borans, but indiscretion of another sort." She gave a little sigh of content. Her eyes challenged him.

"This sounds more interesting," she murmured. "Please go on."

"There is nothing further to tell you except this," he replied coldly. "The indiscretion consists in the fact that you are the only woman whom I have ever met in my life who could keep my thoughts turned away for a moment from the things that count. A coward would send you away. You see I have faith in myself."

"More interesting than I had even dared to hope," she exclaimed. "Have you never really cared seriously for any woman, then?"

"Never," he assured her fervently. "You are the only one against whom I have ever had to steel myself. The only one who has ever made me feel that there are lonely hours in a man's life."

"You were feeling like that, I suppose," she observed quite calmly, but with the ghost of a tremulous little smile at the corners of her lips, "the night you kissed me on the steamer."

For a moment she was afraid. She called back the challenge from her eyes, but it was too late. His arm was around her neck, his lips pressed to hers. She almost lost her senses in a wave of turmoil, of impotent resistance to the torrent of passion which surged about her. The perfume of the roses which decorated the table remained in her thoughts for years afterwards. Just as she had found his arm around her absolutely without warning, so, in the same fashion, she saw him a moment or two later, leaning back in his high-backed chair, gazing at her with steady but burning eyes.

"As your host, I have transgressed," he admitted, "but I have the great excuse. If you had been any other woman and I had been any other man, I should have been your lover."

He lit a cigarette and smoked furiously. Twice she opened her lips and said nothing. The third time she spoke.

"But you are Samara," she murmured, her eyes swimming in the softness of incredible things, "and I am Princess Catherine of Imanoff. Well?"

He rose to his feet, almost with a bound, passed behind her chair, and before she could imagine what he meant to do was standing on the hearthrug, his finger pressed to the bell. It was answered almost immediately by Ivan.

"An automobile for Miss Borans," Samara ordered.

The man bowed low and departed, closing the door behind him. Catherine looked across at her host, still standing upon the hearthrug, and laughed softly.

"Dismissed," she sighed.

"Would you be willing to pay the price of staying?" he asked bluntly.

The laughter passed from her face. Some part of the wave of emotion which had driven him from her side suddenly surged up in her. Whether it was love or hate she scarcely knew, but for the first time in her life she felt herself dominated.

"The President of the Russian Republic," he began hoarsely, "even though it were his desire, could never —— "

"Is it his desire?" she interrupted, with a sudden wild hatred of those heavy footsteps in the hall.

The door was thrown open. Ivan, tall and massive, stood to attention.

"The automobile awaits," he announced.

"Not later than nine o'clock in the morning, if you please, Miss Borans," Samara said, bowing his farewell.

She left the room slowly, — the room which seemed strewn with fragments of a dream. She followed Ivan down the hall and nodded good night to him carelessly as she stepped into the automobile. As she drove across the Square and came within hearing of the night-hum of Moscow, — a medley, it sounded to her, of strange music and hurrying footsteps — she found herself suddenly thinking of Sadie Loyes and the Hotel Weltmore Typewriting Bureau. It was like an anticlimax to her emotions. She began to laugh softly.

ALEXANDRINA breathed a sigh of relief. She was entertaining an unexpected visitor whom she had found a little difficult.

"At last!" she exclaimed, as Catherine entered. "My dear child, what extraordinary accident has detained you? We have telephoned to Government Buildings and every place we could think of. You have met General von Hartsen, I believe."

The General bowed low and raised Catherine's fingers to his lips.

"In Monte Carlo," he murmured. "It gives me the greatest pleasure, Princess, to renew our acquaintance."

Catherine glanced around the room, conscious of an acute sense of mental fatigue, a desire for an impossible seclusion. Kirdorff was there and Cyril Sabaroff, the former in uniform, but if there had been other guests, they had all departed. She sank a little wearily into an easy-chair. She was the only one in morning dress and she was sensible somehow of a complete lack of sympathy with the little coterie gathered around her aunt's chair.

"I was working late," she explained with perverse candour, "and I stayed to dine at Government House."

General von Hartsen was interested.

"Does your work, Princess," he enquired, "still lead you into direct association with Gabriel Samara?"

"At times," Catherine admitted. "I dined with him to-night. I am working with him at Government House to-morrow."

There was a moment's silence.

"At Government House," Kirdorff repeated thoughtfully.

Catherine nodded. Her questioner moved a little nearer towards her.

"Have you any idea as to the nature of the work?" he ventured. "I ask, because we have information ―― "

Alexandrina intervened with a wave of the hand.

"My dear Kirdorff," she complained, "you think of one thing, and one thing only. We admit your zeal, and we quite understand that Catherine's intimate association with Government work just now may prove of great benefit to our cause. At the same time, we would ask you to remember that General von Hartsen's mission is of the first importance with us at the present moment."

"Has General von Hartsen a mission?" Catherine enquired, a little flippantly. "Tell me, General," she went on, "how is that very hot-headed young charge of yours who followed me to London? You will have trouble with that young man when he grows up."

The General stiffened.

"Princess," he begged, "may I ask for your very serious attention to what I have to say?"

"Frankly I could not promise it," was the somewhat unexpected reply. "I am very sleepy and my nerves are all tangled. What about to-morrow, General? I feel, somehow or other, that to-morrow I shall be a different person. You are not hurrying away from Moscow, I hope."

"That depends upon you, Princess," he answered gravely. "My mission here is to lay a certain proposal before you."

"Not the same proposal as before, I trust!" Catherine exclaimed.

The General frowned.

"Princess," he said, "the circumstances and conditions under which I now approach you are entirely different. I asked you then to accept in marriage the suit of a German nobleman of royal descent, whose future was of no great account in the world. To-day I am here to beg for your hand in marriage to Prince Frederick of Wehrenzollern who, I pledge you my word, before twelve months have passed will be crowned Emperor of Germany."

"Matrimonially," Catherine murmured, "my destiny seems to lead me to high places. Have you not been informed, General, that I am already as good as betrothed to Prince Nicholas of Imanoff, the future Tzar of Russia?"

"It is upon that point that I desire to speak with you, Princess," was the earnest reply. "We Germans, if I may say so, are in the last lap of our struggle towards monarchy. The people are only waiting for a word and they will lift the roof off the Reichstag with their cheering. The present parliament is due to be dissolved in two months' time. The Government will then resign and not a single other statesman will attempt to form a fresh one. The President, who is also resigning, will send for Prince Frederick. He will make an announcement. You may hear the roar of German voices even to your frontier."

"Very interesting," Catherine admitted, "but do I understand that the object of your mission here is seriously to revert to the subject of a marriage between myself and Prince Frederick?"

"Dear and gracious young lady," Von Hartsen continued, "the matter now rests upon an entirely different basis. The road to monarchy in Russia will be a long and arduous one in any case. The aid of Germany is the only thing which may shorten it by a span of years. As Kaiserin of Germany you will be able to do more for the cause of monarchy in this country than if you remain the betrothed of Prince Nicholas of Imanoff."

"Plausible," Catherine agreed, "but scarcely convincing. What has Nicholas to say to this?"

"Prince Nicholas," Kirdorff intervened, stepping forward, "was consulted before General von Hartsen left Berlin. He is deeply sensible of the potency of the General's arguments. The royalist cause will gain nothing outside Russia by the intermarriage of yourself and Prince Nicholas. You will indeed be looked upon doubtfully. Marriage between first cousins here is not too popular — especially after a decade of Soviet rule. Your marriage with Prince Frederick, on the other hand, would enable you to ensure the return of the monarchy to this country. Prince Frederick has pledged his word to make this a charge upon his conscience if you should accept his offer."

Alexandrina, who had been watching her niece a little anxiously, motioned her to her side.

"My dear," she said, "I am aware that this suggestion must have taken you completely by surprise. I quite appreciate the fact that you have not had time to think seriously about Frederick as a possible husband. You would furthermore consider yourself bound in honour to conclude your alliance with Nicholas. Nicholas, however, has had a very plain hint dropped to him. He has signified his intention to listen to reason."

"In other words Nicholas is quite agreeable to the transfer," Catherine remarked.

"It is for the good of his country," Kirdorff reminded her. "Nicholas is above all things a patriot."

"At the same time," Catherine pointed out, "this trafficking in my affections seems a little sordid. Nicholas, it appears, is content to do without me. I have, in other words, regained my liberty. I insist upon spending the night in that state. To-morrow I will interview General von Hartsen at the earliest possible moment."

Alexandrina turned towards the frowning ambassador with an ingratiating smile.

"My niece's attitude appears to me to be correct, General," she said. "You must not be over-zealous on account of your young master. Lunch with us here to-morrow."

"Dine," Catherine put in softly. "I shall be away all day."

"Dine with us here to-morrow night, then," the Grand Duchess invited, "and my niece shall be prepared."

Von Hartsen rose a little unwillingly to his feet.

"I should have preferred to have telephoned favourable news at once to my august young friend," he confessed. "You will forgive my pointing out once more that the position he is able to offer his wife is absolutely and entirely unique. However, I am at Her Highness's disposition."

"I shall have made up my mind by dinner time," Catherine promised him. "It really is quite an important matter to me, you know."

"It is of vast importance to all Europe," the General agreed. "On the other hand, I cannot imagine where hesitation could arise."

Catherine smiled cryptically.

"Perhaps not," she admitted, "but then you see you have to do with a woman. I am not sure that I should not find the Court life at Berlin a little irksome."

"You, Princess," the General declared, "would be the Court. It would be for you to set its tone. It is not for me to remind you that the lives of people even in the highest places have their relaxations at which even the historian can only guess."

He made his ceremonious farewells. They all waited until the door had closed behind him. Then a buzz of conversation started.

"My dear," her aunt told Catherine confidentially, "Nicholas has gone further in self-denial than we permitted General von Hartsen to know. He abnegates his personal wishes with joy. A friendly monarchy established at Berlin would assure our own triumph."

"There is not the slightest doubt that the German people are aching for their Kaiser," Cyril Sabaroff observed. "Frederick can scarcely walk the streets in comfort nowadays."

"Every illustrated paper has his picture," the Grand Duchess added. "You can read of his doings every day."

"And every newspaper has anecdotes about him," Kirdorff concluded. "He is easily the most popular young man in Europe to-day."

"I am very much flattered," Catherine pronounced, "and very sleepy. To-morrow I will make up my mind whether I shall be Kaiserin of Germany or Tzarina of Russia or —— "

There was a long pause. Rosa Sabaroff at last interposed.

"Or what, Catherine?"

Catherine looked back from the door towards which she had made her way.

"Or return to the Weltmore Typewriting Agency and my American independence!"

CATHERINE came face to face with Andrew Kroupki as she was leaving her office in Government Buildings at an early hour on the following morning. He stood in the doorway, blocking her exit and his expression was menacing. She realised at once that there was to be trouble.

"One word with you, if you please, Miss Borans," he insisted.

She gave way and he closed the door behind him, confronting her with a spot of angry colour burning in his cheeks, wild-eyed and almost inarticulate.

"It is unbelievable!" he exclaimed. "You must not go to the Chief to-day! Stay here and I will make your excuses."

"What do you mean, Andrew?" she asked coldly. "I am directed to report myself at Government House before nine o'clock. Of course I must go."

"You must have begged for the work," he continued, his tone trembling with agitation. "It is not right that you should have it. It is not safe. It is a wicked thing!"

"Andrew, you are not yourself," she said gently, almost kindly. "Surely you know that I must obey orders."

"Orders! The Chief must be mad," he cried. "A moment's indiscretion with regard to to-day's work and a terrible situation might arise. You are not of us. You are not for the people of Russia. You are for those who are already beginning to plot against us."

"That is absurd," she told him. "You must not talk to me so, Andrew. I have never yet failed in my trust wherever my sympathies may have lain. Besides, it is not for you to interfere. It is your master who speaks the word."

He shook for a moment, as though seized with an ague.

"You dined with him alone last night," he cried hysterically. "What was the argument you used to bring him to folly?"

"I have been very patient with you, Andrew," she said, with a warning flash in her eyes, "but I am reaching my limits. Perhaps if you desire to preserve my esteem, you had better stand on one side."

"I think," he sobbed, "that I would rather dig my fingers into your white throat and wring the life out of you than let you go to Samara to-day."

Sympathy once more chased the anger from her mind. It was obvious that he was unstrung, on the verge of a nervous breakdown.

"You are very foolish, Andrew," she declared. "The work of to-day is better done by me. You are a very bad typist and you are very slow with the new code. It is natural that the Chief should send for me. There are many matters of graver importance, I am sure, that he would leave in your hands."

Her kindness seemed only to throw fresh fuel on the fire of his anger. She suddenly realised that she was in actual physical danger. They were alone on the floor of the great building. No one arrived at the offices until nine o'clock and the cleaners had departed. She moved a little towards the telephone, but he seemed to apprehend her purpose and blocked her passage.

"It is false," he almost shouted. "He has lost his head. There is nothing more vital to the State than the scheme which he is to confide to you to-day. He has lost his head! You have bewitched him as you have done me — Samara, to whom women have been but playthings! — the idlest of all his diversions!"

"You are becoming absurd," she said quietly. "Be so kind as to let me pass."

He shook his clenched fists in the air. His appearance was veritably tragic. Every moment he was more completely losing control of himself.

"You must answer my question or I think that I shall kill you," he gasped. "You know very well what it is. You could have saved me this torture. Is Samara your lover?"

Catherine looked at him steadfastly for a moment; looked at his long narrow face with its high cheek bones, his lips trembling like a woman's, at his eyes from which all the kindly dreaminess had gone. It seemed to take her a few seconds to realise the actual meaning of his words, but when she did, the strain of inherited savagery, which had made for purity amongst the women of her race and bravery amongst the men, leaped into fire in her veins. Her physical strength itself seemed to swell. With her outstretched hand, she struck Andrew Kroupki a blow on the side of the face with such unexpected force that he staggered back half-dazed, blood already commencing to trickle from the place where her ring had bitten into his flesh. Before he could recover himself she had gone. To his reeling senses the slam of the door, the click of her heels upon the polished floor, were full of evil portent.

She made no excuses when she arrived at her destination, though Samara was manifestly impatient. Their meeting of the night before seemed to belong to another world. Never, for a single moment, did he depart from the rôle of exacting and conscientious employer. He did not even trouble to present to her Adolph Weirtz, the semitic, brilliant Minister of Finance, who was present, but plunged at once into their work. At eleven o'clock Weirtz left. At one o'clock her fingers began to stumble. He looked at her sharply.

"What is the matter?" he asked curtly. "Do you need luncheon?"

"I do not think that I need it any more than any one else would," she replied. "Something of the sort is usual. Probably you would have noticed yourself that it is past one o'clock if you had breakfasted at seven and if you had not had the resources of your sideboard."

He suddenly and unexpectedly smiled.

"*Touché,*" he confessed. "I am a selfish brute."

He rang the bell and gave Ivan a brief order. Then he crossed to the sideboard, concocted a strange amber-coloured drink which he forced upon her and pushed cigarettes to her side. He himself had been smoking a huge pipe most of the morning.

"At four o'clock," he confided, "the other two members of the Council will be here to approve. So much for my autocracy which you were talking about."

"And if they disapprove?" she asked.

"The proclamation will be issued just the same," he declared, with a sudden note of belligerency in his tone.

She laughed quietly; a relaxation which a moment or two later he found himself sharing. Afterwards he became almost apologetic.

"The principle is already decided upon by the Cabinet," he explained. "There can be no objection to anything except detail, and, so far as that is concerned, I am more likely to be right than any of them. You gathered that Weirtz was against the whole thing?"

"I tried not to listen," she replied. "I gathered that he was disapproving."

"He looks upon the army as our sole refuge against two smouldering factions of the community — the Royalists and the anarchists," Samara expounded. "He agrees that the anarchist influence to-day is negligible but he has an absurdly exaggerated idea of the significance of the royalist movement."

"So you admit that there is a royalist movement?" she asked him curiously.

He shrugged his shoulders.

"Oh, I suppose so," he assented. "They're making noise enough, at any rate. To return to Weirtz. He thinks that the period of interregnum between the disbanding of the armies and the establishing of a citizen force will be a period of danger. I disagree with him. The idleness of a standing army makes it a constant menace; usually a hotbed for intrigue and conspiracy. They're hard at it now down there. They think I don't know, but I do. Your friend Kirdorff, a cold-blooded, brainy schemer; Orenburg — less brains but more courage. They took their commands willingly enough and drew their pay, and began to plot the next day. I've no great fancy for your friends, Catherine Borans."

She sighed.

"Why should you have? They look at life differently. They follow other gods."

"Eat your luncheon," he invited, as soon as Ivan had finished setting the table. "We must start work again directly. You must have some of this goulash. I never imagined I was hungry. Ivan, some Rhine wine and tumblers. Have you seen Andrew to-day?"

"I saw him at Government Buildings," she replied. "He was very angry and very rude."

"He doubts my wisdom in giving you this work," Samara confided. "He is quite right from his point of view. No one would do it unless it were some one like myself, whose life is governed by instinct and not reason."

She smiled. "Andrew would never understand that."

"I am sorry for him," Samara declared abruptly. "He is jealous of you and at the same time he is in love with you — a painful condition of mind for a highly strung and extraordinarily susceptible young man."

"Were you insensible to all human weaknesses when you were young?" she asked.

"I? Mother of God, no!" he answered carelessly. "I had my fits of weakness and I yielded to them, when I chose, but they never formed part of my life. They were the rest houses in the night. They helped one to draw breath for the morrow. It is these romantic youngsters who seek to weave their follies into the web of durable things who are to be pitied. Ivan, some coffee," he ordered. "A cigarette, Catherine Borans. Now let us start. I have a new vision!"

At four o'clock Samara read the results of his day's work to Weirtz, his Minister of Finance, to Argoff, the Minister for Home Affairs, and to General Trotsk, the Chief of the Police. In an inner room Catherine sipped tea and listened. From the beginning she was conscious of the attitude of deferential opposition existing amongst Samara's colleagues. Argoff was the first spokesman.

"Sir," he said to Samara, "you have faithfully embodied in these proclamations and directions the decision of the Cabinet as arrived at last Thursday. We three were in a hopeless minority then; we are in a hopeless minority now. I personally look upon the action you propose to take as fraught with the greatest danger to the future of the Republic."

"And you, Weirtz?" Samara asked.

"I agree with Argoff," was the unhesitating reply. "The disbanding of the Third Army was sound and brilliant legislation. To go further in the same direction would, I think, expose the country to unnecessary dangers."

"What have you to say, General?" Samara concluded.

General Trotsk — a thin, grey man, with the face of a sphinx

— was in reality the most discomposed of the three, although he did not betray it.

"Gabriel Samara," he said, "before you came into power there were those who called you a visionary. You have silenced your critics in the establishment of what might well become the greatest republic in the world's history. I beg you to beware lest one single mistake should bring to naught all that you have done."

"Aye, and more than that," Weirtz put in, "plunge this country once more into the throes of rebellion and disorder. To all appearance," he went on, "Russia is to-day a contented and happy nation, yet under the surface, as I very well know, there is discontent and grumbling because it is human nature that this should be so amongst the worthless, the Quixotes, the criminals. There is always fuel for a burning brand. Frankly, my agent's report from Odensk is that the great mass of the Second Army do not desire demobilisation. A civilian life does not appeal to them. They like their uniform, the routine of their daily life, the freedom from all personal anxieties and responsibilities. They do not doubt your beneficent schemes for their welfare, but they prefer to remain soldiers. It is this feeling which is making them ready listeners to the propaganda which is going on amongst them."

"The love of the military life," Samara pronounced, "is an unnatural affection. The sooner it is stamped out the better."

"Theoretically very right," Weirtz agreed, "but practically there are difficulties. Can even you, Gabriel Samara, force a million men out of a life which is dear to them, into a new and untried career?"

"Nonsense," was the impatient reply. "Half of them were peasant agriculturists in their youth, with land to till and a homestead to look after. They will soon find themselves. Besides, you and I, General, should know that the Russian soldier is never insubordinate. He will obey orders. There will be nothing else left for him to do. On the day these proclamations are posted, every ammunition dump in the camp will be blown up, and their bayonets withdrawn. It will be simply a million unarmed men, pouring through the great clearing house which will be ready for them next month at the rate of thirty thousand a day."

"It is to my mind," General Trotsk declared, "a most rash and hazardous experiment."

"Where is the hazard?" Samara demanded. "The First Army is within a day's march of the city, fully equipped and fully armed. But far be it from me to suggest such a thing as a conflict. Their mere existence would prevent it."

"There is yet another danger," General Trotsk pointed out. "Supposing word of this projected destruction of their ammunition were to reach the army; it would be easy enough for them to guard against it."

"Such a supposition infers the presence of a traitor amongst us," Samara argued. "Not another breathing soul knows my plans. Peter Tranchard, who controls the private printing press of the Home Office, you yourself would vouch for, Argoff. Not one of his compositors can read, but, as in the case of the proclamation addressed to the Poles two years ago, these men are locked up in quarters for a week after their work is done."

"There is your secretary," Weirtz suggested bluntly.

"I will answer for her," Samara promised, with a flash in his eyes. "I admit the need for secrecy. It is because of it that I dealt with this measure before the Cabinet instead of the General Assembly. You have no reason to doubt the loyalty of the First Army, General?"

"There is some disquiet," Trotsk admitted. "I have only this morning caused seventy of my men to be enrolled in the ranks."

"The plot to reëstablish Soviet conditions," Weirtz remarked, "was never, I think, a serious one. I suspect that the plotting such as it is to-day, emanates from a different source."

"Royalist?" Samara enquired.

"Royalist, beyond a doubt," Trotsk affirmed. "The Russian of to-day hates the very sound of the word 'Bolshevist' or 'anarchist.' It is the reactionary swing of the pendulum which is to be feared. It is my firm belief that there are a million more Royalists in the country to-day than any one imagines."

Samara laughed confidently.

"There may be amazing surprises in store for us in this world," he said, "but I do not think that Nicholas Imanoff, bond seller of New York, will ever be crowned Tzar of Russia. You have read the proclamations, my friends. Apart from the fact that you are not in entire sympathy with me and with the majority of the

Cabinet as to the policy of which they are the outcome, you have no criticism to make?"

"I have none except those I made before the Cabinet," Adolph Weirtz declared. "I maintain that as it seems to be the wish of the Cabinet that the Second Army should be disbanded, it should be done gradually — a hundred thousand a year, the men to be selected by lot."

"Too slow," Samara observed brusquely. "Anything else?"

"I propose," Trotsk said, "that you, sir, visit the district personally, address the soldiers, and study their disposition. I have reports from my subordinates every day which I find disquieting."

"That I have decided to do," Samara assented. "And you, Argoff?"

"I have but one suggestion to make," was the prompt reply. "Burn your morning's work, Mr. President, and expunge the decree from the archives of the Cabinet. You are trifling with destiny."

"Every reformer the world has ever known," Samara answered deliberately, "has sat at the table of chance."

Samara drew back the curtains of the inner room as soon as he was alone. Catherine came quietly forward to meet him.

"Well?" he asked. "You heard everything?"

"Everything!"

"And what is your opinion?"

She shrugged her shoulders.

"I am twenty-five years old," she said. "Twenty-three years of my life have been spent in New York. I am a Russian only by instinct. I have yet to learn the temper of my people."

"Never mind your lack of experience. Answer me from that instinct."

She acquiesced unwillingly.

"You have made Russia a great and prosperous country," she said. "You have succeeded in reducing her army by a million men. I do not see why you take this further risk."

"Sophist," he growled. "Instinct only. I insist."

She shrugged her shoulders.

"Yesterday," she confided, "I looked upon the royalist cause in Russia as a forlorn thing. To-morrow, if you persist, I shall begin to wonder what it would feel like to marry Nicholas and be Tzarina of all the Russias."

Samara seemed afflicted by a curious fit of lethargy after Catherine's departure. He sat in his great bare room till the twilight filled it with shadows; until, in fact, he was disturbed by stealthy footsteps behind his chair. He turned abruptly round. A tall, gaunt figure was standing before the safe. Samara, after a second's scrutiny, withdrew his hand from the butt of the pistol towards which it had sprung.

"Andrew!" he exclaimed. "What the devil are you doing here?"

The young man faced him. Even in the gloom of the apartment the wound on his cheek was clearly visible.

"I was restless, Master," he said. "I entered by the side gate. I have come to ask a favour."

"What is it, and what has happened to you?" Samara demanded.

"I have met with an accident," was the dreary confession. "Something very terrible has happened. I cannot breathe here in Moscow. I must get away."

"Go on."

"We were to start for London on Monday. Let me go by the early morning boat and wait for you there. There are things to be done before you arrive. I can see to them."

"What have you been doing to yourself?" Samara asked, looking at the scar upon his face.

"An accident has happened," Andrew replied. "A very terrible accident! I must get away at once. Give me permission to go to England, please."

"Is this because Catherine Borans has been working for me to-day?" Samara enquired bluntly.

Andrew shivered. He had winced at the sound of her name as though some one had struck him with a whip.

"I have no more feeling of that sort," he groaned. "It is finished. I simply want to get away."

Samara wrote a few lines upon a sheet of foolscap and passed them over.

"Very well," he assented. "There is your order, and the name of the hotel where you will stay when you reach London. If all goes well I shall follow you on Thursday."

"Aye, on Thursday," Andrew muttered.

Samara glanced at him curiously.

"Have you seen your doctor lately, Andrew?" he enquired.

The young man laughed bitterly.

"I am ill," he acknowledged, "but no doctor can cure me."

Samara indulged in a moment's deliberation. Distinctly something had happened.

"Are you sure that you are fit to travel?" he asked.

"If I stay here for another day, I shall shoot myself or some one else. Better let me go. I am of no use to any one just now. I could not work. I could not be trusted. Let me go, please."

"You are talking foolishly, Andrew," his master declared. "I have trusted you with the secrets of my life. You could not betray me if you would. There is something beneath all this. Why not give me your confidence?"

"It is too late," Andrew groaned, shuffling towards the door.

Samara stopped him with an imperative monosyllable.

"Andrew," he asked, "is it a woman who has done this? Well, I see it is. I am going to use the surgeon's knife. Never in this world could Catherine Borans be anything to you."

The young man's face for a moment was like the face of a devil.

"Blast you, don't I know it?" he cried. "Don't I know whose woman she is? That's why I'm getting away — why I choose hell rather than stay here!"

For once his master's call was disobeyed. The slam of the door echoed through the huge half-empty house. Samara's few seconds of spellbound agitation were all the start Andrew needed. He was gone!

CATHERINE, standing that evening in a corner of her aunt's little salon, with Nicholas in close attendance, watched, with a disquietude which she found it hard to conceal, the continued stream of visitors pouring all the time through the open doors. Alexandrina's first "At Home" six months ago had resulted in the visit of less than a dozen rather shabby, melancholy men and women, who seemed like the ghosts of their own unhappy pasts. Conversation had been almost pathetic and had consisted principally of reminiscences. They spoke of the great families which formed the connecting links between them, of the branches which had died out, of others whose members were scattered all over the world. To-day the memory of that first gathering seemed like a dream. There were at least a hundred and fifty visitors in the small suite of rooms, and more arriving all the time. The people, themselves, were different. There was an air of subdued interest, almost excitement, in their demeanour, a new spring in their walk, and a note of suppressed jubilance in many fragments of smothered conversation. Kirdorff was there in brilliant regimentals, surrounded by a little group of eager but cautious questioners. The names of the men and women who came and went so freely recalled all the splendours of a St. Petersburg Court of fifty years ago. Nicholas played with the hilt of his sword and stroked his incipient moustache with an almost fatuous air of self-satisfaction. Nearly every newcomer, after paying his or her respects to their hostess, came to address a few words to him. The presence of Mrs. Saxon J. Bossington, in a dress of magenta velvet with a hat to match, her neck and arms ablaze with jewels, and a priceless ermine stole about her shoulders, seemed the only discordant feature, and even she, through sheer magnificence, presented a striking appearance.

"I wonder if all this is wise," Catherine murmured to her cousin.

He smiled condescendingly.

"You are afraid that it might offend your friend, Samara?" he observed with a superior smile.

"Thanks to whom you are no longer selling bonds in New York," she retorted sharply. "As it happens, I was not thinking of Mr. Samara. Is not full-dress uniform now against the laws of the country?"

"It may be," he admitted. "We shall soon make our own laws. Since that man's name has been mentioned, Catherine," he went on, "I have a word to say to you. The time has arrived when you should cease to be his secretary."

"Why?" she enquired.

He stared at her, as though astonished at her lack of comprehension.

"In the beginning," he explained, "your position was naturally of great benefit to us. Those times are passing. When one thinks of the future, it will not do for people to be able to look back and remember the time when you were his paid assistant."

"You seem quite sure that I am going to marry you," she remarked. "Is this because I have sent General von Hartsen back to Berlin?"

"Not at all," he answered confidently. "It is your destiny to be Tzarina of all the Russias. The other scheme was absurd."

"It seems almost a pity," she sighed, "that I was brought up in New York."

"Why?" he asked.

"One gets so foolishly democratic," she replied. "As a royal wooer I think I rather preferred Frederick. He quite lost his head about me."

Nicholas laughed scornfully.

"Frederick was a little premature," he observed. "Things may not move so quickly in Germany as he imagines. Tell me about General von Hartsen and his ridiculous mission. How did he take your refusal of his proposal?"

"Badly," she answered. "He left before dinner was half over to catch the night boat to Berlin."

"The worst of these Germans," he sneered, in a self-satisfied manner. "As soon as they are thwarted they lose their tempers."

Mrs. Bossington sailed up to them and Nicholas promptly made his escape.

"My dear," she exclaimed, "it's good to see some one who knew me in New York, where we were somebody! I am getting quite confused with all these Princesses and Duchesses and Grand Duchesses, and they tell me that after all, even if Saxon does buy the whole of that Ardenburg estate — dozens and dozens of square miles, my dear — he will only be a Count!"

"Well, that should do for a start," Catherine declared, smiling. "As a matter of fact," she went on, "if I were you, I wouldn't talk about it too much. I think my aunt and Nicholas and all of them here have rather lost their heads. To discuss such things openly, to speak of the future as we continually do, is treason to-day."

"You don't think there's any doubt about this thing coming off?" Mrs. Bossington asked anxiously.

"I prefer not to discuss it," Catherine replied. "I even go farther. I think that it is in bad taste to speak of it as blatantly as my people are doing. After all, we are here on sufferance."

"You came on sufferance, perhaps," Mrs. Bossington amended, "but you should hear what Colonel Kirdorff has to say about the army. Your friend Mr. Samara has been making himself pretty unpopular."

"The army is still not Russia," Catherine reminded her.

Mrs. Bossington smiled cryptically.

"I don't know whether you are aware," she remarked, dropping her voice a little, "that I was admitted to the last meeting of Colonel Kirdorff's secret council. There were delegates from the southern provinces, from Petrograd, and I don't know how many places. They all seemed to agree that the peasants at any rate and the lower *bourgeoisie* all want their Tzar back again. As for the army, there is scarcely an officer who isn't a Royalist, since the Germans got the sack, and the soldiers themselves are all furious against Samara because of this talk of disbandment. Saxon's no slouch, my dear, as you know, and he declares the whole thing's a cinch, as long as it's managed on a business footing. I want him to take an interest in politics. A man with a business head like his would be worth having anywhere. If he were Finance Minister, for instance, he might easily be made a Prince."

"I must go and talk to my aunt," Catherine said abruptly. "I quite realise all that you have done for my family and my friends, Mrs. Bossington, and I hope that some day you may be rewarded for it, but I earnestly advise you not to talk so openly of your hopes."

She crossed the room towards where her aunt was seated, the centre of an animated little group. She was on the point of being surrounded herself when two new guests were announced. As though of a purpose, the major-domo who stood at the doors raised his voice as he spoke the names:

"General Trotsk — Captain Irdron."

The babel of conversation ceased as though by magic. It was amidst almost a complete silence that the two men, both clad in the plain dark uniform of the State Police, approached Alexandrina. The General saluted, as he came to a standstill before the hostess of the little assembly. Everybody seemed to recognise the sombre, almost menacing note which their arrival had introduced.

"Madame," he said, "I have taken the liberty of paying you a visit. I beg leave to present my aide-de-camp, Captain Irdron."

Alexandrina acknowledged the salute of her two visitors a little stiffly.

"You are very welcome, General," she replied. "I do not remember, however, that your name is upon my visiting list."

"Madame," was the somewhat curt retort, "by virtue of my office under the Republic, my name is upon any visiting list where I choose to place it. We will, since you prefer it, consider my visit official."

He saluted again and turned deliberately away, murmuring a word or two to his companion, who appeared to be taking notes of the names of some of those present. He exchanged a few cold words with Catherine.

"You find time occasionally, then, mademoiselle, to attend social functions," he remarked.

"One has one's family duties," Catherine rejoined with faint irony.

The General turned on his heel. The silence in the room remained unbroken. Every one was curious, a little agitated. The Minister of Police approached Kirdorff, who was talking to Nicholas. His expression was grim and official. The atmosphere of the salon became tense.

"Sir," he said, addressing Kirdorff, "I have to inform you that you are wearing a uniform which is contrary to the regulations of the Republican Government of Russia."

"In what respect is it at fault?" Kirdorff enquired.

"In every respect, sir," Trotsk answered harshly. "The uniforms worn by the officers in the Republican Army are supplied by Commissariat Department C. You are wearing a full-dress uniform of the monarchical army, abolished by law in nineteen-nineteen. Your name, sir?" he asked, turning to Nicholas.

"Nicholas Imanoff," was the contemptuous reply. "I was not aware that a policeman had anything to do with the uniform of the army."

The smile of the Minister of Police was gentle, almost urbane.

"Naturally you are ignorant of Russia and its military regulations," he murmured. "You have, I think, lived all your life in New York and been engaged in other pursuits. You will report at the War Office to the Chief of the Staff, within a quarter of an hour. He will give you further instructions."

Kirdorff laid his hand on Nicholas' shoulder in time to check an angry retort.

"By what authority, sir, do you of the police," he demanded, "issue orders to officers in the Russian Army?"

The Minister smiled.

"Your long absence from the country, sir, is your only excuse for such a question," he declared. "I represent the supreme power in the country — the Armies of the Service of the State. You can obey my orders voluntarily or, in five minutes, under escort."

There was a brief pause. Kirdorff turned away, bowed low and raised his hostess's fingers to his lips.

"Madame," he whispered, "we do well to bend. Nothing must prevent my being able to rejoin the army."

"I have confidence in you, Colonel," she assured him.

The two men left the room. As soon as he was sure of their absence, the Chief of the Police himself saluted Alexandrina.

"Madame," he said, "I regret to have interrupted your social gathering and to have deprived you of doubtless honoured guests. I shall now take my departure. For the present," he added, "it is sufficient for me to remind you that in this city you are the guests of the Russian Republic."

"I am a Russian citizeness, Monsieur le Commissionaire," Alexandrina answered, with a touch of hauteur in her tone; "my opinions and my actions are a matter for my own conscience."

The Grand Duchess had at least the triumph of the last word, for her visitor made no reply. He left the room followed by his attendant. There was a little gasp as the door was closed behind them, a silence broken by old Prince Dromidor, eighty-seven years of age, back from his little villa at Kensington after thirty years' absence from his country, to pay his respects to the returned refugees.

"It is the beginning," he cried. "They have shown their fear."

Mrs. Saxon J. Bossington laid her hand upon Catherine's arm.

"My dear," she said impressively, "let me put you wise to one thing. I've lived in New York and I know. Don't you let your aunt get in wrong with the police. What was he, an inspector or an assistant commissioner?"

Catherine smiled.

"As a matter of fact," she confided, "he is a Cabinet Minister. He is one of the three who, with Mr. Samara, rule Russia."

"Really!" Mrs. Bossington murmured, with some chagrin. "And I never met him!"

CHAPTER VIII

SAMARA greeted Catherine with a grin of delight when, in response to his telephone summons, she appeared at Government House on the following morning. General Trotsk's report had appealed immensely to his sense of humour.

"So your aunt is giving royalist tea parties," he remarked, "and your relatives are sporting the uniforms of the Imperial Guard. Were you there when the fun began?"

"I was there," she admitted. "I didn't think it very funny."

"You are quite right," he confessed. "It is not funny. It is pathetic. These people have lived in the past so long that they have taught themselves to believe in its reincarnation. All the same, your aunt seems to have been behaving very badly."

Catherine shrugged her shoulders.

"Is there any reason why she should not entertain her old friends?" she enquired.

"Not the slightest," Samara agreed. "I should not have interfered in a thousand years. Trotsk takes himself too seriously. He speaks already of the royalist movement — as though there could be such a thing."

"General Trotsk may err too much in one direction," Catherine observed. "As an impartial looker-on, I should say that you erred too much in another."

"Are you an impartial looker-on?" he asked quickly. "Trotsk will have it that you are one of the gang."

"I am a Royalist at heart, of course," she acknowledged, "but I am not a conspirator."

"What have you been doing to Andrew Kroupki?" he asked abruptly.

"Quarrelled with him, more or less," she replied. "As a matter of fact, the quarrel was not of my seeking. He insulted me the other morning."

"Is it true that you knocked him down?"

"Perfectly," Catherine admitted. "I was delighted to find how strong I was."

Samara looked at her gravely.

"It is a terrible thing," he declared, "for a man to strike a woman, although she often deserves it. For a woman to strike a man is a tragedy. What was his offence?"

Catherine had seated herself at her table a few yards away. She swung round and faced her questioner.

"He asked me if you were my lover," she said coolly.

"A very natural question," he remarked, taking up a pile of letters and beginning to look them through. "Was that your only provocation?"

She turned away, opened her desk, and drew out her work.

"I have always understood," she reflected, "that the standard of morals amongst the educated portion of the Russian *bourgeoisie* was exceedingly low."

"Meaning me?" he asked cheerfully.

"Yes."

"The cap, alas, does not fit," he assured her. "I have no pretensions to rank amongst the *bourgeoisie*. I am of peasant stock."

"You do not surprise me," she replied.

He rose to his feet and set into operation the machinery which unlocked the great private safe. In a minute or two he appeared with a roll of manuscript.

"Please get on with this manifesto," he begged. "You are at your best this morning. It would be a pity to waste such intelligence."

She took the papers. "I should like to know what has become of Andrew," she said.

"He has gone to London as my advance agent. I do not think that he will ever come back — not unless you leave me. Of course," he went on, "if this little tea-party scheme of your aunt's comes off, you are booked for the part of Tzarina, I suppose."

"There is always that hope," she admitted.

"Heaven preserve me from another woman secretary!" he exclaimed. "One never gets the last word."

Catherine was studiously silent. Samara waited for a moment or two. Then he left the room, slamming the door violently. It was an hour before he returned, and when he did he closed the door behind him and locked it. Catherine looked up questioningly.

"What is that for?" she asked.

"So that you don't leave me before I am ready for you to go," he answered. "Also to make sure that we are not interrupted."

"It seems a little absurd," she complained. "I have no idea of going until I have finished my work."

"How long will that take you?"

"Another half an hour."

"Finish it, then," he directed. "Afterwards I have something to say to you."

She continued her task. Samara studied a handful of the documents which he had brought back with him, signing some and throwing others on one side. Once or twice he spoke on the telephone. Finally Catherine turned towards him.

"I have finished," she announced. "Will you check my transcription?"

"Presently," he acquiesced.

"You had something to say to me," she reminded him.

"I had. I find that after all old Trotsk wasn't such an idiot. There is a genuine monarchist plot afoot."

She sat watching him, without faltering, with no sign of self-consciousness.

"Started in your aunt's drawing-room without a doubt," he went on, "subscribed to and joined in by all that shabby down-at-heel crew I brought home from a second-rate American boarding-house, making its way in the army, they tell me — especially in the Second Army. Do you know that I have to postpone my journey to England and go down to Odensk to harangue these recalcitrant subjects? That's the result of trying to make good Russians of men like Kirdorff and Orenburg. What do they care about Russia? It's their blasted selves they think of."

"They have a right to their convictions," she rejoined.

"And I have a right to have them shot," he answered. "They've been guilty of treason against the State. Trotsk has just given me a copy of one of Kirdorff's speeches to the Fourth Army Corps. He'd have been tried by court-martial and shot a few years ago.

I hate to kill fools, but something must be done. Trotsk would have the whole lot out of the country, or facing the firing line in ten minutes, and I am not sure that he isn't right. Advise me, Miss Secretary. What am I to do with this nest of vipers? Not much poison about them, but enough to hurt, Trotsk says. Tell me how to deal with them."

"Too great a responsibility for me," she replied.

"What if I were to shoot Nicholas Imanoff, or banish him?" he suggested. "There isn't another Imanoff amongst them. They can't make a Tzar out of an ordinary person, can they — even an aristocrat?"

"There is me," she remarked meditatively. "I am an Imanoff. They might make me Tzarina and permit me to choose my consort."

"You had a predecessor," he reminded her scornfully. "A pretty mess you'd make of things!"

"That would depend upon my consort," she replied. "I might choose you. How would you like that?"

He stood like a statue, looking at her across the bare, lofty room. She was not near enough to see the knuckles whiten about his clenched fists or to catch the fugitive gleam of something unusual in his hard, brilliant eyes. She noticed with surprise, however, the slight break in his voice.

"Curse you, can't you ever be serious?" he exclaimed. "I've a good mind to throw the lot of them into prison."

"I should only intercede on behalf of my aunt," Catherine assured him. "She is really quite a dear old thing, but Tzardom to her is very much like his Bible to an English Methodist."

The private telephone on Samara's table rang. He picked up the receiver and listened for a moment or two, frowning. Then he nodded and laid it down.

"Your friends," he said, turning to Catherine, "are beginning to annoy me. Trotsk is outside with an amazing story. You had better stop and listen to what he has to say."

General Trotsk was ushered in shortly afterwards. He entered the room and saluted, looking grimmer than ever.

"Sir," he announced, "I have a report to make."

"I am at your service, General," Samara replied.

The visitor indicated Catherine with a little wave of the hand. Samara only smiled.

"I should prefer you to speak before Miss Borans," he said. "I have a certain amount of confidence in her, but apart from that, she is in a way responsible for my ever having invited this nest of conspirators over here."

"Miss Borans may yet find, then, that her responsibility is a heavy one," General Trotsk declared, with portentous coldness. "I have already reported, sir," he continued, "that I found Colonel Kirdorff and Lieutenant Nicholas Imanoff attending a private function yesterday wearing the uniform of the late Imperial Army. I ordered them to report at once at the War Office. It has now come to my knowledge that they failed to do so. They left the city instead, travelling by motor car in the direction of Odensk."

Samara nodded.

"Well," he remarked, "I suppose you did not allow them to get very far?"

"They were arrested by my orders at Miltou," the General went on, "and were brought back to the city under escort. I am here to ask your instructions, sir. The Minister of War is at Odensk, as is also General Denkers, commanding the Second Army."

Samara glanced at his watch.

"Bring them here at three o'clock," he directed. "I will deal with this matter summarily."

The Minister of Police saluted.

"I have your permission, sir, to speak frankly?" he asked.

"By all means," Samara replied. "You can discard officialdom altogether if you will. Light a cigarette and speak to me as my trusted minister."

The Minister of Police made no movement towards the box of cigarettes which Samara proffered. Catherine was watching him from across the room with fascinated eyes. There was something inhuman about this man's slow, deliberate speech, his waxen complexion, his lack of all earnestness; something sinister about the cold detachment of his words.

"My reports as to the condition of the morale of the Second Army are unsatisfactory," he declared. "These two men in their persons and by their precepts have broken the laws of Russia and are largely responsible for the disaffection. I recommend that under Section Seven of the Military Discipline Act they be shot this afternoon. It is possible that such action will avert grave results."

"I shall bear what you say seriously in mind, General," Samara promised.

The Minister of Police saluted stiffly and withdrew. Samara waited until the door was closed behind him.

"You heard Trotsk's suggestion," he observed, turning to Catherine. "It seems to me that your chances of wearing that crown are slipping away."

SAMARA broke through precedent that afternoon. He consented to receive a visitor who came without an appointment. Alexandrina, her good-humoured face wrinkled with anxiety, her clothes badly arranged, and out of breath already with the exertion of climbing the long flight of steps and crossing the great stone hall of Government House, was ushered into his presence. Nothing of the *grande dame* remained but her manner.

"I owe you my thanks for receiving me, Mr. Samara," she said, as he rose to greet her. "Will you allow me to sit down? I am out of breath. I remember your house and that flight of steps when it was the palace of my cousin, the Grand Duke Cyril. In those days, however, steps meant nothing to me."

Samara placed a chair for her with grave courtesy and returned to his own seat. He preserved his somewhat ominous demeanour.

"I have been trying to find my niece," Alexandrina continued. "At Government Buildings they would not admit me. I thought, perhaps, that she might be here."

"She will arrive in half an hour," Samara confided. "She is now at Government Buildings finishing some work for me. If you would care to wait for her here, my housekeeper shall show you a salon where you may be comfortable."

"Thank you very much," was the grateful reply, "but since I am fortunate enough to have your ear for a moment, I will tell you my mission. I came to ask Catherine to intercede with you on behalf of my hot-headed nephew and Colonel Kirdorff."

"On what grounds, madame?" Samara asked.

"Nicholas is young and he is an Imanoff," she said. "This is his Russia by the grace of God. How can he be expected to yield to the discipline of an artificial constitution?"

A slight smile played about Samara's lips. This was greater candour than he had expected.

"Madame," he reminded her, "I did myself the honour of paying you a visit a few weeks ago. Rumours of the activities of your friends had reached me. I offered you then a warning. You had accepted the hospitality of the Republican Government of Russia. In plotting against it, you or any other were guilty of dishonourable action."

"Mr. Samara," Alexandrina said simply, "I cannot argue with you. I live by my convictions. You are without doubt a great statesman and you have been a great benefactor to this country. I appeal to you only as a man. I beg that you will not treat Nicholas' misdemeanour too seriously."

"I have heard you, madame," Samara replied. "I can make you no promise. I am the servant of the State."

The Grand Duchess rose to her feet. Samara's face was like stone. She knew very well that further speech was useless.

"At least," she concluded, "I thank you for receiving me. I read in New York, and I have been told here, that your régime in this country is one of mercy. I shall pray for your forbearance, sir, and for you, if you extend it to my nephew."

She left the room, escorted by Ivan, and without further word from Samara. He sat in his chair for a time, thoughtfully studying the mass of papers, by which he was surrounded. Presently Catherine entered, carrying her despatch box. She came straight over to his desk.

"The work is finished," she announced. "You will remember that Andrew is not here. Do you wish me to communicate with the Chief of the Ministerial Printing Press?"

"Presently," he answered. "Lock the despatch box in the safe."

"I do not understand the mechanism," she reminded him.

He rose to his feet and began to demonstrate it. She suddenly seized his arm.

"Why do you trust me like this?" she expostulated. "You seem surer of me than I am of myself."

"I must trust some one," he observed. "Andrew was the only other person who knew the secret and he is not available."

"But why me?" she protested. "You know that there are reasons why you should not."

"I trust or distrust by instinct only," he replied. "I govern in the same way."

"Then you make a gamble of life and government," she declared. "Sooner or later the crash will come."

"Meanwhile watch me," he directed. "The combinations you will have to learn."

Presently the telephone bell rang. He took down the receiver and his face hardened as he listened.

"In ten minutes," he decided.

Catherine turned towards the door. He called her back.

"Have you nothing further to say to me?" he asked.

"Nothing," she answered.

"You know that your aunt has been here?"

"I have been told so," she admitted. "I can add nothing to what she has probably already said."

"Your personality might have more weight," he suggested.

She shrugged her shoulders.

"Put it in the scale then, by all means," she enjoined.

"In plain words," he persisted, "you are too proud to ask a favour of me."

"I know you too well," she assured him. "You will do what you choose, what you think fit and right. Nothing that I or anybody else in the world could say would make any difference."

Her hand was upon the door. Again he called her back.

"I desire you to remain during my interview with your friends," he said. "They will be here almost immediately."

"Why should I be present?" she asked coldly.

"So that you may know the truth without perversion. Go to your desk in the alcove. You can hear there but you will be invisible."

She still hesitated.

"I have every instinct towards insubordination," she told him.

"Conquer it," he insisted. "I may need you to bear witness for me in the future."

She had scarcely reached her alcove before General Trotsk was ushered in. Kirdorff and Nicholas Imanoff followed, wearing military greatcoats buttoned to their throats. Behind came a guard of two soldiers with fixed bayonets. The Minister of Police saluted.

"According to your instructions, sir," he announced.

Samara seated himself at his desk. Kirdorff and Imanoff stood opposite to him; on either side of them a soldier, the Minister of Police, immovable and grave, a few feet away.

"Boris Kirdorff and Nicholas Imanoff," Samara began, "less than twelve months ago you accepted my offer to return to this country and become Russian citizens. I gave you both posts in the Republican Army. I told you that I was prepared to view your monarchical principles with toleration. Every one in this country has a right to his own opinions and has a right also to ventilate them. So far as you could influence people openly and honourably, by lectures and literature, you were at liberty to do so. You have ignored the honourable means of propaganda. You have stooped not only to underground conspiracy but to conspiracy with a foreign power. You have made use of your position in the army to initiate a seditious plot amongst the soldiers of the State, directed against this Republic. Do you require evidence? I can give it to you."

"I desire no evidence," Kirdorff replied. "It is quite true that I have endeavoured to awaken the people of Russia to a sense of what is due to themselves and their natural ruler."

"And I," Nicholas added, "being by descent and grace of God, Tzar of all the Russias, can be guilty of treason to no one."

"A very comfortable self-assurance," Samara remarked with a faint sneer. "To proceed to a minor point. You were discovered yesterday wearing a uniform which is contrary to the regulations of the army in which you serve."

"So long as there is a Russian army," Nicholas argued, "so long must there be a regiment of Imperial Guards."

"An entire fallacy," Samara assured him. "To continue. You were directed by the Chief of Police to report at the War Office. You failed to do so."

"We are only subject to military discipline," Kirdorff observed.

"You display a shameless ignorance of existing conditions," Samara said sternly. "The Chief of Police ranks as a Major General in the army. To disobey his orders amounts to gross insubordination, the penalty for which you know."

"On a technical point," Kirdorff admitted, "we appear to be guilty. I have never in my experience connected any part of the civil administration with the army."

"It should be your duty to learn the regulations of the army whose uniform you wear and whose pay you draw," Samara reminded them coldly. "You are both, on your own showing, guilty of military insubordination and treason against the Army of the Republic. The penalty for both offences is death."

"I demand to be tried by court-martial," Kirdorff exclaimed.

"And I," Nicholas echoed.

"Again your ignorance of the regulations amazes me," Samara declared. "I am the Commander in Chief of the Russian Republican Army. I and General Trotsk form an ever-existing court-martial, empowered to deal summarily with any cases which we direct to be brought before us."

For the first time both men lost confidence. Nicholas' air of somewhat fatuous bravado had disappeared and he was tugging nervously at his moustache. Kirdorff was obviously taken aback.

"Your republic, then," he ventured, "is a more autocratic institution than any monarchy which I remember."

"Your criticism may be just but it is irrelevant," Samara observed. "We are a competent tribunal, your offences are acknowledged. The penalty is beyond dispute. Have you anything further to say as to why this sentence should not be carried out upon you?"

"The army will rise to a man," Nicholas threatened, shaking with emotion.

"Young sir," Samara enjoined, "you would be wiser to omit all mention of an army in which you have served merely to gain your own purposes. Furthermore, half-past five is the time at which our firing parties generally parade. Odensk is some distance away."

Nicholas was almost beside himself with mingled fear and passion.

"It is unheard of, this," he cried. "I have still my American citizenship. I appeal!"

"Spare me a few illusions," Samara begged. "For a Russian seeking to obtain a lofty position in his own country by virtue of his birth to attempt to shelter himself in a moment of danger under a foreign flag is scarcely in accord with the traditions of your race. Now, listen to me, both of you. I have addressed you as a judge to the offenders brought before him. Your crime is admitted. The penalty is acknowledged. Now, I am going to speak to you as one human being to another."

A sudden gleam of hope flashed in Kirdorff's eyes. Samara paused for a few minutes as though to collect his thoughts.

"From the point of view of an ordinary human being," he continued, "you two cannot be judged as normal malefactors. Behind everything that you have done there stands, if not an excuse, a reason. How you can justify yourselves as men of honour, I do not know. You have accepted my invitation to come here. You accepted the positions I offered you in the army, and you started at once to plot against the Government of a country which has never been so stable and prosperous as she is to-day. I will still bear with you. I will look upon you as men afflicted with a Jesuitical turn of mind. You believe that the code of honour may be abnegated if the cause itself be great enough. Very well. You believe that monarchy is a great cause. You believe that Russia would be better governed by a monarchy than it is as a republic. I believe the contrary. Very well. Go and preach your doctrines, and I will preach mine. If you can convert this country to Tzardom, do so. Only, do it, in future, openly, not by conspiracies and sedition. Don't pretend to be faithful soldiers of the Republic, when you only wear their uniform to preach treason against it."

The two men stood with their eyes fastened upon Samara. Nicholas was moistening his lips nervously. Kirdorff had already realised that respite was at hand. The most gloomy figure was that of the Minister of Police.

"My decision is this," Samara concluded, turning to the latter. "You will escort these two ex-soldiers of the Republic to your headquarters, where you will strip them of their uniforms and provide them with civilian clothes. You will expunge their names from the Army List, but you will give them passes to cross the lines at Odensk and to travel wherever they will in the country. That is all. Remove your prisoners, General."

"We are to be set free?" Nicholas gasped.

"I hoped that I had made myself clear," Samara observed drily.

"You will permit me to say, sir," Kirdorff ventured, "that you are treating us in an extremely chivalrous fashion."

Samara rose to his feet.

"I do not desire your thanks," he said. "As criminals, I have absolved you. As men of honour, I shall be glad to be relieved of your presence."

The Minister of Police knew better than to argue. He made his protest, however.

"You have allowed yourself the luxury of quixotic altruism, sir," he said, "at the expense of your duty to the Republic."

"That may be the verdict of posterity, General," Samara replied. "If so, I must accept it."

The little procession filed out, Kirdorff and Nicholas alike momentarily drained of dignity, men to whom unexpected generosity had brought a sense of shame. Samara sat still at his desk and waited. There came no sign from Catherine. He rose to his feet and crossed the room at last to her alcove. On the threshold he stood still, amazed. She was leaning forward, her head buried in her hands, her shoulders convulsed. He came a little nearer.

"Catherine," he said quietly.

She held out her hand towards him without looking up. He gripped it tightly. Then he leaned over her. He asked no questions — there was that much of understanding between them. He kissed her fingers tenderly and turned away. Ivan's stentorian voice was announcing the arrival of his Cabinet in the outer room.

CHAPTER X

CATHERINE, a little tired, a little anxious, more than a little unhappy, lay stretched upon the sofa in her aunt's drawing-room, smoking an after-dinner cigarette. Opposite her, Alexandrina, with half a dozen newspapers by her side, her spectacles slipped on to the edge of her nose, her voice unsteady with excitement, was reading aloud occasional paragraphs.

"Listen to this, Catherine!" she exclaimed. "This is from the leading socialist paper in Berlin:

"THE POLITICAL CRISIS STILL CONTINUES

"Herr Brandt has confessed himself wholly unable to form a ministry and Dr. Beither has also refused responsibility. Meanwhile the Imperialist Party have openly avowed that they are in a position at any time to form a government which will command the entire support of the whole country. Prince Frederick is unable to leave his house in the Wilhelmstrasse owing to the crowds which surround it night and day. The announcement of a change of constitution is expected hourly."

Catherine listened unmoved.

"I seem to have missed a great chance," she murmured. "The young man was very much in love with me."

Alexandrina smiled.

"You are one of the fortunate ones of the earth, Catherine," she said. "No other woman in history has quite occupied your position. You could have been Kaiserin of Germany, and instead you will become Tzarina of Russia."

Catherine poured herself out some coffee from the copper pot which stood by her side. She clapped her hands and a somewhat uncouth-looking Russian servant entered.

"Sugar, Paul," she ordered, "and the samovar for Her Highness. See if that is a later edition of the paper they are calling in the street, too."

The man withdrew stolidly.

"Even if the Royalists succeed in Germany," Catherine continued, "I cannot see that our chances are much improved. They have no Samara to deal with there."

"Gabriel Samara is a great man," her aunt admitted, "but his dominion is on the wane. His ministers have allowed all the power to drift into his hands simply because they have had no will to resist. Many have resented it, however. His final proposals with regard to the completion of this demobilisation scheme are unpopular throughout the whole country. They only passed the Duma by less than a dozen votes."

Catherine leaned back thoughtfully, with her hands clasped around her knees.

"He is rash like all great men," she said. "He should have gone more quietly with these altruistic ventures of his. The people do not understand, and he is always a little impatient of opposition. But he has genius, and a man with genius is not easily crushed."

The servant returned with the sugar and the evening paper. Alexandrina glanced the latter through.

"Nothing fresh," she declared. "Samara is to address the last of his series of meetings at Odensk to-night."

The door was thrown open. General Orenburg was announced. They both turned towards him eagerly.

"Any news?" Catherine asked.

"Nothing within the last few hours," the General answered, seating himself by his hostess's side on the divan. "I came, wondering whether you had heard anything from Kirdorff."

"Nothing," Alexandrina replied. "The news from Berlin is amazing."

"Amazing indeed," Orenburg assented. "Six months ago the German Liberal Party appeared to have an ample majority and to be thoroughly established. The Imperialists scarcely dared to let their voices be heard. They were the weakest party in the State. Now a cataclysm seems to have taken place, a fever seems to have spread throughout the country. Every moment one expects to hear that Frederick has been proclaimed Kaiser."

"What do you think about the position here?" Catherine enquired curiously.

"In the light of what has happened in Germany, it is hard to say," the General admitted. "Six months ago Samara was his country's god, and the Duma were prepared to follow him blindly. If there had been another election he could have nominated every candidate. To-day there seems to be a strange undercurrent of political reaction. The people do not understand this demobilisation. The peasants and work-people are afraid of undue competition, the soldiers of privations, the *bourgeoisie* of invasion. They have suddenly begun to wonder whether their idol is only a great theorist. How far the pendulum will swing back, I cannot tell. We know that the Russian people are faithful and dogged. It seems hard to believe that in a few months' time they could forget and discard the man who slew their dragon."

"Samara has ruled Russia for fifteen years," Alexandrina said solemnly — "ruled her for her own good, we must admit, but ruled her like an autocrat. All the same, just as I believe in God as our spiritual Master, so I believe that every human being is born with the reverent instinct and desire for temporal government by an anointed head. Germany's period of madness lasted for a short time only. When France, too, comes to her senses and an Emperor reigns once more at Versailles, then the wounds of the world will be healed and not before. So far as we are concerned, there has never been a time like the present. If we can secure the army, our moment may have arrived."

Once more the door was hurriedly opened, this time to admit a more unexpected arrival. Nicholas Imanoff entered, wearing a long brown leather coat and carrying dark spectacles in his hand. He was still a little breathless and had the air of one who has just concluded a rapid journey.

"Have you heard the news from Berlin?" he cried.

"Nothing for some hours," Orenburg replied.

"Frederick was proclaimed Kaiser early this afternoon!" he announced. "The whole city is *en fête,* and to-morrow has been declared a national holiday!"

"Wonderful!" Alexandrina murmured, the tears standing in her eyes.

"What news of Odensk?" the General asked.

"Samara is like King Canute," Nicholas pronounced. "He has a great following there. He is enthusiastically received, but the men are on our side, and he cannot keep back the tide."

"You have a mission here?" Orenburg enquired.

The young man nodded, threw his coat over the back of a chair, and called to the domestic for brandy.

"I have flown from Odensk," he explained. "All goes well, but one of our recruits insists that there are now in print secret orders to every army corps commander, to be issued some time within the next week, which might affect our plans. It is absolutely necessary that we get hold of those orders."

He looked across at Catherine. She tossed her cigarette into the fire and smiled at him pleasantly.

"You seem to have established a secret service already, Nicholas," she remarked.

"Kirdorff is organiser," he acknowledged. "I speak in his name. It is he who has found out about these proclamations and secret orders. They are in code at present, but I think we could find some one who could deal with them. Do you know anything about them, Catherine?"

"Very likely," she replied.

"Splendid!" he exclaimed enthusiastically. "Kirdorff hates mystery. He had always felt that Samara had something up his sleeve or he would never have dared to make this an open struggle."

" 'Dare' is scarcely the word to use in connection with Samara," Catherine observed. "He may have made glorious mistakes but he has the courage of a lion."

"No one wishes to deny that Samara is a great man," Nicholas declared, a little impatiently. "His time is over, though. If he behaves sensibly and leaves the country without provoking a conflict, no harm will happen to him. Catherine, I want a copy of that secret order. I shall fly back with it to Odensk to-night."

"How do you know that I can give it to you?" she demanded.

"That is of no consequence," he answered. "The knowledge has come to us. It was you alone who worked for Samara on the day when he thought out his scheme. Why do you hesitate? What other reason had you for working for this man than to aid the cause?"

Catherine rose from the sofa and stood by her aunt's side.

"Aunt," she said, "what is your opinion? I became Mr. Samara's secretary intending to betray him at the first possible opportunity. I am still a Royalist, I am still as anxious as any of you to see Nicholas Tzar of Russia. On the other hand, Samara is a great and honourable man. Shall I do well — I, a Princess Royal of Russia — to betray his confidence?"

Alexandrina looked a little disturbed. She was almost brutally frank.

"My dear," she confided, "I never dreamed that you would hesitate for a single moment."

Catherine turned to Orenburg.

"What is your opinion, General?" she asked him.

"I sympathise with your position, Princess," he said, "but the Cause must come before everything."

Catherine was standing in the glow of a tall rose-shaded electric standard. Her expression was unusually serious. Nicholas, fresh from the drab barbarities of a huge garrison cantonment, thought that she had never appeared so desirable.

"The best friends in the world," she said, "must sometimes agree to differ. I am a Royalist and by any honourable means I would try to help Nicholas. The thing you ask of me I will not do."

"You desert us?" Nicholas exclaimed with passionate emphasis.

"I do nothing of the sort," she replied. "I am against Samara; I am for you, but let us fight fairly. Samara himself has set you a great example."

Nicholas poured himself out more brandy. His fingers were shaking. He dared not trust himself to speech. Alexandrina stretched out her hand and took up her knitting.

"If Catherine has made up her mind," she remarked, "it is of no use trying to change her."

"The young are like that," General Orenburg agreed with quiet resignation. "As they grow older, the light they carry burns less brightly, and the journey becomes easier. The Princess must have her way."

Nicholas indulged in one final outburst. He set down his tumbler empty and caught up his coat.

"I am to go back, then, and report failure," he protested. "I am to report that whilst we may sell our souls and bodies for the Cause my affianced wife has scruples about betraying the confidences of a usurper. We shall find another way into the secret, though. Be sure of that."

"I doubt it," Catherine rejoined coldly.

Nicholas forgot for a moment to be cautious.

"You think that it is your secret and his alone," he sneered. "You are mistaken. There is another."

"There is only Andrew Kroupki," she declared, "and he is in London."

Nicholas buttoned up his coat without a word.

"I had hoped to stay a little longer," he said, kissing his aunt's fingers. "Catherine's decision drives me back to the camp at once, however. I must let them know of my failure."

He hurried off. Between Catherine and him there passed only the slightest of farewells. They heard the front door slam and the sound of his automobile driving away. Alexandrina rose with a little sigh, fetched the cribbage board and sat down opposite to the General. Catherine moved to the window and stood listening to the cry of the newspaper boys in the street.

THE mind of Europe was suddenly swayed and distorted by an avalanche of strange happenings. Once more the Imperial flag flew from the Royal residences in Berlin and Potsdam. A proclamation, studiously moderate in tone, almost democratic in its general outline, and without a single bombastic reference to the military powers by whose machinations his success had been achieved, had marvellously consolidated the young Emperor's position. Austria was reported to be on the point of begging for inclusion in the German Empire. Italy, with the grasp of the Socialists upon her throat, could only look on and wonder. France, with a deep groan, went at once into military conclave, counted her armies and found them insufficient, inspected her forts and found them vulnerable, but with the amazing and patient heroism of her race, set herself to face the inevitable. England, the most faithful subscriber to the Limitation of Armaments which Germany had so flagrantly disregarded, postponed the Peace Conference and sent out half a dozen commissions of ingenuous and credulous men to study conditions in the various countries which had subscribed to the League. America looked on from afar and tried not to feel the thrill of gratitude and superiority with which her great ocean barrier usually inspired the less far-seeing of her citizens. Russia itself, after twenty years of peace and content, felt the throb of political emotion — a new sensation in her giant body. She was bewildered at the strength of her own feelings. The more intelligent portion of the community looked with something like reverence upon that amazing rekindling of monarchical, almost religious sentiment on the part of the peasant class. Only a minority of them could remember rule under Tzardom; could remember the whispers of "a little father," a being nearer than God in their thoughts, as making a more tangible and real appeal to their imaginations. Samara's action, regarded with wondering admiration in other countries, almost stunned his own supporters. He dissolved the Duma as soon as he recognised the strength of the monarchist movement and issued a proclamation in every electoral district requiring the people to nominate their representative on the question of the constitution of the country. He himself, immersed in the one scheme so near his heart, yet the scheme which had temporarily shaken his power, remained at Odensk and in the neighbourhood, patiently addressing audience after audience of his dissatisfied soldiery, trying to convince the most difficult race upon the earth, realising his slow progress, yet fascinated with his task and deaf to the pleadings of his advisers to seek a wider field. The acme of his quixotism, however, was yet to come.

Catherine found herself living in an atmosphere of excitement from which she was to some extent excluded. Alexandrina, after Nicholas' visit, had never once alluded to its purpose. Nevertheless, Catherine had felt the veil fall. She discussed the situation with no one but she pondered over it. She compared the Russia of her dreams with the Russia which Samara had created; compared the man in his daily life and ideals as she now knew them with the narrow monarchical judgment which branded him simply as a usurper and a demagogue. Tzardom she had accepted very much as she had accepted the Bible. Both, it seemed to her, were fundamentals. The atheist was by the very fact of his existence a debased creature; the anarchist, vermin of a different race to human beings; the republican or antimonarchist of any type, a person outside argument or consideration. Monarchy was God's system of government. Any other form was a species of blasphemy. It was really after all a somewhat clarified vision of the point of view once held by fifty million peasants. Samara, in the days of her earlier acquaintance with him, she had looked upon with a certain toleration, simply from the fact that she regarded him as one of the milestones on the way from the ruin of her country to its regeneration, to be disregarded ruthlessly enough when the whole light of sanity once more returned to the people. The ethics of his system of government she had never even considered. She had marvelled at its results, but all the time with the feeling that the same and better results would have been attained under monarchical rule. She had never even doubted that if the longed-for day of reëstablishment should come, she would marry Nicholas and reign over Russia. She scarcely doubted that even now, although for once their wills had crossed.

Yet, in these days, she found herself comparing the two men. She found herself asking, in the spirit of a new-born heresy, whether Nicholas indeed possessed a single one of Samara's gifts, whether indeed it were possible for him, ruling by divine grace, to attain similar results to those which Samara's genius had achieved. In those days of disquiet after her few hours of daily work' at Government Buildings, necessarily restricted, owing to Samara's absence, she took to walking the streets in the late afternoon, when twilight offered a sort of shelter — streets now as safe as the thoroughfares of any European capital of the world, thanks to the wonderful system of police. Nearly always her way led her past Government House. One evening, to her surprise, she found a crowd collected in the street — a patient crowd, watching a thin thread of light through the curtained windows of a room on the lower floor. She paused for a moment and listened, gathering from the whispers that Samara had returned. In front of the door stood a high-powered motor car. She retreated a little from the throng and passed into a side street, unlocked a postern door in the wall with a key which she carried always with her, and made her way up the narrow strip of artificial garden to the back of the house. A manservant admitted her without question, and she hastened towards Samara's room on the ground floor. Ivan stood on duty outside the door.

"One may enter?" she enquired.

Ivan shook his head.

"General Trotsk is within," he replied, "and Minister Argoff. There is to be no interruption."

Catherine fetched herself a chair and sat down. The conference was obviously of a disturbed nature. Often she heard Argoff's voice raised almost to passion, and more than once the cold anger which burned at the back of Trotsk's measured words filled them with unusual and ominous volume. Samara's voice, alone, seemed unchanged, but sometimes in his intonation she detected a sign of the strain from which he must be suffering. At last came silence — then the throwing open of the door. The Minister of Police and Argoff came out together. The former glanced steadily at Catherine, saluted, hesitated and passed on. Ivan stood on one side and she crossed the threshold. As the door was closed behind her, she stopped short. Samara's head was buried in his hands. Instinctively she felt like an intruder, and hesitated, wondering whether she could withdraw unheard. Samara, however, with his amazing sensibility, seemed to be suddenly conscious of her presence. The flutter of her skirt, a waft of perfume from the bunch of dying violets she wore, or perhaps the sound of her quick indrawn breath, warned him of her coming. He looked up, rose an inch or two from his chair and nodded in friendly fashion.

"The light tires my eyes," he said, as though in explanation of his posture. "How did you know that I was here?"

"By the people outside, not from you," she replied a little reproachfully.

"I nearly sent for you," he admitted, "just to indulge in the very weakness of sharing my woes."

"The Peace Conference, I am told, is postponed," she said. "Why is Andrew not back from London?"

The question seemed to perplex him.

"I wish I knew," he admitted. "I cabled him to return. For ten days I have had no word from him. He is perhaps ill."

"It is I who have robbed you of the one person who should have been by your side," she exclaimed remorsefully.

He shook his head.

"I am not sure whether Andrew would be any comfort to me if he were here," he confided. "He behaved most strangely before he left and he never sympathised with my demobilisation schemes. I rather fancy that he would go over to the great majority and side against me."

He sat quite still for a moment, as though deliberating. Catherine, venturing to watch him a little more closely, was shocked at the change in his appearance. There were hollows underneath those always somewhat high cheek bones. His mouth, in its straight firm lines, seemed to have lost the possibility of any tenderness or humour. His eyes had surely receded a little and hardened. The wistful gleam of the visionary was still lurking in their depths, but the light of hope seemed to have grown weak.

"This room is insufferable," he declared wearily. "I dare not open the windows because of the people. Come up to the top. I have a fancy to talk with you there."

She followed him from the room by a door opening out of the alcove, along a narrow passage and into the self-adjusting lift, then up the final flights of stairs, on to the leaded parapets. From the recess to which he presently led her the whole of the city westwards was visible, enclosed in an arc of lights, with a glimpse beyond of the great plain rolling and falling to an indefinable horizon. The new city was tangled with the old, high buildings and straight-hewn streets cleaving their way through the jumble of ancient tenements, decayed mansions, half palaces, half hovels, the churches with their strangely shaped roofs and towers, the gimcrack lodging houses of Soviet erection. In the half light one seemed to be able to visualise the eternal struggle between modernity and antiquity; the utilitarian triumphing, magnificent in victory, here and there an old street or square left only partially destroyed, lending a touch of beauty to the stern and intruding materialism of brick and iron. Samara laid his hand upon Catherine's sleeve, his other arm outflung to where the canopy of lights ended.

"This has been my hardest task," he said, "and this has become the city I love. When they asked me to do what I could for Russia there was scarcely a light to be seen from here, scarcely a sound building. The streets were full of holes and ruts, the sewers were open, no man or woman could walk safely for a hundred yards in any direction. There was scarcely a shop doing business, prices were ridiculous, people died of starvation in the street. And to-day, see! Even this below is only the birth of a great city, but it grows hour by hour. The stores are full, prices are normal. Look at that blaze of light westward. Those are factories working overtime on American contracts."

"Russia will never forget what you have done for her," she assured him softly.

"History may remind her in the future," he answered. "Your passer-by in the streets below to-night has forgotten. Strange things are happening hour by hour. Marshall Phildivia, Commander in Chief of the Russian armies, received instructions to report here to-day. He failed to do so. They tell me that after receiving the mandate he flew instead to Odensk. Trotsk, my one really strong man, has asked to-night for permission to resign his position."

"I do not understand," she confessed. "Are you preparing to abdicate without even a fight?"

"A fight!" he repeated. "I have been fighting every minute of every day for the last three weeks. I shall fight to the end, but concerning one thing I have sworn an oath in heaven, and no one shall make me perjure myself. Enough blood has been shed in Russia. What there is left is best preserved. I shall resist monarchy with the last breath of my body, but not a single Russian soldier shall lose his life for or against me."

"It is a wonderful decision," she murmured. "What about the First Army, then?"

"It is because of the First Army that Trotsk deserts me," he replied. "I will not have them mobilised. I will not have them fight against their fellows. While I live, Russia shall not fight Russia."

"But surely you need a certain measure of defence," she protested. "May I be quite frank?"

"Naturally," he answered.

"From what I can learn," she went on, "I think that your mission to Odensk has been more or less a failure. What you can demonstrate to a logician you cannot hammer into the head of a Russian peasant. I·have read some of your speeches. They are wonderful. They have almost convinced me — a Royalist from the cradle. They are utterly wasted upon the men of the Second Army to whom you have addressed them."

"I believe you are right," he admitted gloomily. "Yet, what does it matter? It is not the Second Army which will decide this problem. It is the whole electorate. Trotsk wants to mobilise the

First Army and bring them across the river to the city. Why should I? The danger from Odensk is less than they have any idea of. Only you and I know that secret. But if it were greater, I would never see army against army. The people of Russia shall judge between what I have done and what Nicholas Imanoff may promise them."

"You are a Quixote amongst rulers," she exclaimed. "The First Army is still yours, uncorrupted and patriotic. With their help you could hold your own against anything the others could do. Why do you hesitate? It is without a doubt your best chance."

"If it were my only one," he answered, "I should not change. The people shall decide."

"There is something tragical about it all," she sighed. "You do not mind if I continue to speak frankly?"

"Mind? Go on, please."

"If it were left to the class you despise most — the *bourgeoisie* — there would be no doubt of the result. These are the people who read a little and think a little, who study foreign politics and realise the amazing change in their own country. You are sure of them. Their vote is yours to a man. It is the peasants whom you love — the peasants to whom you have spoken as a father to his children — who are the doubtful quantity. They are superstitious, at heart deeply religious, but very, very narrow; very prone to rely upon a passing feeling."

"I know them," he admitted. "I must confess that they are the doubtful quantity. I am still content to leave the issue to their judgment."

"So you have announced," Catherine said. "But has it ever struck you that it may not suit the other side to wait? The electorate is, after all, unreliable. If they believed that it was in their power to seize Moscow without the possibility of any resistance, don't you think that they would do so?"

"There is no chance of that," he answered. "You and I best know why."

"Supposing the corps commanders should refuse to destroy the ammunition dumps?" she persisted.

"They will not refuse," he assured her. "They are all my men.

You must not imagine either that it will be a matter of hours. It will be a matter of seconds — the turning of a single prepared switch."

"Supposing the Royalists should get to know your plans and save the ammunition?"

"It would have to be a very wonderful betrayal," he observed. "The secret is known to exactly three people in the world — yourself, myself and Andrew. Problem — find the traitor!"

"I am on the side of the Royalists," she reminded him. "It is absurdly rash of you to trust me with such a secret!"

"You might fight," he answered, "if you were a man. You would never betray."

For some reason unintelligible to either of them, they both relapsed into a curiously prolonged silence. Samara, a few feet back from the edge of the parapet, was leaning against a great block of masonry, his arms folded, his eyes fixed first upon the dark pall of clouds which had suddenly risen up on the horizon, but later on Catherine, whose face was a little turned from him. She stood on the extreme edge of the parapet, the upper part of her figure outlined against the black chasm of sky and space; a curiously effective background. She was like a pastel in real life, something fine in line and exquisite in conception, but amazingly human. She looked into the empty places, but without the air of a visionary. There were human thoughts which throbbed in her brain; human passions which stirred in her veins. Life, which since her departure from New York had moved so swiftly for her, seemed all the time to be piling up problems which even at that moment filled her mind — problems which she faced without a touch of neurotic disability but with a simplicity and breadth of vision essentially racial. Even her smooth and beautiful forehead was unruffled as she studied the issues which had risen up before her. Samara, watching more and more intently, was puzzled. He remembered ever afterwards that in these, his hours of fate, the most strenuous effort of his mind was directed towards a wistful, intense desire to read the thoughts of one who certainly might have been counted outside the cycle of his fate.

The breaking of the storm disturbed them. The whole of the black curtain of clouds seemed suddenly to open and disclose a background of fire. For a moment the light on her face appeared to him almost unearthly. Then she turned towards him with a very human little exclamation.

"Come along down," she cried. "The rain will be here in a moment."

The end of her words was lost in the crash of thunder which seemed to shake the building around them. She grasped his arm. He held her tightly and for a moment he did not move.

"An allegory," he whispered. "I came to look out upon this city because its splendour is mine. I made it, brought it into being. All this is nothing to the meeting of the clouds. To-morrow the sun will shine down again on my work."

Suddenly he felt the cling of her arms, the touch of her body against his. A spell of forgetfulness swept him off his feet as his lips were pressed to hers. There was a moment of deep, intense silence, then the blaze of light again all around them. She broke away, with a perfectly human, unembarrassed laugh, though underneath was a curious new undertone.

"Another second," she warned him, "and all Moscow would have seen us. Perhaps they did, as it is. Come!"

She ran with flying footsteps across the leads, down the iron ladder and along the passage. He was breathless when he rejoined her in the great wainscotted library. The telephone bell on his desk was ringing without intermission. She pointed to it silently. He took off the receiver, listened for a time, spoke again and hung it up. Then he turned to Catherine.

"The Cabinet are holding a private session at Government Buildings," he explained. "They have heard that I am back from Odensk and they have done me the courtesy to desire my presence. I must go there at once. Except for Trotsk, Argoff assures me that they are perfectly sound."

"Have they to seek election?" she enquired.

"Only by the Duma," he answered. "They are in office until Parliament reassembles."

"Are you coming back here afterwards?" she asked.

He shook his head.

"This must be good night," he told her. "I am addressing the officers at Odensk to-morrow morning and I shall fly back as soon as the storm is over. Before I go, I want to ask you one question."

"Well?"

"What were you thinking of to-night when the thunder crashed down upon us?"

She smiled reminiscently.

"Of you," she admitted. "I will tell you what I was thinking. I was remembering first of all a saying of Voltaire's that 'Every great man in the world at some time or another makes one huge mistake.' Do you know what yours is?"

"No."

"You have despised women. You have been too proud to share yourself, to live anywhere else except in the unalterable ego. You have classed women with flowers and wine and sunshine — a great mistake, Gabriel Samara!"

"There are not many women like you," he said, after a moment.

"That is part of your folly," she insisted. "A woman is what her own love makes her, or the love of the man she loves. You know what yours would have made of any woman whom you had taken into your life? It would have made her practical, far-seeing. She would have supplied just that leaven of common sense, of human outlook, which would have kept your feet on the ground. You have kept your head turned to the skies just one hour too long. The woman would have pointed across the plain. You could have had this, Gabriel Samara, and the wine, and the sunshine, and the flowers."

He shook his head a little sadly.

"You may be right," he confessed, "but if you are, salvation would still have been impossible for me."

She smiled across at him delightfully.

"I am too much of a woman to refuse the compliment," she murmured.

At the door, he turned back. He pointed to the safe with its marvellous array of bars and cross-bars.

"I have never asked you for an assurance before," he said, "but I ask you now — will you hold that secret for me for forty-eight hours?"

"I promise," she answered readily.

CATHERINE, on her homeward way that night, paused at the corner of the Square, astounded. Streets and pavement alike were closely packed with a surging crowd, many of them, as she saw at once, students from the universities, but the great majority of the working class. They waited very patiently, almost in silence, always gazing at the upper windows of her aunt's house. Even whilst she lingered there for a moment, the windows leading out on to the balcony were opened and Nicholas, not for the first time, she gathered, made his appearance. With a little catch of the breath, she noticed that he was wearing the old uniform of the Imperial Army. The people realised it too, and there was a low, hoarse murmur of restrained applause. Nicholas stood at the salute. The applause swelled and grew, but only one or two amongst the crowd were venturesome enough to dare the spoken word.

"Long live Nicholas Imanoff, Tzar of Russia!" some one cried shrilly from the centre of the throng.

The applause increased still further to a roar. Catherine turned to one of the great policemen who was standing, placid, by her side.

"Is this allowed?" she enquired.

"All this is permitted, lady," was the respectful reply. "Save the anarchists, every one in the city has the right of free speech. An edict confirming this has just been issued from the Home Office, signed by Samara himself."

"Do you think I could get to my home?" she asked.

"Where is it that you wish to go?"

"To the house where Nicholas Imanoff is standing upon the balcony."

"You are a member of the household?"

"I am his cousin, Catherine Zygoff of Urulsk."

"In that case, gracious lady," the policeman assured her, "a way shall be made."

He held his baton above his head and shouted in strident Russian at the top of his voice.

"Way for the Princess Catherine Zygoff of Urulsk, who seeks to return to the house of the Grand Duchess. Give way for the gracious Princess! Give way, you loiterers!"

The spirit of orderliness was in the crowd, perhaps because it was so seldom questioned. A lane was made for Catherine at once. People in the background stood on tiptoe to see her. From the heart of the assembly came the same shrill voice.

"Way for the Princess Catherine Zygoff of Urulsk, cousin of Nicholas Imanoff, future Tzarina of Russia."

There was a moment's breathless pause. Liberty of speech was a new gift to Russia and something of the old dread lingered. In a few seconds, however, hesitation vanished. Catherine regained her roof through an avenue of wildly applauding, hat-waving youths. She passed into the house without a sign. At the top of the stairs Nicholas met her, his face flushed.

"Come and stand by my side, Catherine," he invited. "The people demand it. It is our betrothal."

"Do not be absurd," she answered scornfully. "What are these but a few handfuls of sight-seers, out for any sensation they can get hold of. There are just as many yelling themselves hoarse at Samara's gates. One loses dignity in accepting such tribute."

The young man's eyes flashed with anger.

"It is from the small beginnings that the great things come," he cried. "These people have sought me out of their own will. You have not heard. We bring news from Odensk. There have been demonstrations at Petrograd. The country is with us!"

"It will be quite time enough for us to accept the homage of the people," Catherine insisted, "when the elections have convinced us that it is the people's will that we should be restored to our proper places."

"You talk like Samara himself," he sneered. "Have you no Russian blood in your veins?"

"Catherine!"

The suddenness of the interruption startled her into momentary silence. Alexandrina had pushed her way past Nicholas and stood below him upon the stairs. She was like a woman transformed. The disabilities of her figure seemed to have vanished. It was the voice of a great lady who spoke.

"You have forgotten what is due to your cousin and to your destiny, Catherine," she said. "These are the first of the millions who will yet claim you. Do not hesitate for another moment. Let these people see you standing by Nicholas' side. All Russia will hear of it and know."

Catherine was torn with a terrible indetermination. Nicholas made room for her to pass and followed her as she slowly ascended the stairs. She was in a state of furious revolt, but she had somehow the feeling that she was obeying an immutable law. They entered the salon and moved towards the wide-flung window.

"This is no small matter, Catherine," Nicholas exclaimed eagerly. "We bring wonderful news. People are flocking here from all parts of the city. There are students there, too — the class we want. Smile at them and at me, Catherine. This is the beginning of the greater days."

She took her place beside him on the balcony and looked downwards into the upturned faces. Once more hats were waved; a roar of voices seemed to come to her from an indefinite space. She felt her hand grasped tightly by Nicholas, and the volume of applause suddenly increased. Her fingers were limp and passive and cold. She seemed to remember that earlier in the evening she had stood in a windier paradise and on a greater height.

Dinner that night at Alexandrina's flat was a disturbed and tumultuous meal. Nicholas was full of his personal triumphs at Odensk. Even though he had been compelled to appear there as a civilian, the common soldiers had broken all rules of discipline and saluted him. The meetings which Kirdorff had arranged had been packed, the enthusiasm enormous. The excitement seemed somehow to have benefited Nicholas, to have raised for a few moments his feet from the ground. He was vainglorious, but confident.

"I have promised the people," he announced, "a government

which shall give them as much liberty as the present one — liberty
of speech and liberty of religion. I have promised them to alter
nothing which is for their good. In return, they will know that
they are being governed, not by a usurper, but by divine and
moral right."

"You are becoming amazingly eloquent, dear cousin," Catherine murmured. "To tell you the truth," she went on, "your
eagerness for my presence to-night astonished me. I had fancied,
from our last parting, that I was written out of your scheme
of things."

"That could not be," Nicholas replied solemnly. "It could not
be in the first place because our alliance is the one thing necessary
to make our position sure in the face of the Russian people. You
and I represent all that is left of our great House."

"The union," Alexandrina declared, "has been blessed in
heaven and sanctioned by the Head of our Church. It is one of
the great and happy features of the new day."

"As for our last parting," Nicholas concluded, "I remember
very well my anger. That, however, is finished. We ask no
further service of you, Catherine. To-night we start afresh."

Catherine looked at him reflectively. A vague sense of trouble
was gathering in her mind. To cross-question him further at
present, however, was impossible. They had finished dinner now
and moved into the small salon, where all the time a little stream
of callers presented themselves and, having paid their respects,
passed on to make room for others. Nicholas accepted the homage
paid him readily and with dignity. Catherine was gracious but
noncommittal.

"We move too fast," she insisted more than once. "Later,
perhaps."

She sought her opportunity for speech with her cousin. Towards
the end of the evening it came.

"Nicholas," she said, "I must ask you what you meant when
you assured me that you would cease your attempts to persuade
me to betray Samara's confidence? You know that I have in my
keeping a secret. When you left the house that evening you were
very angry because I refused to divulge it."

He smiled at her in condescending fashion.

"Put the matter behind you, my dear Catherine," he begged. "It is finished. The world itself is opening before us. All that we seek to learn we shall learn, and that without delay."

He moved away to greet some fresh arrivals. The cloud of uneasiness in Catherine's mind increased. She was seized with a very definite and persistent apprehension. As soon as it was possible she slipped unnoticed from the room and made her way to her own apartment.

There were still people in the Square when, at a few minutes after midnight, Catherine left the house by the back entrance and turned towards Government House. She had changed her gown for a plain walking costume of dark material, and she wore a small hat with a thick veil. There was something hard and comforting in her pocket and the thrill of adventure in her pulses. The back streets through which she passed were almost deserted, but in the broader thoroughfares the lights were still flaming and people were promenading in such numbers that the tread of their feet sounded like the march of a distant army. Samara's boast, however, that the streets of Moscow were now as safe as the streets of New York and London was justified in her person that night. Except for a few good-humoured greetings she passed on her way unnoticed until she reached the side entrance to Government House. She entered by the postern door, closed it behind her noiselessly, and stood for a moment peering into the shadows of the courtyard. There was no one stirring, no sound of following footsteps from the street outside. Yet, for the first time, Catherine was unaccountably nervous. She moved forward reluctantly. She paused at every other step to listen. There were two tall elm trees on her left through which the wind seemed to pass with a sort of shuddering sigh, sending pattering down upon her drops of rain from the recent storm. The house itself presented a great white blank, the blinds drawn and the shutters tightly fastened. She approached nearer and nearer to it, climbed the steps and stopped once more to listen. The silence was still unbroken, save for the dull reverberation of those ceaseless footsteps in the distance, the sharp honk of a motor horn on the boulevard, an occasional murmur of voices. She entered the house, shut the door behind her, groped her way for a few steps into the gulf of darkness, and found the switch. The great hall was flooded at once with light — an instantaneous though unaccountable relief to her. She passed on and opened the door of the anteroom, itself furnished as a library, at the further end of which lay the entrance to the room she sought. One light only was burning here from the ceiling; so inadequate an illumination of the lofty chamber that she could scarcely see across it. By degrees, as her eyes became accustomed to the gloom, she could dimly discern the great table round which the counsellors had been used to sit, the plain wood panels reaching to the ceiling, with here and there fragments of the ancient tapestry, and, most reassuring sight of all, at the end of the room, seated on guard before the closed door of his master's private apartment, Ivan. She recognised him with a throb of relief and moved at once towards him.

"Ivan!" she cried.

He took no notice. He was bending a little forward, motionless and apparently asleep.

"Ivan!" she called again.

Still he did not reply. She stretched out her hand and gripped him by the shoulder. Her fingers fell upon something hard and as she leaned over him she saw the horror in his distorted face. Her lips parted. It was the effort of her life to keep back the shriek which rose to her lips. In Ivan's back was a dagger. There were some faint drops of blood upon his coat. His face was the face of a dead man and from underneath the chink of the door in front of her, she could distinguish a pale shaft of light.

CHAPTER XIII

THE first shivering moments of panic were past and Catherine was comparatively calm, almost collected. In her right hand she held the small revolver which Samara had given her on the steamer; with her left she turned the handle of the door and entered the room. She entered so softly that the man busied with the safe, his back turned towards her, proceeded with his task undisturbed. She drew a little nearer. Then surprise forced from her the exclamation which terror had failed to wring from her lips.

"Andrew!" she cried. "Andrew Kroupki!"

He turned round quite slowly; stiffly, as though it were against his will. The change in him was so startling that she almost wondered that she had recognised him. His face had grown lanker and thinner than ever, his mouth seemed to have taken to itself the character of a wolf's, his sunken eyes seemed at once to have lost expression and yet have gained in brilliancy. With a little thrill of horror she saw the scar upon his cheek. He drew himself gradually upright.

"Catherine Borans!" he muttered. "What do you want?"

"When did you come back from England?" she asked.

"I did not go to England," he answered. "Samara thought that I was there. He was wrong. I went to Odensk."

"Odensk!" she repeated incredulously.

"Yes. You haven't heard, then? But how would you? I swore them to secrecy. I have betrayed Samara. I am selling his secrets to your friends, the Royalists — selling them day by day. They tell me you have some foolish scruples. So they sent me here for the great one. Scruples! I have none, but I thank the Father of Russia that you came to-night."

"Why?"

He struck himself on the side of the head. He had the appearance of a madman.

"Because my mind is going," he groaned. "My memory is failing. I remembered the hiding place of the key. I remembered the adjustment of the bars — four panels to the left, three to the right, two back — I remembered it all as well as ever — the combination for Monday, Tuesday, Wednesday and Thursday — I know them by heart. To-day is Friday, and I have forgotten. Here I stand, with those proclamations only a few inches off, the secret orders I have promised there within my grasp — and I have forgotten. It is well you came. Tell it me quickly. The password for Friday? My head is hot with the emptiness of it. Quick!"

"To whom are those secret orders going when you have them?" she asked.

"To your friends, the enemies of Samara. Quick!"

She made no movement.

"What has Gabriel Samara done to you," she demanded, "that you should betray him like this?"

"Robbed me," he shouted fiercely. "Robbed me of you!"

"You poor fool!" she scoffed. "Do you know who I am?"

"Catherine Borans," he answered. "The Chief brought you from New York. But they tell me that you are a Russian — a Monarchist. Well, I am a Monarchist too. Damn Samara!"

"They might have told you the truth," she said. "It really doesn't matter. I am the Princess Catherine Zygoff of Urulsk, betrothed — if I carry out my contract — to Nicholas of Russia, whom you say you serve."

He glared at her, speechless for several moments.

"Now I know that I am mad," he muttered at last. "A Princess of the Royal House! You were in the Weltmore Typewriting Agency!"

"Quite true," she admitted. "So was Nicholas selling bonds on commission. Kirdorff was secretary to a foreigners' club. My aunt, the Grand Duchess, designed artificial flowers. It is none the less true that we are what we are."

He sank into Samara's chair. For a few moments he seemed to have forgotten his mission.

"Did Samara know?" he gasped.

"He knew at Monte Carlo," she answered. "General von Hartsen told him."

He sat at the table perfectly limp. Something in his attitude reminded her with a little thrill of renewed horror of the man outside.

"Now that you know who I am," she continued quietly, "you know that I have a right to speak on the matter of those papers. You and I are the only two whom Samara has trusted. Royalist though I am, I have no mind to betray him. Neither shall you. Close up the safe, Andrew Kroupki. Go home and ask your God to pardon you for the terrible thing you have done to-night, and the terrible purpose that was in your mind."

He stiffened slightly in his place. Something from which she shrank came into his expression.

"I have finished with Samara," he announced. "He is only a woman. He has not the courage to fight for the people. He is a coward."

"Samara is a great man and you are a liar," she answered.

The fury was back in his face.

"It was always true what I feared," he went on. "You love him. You cannot deny it. In your heart — even though Nicholas takes you to his throne — you are Samara's woman."

"You are becoming a little absurd," she said quietly, struggling against what seemed to be a shortness of breath. "Do as I directed. Leave this room and go home."

He rose from his chair and began moving slowly round the table which separated them.

"No," he decided, "I shall not do that. I shall fulfill the purpose for which I came. Tell me the password for Friday, Catherine Borans."

"I shall never tell it to you," she retorted with determination.

He was clear of the table now, within a dozen yards of her.

"You shall tell me the password," he insisted, his voice rising, "and you shall do other things that I bid you. I have lost my soul since I bore the shame of a woman's blow. There is a little left in life and I will take it. First tell me the password."

Her hand came from the folds of her dress. The feeble light

shone on the bright metal of the revolver she held before her.
"I shall tell you nothing," she warned him, "and I will not
have you a step nearer."

He laughed.

"Those who are sold to the devil," he cried, "have no fear of
hell!"

She would have aimed at his mouth but a chance word of
advice of Samara's, never to aim too high, came into her mind.
She dropped her arm a few inches and fired. Within the four
walls of the room the report seemed to her tremendous — almost
deafening. He came on another couple of paces, undeterred. Her
finger was on the trigger again, when he suddenly faltered and
spun round. He clutched at the air, grasping as though for something to seize hold of, and fell a crumpled heap upon the floor.
Catherine stood for a moment looking at him. She watched the
slight colour drain from his cheeks, saw the little hole just underneath his shoulder from which a dark spot of blood was oozing.
She felt no pity for him; only a great and wonderful relief. If
by any chance she had missed! The thought was paralysing in
its horror! She retraced her steps for a minute to the door and
stood listening. The domestic part of the establishment was some
distance away and no one apparently had been disturbed by the
report of her revolver. Ivan was still there, terrible in his limp
inertness. Again she retraced her steps, made her way to the front
of the safe, laid her revolver down upon the table and began
the task of securing the intricate fastenings. Once she paused
and listened. She fancied that there had been some movement in
the room. There was nothing to be heard, however, except the
muffled and distant sounds from the street. The safe itself was
a miracle of ingenuity, the work of one of Russia's foremost
engineers, and familiar though she was with its mechanism, it
still absorbed her whole attention. Her task was approaching completion. There was only one more bar to coax into its place.
Then the horror came again. She felt her heart almost cease to
beat. There was a hot breath upon her cheek. She turned around
fearfully, and this time she shrieked as one who looks into hell.
It was Andrew's face, white and drawn with pain and passion

—Andrew who had dragged himself to his feet and found strength in his madness.

"Nothing but a flesh wound," he muttered. "I'll have the password from you, and then — the password first. Tell it to me!"

She struck at him with all her force, and for a moment it seemed as though her blow had gone home, for he reeled upon his feet and his new-found strength appeared to have left him. With a fierce effort, however, he recovered himself. His fingers were upon her throat. His knee pinned her to the safe door.

"The password! The password first!"

She put forth all the strength of her youth and supple limbs, and suddenly realised that it was hopeless. His fingers were like burning pincers; his arm like a band of iron. Already the room seemed to be going round, the light must have been extinguished. Then there was another sound — a roar at first, a whisper, a roar again. Where had she heard it before, she wondered with the last efforts of her ebbing consciousness? The steamer! Samara with the would-be assassin in his grasp! The body hurtling through the air! Then she opened her eyes and tried to smile. She was filled with an ineffable sense of relief. The arms which were holding her so firmly and yet so tenderly were Samara's.

CHAPTER XIV

THERE followed days during which Moscow scarcely knew itself; days of excitement and processions, rumours and counter rumours, meetings in every public hall, at every street corner; telegrams and wireless messages in the plate-glass windows and in nearly every one of the great shops. Curiously enough, all the time business went on almost as usual. The restaurants and cafés were packed with surging crowds, who thronged the boulevards at night singing patriotic songs. Sometimes the crowds were thickest outside Government House, sometimes outside Alexandrina's modest abode. Everywhere people were asking themselves what it all meant. Was it a military rising of the Royalists? If so, why was Nicholas Imanoff, in civilian clothes, to be seen day by day on the balcony of his aunt's house, alighting at the aerodrome on hurried visits from Odensk, driving in an automobile through the streets?

Then Samara addressed two great meetings, one at the Skating Rink, and another at the Opera House, and on the following morning the city awoke to find a proclamation signed by him on every wall. At last they began to understand. It was theirs to make the choice; the restoration of the monarchy under Nicholas Imanoff, or the continuation of the republic under Samara and his Council. The people should decide, Samara promised with persistent passion. No portion of the army should be used even to defend the city against any possible military coup. No blow should be struck, no blood be shed. Samara's invocation to the Russian people was:

CHOOSE WHO SHALL GOVERN YOU

As the days passed on, Catherine became conscious of a sense of growing excitement in her aunt's disturbed household. Kirdorff, Orenburg and most of the younger men of the party were now absent. Finally Nicholas himself departed. The air was filled with rumours. It was the quiet before the storm. In two days the initial electioneering results would be proclaimed. Catherine, who for the first time in anybody's recollection had been confined to her room with a bad throat, came down late one afternoon, with a red rose in her waistband, and a great bundle of papers under her arm. She passed smiling amongst the little groups of her aunt's visitors. She wore an unusual band of velvet around her neck, but seemed otherwise very much as usual. Only the immediate members of the household who had not retired on the night when she had been brought home by Samara's physician in his own car had any idea that she had been suffering from anything but an ordinary indisposition.

"So after all," she remarked, "this great Samara will keep his word. It seems too amazing to think of a change like this without a gun being fired or a blow struck."

An octogenarian baron, once the owner of vast estates in Southern Russia, and now a pensioner at Monaco, took snuff and grunted.

"You forget, Princess," he reminded her, "there may be no change at all. Samara may prove to have been too clever for us. If I had been Kirdorff and the others, I would have let Samara talk of peace and then asked him to look down the barrels of a hundred thousand rifles from Odensk."

"The Baron is right," a woman from the other end of the room declared eagerly. "The whole of the army at Odensk is almost in a state of mutiny at the idea of demobilisation. Nicholas has made no compact with Samara. He could march into Moscow at the head of a quarter of a million of soldiers in two days, and the victory would be won."

The Grand Duchess smiled. She looked across at Catherine and smiled again.

"One never knows," she murmured.

But Nicholas had not the chance of marching into Moscow at the head of even a hundred thousand soldiers. He arrived instead, very sulky and wet, about half-past eleven that night, soon after the last of the guests had departed. His anger blazed up at the sight of Catherine.

"It is you whom we have to thank for this failure," he exclaimed furiously. "You and that lunatic, Andrew Kroupki, who seems to have tumbled off the edge of the earth."

"What has happened?" his aunt cried. "All day long we have been listening for the rumbling of the trains and the sound of your guns."

"Guns!" he scoffed. "Samara's secret was simple enough. It has paralysed the entire army. Yesterday the whole of the ammunition within five hundred miles of us was destroyed, and the men's bayonets seized. There is an army still, it is true — armed with walking sticks!"

"Samara has at least been consistent," Catherine pointed out. "He fights harder to avoid bloodshed than for his own cause. Do you realise that if he chose to, he could bring the First Army into the city, fully armed and equipped?"

Nicholas sprawled in an easy-chair and drank brandy.

"How could he?" he asked cynically. "After his declaration of pacifism? We could show fight — not he."

"My opinion of you and your counsellors is that you are a brainless lot," she retorted. "You have lost a magnificent opportunity of impressing Moscow and the whole world."

"What do you mean?" he demanded.

"Simply this. You say that practically the whole of the Second Army are on your side."

"Except for a percentage of the officers, they are."

"You have your hundred trains waiting and your commissariat," she continued. "Why don't you bring your soldiers up unarmed? You can issue a proclamation and say that, agreeing with Samara in his great desire that not a single life should be lost, you are content to show by peaceful illustration the will of the army."

Nicholas looked across at her for a moment blankly and afterwards in almost fervent admiration. Then he rose to his feet.

"I'm going to the telephone," he declared. "You are a genius, Catherine!"

Catherine herself waited until the small hours of the morning. Then she stole downstairs to the room on the ground floor where the telephone was, and asked for that secret number which only she and a few others knew. Almost immediately Samara answered her.

"You should be in bed," she told him severely.

"One does not sleep these days," he answered. "You are better?"

"Absolutely," she assured him. "What about Andrew?" she added, after a moment's hesitation.

"He died in hospital this morning," was the cool reply. "I only wish that he had died in New York twelve months ago."

"I have news for you," Catherine confided.

"Well?"

"The Second Army are going to march on Moscow just the same, but as pacifists. They are coming to protest against being demobilised and to shout themselves hoarse for Nicholas. My idea entirely."

"A very excellent one," Samara admitted after a moment's pause, "but I'll counteract it. Some busybody has mobilised the First Army against my orders. I'll disarm them and bring them in also."

"I gather that Moscow will be becoming lively during the next few days," she remarked. "How do you think things are going?"

"In the direction of change," he answered a little sadly. "It is always like that. The pendulum of political impulses will never cease to swing. Are you to be crowned in Moscow?"

"It has been suggested," she assented. "Shall I send you a card?"

"I shall escape from your magnificence," he declared. "There is that little villa down in the South of France which I showed you on our way back from America. I fixed upon it then as my ultimate retreat. I scarcely thought, though, that it would be so soon."

"Nothing is settled yet," she reminded him. "You may win at the polls. If you do, there is only one way to avoid trouble in the future. Send Nicholas back to New York to sell bonds and my aunt with him to make her artificial roses."

"And you?"

"Back to the Weltmore Typewriting Agency. I am sure they'd take me. It was such a good advertisement for them when I left New York with you."

"Are you by any chance being flippant?" he asked.

"No, I'm just sleepy," she confided. "Good night!"

Two days later a new sensation presented itself to the already distracted inhabitants of Moscow. Soon after dawn from every railway terminus and even along some of the main thoroughfares outside, columns of soldiers in blue-grey uniform came creeping into the city. By noon it was estimated that there were nearly a hundred thousand from the Second Army alone encamped in the streets and squares. To add to the bewilderment of the people, from northwards came a steady stream of soldiers from the First Army, also unarmed. The streets were hung with a proclamation:

> A portion of the Second Army will arrive in Moscow to-day to protest against demobilisation. Anxious in every way to show my accord with the desire of your President to avoid bloodshed, the troops at my advice will come unarmed.
>
> (*Signed*) NICHOLAS.

Samara showed his first signs of anger when a copy of this proclamation was brought to him. He tore it promptly in two and flung the pieces across the table.

"It is untrue," he told the little conclave of ministers who were with him in almost hourly consultation. "If a woman had not been faithful, Nicholas would have made a shambles of the city. As it is, under whose orders do these troops march? Where is General Denkers?"

It was a Cabinet Meeting but there were many vacancies down the long table. Argoff leaned forward in his place.

"The General telephoned half an hour ago to say that he would call at Government House on his way into the city," he announced.

"If he is here, admit him," Samara directed shortly.

Argoff left the Council Chamber and returned a few moments later ushering in the Commander in Chief of the Second Army — General Denkers. The latter saluted gravely and stood with his hands resting lightly on the back of the chair to which Samara pointed.

"By whose orders, General, have you brought these troops to Moscow?" Samara demanded.

"I have to report, sir," was the momentous reply, "that in common with a large majority of the officers under my command, I, two nights ago, took the oath of allegiance to Nicholas Imanoff, future Tzar of Russia."

"Are you not anticipating a little, General?" Samara enquired imperturbably. "It is true that I have issued a proclamation that the constitution of this country shall be according to the desire of the people. The people as yet have not spoken."

"Sir," the General answered, "the army has spoken."

Samara smiled with faint sarcasm.

"And, but for an unexpected shortage of ammunition," he remarked, "I imagine that the army would have spoken in a different tongue. It is perhaps fortunate that my agents advised me of your probable attitude."

The General remained silent. He had been a soldier of Samara's own choosing, a fine disciplinarian, a strong, conscientious man. It was very certain that if he had declared for the Tzar, it was because he had believed in Tzardom.

"Supposing I order the First Army to march upon the city?" Samara suggested. "They are perfectly armed, accoutered, and loyal to the Republic."

"Such a step would be contrary to your own proclamation, sir," General Denkers rejoined quickly. "You have announced your earnest desire to have the future of this country decided upon without the shedding of blood."

"I wonder," Samara asked, looking at him steadily, "whether you would have respected my appeal if the bombs had been there for your aeroplanes, the cartridges for your rifles and machine guns, and the ammunition for your heavy artillery?"

The General made no reply. His silence was in itself a confession.

"You are dismissed, General," Samara concluded. "In the name of the State, I charge you to issue orders to your officers that all property be respected and that any acts of insubordination are immediately punished."

"We shall use our most strenuous efforts in that direction, sir," were the General's final words.

Samara looked down the table. There were eight ministers present; five others, including Trotsk, already deserters.

"Gentlemen," he announced, "the Government of this country is in suspense. Until the new Duma is elected and meets, constitutionally we are impotent. Such measures as must be taken for the good of the country can be left to my associates, Weirtz and Argoff, together with myself. You are dismissed."

The Minister of Finance rose to his feet.

"Sir," he said, "we are passing through one of the strangest upheavals of history. It may be that we shall none of us meet again in this chamber as officials of the Russian Government. Before we part, let me say on my own account, at least, that if we and the rest of the country should yield to the popular desire for a change of constitution, there will still be not one of us who will not think of you, Mr. President, with the deepest gratitude and respect. You have been a great ruler of this country in troublous times and a patriot in this hour of adversity, as these days of bloodlessness prove. I claim the privilege of shaking hands with you, sir, even though I venture to tell you that if the people's call for a monarchy is, as seems at present, unanimous, I shall tender my services to Nicholas Imanoff."

There was a chorus of assent. Samara shook hands with every one. They filed out a little reluctantly. At the very last moment one of the official secretaries rushed in with a telephonic dispatch.

Samara read it through.

"Gentlemen," he announced, raising his voice a little so that every one might hear, "the result of the elections in twenty-three districts is herewith proclaimed. Twenty-one have voted for the representative pledged to the restoration of the monarchy."

A murmur of amazement, almost of consternation, was clearly audible. Nothing so sweeping as this had been expected. Argoff and Weirtz would have lingered with their Chief, but Samara waved them away.

"It is useless," he said, "to discuss affairs of state. You will find me here if I am wanted."

He retired into his inner chamber — the faithful Ivan no longer there to guard the door — telephoned to the servants outside, denying himself to all callers, and spent several hours looking through his private papers. Once a privileged servant came silently in with the samovar upon a silver tray. He waved him away.

"A bottle of brandy," he ordered.

He helped himself liberally, refilled his glass and sent over to Government Buildings for one or two minor officials with whom he completed some unfinished business. Later on an official from the Home Office presented himself with another list of election results. The young man handed him the sheet almost apologetically and Samara read it with genuine astonishment. The returns were now in for over half the seats in the Duma, and out of a hundred and thirty districts, a hundred and seven had voted for the monarchist representative.

"What does it mean, Paul Metzger?" Samara asked curiously. "Where did it come from, all this fever for a monarch? Why was there no evidence of it before?"

"There isn't a man in Russia who isn't asking himself the same question, sir," the young official declared. "In the cafés, on the streets, and in the clubs, there is nothing but sheer amazement. All that the most clear-sighted can say is that it is the swing of the pendulum. The army started it, of course, but why the country districts should all be on fire to see the monarchy back again is inexplicable."

"I wonder whether Bromley Pride is still in Moscow?" Samara ruminated.

"He is one of about a hundred waiting in the ante-room, sir," Metzger replied.

"I will see him," Samara announced. "Send the others away."

Pride came lumbering in, as breezy and cheerful as ever. He was too much a man of the world to pull a long face and offer sympathy.

"You've earned immortality, Mr. President," he said, as he shook hands. "I'm just from Berlin. I was at the start of things there. I've seen half a dozen South American republics come and go, although perhaps they don't count any. I'm supposed to be an authority upon revolutions and changes of constitution in a country, but I want to tell you this is the most astounding business I ever knew. No one could conceive of such a thing. There are a hundred thousand unarmed soldiers in the city, hobnobbing with a hundred thousand civilians; there are gala dinners at all the swagger restaurants, you can't get within a dozen yards of a table at any of the ordinary cafés, and I haven't heard an angry word or seen a blow struck. I was out early this morning. There the crowds were, as patient as you please, waiting for the election returns. I met dozens of people I knew slightly and I asked them all the same question. 'Which is it going to be?' I got the same answer right away from every one of them. 'The elections are to decide,' they said. And I tell you this, Samara," the journalist concluded impressively, "if the country had voted the other way, they'd have taken it all right. Talk about a bloodless revolution! I never believed in such a thing before. I didn't think human nature could stand the strain."

Samara pushed over the bottle of brandy and lit a cigarette.

"Pride," he said, "you are one of the few men in the world whose judgment I would believe in as soon as my own. You are there amongst the people, and you see the truth. What does it all mean? I have governed these people for fifteen years. No country in the history of the world has prospered as Russia has done under my rule. Yet along comes this young scion of the Imanoffs, whom I found selling bonds in New York, shows himself to the people, makes use of a little propaganda in the army, and behold, he seems suddenly to have become a god. You have seen the voting?"

Pride nodded.

"When you've learned not to care, Samara," he said, "you'll

understand it better. This is at the root of the whole thing. The commonest evil quality in all human nature is ingratitude. It isn't a conscious evil quality. It's the philosophical evolution of the profound egotism of human nature. The whole country's prosperous and happy and cheerful. The people don't stop to realise that it's your administration which has brought that about. They honestly believe that they have done it all themselves. You've had the privilege of being at the head of the government. They don't grudge it to you. They have no ill-will towards you. They're simply dazzled by the prospect of a more picturesque form of government. It never enters into their heads for a moment that the present prosperity might not continue. They have accepted it as a matter of course. They think it will continue as a matter of course. That's as near as I or any one else can get at an explanation of what is going on to-day. It has nothing to do with you. You made just one mistake and only one."

"Demobilisation," Samara murmured.

Pride signified his assent.

"You will remember I warned you in New York," he continued. "A soldier doesn't look far enough ahead. Your men were well-fed, well looked after, well pensioned. They weren't philosophers. They didn't appreciate the fact that theirs, from your point of view, was an unnatural existence. You tried to pitchfork them out into civil life without preparing them sufficiently for the change. Then arrived that little nest of conspirators you brought back from New York, and the whole thing was easy. You went too fast, Samara. You brought it off with the first million, but you ought to have waited for a year or so afterwards."

Samara nodded and changed the subject almost abruptly.

"What's the last move in the city?" he asked.

Pride shrugged his shoulders.

"This is such a kid glove sort of affair," he observed, "that I should have thought Nicholas Imanoff would have been round here to consult you. There's some talk about a ceremony to-morrow of some description. I heard there were a hundred men working upon the cathedral bells."

Metzger reëntered with the air of one who brings tidings.

"Sir," he announced, "the Archbishop is here and begs to be received."

"You can show his Lordship in at once," Samara directed. "Don't go away, Pride. It's as well there should be some historian of the period present. Sit at the other end there and listen if you wish to."

The Archbishop, followed by a chaplain, was shown in with some formality. He was a large, bulky man, with a black beard, commanding physique, a splendid forehead and piercing eyes. Even in his strangely fashioned vestments he was a person of dignity.

"Mr. President," he said, as Samara rose to receive him, "you will permit me to explain the reason of my visit."

"If your Lordship will be seated," Samara begged.

The Bishop leaned his elbow upon the table and played for a moment with one of his rings.

"You are doubtless in touch, sir," he proceeded, "with the trend of events. I have been asked to-morrow morning to open the cathedral and to administer the sacrament to Nicholas Imanoff and the Princess Catherine of Urulsk, his intended bride."

Samara made no movement. He sat quite still, looking beyond the walls of his room.

"You and I, sir," the Archbishop went on, after a moment's pause, "have had little to do with one another during the years of your office—much sometimes to my regret. From the material point of view, Russia will never be able to forget what it owes you. You have brought the country out of a state of pitiful misery and filled her veins with new and vigorous health. If it has not seemed good to you, or according to your convictions, to think also of her spiritual welfare, that, alas, in these days, is no uncommon thing. You cannot blame me, however, if, as the head of the Church, I welcome frankly a new régime which incorporates at least the outward observances of the Christian faith with its ceremonies of state."

"I do not blame you, indeed, Archbishop," Samara acknowledged. "From your point of view, this must be a wonderful change. The pageantry of monarchy needs the background of ecclesiastical ceremony."

"Not only the outward form, I trust," the Archbishop ventured earnestly. "The ceremonies of our Church, even that one which will take place to-morrow, are as nothing if they are not symbolic of spiritual things."

Samara bowed.

"Your Lordship has done kindly in coming to visit me," he said. "My work for Russia is over. The new government will bring you a larger sphere of action and greater responsibility. You have my best wishes."

The Archbishop rose to his feet.

"You, sir," he pronounced, "stood shoulder to shoulder with the Church when you struck at the great dragon of atheism, and for that reason I beg you to accept my blessing."

Samara bent his head. For a moment the sonorous voice of the priest seemed to be attuned to some deep note of music. Then his hand flashed back and followed by his chaplain, he was gone. Samara looked after him like a man in a dream.

Presently Pride came up to offer his adieux.

"What are your plans?" he asked.

"I am going abroad at once," Samara confided. "I am going to live in the most beautiful country I know; grow olives and grapes, farm a little, read a little, write a little. After all, I have earned a rest."

"What part of the world do you choose?" Pride enquired.

Samara shook his head.

"When my wine press makes its first revolution," he replied, "and I gather my first crop of olives, you shall know."

No PERSON had a finer view than Samara himself of the great pageant which transformed Moscow on the following day into a city of amazing beauty and splendour. He stood upon the roof of Government House, leaning against the solid parapet, looking down upon the great thoroughfare below, at the streets beyond, at the great dome of the cathedral above which the bells, silent for many years, were making clamorous music. Every house was decked with flags, every person in the crowded streets seemed to be carrying flowers or waving banners. With a grim smile he watched Trotsk, with an escort of mounted police, pass up towards the cathedral, pushing the people back on either side. They stood eight or nine deep upon the pavement — a solid phalanx; soldiers and civilians mixed together, good-humoured, cheering at everything, festive with the joy of a great holiday. Samara gazed down at them a little wistfully. After all it was his city; it was his brain which had made her what she was. Those two universities, the finest in the world, had been his conception. The hospitals, white-fronted, flower begarlanded and hung with hundreds of flags, were of his building. It was he who had cleared out the dreaded foreign quarter, which the Soviet Government had allowed to become a very sewer of humanity, and erected the great warehouses there, every one of which was filled now to the topmost storey. It was he who, with a mayor of his own choosing, had studied deeply the question of civic administration, who was responsible for the wonderful transport, the perfect sanitary system, the broadening of the streets, the wonderful schools. All these things had come under his rule, almost at his instigation. Pride was right. It was unconscious ingratitude. The people had these things — they belonged to them — all thought as to their source had passed. Not once for him had those cathedral bells rung out their almost barbaric note of welcome. Not once had any crowd, such as he saw now, filled the streets and waited for his coming. Blazoned upon a hundred huge banners reared in prominent places he could read from where he stood the amazing electoral results. Nobody wanted anything more to do with the government which had brought prosperity to their doors, which had reëstablished them in twelve short years amongst the nations of the world. Nobody even thought of these things. There must lie somewhere engrained in the minds of men, he reflected, a sort of craving for the pageantry of life; to see life itself decked out with the trappings of ceremonial usage, an unconscious survival of the delight of savage ancestors in processions and drum-beatings. When the time came for the natural revulsion of sentiment, people would think of him without a doubt, historians would praise him, they might even raise a statue to his memory. And in the meantime those hideous figures telling their humiliating story of his defeat, and a crowd beside itself with delight!

Trotsk and his men, who had ridden back, reappeared. In the distance, coming nearer, was a slowly breaking wave of sound, of rapturous welcome. Samara felt a sudden quietness steal over him. He had come to this place that he might fully realise and ever afterwards forget this great blow of fate, that he might never look upon it as in any way accidental or dubious in its import. He was discarded by the will of the people. The hurt and grievousness of his humiliation seemed to him just then as nothing compared to the sharp pain at his heart when, from the sudden baring of heads, he knew that the moment had arrived. He gazed down, tense and motionless. The open automobile came into sight. Inside was a solitary figure — Nicholas Imanoff, in his prohibited uniform of white and silver, his hand to the salute, looking to the right and to the left — Nicholas, alone!

"I am afraid," a familiar voice said behind him, "that I have rather spoilt the procession."

Samara turned slowly round. He gripped the iron bar above his head until he almost fancied that it bent in his grasp. He stared incredulously at this impossible vision.

"Such a beautiful gown it was they had for me to wear!" Catherine went on. "White, all covered with pearls, and a real Russian headdress. It would have suited me wonderfully!"

"What are you doing here, like this?" he asked, and for once in his life his voice was broken and choked.

She laughed up at him. She was wearing the plain dark clothes and small hat with the rather faded flower, in which he had first seen her. On the ground by her feet was a square black box, she had just set down.

"I am Miss Catherine Borans, from the Weltmore Typewriting Agency," she announced. "You observe that I have not forgotten even the typewriter. Like a perfect secretary," she went on, "I have made all the arrangements. I have an automobile waiting at the side entrance. The streets at the back are absolutely empty. Your bag is packed and in the car with mine. We have just twenty minutes to catch the train."

"Where to?" he asked, a little dazed.

"The perfect secretary," she whispered, with a wonderful smile, "knows exactly where to go. A little way beyond Monaco, a little way into the hills, a few yards down a rose-entwined avenue of olives! We have plenty of time, but I think we ought to go!"

Nicholas Imanoff was mounting the steps of the cathedral. The bells, which had ceased for a moment or two, suddenly pealed out in their widest clamour.

"For us," she murmured, her arms stealing out towards him. "Wasn't it wonderful for that to happen just as you are going to kiss me!"

MR. BILLINGHAM, THE
MARQUIS AND MADELON

I

THE BAMBOOZLING OF MR. GASCOIGNE

MR. SAMUEL T. BILLINGHAM of New York, recently landed from the great liner anchored a few miles out, walked along the Terrace at Monte Carlo, serene, light-hearted, beatifically content. His yellow shoes and his variegated socks might be described as a trifle vivid, but the rest of his attire — his well-pressed grey suit, his irreproachable linen, and his well-shaped grey Homburg hat — was beyond criticism. He was a man of medium height, thick-set, inclined a little, perhaps, to *embonpoint*. His complexion was pink, his flaxen hair only slightly streaked with grey, his eyes filled with the light of good-humour. He was possibly about forty-five years of age, but he walked with the spring of a young man. In his pocket was his *carte de saison* for the Cercle Privé and card of membership of the Sporting Club, taken out an hour or so before. In the same pocket was also a well-filled money case, and in his mind the consciousness of pleasant quarters in his favourite hotel, and the knowledge that he was in the spot which he loved more than any place on earth. Furthermore, he was pleasantly aware of the fact that he was in the immediate neighbourhood of various interesting little *rendezvous* where restrictions as to any refreshment he might deem advisable for his welfare were non-existent; where compatriots were always to be found and amusement plentiful. Mr. Samuel T. Billingham, brimming over with good-humour, was certainly an agreeable circumstance in a wonderful setting.

At half-past eleven o'clock — Mr. Billingham was a man of regular habits — he quitted the promenade, crossed the Place in front of the Casino, and selected a table outside the Café de

Paris. He selected it simply because it happened to be the nearest empty one and without even a glance at his neighbours.
It was nevertheless, without a doubt, by the direction of that
mysterious influence called fate that he should have chosen that
particular chair and ordered his champagne cocktail with that
clear and pleasant directness of speech which caused the two
people at the adjacent table to turn and focus their attention
upon him.

"A champagne cocktail," he enjoined confidently, frankly
ignoring the fact that he was addressing a foreigner, "and some
of them little salted nuts — and say, get a move on!"

The waiter hurried off. Mr. Samuel T. Billingham looked
around him genially and met the faintly amused, gently enquir-
ing gaze of his neighbours. Mr. Billingham smiled back again
but at that moment no words were exchanged.

The man and the girl were of ingratiating, even distinguished
appearance. The former seemed to be about fifty or perhaps
fifty-five years of age. He was tall and thin, dressed in dark
clothes from which the first freshness had gone, and though no
fault could have been found with his linen or the less important appurtenances of his toilette, it was noticeable that his shirt
cuffs were a little frayed, his patent boots a little cracked, his
coat a little shiny at the seams. His face was gaunt, his eyes
were deep-set, but his mouth had a most attractive and humor-
ous outline. The girl with whom he was seated and at whom
Mr. Billingham had permitted himself a single glance of admiration, was young enough to be his daughter, but bore him
no resemblance. Her hair was of a most attractive shade of
brown and her eyes were of the very darkest shade of blue. She
seemed pale from the absence of all cosmetics, but her lack of
colour was, as a matter of fact, healthy and natural. There was
something a little insolent about her expression, as though she
were one of those often at war with the world and circumstances, but amongst the cosmopolitan little crowd by which
they were surrounded she preserved an air of distinction which
a keen student of his fellow-creatures, such as Mr. Billingham,
was not slow to recognise. He waited for his cocktail without
impatience and with the air of one entirely satisfied with him-

self and his particular corner of the world. Meanwhile the man and the girl talked — the former in broken English — and, although they never seemed to raise their voices, every word they said was audible to their neighbour.

"It is incredible, Madelon," her companion exclaimed irritably, "that you should have been so careless! Our day is spoilt."

"I am very sorry," she replied humbly. "It is not often I forget such things. As you told me, I put three mille notes in my little sacque early this morning. Then, alas! the sun came out, I wore a different dress, and I brought the other sacque. There it is upon my dressing-table!"

"And here are we," the man grumbled, "without a penny to pay for our *consommation,* to say nothing of luncheon. Furthermore, there are the Rooms and perhaps a fortune waiting. Last night I dreamed of fourteen, three times following."

"It is not so wonderful," she declared a little pettishly. "You always dream of fourteen, but it never arrives."

The champagne cocktail, well frosted and with a thin line of sugar around the rim of the glass, was brought to Mr. Billingham, who accepted it with an air of content. The eyes of the man and the girl rested for a moment upon the glass with a veiled expression of envy. Mr. Billingham lifted his hat and leaned forward.

"Sir," he said, addressing the man, "I am blessed, or should I say cursed, with acute hearing. From what you were saying to the young lady I gather that you have left your money at home."

His neighbour, also with his hat slightly uplifted, listened with an air of grave embarrassment.

"Sir," he rejoined, "I regret that, in some temporary excitement, owing to the discovery of my niece's carelessness, my voice was a little raised. May I venture to suggest, however, that my conversation was not intended to reach the ear of a stranger, nor can I — pardon me — understand what significance it can have for him."

"That's very well put," Mr. Billingham commented approvingly. "I'm rather a plain-spoken man myself, but what I figured out in my own mind was that this being my first morning in

Monte Carlo after an absence of a good many years, and this being my favourite spot upon the earth, and the sun shining and my cocktail looking pretty good, I thought perhaps I might take the liberty of inviting you and the young lady to join me."

The elderly gentleman rose to his feet, hat in hand, and bowed.

"Sir," he said, "we shall accept your courtesy in — may I say — a spirit of reciprocity. Permit me to present my niece, Mademoiselle Madelon de Félan. I myself am known as the Marquis de Félan."

Mr. Billingham rose also to his feet, lifted his hat, fumbled in his pocket and produced a card.

"Samuel T. Billingham is my name, sir," he announced. "I come from New York and I'm interested in linoleum — that is to say, I was, only I've recently sold out. Pleased to meet you both. . . . *Garçon!*"

Their prospective host accepted an invitation to bring his chair to the table of his new acquaintances, and the succeeding half-an-hour passed agreeably enough. Certain orders concerning champagne cocktails were given and repeated whilst the usual amenities of general conversation were exchanged.

"I was thinking of moving on to Ciro's presently," Mr. Billingham announced, glancing at his watch. "We might try one there and, say, why shouldn't you and the young lady join me in a bite of luncheon."

The girl laughed at him pleasantly — and it was a very pleasant laugh indeed.

"I'm so hungry," she murmured.

The Marquis was touched.

"Really, sir," he said, "your kindness is astounding. We will join you on the distinct understanding that we are allowed within the course of the next few days to reciprocate your hospitality."

"Good enough!" Mr. Billingham assented. "That goes, then! We'll move on as soon as the *garçon* has brought me my change. Now promise you won't go back on our luncheon engagement, whatever happens."

"Not a chance," the girl assured him, with that twinkle in her eyes which Mr. Billingham was already beginning to love. "I'm far too hungry, and Ciro's is my favourite restaurant."

"Very well, then," Mr. Billingham concluded, drawing his chair up a little closer. "So long as it's understood that you don't take offence, I just want to ask you one thing. Do I look such an almighty hayseed that you should pick me out to try that old wheeze on?"

There was a moment's silence. The orchestra rattled on, corks still popped, a pleasant murmur of conversation swelled and flowed around. The man and the girl, however, remained speechless. The latter had lost that smile of pleasant anticipation; her face was suddenly a little drawn and troubled. The man seemed older. His manner, however, preserved its dignity.

"Sir," he began——

"Cut it out," Mr. Billingham begged. "I know pretty well what I look like, but you see it's my job to look like it. Any one would think I was what I want them to think me — an American traveller, over here, probably for the first time in his life, with plenty of the stuff. Well, I ain't! I'm from the United States all right, but I'm looking after a little bit of that stuff myself. Perhaps that's why I sized you two up so easily."

The Marquis half rose to his feet. Mr. Billingham pulled him back into his chair.

"Look here," he insisted genially, "cut out the starch. I'm a bit of a crook — I'll admit that — but I'm not a bad sort and I've taken a fancy to you two. We're going on to Ciro's and we're going to have that little lunch together. I can pay for it all right, and dinner afterwards, most likely. No reason why we shouldn't have a pleasant day together. We might even get to talking business."

The Marquis coughed. He was beginning to recover himself.

"We will certainly accompany you to Ciro's — er — Mr. Billingham," he assented. "In the meantime tell me, I beg of you, why you arrived at the conclusion that my niece and I were — er —— ?"

"I figured it out this way," Mr. Billingham interrupted. "You

are both French. What did you want to talk in English for
except that you wanted me to understand? That was enough
for me to be going on with!"

"Our story is a sad one," the Marquis commenced.

"Say, we'll have that after luncheon," Mr. Billingham suggested, rising to his feet. . . .

The cocktails at Ciro's were equal to Mr. Billingham's anticipations, and the luncheon which he presently ordered was
entirely satisfactory. Conversation, so far as his two guests were
concerned, was a little stilted and diffident. Their host, however, was absolutely at his ease.

"I guess you wouldn't believe it, you two," he recounted, as
they attacked a wonderful selection of *hors d'œuvres,* "but I
was once a rich man, and I never got such fun out of life in
those days as I am helping myself to now. I figure it out like
this. When you've got your money in the Bank, and the bits
coming in, you're kind of tied up with respectability. Now,
since I was a lad I've always been for adventures, and there's
only one sort of adventure that counts, and that is the adventure which sets your brain against another man's and brings
you in the stuff if you come out on top. It don't seem to me
that a rich man has got any fighting outlook on life. . . . Do
you get me, Miss de Félan?"

"I understand what you mean?" she replied, a little dubi-
ously, "but I am afraid I do not agree with you. You see, I have
always been poor, and I hate poverty."

"Might be kind of different for a young woman," Mr. Billingham conceded thoughtfully, "but for a man, to go about the
world doing no one any particular harm but living by his wits
and what he can make by being a trifle smarter than other
people, that's my idea of a happy time! I don't mind telling you
that my present job over here is to swindle a man out of half
a million dollars."

"Half a million dollars!" the Marquis gasped. "It is incredible!"

"What an imagination!" the girl sighed. "What courage!"

"I guess I'm not out for pinching old ladies' reticules," their
host confided. "I like a big deal. And," he went on, leaning a

little across the table, "if I can make up my mind that you two are to be trusted—I'm not saying I mightn't let you in on this little affair. I need just the sort of help you might be able to give, and that's a fact!"

The Marquis concealed his impatience with all the restraint which was doubtless an inheritance of his breeding. He polished a worn and scratched horn-rimmed eyeglass with a clean but frayed handkerchief and prepared to listen with tolerant partiality. The girl, however, was frankly eager. She leaned across towards her host, her elbows upon the table, her chin supported by her two hands. There was a light in her very beautiful eyes which was almost adoring.

"Tell us about it, Mr. Billingham," she begged. "We are so very poor and I am tired of being poor."

"My niece has the natural desire of the young for luxuries," the Marquis observed. "Frankly, I have outlived the necessity for wealth. My modest *déjeuner* here or at the Hôtel de Paris, my dinner, my bottle of Burgundy, my choice of brandies, *carte blanche* at my tailors, a mille or two to play with when the fancy seizes me, are all I wish for."

"You don't aim at putting together a pile for later on in life?" Mr. Billingham queried.

The Marquis sighed.

"That is beyond my hopes," he admitted.

"And you, Mademoiselle?"

The girl was terribly in earnest.

"If I had the chance," she said, "I would save. I love all the things which go to making life here so delightful, but more than anything else on earth I should love my independence. I should love to feel that it was no longer necessary for me to worry to-morrow as to how I was going to pay the next day's bills."

"Good spirit!" Mr. Billingham approved. "Good spirit, that!"

"Madelon is more practical than I," the Marquis sighed. "And now concerning that little affair of business, Mr. Billingham, you were about to place before us."

Mr. Billingham's attention, however, had wandered. He was watching the approach of an obvious compatriot—a man the very antithesis of himself, but with equally distinct transatlantic attributes; a small man with a sallow face and little hair, teeth stopped plentifully with gold, a wizened expression about the mouth, a short-sighted squint, neat clothes and square-toed shoes. Mr. Billingham welcomed him as a long-lost brother.

"Say, if this isn't Joe Gascoigne!" he exclaimed. "Well, well, when did you come along?"

Mr. Gascoigne's reciprocating smile was frosty. His manner showed him to be a man of reserves.

"Paris, last night," he answered. "How's oil?"

Mr. Billingham shook his head gloomily.

"Can't say those new lands are panning out quite as we expected," he admitted.

"No gushers?" Mr. Gascoigne enquired.

"Nothing of that sort reported up to the present," was the cautious but somewhat depressed reply. "Still, one never knows. Where there's oil there's hope! Where are you staying?"

"Hôtel de Paris."

"Fine!" Mr. Billingham commented. "Sold your option yet, Joe?"

"I guess I didn't come to Monte Carlo to talk business," the other rejoined, as he turned to pass on his way down the room.

Mr. Billingham was thoughtful for a moment or two after his friend's departure. The fact, however, did not impair his appetite.

"Why did you not present your friend?" the girl enquired. "I thought Americans always introduced everybody."

Mr. Billingham smiled.

"That," he explained, "is the man whom we are going to rob. In case you come into the game, I didn't ask you to shake hands with him. He's as near-sighted as a clam and too vain to wear spectacles."

"He is presumably wealthy," the Marquis ventured.

"He is of the genus known as 'millionaire,'" Mr. Billingham acquiesced.

The Marquis nodded approvingly.

"To rob the rich," he murmured, "is a reasonable hobby."

"When you add to that," Mr. Billingham continued, "that Joe Gascoigne is the doggonest, meanest cuss that ever drank water and preached prohibition, you've got him sized up about right."

"To rob such a man," the Marquis suggested hopefully — "or shall I say to assist in the redistribution of his wealth — would seem to be a charity. Five hundred thousand dollars, I think you said, sir?"

"Maybe more," Mr. Billingham assented. "It's like enough I'll take you two in, but we'll quit it now until later on. I've got to size you up a bit more first. . . . Some salmon, this!" he added, almost reverently, as he laid down his fork. "The sauce tastes good to me, too!"

"Loire salmon," the Marquis confided. "Very good fish, but short season."

"Supposing you get on with that sad story of yours, Marquis," Mr. Billingham proposed, as they waited for the next course. "I don't say as I'm going to believe every word of it, mind you, but I'd like to hear your own account of yourself and the young lady."

The Marquis was a little stiff at first, but he gradually warmed to his task. He came, it appeared, of a noble but impoverished family, and his various attempts at earning an honest living had met with a singular lack of success. He had been, in turn, a vineyard proprietor, a vendor of wines, an insurance agent, and had interested himself in a cigarette business. In all of these undertakings he had suffered from lack of capital. A year ago the daughter of his only brother, who had married an Englishwoman, was left with practically no one else to look after her. They had lived in Paris for some short time upon the very trifling sum of money which she had brought with her. A small investment in a lottery business had been a failure. Behold them at Monte Carlo, practically destitute! It was becoming indeed a question of money sufficient for a meal between them. Mademoiselle Madelon ·was ready to give French lessons, and she had some knowledge of typing. The Marquis had even gone so far as to offer himself as a sort of super-guide to strangers of wealth to whom the best restaurants and manifold pleasures of the place were unknown.

"Ever any trouble with the police?" Mr. Billingham asked.

"Not in these parts," the Marquis hastened to explain. There had been some slight misunderstanding in Paris, he added, with reference to his mismanagement of a gambling club, and the investigation into his lottery business had made a hurried departure from the city advisable. Here, however, they had a clean sheet; had modest rooms at an unpretentious hotel, and so far had paid their way.

"I sized you both up as being amateurs in this crook business," Mr. Billingham observed. "You may make good at it, of course, but I am not so sure about the young lady — kind of dangerous, with her appearance!"

"Sir," the Marquis replied, "I am a man of honour, but frankly I think that my niece should make more use of her undoubted attractions. She receives many invitations to lunch or dine with acquaintances, all of which she refuses. I think that she is wrong."

Madelon remained undisturbed. The frank admiration with which her host was contemplating her brought only a slight tinge of colour into her cheeks.

"My uncle thinks always," she explained, "of some millionaire or nobleman who will invite me to lunch and find me so charming that he will propose marriage to me. Our acquaintances, unfortunately, are of the bar or the Casino, and I do not fancy that they are quite of the class likely to propose marriage to an honest but impecunious young woman."

"One never knows," the Marquis grumbled. "This is the land of chance, and in case of trouble you have always me to protect you."

Madelon preserved a tactful silence and the luncheon drew on to its close. After he had paid the bill, Mr. Billingham produced five hundred-franc notes.

"What about dining with me to-night?" he enquired.

"Two goods meals in one day!" the girl exclaimed blissfully.

"We shall be charmed," the Marquis assented, with a courteous wave of the hand.

"I have only one evening dress," the girl observed thoughtfully.

"One will be all you need," was her prospective host's cheerful rejoinder. "I'll get a corner table in the Sporting Club. And if I can see my way to letting you in on this little job of mine I'll tell you about it. In the meantime if five hundred francs——"

"As a loan, my dear sir—a loan!" the Marquis interrupted, stretching out his hand eagerly.

"Precisely," Mr. Billingham agreed. "Three for you, sir, and two for the young lady."

The Marquis clutched his three without hesitation; Madelon made no movement.

"I do not think that we ought to take this money until we are sure that there is something we can do to earn it," she said, looking at Mr. Billingham with doubt in her beautiful eyes.

"It is for—how you say it?—a lien upon our services," her uncle declared, thrusting the notes deep down into his pocket. "We are now at Mr. Billingham's commands. You look at the affair in that light, I am sure, my dear sir."

Mr. Billingham lit a cigar and smiled.

"I guess that's the idea, sir," he acquiesced. "Don't let me keep you. I see you are kind of fidgety to be off."

The Marquis rose to his feet; Madelon laid her hand upon his arm.

"Not to the Rooms just yet," she begged.

"My dear," he replied tolerantly, "have no fear. I shall play carefully; start with the little gold pieces, force my luck as I win. Later on I will show you something!"

"Meanwhile," Mr. Billingham reminded them, as he took leave of his guests, "at eight-thirty at the Sporting Club."

Perhaps because of the smallness of the room and the absence of any orchestral music, the babel of conversation at the Sporting Club was that night almost deafening. Under its cover Mr. Samuel T. Billingham took his two guests into his confidence.

"It ain't worth while," he began, leaning forward so that the three heads nearly touched, "to try and put you wise to all the details but, as a business proposition, this is how the matter stands. That swab of a fellow, Joseph Gascoigne, whom you saw at luncheon time, has got an option on ten thousand shares in an oil tract out in Arkansas — the 'Great Divide,' they call it. He lent 'em some money for a new plant a year ago and insisted on the option in return. The option's up on Saturday. Last month they struck oil in eleven different places. Luckily the boss of the company was down there and he had all work stopped at once. It's a big find, though, and if Joe Gascoigne gets to hear of it and exercises the option, it means that he'll buy ten thousand shares at a hundred dollars that are certainly worth a thousand dollars and maybe worth twice as much."

"What happens to the shares if Mr. Gascoigne does not exercise his option?" the girl asked.

Mr. Billingham looked at her with a smile of admiration.

"A cute question," he admitted. "Those shares are divided equally amongst the five directors — or, rather, they are allowed to buy them at a low price. Now, I'm well in with the boss of this company and he knows I don't mind a bit of crooked work occasionally. If I, or we, can stop Joe Gascoigne cabling to America before Saturday and taking up his option, there's fifteen thousand dollars coming to me."

"Fifteen thousand dollars!" the girl murmured.

The Marquis rolled his eyes in silent ecstasy.

"An affair of two hundred thousand francs!" he gasped.

"What makes me look for a trifle of help in the matter," Mr. Billingham continued, "is that Joe is kind of wise to my being in with the crowd, and if he sees too much of me he'll be suspicious."

"You have some sort of a plan?" Madelon demanded abruptly.

"I'd like his code," Mr. Billingham confided. "It's the simplest affair — two typewritten pages inside blue cardboard covers with just paper fasteners through. There ain't more than twenty or thirty sentences there, and the only other man who has a copy is his partner in New York. I know he means to sit tight until the last moment, and I know he's moving heaven and earth to discover whether there's any truth in the rumours of a gush, or whether it's a rig to make him buy the shares. He's getting cables most days, and he won't send his off until Friday. I had a man on the boat," Mr. Billingham went on reflectively, "who could have had the code in a minute, but Joe was too artful for him. He handed it over to the purser with his valuables directly he boarded the steamer. In Paris he changed his hotel, so we didn't get a show there. That didn't worry me any, though, for I knew he was coming here. He's in room number 246, Hôtel de Paris, and he uses the code book every day. What I want is to get hold of the book for an hour without his knowing, and then replace it."

"You don't want the book destroyed, then?" Madelon enquired.

"Not on your life," was the prompt response. "Joe would tumble to it right away that there was something doing, and he'd cable out directly for the shares."

"It is a deeficult matter," the Marquis mused.

The girl said nothing. She was looking down at her plate with a thoughtful smile upon her lips. Mr. Billingham watched her. He had noticed that smile once before during the last few minutes.

"You have an idea, Mademoiselle?" he ventured.

She nodded.

"This morning," she confided, "I went to a bureau here to try to find a post as lady's companion or secretary. There was nothing of the sort to be had. The only vacancies were for chambermaids at the Hôtel de Paris."

The Marquis burst into excited and fluent French. Madelon stopped him with a superb little gesture.

"You have perhaps made a fortune this afternoon with the money lent you by monsieur?" she demanded.

Her uncle's excitement subsided. He sighed mournfully.

"I chose the wrong tables," he confessed. "My numbers were everywhere, all around me, save at the tables where I played."

"That means," the girl pointed out, "that you have lost everything. We have no money, we cannot pay monsieur what he has advanced us. I find that situation more humiliating than to figure as a chambermaid for a week at the Hôtel de Paris."

"It's an idea," Mr. Billingham admitted, "but the Hôtel is a big place. How do you know, supposing they take you on, that you will be anywhere near Joe Gascoigne's rooms?"

"I have spoken several times to the housekeeper," Madelon explained. "I may be able to arrange it. It seems to me worth trying. I can think of nothing else."

"To-day is Monday," Mr. Billingham reflected. "We have until Friday at least. Joe has promised to cable on Friday. He'll wait until then for the latest information. What I'd like to see you do, Mademoiselle, is to go back to your rooms, change that very becoming frock, put on your old clothes, and try and land the job at the Hôtel de Paris. There's no sense in wasting time."

"Supposing I get the book, what do I do with it?" Madelon enquired.

"You will bring it right to me in room number 114 of the same hotel," Mr. Billingham replied. "You will let me have it for about half an hour. Then you'll fetch it away again and try to leave it where you found it."

The Marquis sighed.

"I much regret the fact," he said, "that my niece is subjecting herself to indignity and perhaps trouble in this affair. I wish very much that it were possible for me to take a more active share in the business."

"You may do your bit yet," Mr. Billingham promised him, dryly. "Now, say, how much have you left of that five hundred francs?"

"Not a centime," was the dismal reply. "My niece, however——"

"I have a hundred francs," the young lady interrupted, "and I am sorry, Uncle, but I mean to keep it. I cannot go to this place penniless."

"Of course not," Mr. Billingham agreed, drawing out his pocket-book and extracting from it a five-hundred-franc note. "You can have that for your evening's amusement, Marquis, on account of what may be coming to you when we succeed. When you have lost that, however, nothing doing! Remember that!"

The Marquis' smile was one of superb confidence. The note was already buttoned up in his pocket.

"I shall win!" he declared.

Mr. Joseph Gascoigne, although not in the strict sense of the word a susceptible man, was not wholly insensible to feminine attractions. Seated at his desk with a pile of cable forms before him and an open manuscript code book on his left-hand side, he heard the soft ingress of his very attractive-looking chambermaid into the bathroom. He laid down his pen and listened. It was she beyond a doubt. It was an occasion to progress a little in the flirtation which he had already essayed. He crossed the room.

"Hullo! Late this morning, aren't you?" he remarked, looking into the bathroom.

Madelon glanced at him from behind a barricade of towels.

"There is so much to do," she complained. "One fatigues oneself here terribly."

Mr. Gascoigne smiled palely. It was an opening.

"The work is too hard for you," he declared. "How would you like to leave it and let me find you something easier?"

"Ah, Monsieur!" she sighed.

He advanced a little nearer.

"I've had my eye on you all this week," he confided. "You're too good for this job. Give 'em notice. Leave right away. Say where you live and I'll come round this afternoon, and I bet you we fix up something a good deal better than this."

Madelon was half-distressed, half-overcome by some sort of emotion. Mr. Gascoigne smiled and drew out his pocket-book.

"Say, do you know what this is?" he asked. "Guess you don't come across many of them. It's a mille note! Put it in your pocket, drop those towels, give me a kiss, and go and tell the housekeeper you've found a better job."

Madelon gazed at the mille note ecstatically.

"But Monsieur is generous!" she exclaimed.

Monsieur's telephone-bell rang. He turned away with annoyance.

"Wait one second," he begged. "I'll be right back. . . . Well, what's the matter?" he demanded down the telephone.

It was the hotel clerk who spoke. A gentleman was below begging that Mr. Gascoigne would spare him five minutes on a matter of urgent importance. The gentleman declined to

mount. He would only say that his business had some connection with America.

"I'll be right down," Mr. Gascoigne announced, and hastened
back to where Madelon was still engaged with the towels.

"Say, you're not in a hurry, are you?" he enquired.

"I do what you tell me," she assured him, clutching the mille
note tightly in her fingers and smiling at him bewitchingly.
"I go home now — 15, Avenue de Mimosas. I wait until you
come."

Mr. Gascoigne hesitated. Madelon was looking very attractive,
but the door was open and the visit of the gentleman downstairs intrigued him. He patted her on the shoulder.

"I'll be round directly after lunch," he promised. "We'll fix
up something right away. . . ."

In the hall the hotel clerk directed his attention to the Marquis,
who, with sundry of the slightly shabby details of his toilet
now amended, presented an impressive appearance. His manner,
however, as he stepped forward to accost Mr. Gascoigne, was
a little furtive. He had the air of not being entirely at his ease.

"Mr. Gascoigne, I believe," he murmured.

"That's my name," was the somewhat surprised admission.
"What can I do for you?"

"I am the Marquis de Félan," the visitor announced. "I desire
a few minutes' conversation with you — not here, if possible.
Will you step across with me to the Café de Paris?"

"But I don't know you," Mr. Gascoigne objected. "What
business can you have with me?"

"Business of little importance to myself, perhaps," was the
guarded reply, "but of the utmost importance to you. I can put
you in possession of information with regard to some business
which you propose to transact to-day or to-morrow — very important information."

A light began to break in upon Mr. Gascoigne.

"Say, didn't I see you lunching with that fellow Billingham?"
he demanded.

"You did," the Marquis acknowledged. "It is in connection
with something which transpired at that luncheon —— "

"I'll come right along with you," Mr. Gascoigne interrupted.

"I've got a hat in the cloak-room here. One moment! . . ."

The two men left the place together, the Marquis still with the air of one desiring to escape observation. He glanced to the right and to the left in constant disquietude. At the Café de Paris he led the way to a corner of the bar. Then he sat down with an air of relief.

"Now let's get to business," Mr. Gascoigne begged.

The Marquis glanced towards the bartender. His companion accepted the hint and ordered refreshments.

"My business," the Marquis commenced, "is that I have been insulted by a person who is, I believe, a fellow-countryman of yours."

"Samuel Billingham?" Mr. Gascoigne muttered.

"That is his name," the Marquis admitted. "You will understand, sir, that I am not a man of wealth, that I am indeed a very poor man. Under circumstances which I need not detail, I invited Mr. Billingham to oblige me with a small loan — no more than ten milles. It is there that he insults me."

"Wouldn't part, eh?" Mr. Gascoigne queried.

"On the contrary," the Marquis rejoined, "he offered to increase the amount, but on a condition so loathsome that to mention it gives me pain. He wished me to join in a plot to deceive you concerning the value of some shares in Arkansas."

"The devil he did!" the other exclaimed. "Say, this is interesting!"

"To me it was a situation most humiliating," the Marquis declared. "Tears were in my eyes as I listened to his infamous proposition. I made no promise. I left him. He confided in me the value of those shares and all about them. I say nothing. I make him no promise. He tempted me with the money. It is a terrible thing, Mr. Gascoigne, to be poor. Then I asked myself what an honourable man would do. I decided to come to you."

"How much did you say that loan was to be?" Mr. Gascoigne enquired.

"Ten milles — a paltry ten milles," the Marquis groaned.

Mr. Gascoigne was not a man who loved parting with money, but there were times when he was prompt in action. He opened his pocket-book, counted out ten milles, and folded them up.

"Look here, Marquis," he said, "I'll be on the square with you. Tell me just what Samuel Billingham said about those shares and you can accept the loan from me instead of from him — accept it, too, with nothing on your conscience."

The Marquis finished a cocktail and made signs towards the bar.

"I will disclose the situation to you," he promised. "It gives me pain, but it is just retribution. One month ago, oil — how you say that? — gushed — from eleven wells on this property. The chairman of the company was there. He ordered everything concealed. No one was to work, the secret was to be kept until after Monday. I know why — Mr. Billingham told me why. It is because you have the right to buy most of these shares at a low price."

Joseph Gascoigne leaned back in his chair. He thrust both hands into his trousers pockets, turned over his keys, and chuckled. He remained chuckling until the waiter directed his attention to the cocktails which he was serving.

"Say, this is great!" he declared, as he banished the man with a twenty-franc note. "I don't mind telling you, Marquis, that I couldn't get any definite information, but I had a sort of a feeling there was something doing down there. So old Samuel was going to do me out of my little deal, eh? Do you know what I shall do, Marquis?"

The latter shook his head politely.

"I shall go right back to my sitting-room," Mr. Gascoigne continued, "and send that cable straight away. I shall take the whole of the ten thousand shares. I'll risk your information being O.K. I believe in it anyway. Stick that ten milles in your pocket-book, Marquis, and if this comes off there will be another ten milles on the top of it, and you can pay me in the year two thousand."

The Marquis buttoned up the money; his expression was one of chastened content.

"It will remain for long on my conscience," he confided, "but I have felt it right to adopt this course. I regret it — I regret the disappointment to Mr. Billingham very much. Still, he should have known better than to have made suggestions to me of so infamous a nature."

Mr. Gascoigne sipped his second cocktail — an indulgence which he seldom permitted himself — and the world seemed a very pleasant place to him. He leaned still farther back in his chair and listened to the music, and he thought of that other very pleasing little adventure soon to be prosecuted. It was quite some time before he and the Marquis parted; the Marquis on his way to the Casino, Mr. Gascoigne to his sitting-room. Arrived there, he found everything as he had left it, but there was a little note addressed to him. He tore it open.

Would monsieur kindly come to 15, Avenue de Mimosas, on Monday — not before. My aunt is there. She leaves midday Monday and I shall be alone.

Thanking monsieur for his generosity and anticipating,

MADELON.

Mr. Gascoigne's first impulse of disappointment hastily passed. After all, it was not long to wait. He drew the code book towards him, ran his finger down the first page, and selected a phrase.

HUNGERING. . . . Have decided to avail myself of option in Great Divide shares. Secure the whole ten thousand on my account.

Mr. Gascoigne smiled. He wrote the word "Hungering" upon the cable form and took it himself to the office.

"What a dinner!" exclaimed François, the chief *maître d'hôtel* at the restaurant of the Sporting Club.

"What a prince!" murmured his assistant, glancing at the hundred-franc note in his hand.

There was a great cluster of red roses in the centre of the table; a magnum of Cliquot in an ice-pail by its side; an amazing menu on each of the three plates. Behind the screen an emissary from the bar waited with a cocktail shaker in his hand, ready to rush out at the psychological moment. There was caviar in ice, *langouste* from the Mediterranean, pheasants which had known no cold storage, a *vol au vent* of which the *chef* had spoken with tears in his eyes. Nevertheless, the Marquis and Madelon entered the room a little anxiously. One glance, however, at their host's face and all was well. Mr. Samuel T. Billingham was very happy, and when he was happy he showed it.

"Mademoiselle, no guest so charming has ever graced my table," he murmured, as he bent over her hand. "If dresses like this are to be bought ready to wear in Monte Carlo it is indeed an amazing place. Marquis, success! The time has passed. I have my cable. To the surprise of many people in New York, Mr. Joseph Gascoigne cabled his decision not to exercise his option on those ten thousand shares."

"You relieve my mind greatly," the Marquis confessed. "I was afraid of some slip at the last moment."

They took their places. The details of the repast unfolded themselves. The Marquis and his niece exchanged ecstatic glances. Madelon, also, in her way — like most well-brought-up young women — approved of good food and the best wine.

"It is a feast of celebration, this," Mr. Billingham declared, scarcely able to take his eyes off his beautiful guest. "We have achieved a veritable triumph. We have perpetrated a swindle for which the law cannot touch us. We have robbed a miserable, mean, miserly old skunk of what I think in the end may turn out to be the best part of a million dollars. Let us see how we stand."

The Marquis' fingers shook as he lit a cigarette and sipped his wine.

"Your *douceurs,* up to the present," this prince of adventurers continued, "are insignificant. The few francs I have advanced we will forget."

"There was my tip as chambermaid," Madelon murmured. "He gave me a mille note."

"A stingy business!" was her host's criticism. "We take no account of that either."

"I did a little better," the Marquis confessed. "I got ten milles for betraying your secret and informing him of the worth of his option."

Mr. Billingham waved his hand.

"You introduced a note of humour into the situation, Marquis," he declared. "It was a brain-wave, that! That ten milles, also, we ignore. You are welcome to it. The *douceur* which I receive is fifteen thousand dollars. I myself will retain five thousand, there will be five thousand for you, Mademoiselle, and five thousand for you, Marquis."

"It is princely!" Madelon gasped.

"It is seventy-five thousand francs," the Marquis faltered.

"It is some money," Mr. Billingham admitted, "but I tell you right here that without mademoiselle I might have found great difficulty in getting hold of the code. Of course, all that I did was to alter the terms. You, Marquis, kept Mr. Gascoigne engaged at the Café de Paris whilst I worked hard with my typewriter. I can say no more than that I consider myself highly fortunate to have come across two assistants of such intelligence and," Mr. Billingham concluded, with a sigh, "such charm."

"You are what we used to call in England 'a great dear,'" Madelon whispered. "I hope before long you will find something else for us to do."

"Sure," Mr. Billingham assented fervently. "Five thousand dollars is a pretty good sum, but it don't carry a man very far in Monte Carlo, and apart from the money there's the adventure. I don't look the part, but I guess I was born to be a pirate. I'm all for taking chances, for looking out for some skunk or another who's got more of the stuff than is good for him. I guess something else ought to turn up before very long."

"And meanwhile," the Marquis suggested, watching the refilling of his glass, "I think that we should drink a toast to our very dear friend who must now be in great distress of mind."

"Poor old Joe!" Mr. Billingham murmured, as he raised his glass.

The first glimmering of uneasiness came to Mr. Joseph Gascoigne when he demanded a *petite voiture* and asked to be driven to 15, Avenue de Mimosas. The driver looked blank, and appealed to the concierge, who shook his head.

"*Je ne le connais pas,*" the driver declared.

"*Ni moi non plus,*" the concierge echoed.

"What do you mean? What's the trouble?" Mr. Gascoigne demanded.

"There is no such street, sir," the concierge announced. "I have lived in Monte Carlo for many years and I can assure you that there is no such place as the Avenue de Mimosas."

Mr. Gascoigne hesitated for a moment, bestowed an inadequate *pourboire* upon the coachman, and stepped back into the hotel. Was it possible that the girl was fooling him — had taken his mille and gone off? He ascended to his room and made cautious enquiries of the valet. Yes, the young woman had left unexpectedly. She had made no complaint but simply stated that she could not continue the work. As for her address, she had given none. The valet was quite sure that there was no such street as the Avenue de Mimosas in Monte Carlo. . . .

Mr. Gascoigne opened a cable, brought in at that moment, with eager fingers. As he read it his face grew first bewildered, then white and evil.

Am astonished that you have decided not to exercise option but have acted according to your instructions. Venture assure you that you have made great mistake.

Mr. Gascoigne almost snatched at his manuscript code book, and tore open the pages. There it was, without a doubt:

HUNGERING. . . . Have decided to avail myself of option in Great Divide shares. Secure the whole ten thousand on my account.

He sat down at once and wrote a cable:

What the hell do you mean? Cabled HUNGERING. Word for word translation, "Have decided to avail myself of option in Great Divide shares. Secure the whole ten thousand on my account." Reply.

It was about twelve o'clock next morning when the reply came. It was given to him just as he was leaving the Hôtel de Paris for a restless stroll along the Terrace. He tore it open and read:

Exact translation HUNGERING, attested here by whole office. "Have decided not to exercise option on shares in Great Divide. Please inform Company."

Mr. Gascoigne clutched the cablegram in his fingers. He looked across the Square with vacant eyes. Such a mistake in transcription seemed incredible. And then there turned the corner Mr. Samuel T. Billingham, resplendent in a suit of light grey, with a carnation in his buttonhole, and a cigar in his mouth. On one side walked the Marquis, looking very spruce and smiling, and on the other, very becomingly dressed, and not in the least like a chambermaid, was Madelon. Suddenly something in one of her graceful movements, or perhaps the ripple of her laughter, was startlingly reminiscent of Mr. Gascoigne's disappointed hopes. A hideous clear-sightedness seized him. He remembered the manuscript code book open upon his table, his absence for the best part of an hour with the Marquis, some slight surprise at the freshness of the type the next time he had consulted the code book, and finally Mr. Samuel T. Billingham's connection with the Great Divide Oil Company and his reputation. They passed him; Mr. Billingham with a little wave of the hand and a solemn wink, Madelon with a frank laugh into his face, and the Marquis with a patronising nod. He looked after them and he shook his fist. He was cold with fury, but with a mighty effort at self-restraint he remained silent.

For, although it was very certain he had been robbed, there was really nothing he could do!

II

THE NUMBERS OF DEATH

WHEN the mists roll down from La Turbie and the grey clouds hug the sides of the mountains, Monte Carlo is very far from being itself. The red-coated members of the orchestra at the Café de Paris move inside the building, the waiters stand like wraiths amidst a deserted wilderness of tables. Even a winner leaving the Casino — most easily recognisable of all human beings — forbears to whistle as he descends the steps. But when the sun shines down from a cloudless sky of perfect blue, and the women have trooped out like butterflies to drink *apéritifs* under the umbrella-sheltered tables, and the orchestra is playing an Italian love song, and there is a lively murmur of conversation, and the chink of ice against the glass, all is well with life, and Monte Carlo is a very different place.

Mr. Samuel T. Billingham, with Madelon de Félan for his companion and a pleasantly clouded wineglass on the table by his side, submitted cheerfully to the relaxing influence of his surroundings. He even viewed the approach of the Marquis, Madelon's uncle, with toleration, if not without some apprehension.

"I can't say that I like that fixed smile on your uncle's face," he remarked.

She watched her troublesome relation critically, and sighed.

"Jaunty, too," she murmured — "always a bad sign."

The Marquis came up with a wave of his hat. Mr. Billingham made signs to a waiter.

"Just one cocktail, perhaps," the newcomer conceded, "although it is a little early for me. . . . I foolishly came out this morning with almost empty pockets. Have you such a thing as a mille, Madelon?"

She laughed scornfully.

"Am I the sort of girl," she asked, "who goes about with milles in her pocket? I have no money at all with me."

"Perhaps Mr. Billingham," the Marquis proposed tentatively.

Mr. Billingham considered the matter.

"How much have you lost this morning?" he enquired.

The Marquis coughed.

"Very little," he declared, straightening his tie. "I brought very little with me. My numbers are turning up, though. I have fixed upon a table where my luck seems to have definitely established itself."

Mr. Billingham withdrew a five-hundred-franc note from his pocket-book and handed it to the Marquis, who departed hastily, after gulping down his refreshment.

"Seems to me that game's got quite a hold upon your uncle," his benefactor observed thoughtfully.

"It is the one curse of the place for us," Madelon assented, with a sigh. "It keeps us always poor. If he cannot go to the Casino he is miserable — like a child in trouble or disgrace. If he goes, he loses. It is always the same. If we had not met you a month ago I cannot imagine what would have become of us."

It was not often that Mr. Billingham's attention wandered when Madelon was speaking, but at this moment he certainly had a lapse. His eyes were fixed upon an approaching figure — a man, tall and thin, with a long, hatchet-shaped face, a terrible mouth, and deep-set eyes. He was dressed with unusual sombreness, in clothes of a transatlantic cut, surmounted by a black Homburg, and he walked towards the outskirts of the scattered company, looking neither to the right nor to the left. Mr. Billingham half-rose to his feet.

"Hullo, Ned!" he exclaimed in welcoming fashion.

The behaviour of this presumed acquaintance of his was, to say the least of it, singular. He scarcely even glanced at Mr. Billingham, whose hand was already outstretched, and passed on, ignoring his greeting. His right hand was in his jacket pocket, and Mr. Billingham, who had formed the habit of quick observation, saw something menacing in the fact.

"Who is your friend who doesn't know you?" Madelon enquired.

Mr. Billingham, recovered from his first surprise, was deeply interested.

"That's Ned Gunby, the biggest man they've got in the New York police," he confided. "I've never known him abroad before. I'd like some to know who he's after!"

"I should be sorry to be that person," Madelon confessed, with a little shiver. "I think he is an awful man."

"Ned hands out the goods all right," Mr. Billingham affirmed. "They say that from the start he has arrested more dangerous criminals than any man in the police force."

"He seems to be very much in earnest about something just now," Madelon observed.

They both watched his progress with riveted attention, whilst he threaded his way through the maze of tables. At the farthest table, close to a shed in which was displayed an automobile for which lottery tickets were being sold, a man was seated alone, leaning back in his chair and with his face half concealed by a newspaper which he was reading. He showed no signs of being aware of the detective's approach, and even Mr. Billingham failed to catch that surreptitious movement of the paper and stealthy glance. What followed was a matter of seconds. The detective, with his hand half-drawn from his jacket pocket, had reached his destination.

"Jim Robin," he said, in a harsh, unpleasant voice, "throw 'em up! Quick as hell! I want you!"

The answer was a tiny flash of fire, a sharp report and an empty seat. Ned Gunby, for once in his life late in the draw, spun round like a teetotum and collapsed against the table. For a single second conversation all around was entirely suspended. There was a tense stillness, with only the music as a background. Then there was a rush from all quarters. A gendarme from across the road was actually betrayed into running. A few women screamed. Every one asked breathlessly what had happened. Mr. Billingham shook his head as he leaned over the body of his acquaintance

"He's sure got his," he decided. . . .

The authorities at Monte Carlo are adepts at wiping from the face of the earth all traces of tragical events. In a few moments the body of the wounded man was whisked away in a closed motorcar. A functionary in plain clothes, who seemed to have arrived by magic, patiently interviewed the few spectators, with indifferent results. No one appeared to have seen the fugitive distinctly. He had, without a doubt, escaped by passing behind the shed where the car was exhibited and mingling with the crowd of people entering the Casino, but, although several had seen him disappear, there was not a single credible item of information as to his later movements. The hand of justice was temporarily, at any rate, baulked.

Late that afternoon, Mr. Billingham, in response to an urgent message, was driven to the little whitewashed hospital on the slopes of the hill and listened to the last words of a dying man. The bullet had found its way into the detective's lungs and speech was difficult. Nevertheless, he said what he had to say.

"Reckon I'm too old for the job, Mr. Billingham," he confessed, "but I'll hand it to him that it was the quickest draw I ever saw."

"It was that, Ned," was his visitor's sympathetic assent. "You don't want to talk too much. Tell me who he was, what you wanted him for, and what I can do for you."

"That was James Robin, who murdered Hammon, the banker, last year — got him fixed on that Bundell poisoning case, too," the detective announced. "I've got all the papers on the table there — the extradition warrant, and there's this," the suffering man added, lifting his badge from under his pillow and passing it across. "You've puzzled me more than once, Billingham, but if you're a crook you're a straight one. Take this on for me. James Robin ain't got no right to live. He's a white-livered skunk. Gave his own pals away in the Bennett case, or he'd have been sent to the penitentiary then."

"I guess that's so," the other acquiesced. "I remember the whole affair. Anything you know likely to help about his movements here?"

"He's been going by the name of Braund — James Braund,"

the detective confided. "There's a woman with him — picked her up on this side, I reckon. They had rooms at the Boston Hotel, up at the back. The police here are watching it, but I've told them you're in the force and will take over. Shake hands, Billingham. Glad to have an American round, anyway."

The two men shook hands solemnly, and the nurse, who saw the things which Ned Gunby felt, hurried up. Mr. Billingham stepped back into the world of sunshine and flowers and music, with a mist before his eyes. Death in such surroundings was so unrealisable. There was suddenly a chill in the air and a note of discord in the music, which seemed to have become blatant. Mr. Billingham entered upon his task with a heavy heart.

With Madelon's help as interpreter, Mr. Billingham had several long conversations with the local functionaries, and was enabled to make certain arrangements towards the prosecution of his mission. He spent that night seated in an easy-chair in the bedroom which had been allotted at the Boston Hotel to Monsieur and Madame Braund, and which had remained unoccupied since the time of the tragedy. At three o'clock, however, there was the sound of feminine footsteps outside and the turning of a key in the door. Mr. Billingham switched on the lights, and the woman who had entered screamed.

"Don't disturb yourself, madame," he begged. "I've taken over Ned Gunby's job. Where's your husband?"

The woman, after a moment's hesitation, slipped off her cloak, seated herself in an easy-chair, and lit a cigarette. She was a person of somewhat flamboyant type, with hair of an almost startling shade of red, and eyes unnaturally darkened.

"Who are you, anyway?" she demanded.

Mr. Billingham disclosed his badge.

"I'm out to get Braund," he declared, "and I'm going to have him."

She shrugged her shoulders, crossed her legs, and leaned a little farther back, with her hands clasped behind her head.

"Seems to me you're looking for trouble," she remarked. "What do you know about Braund?"

"Your husband," Mr. Billingham observed.

She laughed shrilly.

"Not much," she scoffed. "If you want to know the truth, I picked him up at the Carlton three weeks ago."

Mr. Billingham was silent for several moments. He took out his cigar-case.

"Guess I'll smoke, too," he observed. "Anything to drink up here?"

The woman went to a chiffonier and produced a bottle of brandy, a bottle of whisky and some soda water. She helped herself liberally to brandy, and Mr. Billingham mixed himself a whisky and soda.

"So you ain't his wife?" he said at last.

"Thank the Lord I'm not," she answered. "I shouldn't care to be, in this mix-up. I've come here to get my things, and I'm going to move into a little flat round the corner."

"Where is Braund?" Mr. Billingham asked abruptly.

The woman laughed.

"How should I know?" she retorted. "And if I did know, can you see me telling you?"

"You might avoid a heap of trouble that way," was the suggestive rejoinder.

The lady smiled.

"Look here," she said, "I'm no chicken, Mr. Billingham — or whatever your name is. There's nothing wrong with me, except that I took up with a man who turned out to be a criminal. That don't make me one. There's nothing coming to me from you or anyone else."

"What sort of a chap is he, this Braund?" Mr. Billingham enquired.

The woman hesitated for a moment. Her tone was a little more serious.

"A devil!" she answered. "Hard as they make 'em!"

"Treat you well?"

"No better than he ought to," was the somewhat indifferent reply. "I shouldn't call him a spender."

Mr. Billingham sipped his whisky and soda.

"I want Braund," he confided. "I want him badly."

"How's the detective he shot?" the woman demanded.

"Dead," Mr. Billingham told her solemnly.

The woman was a little shocked.

"I suppose it had to be one of them," she mused. "They tell me that if my friend had been arrested it would have been the chair for him."

"It certainly would have been, and it will be," Mr. Billingham assented.

"You think you'll get him, then?" she asked curiously.

"I do," was the confident reply, "and you're going to help me."

She stared at him.

"Seem to have got me sized up," she remarked. "Do you think that I'd give him away if I knew where he was?"

"You're not a fool," her companion argued. "You're a woman of the world. Braund's no more use to you. You're through with him all right. Sooner or later we shall get him. Why not have your bit out of it?"

The woman shivered. It seemed as though Mr. Billingham was being wilfully callous.

"You must think I'm as cold-blooded as Ned Gunby himself," she muttered, throwing away her cigarette.

"I sized you up as having some sense," Mr. Billingham answered slowly. "This man ain't been anything special to you, and you can take it from me he's a real out and out, downright bad 'un. He'd throw you or any other woman on the dirt-heap if it helped him any. He's not going to worry any more about you. All he's thinking of is his own skin. As for you, the thing's come your way. You haven't been out to look for it. Why not put a matter of five thousand dollars in your pocket?"

The woman sat for a moment transfixed. Mr. Billingham, watching her closely, found it difficult to follow her train of thought. Presently she sat up a little in her chair, helped herself to another cigarette, and drank her brandy slowly and deliberately.

"I've never done any one a dirty trick like that," she said.

There was a gleam in Mr. Billingham's eyes. She knew, then!

"It isn't a very dirty trick," he protested. "James Braund in Monte Carlo is like a rat in a pit. He can't get out. We shall have him all right, but the sooner the better. There's ten thousand dollars' reward for him. I'm offering you half."

"Cash?" she demanded.

"Cash," he assented, tapping his pocket-book.

She had the air of a woman tortured by ugly thoughts. Presently she helped herself to more brandy.

"It doesn't matter what you say," she declared. "It's a dirty piece of work."

"Life here," Mr. Billingham reminded her, "is expensive for a woman like you who needs jewellery and swell clothes and that sort of outfit. Bit anxious sometimes, eh? Why not make yourself sure for a time? Five thousand dollars at to-day's exchange is a lot of money."

She sat for a moment looking at her over-manicured fingers.

"What is it you want me to do?" she enquired, in a voice to which she seemed afraid to listen.

"You know where Braund is," Mr. Billingham said. "Help me to put the irons on him."

"You are sure he'll go to the chair?" she asked, with a queer little quiver in her voice.

"He'll go there anyway," was the confident reply. "The only question is whether you make five thousand dollars out of it or whether you don't."

"Five thousand dollars!" she repeated slowly.

She seemed to be thinking about the sum. Presently she picked up a piece of paper, and, with a gold pencil which hung from her reticule, she worked out the amount in francs. There was a covetous gleam in her eyes.

"I'll do it," she decided.

"Of course you will," Mr. Billingham observed, in a tone which was almost matter of fact. "You'd be stark, raving mad if you hesitated. . . . Go on!"

She looked at him curiously.

"I've heard of you," she reflected. "Samuel Billingham, isn't it? You've been mixed up in some queer cases, but no one seems to know whether you're on the straight or the other side of the fence. How's your nerve?"

Mr. Billingham smiled.

"I guess that's all right," he assured her.

"Got your gun handy?"

He tapped his hip-pocket.

"Would you like to take him right now," she asked — "in a quarter of an hour's time, that is?"

"Suits me O.K.," Mr. Billingham acquiesced. "I've handcuffs in my pocket and a car on the other side of the Square."

The woman rose to her feet. She seemed in some subtle sort of way to have changed, to have lost her airy — almost brazen — ease of manner, to be anticipating already grave things. Mr. Billingham watched her and it seemed to him that she was still hesitating.

"Five thousand dollars," he said reflectively, "at to-day's rate of exchange, is seventy-five thousand francs."

She sighed like one who faces the inevitable. Then she glanced at the watch on her wrist.

"Braund," she confided, her voice lower and thicker, her eyes fixed upon the ground, "has papers or money — perhaps a large sum of money — in this room, which he would not trust me to fetch. I came on to see whether the coast was clear. If I lift that blind at four o'clock and turn on the electric light, he will ascend."

"They will be waiting for him below," Mr. Billingham reminded her.

"The front door is locked," she told him, "and we all have latch-keys. The concierge is not on duty. I have seen to that — I and a hundred francs. At four o'clock he will enter if I turn the lights on and lift the blind, but when you hear his step on the stair, be ready."

Mr. Billingham nodded.

"What about you?" he asked.

She shivered.

"He is watching now," she replied. "I dare not try to get away. I shall hide in the corner there, behind the wardrobe. Remember that if you make a mess of this," she went on anxiously, "it will be my life as well as yours. You know what sort of man James Braund is. You know how he treated Ned

Gunby. You get no more mercy from him than from a stone."

"Nor he from me," Mr. Billingham assured her grimly.

They compared watches. It was ten minutes to four. The woman helped herself feverishly to more brandy. Mr. Billingham followed suit with another whisky and soda. Then he took out his gun and looked at it, laid a pair of handcuffs on the table, and lit another cigar. The woman watched him and apparently she was satisfied. The fingers which held his match did not once quiver, his face seemed somehow to have hardened and tightened. He had all the air of a man who expects to confront a crisis and is prepared for it. Of the two, the woman was by far the more nervous. Nevertheless, when four o'clock came she turned on the other switches of electric light, touched the spring of the blind and threw open the shutters.

"Good luck!" she muttered — "to both of us!"

The seconds passed, perhaps a minute — then the step upon the stair. The woman crept into her hiding-place. She had dabbed her face plentifully with powder, but little drops of perspiration had broken through on to her forehead, her lips were vivid streaks of scarlet, in her eyes was fear. Mr. Billingham stood with his left hand upon the bedpost, and in his right hand was his gun. The footstep was nearer now. The door was suddenly pushed open and Mr. Billingham's voice rang out, crisp and terse.

"Hands up — right up above your head! Up, I say!"

For a single second the man who stood upon the threshold seemed as though his right hand would dive downward. Then he looked into that tiny black space, saw the lights flash upon the plating of the revolver, and saw behind, Billingham's face. His hands went up.

"Who the hell are you?" he demanded.

"Billingham of New York, and I've taken on Ned Gunby's job," was the quick reply.

The man with his hands upraised was still a formidable-looking person. He was of little more than medium height, but strongly built, dark, with crisp, black hair, olive complexion and eyes with violet rims underneath, which spoke of sleepless nights. There was about him, somehow or other, an air of fastidiousness, although his linen was crumpled and his boots ill-brushed. All the time it seemed as though his brain were working — his eyes searching the room.

"Where's Anna?" he enquired.

Mr. Billingham ignored the question. With his left hand he picked up the handcuffs and came a step nearer.

"Lower your hands slowly," he enjoined, "until they point towards me. Keep your wrists together!"

The man obeyed. He was breathing heavily.

"Stop there," Mr. Billingham ordered.

He stopped, but his eyes seemed filled with a tortured light. He seemed to be wondering, speculating. Suddenly, with a movement incredibly swift, he was in Mr. Billingham's grasp, Billingham's left arm underneath his hands to keep them from that downward dive. A moment later there was a click, and the handcuffs were on. Mr. Billingham coolly produced the gun from the man's hip-pocket and thrust it into his own.

"That seems all right," he said. "What did you come back here to look for, Braund?"

"Find out," was the contemptuous reply.

There was a sob from behind the chiffonier. The man turned his head slowly. The woman crept into sight. Braund only nodded quietly.

"Like all the rest," he muttered. "You couldn't be trusted. Do you know, woman, that it is my life you've given away — my life for a few dirty dollars."

"I'm sorry," she gasped. "You shouldn't have killed him, James. They'd have got you, anyhow."

Mr. Billingham, with the situation arranged to his liking, felt completely at his ease. He took out his pocket-book and, from a wonderful pile of bills, counted out seventy-five mille notes. Notwithstanding the tenseness of the moment, the woman could not keep the covetous gleam from her eyes.

"I guess those are yours," Mr. Billingham said. "You needn't worry that you've done anything dirty, either. He was my man from the start. Come along, James Braund. We'll put you somewhere until we can arrange to get you across the pond."

The woman fingered the bills and watched them depart, Mr. Billingham holding his captor by the arm. As they passed through the door, she called out.

"I am sorry, Jim," she cried. "I'm sorry I did it."

"You can go to hell!" was the bitter rejoinder. . . .

The two men walked down the narrow stairs and across the darkened hall, Mr. Billingham with his revolver in his hand, and every sense alert. They reached the street, however, in safety, reached the automobile, and drove to the stern-looking police-office down in Monaco, where a little crowd of functionaries was awaiting them. Mr. Billingham remained until the iron door of a very formidable-looking cell was locked upon his captive. Then he drew a sigh of relief, mingled with some other less comprehensible emotion.

"Well, well!" he exclaimed. "Some evening!"

The trio — Madelon, her uncle, the Marquis, and Mr. Billingham — were seated at their favourite table in front of the Café de Paris. An unusual silence had reigned for some minutes, which was broken at last by Madelon.

"I am dissatisfied with life," she sighed, sipping her Dubonnet.

Her uncle glanced at her reprovingly.

"My dear Madelon!" he protested. "Surely that is ungrateful to our kind friend who has provided so generously for our entertainment."

She made a little grimace.

"I have a complaint against him," she declared. "He provides me with no one to flirt with and he ignores me himself. He has become a hero and he is all the time distrait. I think that his head is turned."

"Why should I provide you with any one to flirt with?" Mr. Billingham objected. "I guess that's my privilege."

"It might have been," Madelon admitted, "if you had been persistent, if you had shown rather more desire to be in my company, to whisper things in my ear, to look as though my presence made the difference to you of happiness or misery. But behold, for five minutes this morning after my arrival, you sat and you looked towards the Casino and you said nothing. You might even have held my fingers — I purposely let them stay in your hand. And there are other things."

Mr. Billingham groaned.

"Go on with it, then," he begged. "Let me know the full extent of my misdeeds."

"Your passion for me," she complained, "has given way to another. You are as bad as my uncle. You spend your time in the Casino. You have become a gambler. When you might be taking me for a little drive to the hills — I love motoring so much that there is no telling how gracious I might be — you stay in that terrible Casino, gambling — not even like a man who seeks the great things, one who deals in maximums in the Cercle Privé or at the Sporting Club, but playing for louis in the 'kitchen.' Bah! It is incredible! Why do you do it? I demand an explanation!"

Mr. Billingham's attention had wandered away. His eyes were fixed upon the little crowd entering the Casino. For once in his life he was almost indifferent to his charming companion.

"I guess I'll go and play a coup or two before luncheon," he announced, rising to his feet. "Don't wait for me if I'm late. Henry will see that you are well served."

He rose to his feet. Madelon made one last attempt to understand.

"Is it possible," she demanded, "that you have embarked upon another adventure without our aid?"

"If I do not return for luncheon," was the evasive reply, "I will tell you everything at dinner-time."

He crossed the Place — a trifle burly in appearance, but walking with the spring of a young man; erect, self-confident. A commissionaire saluted him, the cloak-room attendant recognised him as a generous donor of *pourboires,* the ushers at the door bowed at his coming. He staked a coup or two at the table on the right. Then he turned to the table on the left. Every place was occupied and there was a row of people standing looking on. Mr. Billingham took his place amongst them. This time he staked nothing, however. He stood behind the chair of a slim, elderly man, who wore dark tortoise-shell spectacles and who had just taken a vacant place. By his side sat Anna, the woman who had betrayed her lover.

"*Faites vos jeux, messieurs,*" the croupier invited.

The man in front of Mr. Billingham threw four louis on the table.

"*Sept, quatorze, vingt-huit — vingt-neuf, vingt-neuf en plein,*" he said.

Mr. Billingham glanced meaningly towards a tall, dark man who had moved stealthily to his side. A quick nod was exchanged. Then a singular thing happened. Mr. Billingham, whose arms were almost as powerful as the arms of a prize-fighter, suddenly gripped both wrists of the man seated in front of him and held them together as though in a vise. The tall, dark man leaned over and touched him on the shoulder.

"In the name of the police, Monsieur," he whispered.

The woman looked round, recognised Mr. Billingham and shrieked. The man turned towards her. His teeth were suddenly parted. He seemed about to rise, making no movement of resistance. The woman thrust her hand into her handbag, her fingers towards his mouth. His teeth closed with a snap. Then he rose calmly to his feet.

"If you have a car or anything," he said, "you had better get me into it. A person of brains, Mr. Billingham. I congratulate you."

Mr. Billingham's grip upon the man's wrists was never for a moment relaxed. Play had ceased and people were crowding up only to be kept away by two plain-clothes gendarmes who had suddenly made their appearance, and a small army of the Casino functionaries.

"The gentleman is taken ill," some one announced. "Make way, please."

The handcuffs clicked upon the man's wrists but he only shrugged his shoulders. He commenced his passage towards the door with Mr. Billingham on one side and the man who had arrested him on the other. His steps, however, became uncertain. He turned and looked back at the woman. She was standing, a terrible figure of misery, a few yards off. He forced a little smile into his face.

"Don't take her money away, Billingham, even if she fooled you," he begged. "You've come out on top, you see."

"What's wrong with you?" his captor demanded suspiciously.

"Cyanide of potassium," was the grim reply. "Anna had it ready for me in case we didn't make a get-away. You'll have to carry me down the steps. What about it, Billingham? If she fooled you, it was life or death for me."

"That's all right," Mr. Billingham promised. "I've nothing against her. I guess she can keep what she's got."

Madelon and her uncle had finished their *hors d'œuvres* and commenced the grilled chicken when Mr. Billingham joined them. He took the vacant place opposite Madelon and signified his pressing need of some alcoholic refreshment. He was looking very grave and he had lost a good deal of his healthy colour.

"Something has happened!" Madelon exclaimed.

"We have just arrested Braund," Mr. Billingham confided. "Touch and go it was, too. They were off this afternoon."

"Arrested Braund?" Madelon repeated incredulously. "Why, you arrested him ten days ago! The papers said they were taking him back to America to-morrow."

Mr. Billingham was slowly recovering himself. He was still, however, very grave.

"I haven't let you two in on this," he explained, "because there was nothing you could do. I had to play, as it were, a lone hand. When I promised Ned Gunby I'd see this thing through, he gave me a little pile of papers about Braund and a note of a few of his weaknesses. He didn't tell me much about the woman, though, and I honestly believed that she was on the straight when she offered to sell me Braund for half the reward."

"But the man you arrested at the Boston Hotel —— "

"Braund's brother-in-law," Mr. Billingham interrupted — "the decoy whilst Braund made a getaway. He didn't run any particular risk. There were dozens to identify him the moment he was hauled up in New York. I thought it was all right until I had the handcuffs on him. Then I saw that he wasn't anything like the description of the man I wanted, and besides he put up no sort of a fight. I pretended to be fooled all right, and we've kept him in prison. In the meantime we've watched Madame. She's been damned artful, pretended to be playing the restaurant game at the Carlton and those places, but she was continually disappearing. Then I got her dossier. She was Braund's wife right enough, but wherever he was hiding in Monte Carlo she never went near him. I noticed, though, that she spent a lot of time at the Casino, and amongst Gunby's papers was a little note that the passion of Braund's life was roulette, and that if anything could bring him out of his hiding it would be to gamble. He played on four numbers only — seven, fourteen, twenty-eight, and twenty-nine. I sort of hung around and waited for some one sitting near Madame who backed on those numbers. We very nearly brought it off yesterday morning, but this morning it was a cert. They entered almost at the same time, went to the same table, sat side by side. I gave 'em the office outside and pretty soon — well — seven, fourteen, twenty-eight and twenty-nine. I got him by the wrists so that he couldn't move whilst they took his gun away — got him from behind."

The Marquis looked longingly towards the Casino.

"And we missed it!" he murmured.

"I shouldn't have let you be there," Mr. Billingham assured him. "There's no knowing how those things are going to turn out till they're over. After all, in a way he tricked us."

"How?" Madelon asked.

"The woman again! A common-looking bit of goods but Braund was her man and she saw him through it. The moment they realised that he was done she handed him the poison — put it into his mouth herself, in fact. It was all over before they got him into the auto."

"Horrible!" Madelon exclaimed with a little shudder.

Mr. Billingham ordered his lunch.

"Horrible it is," he admitted, as he laid down the menu, "but there is just one thing that makes me glad of my morning's work."

"One thing?" the Marquis murmured politely.

Mr. Billingham inclined his head towards the hill.

"That little hospital," he confided. "Poor Ned Gunby with

a bullet in his chest, shot on sight for doing his duty. I guess Braund has got what was coming to him."

Nevertheless the shadow remained — the shadow of tragedy, which never leaves the atmosphere of sudden death. Mr. Billingham called for the winelist and revised his order.

"I should like our next adventure," Madelon confided, a few moments later, "to end in a laugh instead of a tragedy."

Something of the grimness passed from Mr. Billingham's face. He watched the pouring out of the wine.

"I guess I have an idea of that sort myself," he agreed. "Supposing —— "

III

MRS. BLOCK CONTRIBUTES

"That horrible woman!" Madelon exclaimed, gripping Mr. Billingham's arm, as they sat in a retired corner of the Sporting Club bar.

"She is indeed deplorable," the Marquis agreed, from the other side. "To-day, at one of the tables in the Casino, before the opening of the Cercle Privé, she created a scene. She plastered the board with plaques. She utterly failed to remember. She claimed everything. Her voice — a horrible memory! The croupiers had no choice. They gave in. She took what she wished. When she departed every one was overjoyed."

"She carries some of the stuff about her," Mr. Billingham observed judicially. "Fine woman in her day!"

The woman to whom they referred, Mrs. William Block, of Leeds, England, stood looking around for a seat, and, finding none, scowled. She was florid, fat, notwithstanding the desperate efforts of a world-famed costumier, and vulgar. She swung in her hand a gold bag, adorned with precious stones. She wore upon her person two pearl necklaces, a pair of large diamond earrings, a succession of diamond bracelets, and several glittering hatpins. Her costume was white and bulgy. She was a well-known *habitante* of the Hôtel de Paris, whose friends were sycophants and whose acquaintances fugitive, and she was reputed to be the widow of a leather merchant who had made a million pounds in hides.

"She is one of the people," Madelon confided, "who upset all my ideas of conventional morality. I should like to rob her."

The Marquis dropped his eyeglass and twirled the corner of his moustache.

"It is an idea," he admitted.

Mr. Billingham considered the matter.

"If one could hatch out a deal," he confessed, "I guess this is a case where one wouldn't need to be too darned particular. That woman don't deserve to be allowed to go about alive, looking the way she does, and with half a million dollars' worth of jewels missing their opportunity in life."

Madelon smiled up at him in intriguing fashion.

"Do something about it, Mr. Billingham," she begged. "You are already in favour with her. Do you not remember giving her your seat yesterday evening?"

"Say, that don't count for much," Mr. Billingham protested. "She was leaning over me with a kind of blend of lily of the valley and patchouli scent, pretty well stifling me, brushing my hair the wrong way, pushing her plaques on and shouting out her stakes till I was glad enough to make myself scarce."

"Nevertheless," Madelon reminded him in a whisper, "you gave her your place, and she is smiling at you now."

It was an incontrovertible fact. Madelon rose to her feet with a sudden graceful movement.

"I have an idea that there is a place for me at my favourite table," she confided. "I'll go to see."

Mrs. William Block advanced a few steps and beamed at Mr. Billingham. He rose at once.

"*Vous désirez une chaise, madame?*" he demanded.

"I'll sit down all right," the lady replied, dropping heavily into the chair, "but I ain't French. Waiter, I'll have a gin fizz."

"An excellent drink!" Mr. Billingham murmured.

"I like a glass of champagne most times," the lady confided, "but I'll have to drink so much for dinner that perhaps I'd better lay off for a while. I'm dining with the Higginsons — Jim Higginson and his wife. You know them, I dare say."

The Marquis felt himself included in the query.

"I have not the honour," he murmured.

"Can't say that I know them," Mr. Billingham confessed.

"Jim's father made his money in wollens at Huddersfield," the lady explained, "and Jim got into that cotton scheme somehow. . . . Why," she went on, smiling at Mr. Billingham, "you must be the gentleman who gave me his seat yesterday evening."

"I had that pleasure," Mr. Billingham admitted.

The Marquis rose stealthily to his feet. He was fond of his friend, he was very fond of his niece, but like all real aristocrats he was in his way a snob. He did not care to sit next Mrs. William Block.

"I wait for you," he explained, with a wave of his hand. "I have an affair." . . .

"Jumpy little person, your friend," Mrs. Block remarked. "Never mind! All the more room for us. Where are you staying, Mr. — Mr. — what is your name?"

Mr. Billingham produced a card.

"My name is Billingham, ma'am," he said — "Samuel T. Billingham of New York. I was interested in linoleums but I've sold out."

"Retired, eh?" the lady remarked.

"That's how you put it over here," Mr. Billingham conceded cautiously. "I'm not saying that I'm right out of the game yet."

"My name's Block," the lady confided — "Annie Block. My husband was in hides. Nasty dirty things, I always thought, but he made a cool million at it."

"Pounds?" Mr. Billingham enquired, in an awed tone.

"Pounds sterling," was the definite reply. "None of your silly dollars!"

"I trust," Mr. Billingham continued, "that your husband remembered to whose inspiration his success was due?"

"I don't know what you're getting at," Mrs. Block observed, "but if you want to know what he did with his money, I'll tell you straight, he left it to me. It will cost you one bob at Somerset House to find out that I ain't a liar, and if you happen to know a word or two of French, just rub it into that flunkey there that a lady doesn't want to wait for a gin fizz half the evening."

Mr. Billingham proved equal to the occasion. The gin fizz was produced, and the lady, notwithstanding her colossal inheritance, showed not the slightest objection to her companion paying for it. They conversed for a time with growing intimacy.

"Are you married?" she asked, a little abruptly.

Mr. Billingham scorned the suggestion.

"Put it off till too late, I guess — a great mistake!"

She sighed, and scrutinised him benignly.

"What do you mean by 'too late'?" she demanded. "You're in the prime of life."

Mr. Billingham shook his head gloomily.

"I am healthy," he admitted. "I'm only just round the corner of fifty, but I guess I'm still a little particular. The women I care for seem to want something younger."

"Rubbish!" the lady asserted.

"Take your own case now," he went on earnestly. "You are a widow, I understand. You are bound to marry again — any one can see that. You wouldn't care to have anything to do with a man of my age."

Mrs. William Block laid four chubby fingers and a fat thumb upon his arm. So far as her double chin would allow her, she looked arch.

"You are a funny person!" she declared. "Come on — I dare you! Ask me, now. I might be tempted."

Mr. Billingham bore the assault stoically.

"If I did make such an idiot of myself," he observed, "I know very well what would happen, and so do you."

"I'd have you," she assured him.

Mr. Billingham contemplated that wonderful array of jewellery with which she was decked, remembered his pledge to Madelon, heaved a deep sigh, and permitted himself to touch the massive arm which leaned against his.

"What are you doing for luncheon to-morrow?" he asked.

"That depends upon what you want me to do," was the brilliant reply.

At the end of a week Mr. Billingham had lost half a stone. He escaped one morning from the Hôtel de Paris at an early hour and met his friends, the Marquis de Félan and Madelon, his niece, at one of the smaller cafés at the back of the town.

"Some one else," he complained, "will have to take a hand in this game."

The Marquis stroked his moustache.

"My turn, I gather," he observed, "is to come later."

"What can I do, dear man?" Madelon asked, patting his hand.

"I am here. I am anxious to help. I must confess that at first I watched your sufferings with heartfelt sympathy. Lately I am not so sure. You are either getting callous, or you are becoming an admirer of the Gargantuan in my sex."

Mr. Billingham groaned.

"Listen," he announced; "we approach the end. I am veritably the accepted suitor of Mrs. Annie Block, widow of a defunct dealer in hides. The million is in her own name."

"It is incredible!" the Marquis declared.

"A million? Is it worth the trouble?" Madelon murmured inscrutably.

Mr. Billingham smiled for the first time for days; a smile that spread and extended to the wrinkles around his eyes.

"Well," he continued, "I guess I'm about through with my part. It is your uncle who takes the floor now."

The Marquis coughed.

"But supposing the lady should object to this — er — substitution of attentions?"

Mr. Billingham's smiled broadened.

"I should worry," he murmured. "Play your part as I have played mine, Marquis — and there must be no shirking, mind — and the thing is accomplished. This morning we meet at the Café de Paris and I shall present you. Then I talk to Madelon. The rest — well — some cinch, I can tell you!"

The Marquis was a little uneasy. He was haunted with visions of a magenta dress which the lady had worn on the previous evening.

"I am not sure," he ventured, "whether my methods may appeal."

Mr. Billingham struck the little table with his fist.

"See here," he announced, "it's a closed pocket-book on this trip if you show the white feather. The game's as easy as pie.

You've got to sail right in. I come along with the finesse later. Madelon!"

She nodded understandingly.

"Uncle," she warned him, "remember that everything depends upon your playing your part properly. You want to have something to take to the Casino to-morrow, don't you?"

The Marquis breathed a deep sigh. He seemed to be able to visualise the moment of suspense, the click of the ball falling into its niche, the croupier's monotonous announcement. He drew himself up.

"I am a man of honour," he declared. "I shall not fail you. Let us start at once. . . ."

Outside the Café de Paris, seated before the most conspicuous table, and looking larger than ever, they found the lady of whom they were in search. Mr. Billingham marched boldly up.

"Mrs. Block," he said, "my friend, the Marquis de Félan, has asked me to present him. The Marquis de Félan — Mrs. Block — also Miss de Félan, the Marquis' niece."

Mrs. Block was fluttered but gratified. The Marquis rose splendidly to the occasion. He kissed her pudgy fingers with an air which evoked her wondering admiration, and accepting a chair by her side he plunged at once into a conversation of a more or less intimate nature. He played the host to the little gathering, ordering refreshments and paying for them with an air of great liberality. After a time Mr. Billingham rose tentatively to his feet.

"I guess Miss de Félan and I are going to walk along and see about that table for dinner," he announced. "We'll find you here when we come back, or else meet in the Casino."

Mrs. Block smiled gracefully; the Marquis for a moment felt his heart sink, but he stuck to his guns.

"A very delightful man, Mr. Billingham," the lady remarked, looking after his departing figure.

The Marquis nodded without enthusiasm.

"Why not?" he replied. "He has in the world all that he desires. He has money, and above all he has a facile disposition.

It is a great thing, that! He makes friends easily. He never suffers from loneliness."

"And do you?" the lady asked softly.

The Marquis sighed. He looked dreamily away towards the hills. He was quite at his best.

"All my life," he confided, "I have been lonely. I lost my wife when I was young. I was foolish not to remarry. Now, alas! when it is too late, I feel the need of a companion."

"Why is it too late?" she enquired tenderly.

"The women of to-day," the Marquis complained, "all prefer young men. Where should I find a woman attractive enough to be agreeable to me who would be willing to marry a man of fifty?"

"Very easily, I should think," Mrs. Block declared with portentous emphasis. "But of course if you want one of these young fly-away hussies —— "

"But I do not," the Marquis interrupted. "I prefer a woman of — of experience. A woman," he went on, leaning a little towards her — "may I venture to say — of something like your age — thirty-eight or so."

It was a moment of ecstasy for Mrs. Block. She was wearing a gown in which she fondly believed that she resembled the mannequin from whom she had bought it. She was sitting alone with a Marquis and quite casually she had been taken for thirty-eight.

"How did you know my age?" she asked, almost archly.

"I am a great diviner of ages," he replied. "It is very seldom that I make a mistake."

"Well, then, I think there are very few women of my age, Marquis," the lady confided, "who would not be glad to try and bring a little sunshine into your life."

The Marquis sighed once more.

"A beautiful way of putting it!" he murmured. "You cheer me up, dear lady. May I," he added significantly, "do myself the honour of calling upon you?"

Mrs. Block was more and more fluttered.

"Come this afternoon," she invited. "I have tea in my sitting-room at four o'clock. Mr. Billingham sometimes drops in, but this afternoon I shall say that I am engaged."

"Mr. Billingham is a great friend of yours, is he not?" the Marquis enquired gloomily.

"Nothing special," was the indifferent reply. "We're friends in a way, of course, but he's not quite my fancy. By the by," she went on, "are you and your niece doing anything to-night?"

"Nothing of any consequence," the Marquis confessed.

"Come and dine at my hotel — the Hôtel de Paris," the lady begged eagerly. "Mr. Billingham's coming, and to tell you the truth, I'd just as soon not dine with him alone. He is very nice, but people do talk so, and when you've made up your mind as I have — well, I don't want to seem to be encouraging him. You *comprenez?*"

"*Parfaitement,*" the Marquis assured her with a little inward chuckle. "About half-past-eight, I suppose. Permit me to escort you across the Place. . . ."

The Marquis strolled down the terrace to Ciro's a little later with the remains of a smile still lurking about his lips. He handed his coat and cane to an attendant and crossed the room confidently towards the table where Madelon and Mr. Billingham were already seated.

"My friend," he announced, "you no longer exist. I have achieved a great success. La belle Block is no longer for you. I take tea with her in her *salon* this afternoon. You are to be told that she is engaged. We dine at the Hôtel de Paris to-night — Madelon and I. A million pounds! It is incredible! One might be disposed to take this affair seriously."

Madelon shook her head.

"Impossible," she insisted. "You may eat her dinners and rob her if you will of that staggering jewellery, but more would not be possible."

The Marquis shivered a little as he glanced down the menu.

"You are right," he assented. "Besides, even if one had the courage, there would be disagreeable people like executors. You might find that there were difficulties about the money and settlements."

"The man who marries a woman like that," Mr. Billingham

declared firmly, "would deserve what he got, and I guess we'll leave that out of the question. She's one of the people in the world, though, the Lord meant to be robbed. She goes about asking for it."

"The scheme itself is as yet scarcely clear to me," the Marquis murmured.

"Nor to me," Mr. Billingham confessed, attacking his *hors d'œuvres* vigorously. "The stuff's there all right, though, and we're going to touch it. Make the running as strong as you can this afternoon, my son. We'll get to work before the week's out."

The Marquis played with his eyeglass a little nervously.

"You will not suggest, of course, anything in the nature of — er — direct larceny?"

"Not I," Mr. Billingham acquiesced. "Jewel lifting's too difficult, and besides, we ain't professionals. Something a little more subtle. I haven't got it quite fixed yet, but I'm not worrying any."

The Marquis escaped from his afternoon tea entertainment, still triumphant but shattered. He drank a large whisky and soda at the bar of the Sporting Club before he felt sufficiently recovered to make his appearance in the Rooms. By dinner-time, however, he was entirely himself again. He sat at Mrs. Block's right hand, and endured stoically the pressure of her immense foot. The burden of conversation devolved mainly upon him, for Mr. Billingham was noticeably silent, and, for him, almost morose.

"Jealous!" his hostess whispered to the Marquis as they left the dining-room. "Jealous of you, dear!"

The Marquis felt his fingers lightly pressed and received a languishing glance.

"You have encouraged him," he rejoined.

"Not more than the others," she declared, airily and mendaciously peopling her environment with the forms of many suitors. "Men are so difficult nowadays," she sighed.

"A beautiful woman has always her embarrassments," the Marquis sympathised. . . .

The evening progressed according to plan. The little party had made their way to the Sporting Club, but Mr. Billingham, becoming more and more silent and depressed, presently withdrew. Madelon followed shortly afterwards and in a little voiture they drove to the Carlton. Mr. Billingham's depression had vanished as though by magic.

"Say, your uncle is getting away with this fine!" he declared. "It took me a week to get where he's got in less than a day. He's got the knack of it."

Madelon was looking up at the moon. Mr. Billingham was suddenly conscious that the night held a charm which was not altogether pagan. The sky was perfectly clear, the music from the cafés reached them faintly, in the dim light the crowds of moving people were like shadows.

"After all," she murmured, "it is rather terrible."

"I don't quite get you," her companion confessed.

"Having to live like this," she explained. "This living on one's wits. The insecurity of it is horrible. Sometimes it is amusing, it appeals to one's sense of humour, but it destroys one's dignity. In time we shall all three become really bad."

"Not you," Mr. Billingham rejoined softly.

"Why not me?" she asked, turning abruptly and looking at him. "What do you suppose will be the end of me?"

"I guess you'll marry."

"Who would marry any one like me—who worth marrying?" she demanded, with a little note almost of passion in her tone. "Of course I want to marry—every girl does. I want a home of my own and a man to look after me. What sort of a husband do you think I am likely to find living this kind of a life?"

Mr. Billingham, too, was very serious.

"I guess it's hard on you," he admitted, taking her hand in his.

"It is hard on all of us, I suppose."

"Say, shall we lay off for a bit," he suggested. "I can make money on the Square. There's my old Company. They'd have me back as a Director."

She withdrew her fingers and patted his hand.

"You are very foolish," she said. "Of course you can make money. You are clever — but that would not help us. We would not live upon your charity. And yet, without you we should probably slip back into helplessness."

Mr. Billingham leaned towards her and coughed. His voice was a little husky.

"Madelon," he began.

She turned her head.

"Well?"

The carriage pulled up with a jerk outside the Carlton; the commissionaire threw open the door.

"Damn!" Mr. Billingham exclaimed. . . .

At supper-time Madelon became unexpectedly gay. She insisted upon dancing most of the time and resisted any attempt at serious conversation.

"Of course you know that you dance absurdly well," she told him once. "You must be very fond of it."

"For a fat man," Mr. Billingham admitted, as he wiped his forehead, "I fancy I can move some. But dancing with you, Miss Madelon, is pretty easy going. Let's sit and talk for a bit."

She shook her head.

"I could not," she objected. "To-night I am nervous. If I talk I shall weep. Go and fetch me that dancing instructor — the dark one. You will have to give him a hundred francs. I like that little side-step he does. You can either rest or try your fortune with the little danseuse."

Mr. Billingham obeyed orders so far as the dancing instructor was concerned, but made no effort towards securing the companionship of the little danseuse. Instead, he leaned back in his corner and watched. He seemed to be watching all the room, but as a matter of fact his eyes never left Madelon. She was very simply dressed, as usual, in a plain black georgette frock, but there seemed to be some new quality in her face — something a little haunting in her eyes, a dash almost of recklessness in her graceful movements. She danced like a devotee, without a word to her partner. Once her eyes met Mr. Billingham's and she smiled, but even her smile seemed to possess an indefinable and unrealisable quality. As soon as the dance had finished she

thanked her partner briefly and returned abruptly to the table.
"I want to go, please," she begged. "We will see how Uncle
is getting on."

Mr. Billingham paid his bill. They stepped outside and into
a voiture. Mr. Billingham's voice was once more a little husky.

"Madelon," he began ——

She laid her hand for a moment on his.

"You must please not speak to me all the way back," she insisted. "And don't mind if I am a little foolish."

Her head disappeared between her hands. Once he saw her
shoulders shiver as though she were sobbing. When they reached
the Club, however, she sat up with a little weary smile. There
were no signs of tears in her eyes.

"You see, after all I am not a finished adventuress," she said.
"I am just a silly girl, who is liable to these sorts of moods. I
think being with this horrible woman has affected me to-night.
I hate ugly things and ugly people. If we continue our life of
crime I insist upon it that our next victim is not of this type."

Mrs. Block was, for her, almost nervous when on the following afternoon, in response to an urgent telephone call, she
received a visit from Mr. Billingham. Mr. Billingham seemed
to have lost entirely that spirit of bonhomie which he generally
presented to the world. Even his attire was more sombre than
usual. He shook hands without a smile and declined a chair.

"Annie," he said, using her Christian name boldly, "I have
come for an explanation."

"What sort of an explanation?" she enquired, toying with her
rope of pearls.

"I guess you know," was the stern reply. "We Americans
don't waste words. You know very well you're engaged to
marry me and you're flirting with my friend. It's got to stop
right now!"

The situation had its embarrassments, but also its delights.
Mrs. Block felt a thrill of joy as she once more invited her visitor to seat himself by her side. She had all the sensations of a
heroine of some modern romance.

"Samuel," she said — "or rather, Mr. Billingham, because I

am not going to call you Samuel any longer — you will have to be very generous. I wish to break off our engagement. It was never announced, as you know."

"Because of the Marquis?" he demanded.

Mrs Block admitted the fact.

"It's no use wasting words about it," she went on. "I promised to marry him last night. We're keeping the engagement secret for a fortnight and then I'm going back to England to arrange my affairs."

"And what do you expect me to say?" Mr. Billingham asked.

"I expect you to be a dear and — give me up," she declared.

"I shall do nothing of the sort," he replied firmly.

"You can't hold me to that promise," she insisted. "There's nothing on paper, anyway. You wouldn't have me marry you without loving you, Samuel?"

Mr. Billingham flinched but persevered.

"You are engaged to marry me," he rejoined doggedly. "I may not be an aristocrat like the Marquis; I may not even be so well off, but you promised."

Mrs. Block shook her head.

"I can't help that," she said. "If you don't like it you can — do the other thing. That's all there is to say about it. I'd rather be friends."

Mr. Billingham remained unmoved.

"I am not to be got rid of like that. I shall appeal to the Marquis himself," he threatened.

"What do you mean?" she demanded.

"The Marquis is a man of honour," Mr. Billingham explained. "I shall go to him. I shall tell him the truth. I shall say 'Mrs. Block was engaged to me. I introduced you as my friend. As a man of honour I require you to withdraw.' I know my friend," Mr. Billingham continued. "He will do as I desire. He will leave Monte Carlo the same day."

Mrs. Block was pale with anger. Her visitor's words carried conviction. The phrase "a man of honour" daunted her. In her fancy she could already see the Marquis seated with folded arms in his little voiture, with his portmanteau on the seat in front, on his way to the station.

"You must do nothing of the sort," she insisted.

"What is to prevent me?" he retorted. "Besides —— "

"Besides what?" she interrupted eagerly.

Mr. Billingham was shamefaced but determined.

"I am poor," he confessed. "I am tired of being poor. I have lost heavily at the tables."

Mrs. Block came up to scratch at once.

"For how much money," she asked, "will you leave me and the Marquis alone?"

"Two thousand pounds," Mr. Billingham replied without hesitation.

She was a little staggered, but she was a woman of action. She wrote out a cheque and handed it to him. He shook his head.

"It would take weeks to get the money for that," he pointed out.

"They will cash it downstairs," she assured him.

"You get the money and bring it in mille notes," he insisted. "That's all I ask. You can marry the Marquis as soon as you like then."

She motioned him to a chair.

"Wait," she ordered.

In a quarter-of-an-hour she returned, slightly breathless, with a great pile of mille notes in her hand.

"They had to send to the Bank," she explained. "There's your money. Now you just leave me and the Marquis alone."

Mr. Billingham picked up his hat sadly.

"You may be choosing the better man, Annie," he said, "but this is a great disappointment to me."

Mrs Block sneered a little. She was not really fond of parting with her money.

"You've got something to console yourself with," she snapped out. "Hurry off, please. I am expecting the Marquis at any moment."

Thereafter the Marquis played his part manfully for a week. At the end of that time he made an abrupt appearance as Mr. Billingham and Madelon were finishing their dinner in a secluded corner of the Sporting Club Restaurant. He had all the appearance of a man on the verge of a nervous breakdown.

"My friend," he exclaimed, sinking into a chair which a waiter had brought from a neighbouring table, "order me a liqueur brandy. This must cease. I have reached the limit."

Mr. Billingham wisely ordered a double liqueur brandy hastily and forbore to question his friend.

"I have stood the amused ridicule of a crowd of strangers," the latter went on. "I have put up with the agony of being drenched with intolerable perfumes, of listening to that strident voice, of —— "

"Cut it out!" Mr. Billingham interrupted. "What's the trouble?"

The Marquis looked around him wildly.

"The lady," he confided, "is becoming amorous. She has held my hand, she has pressed my feet, until the thing has become monotonous. Now she has, I fear — other designs upon me."

The creases around Mr. Billingham's eyes began to deepen, his mouth quivered, his efforts at self-control became useless. He joined in Madelon's ecstatic outburst of amusement. When he had recovered sufficiently to wipe his eyes, the Marquis had drunk his brandy and was looking thoughtfully at the bottle.

"We dined," the Marquis explained, "at the Hôtel de Paris. She insisted — declared that it was too quiet there and that she wanted me alone. She wore white satin, — not enough of it by yards. She wore jewellery which made the people blink when she came into the room. She sat next a party of your compatriots and she called me 'Marquis' at the top of her voice every few minutes. When at last I thought my hour of comparative release had arrived, she declared that she had a headache and would spend the evening in her sitting-room. She has ordered me to follow her. I am to return — to sit with her there alone! She has whispered in my ear that we are engaged."

Mr. Billingham made signs to the waiter, who filled the Marquis' glass.

"You've got to go through with it, Marquis," he declared.

"But what is to be the end?" the Marquis demanded, almost

passionately. "People are beginning to smile when they see us together. Our engagement has even been announced in some of the papers. One day she will march me into a church or registry office and I shall emerge a married man. She is masterful — overwhelming! What is your plan? It is time to announce it."

Mr. Billingham reflected.

"There have been a few little pickings," he mused.

"It is true," the Marquis assented. "I have jewellery for the first time for many years; pearl studs like blobs, and some sapphire sleeve links and waistcoat buttons which are admirable. These things are so much to the good, but I cannot go on collecting them. There is a certain definiteness," he added, "in the woman's intentions towards me this evening, which is horrible."

Madelon, wiping the tears from her eyes, leaned forward.

"There must be a rescue party," she suggested.

"I agree," Mr. Billingham assented. "In ten minutes your sufferings shall be at an end; temporarily, at any rate. I will find some excuse. We will break in upon you."

"With that promise and under those conditions," the Marquis said, "I will return. . . ."

The Marquis kept his word, and Mr. Billingham carried out his share of the bargain. In less than a quarter of an hour he presented himself at the sitting-room of Mrs. Block's gorgeous suite. He was immediately aware of tragical happenings. The Marquis, looking a little dazed, was standing upon the hearthrug. Mrs. Block, grasping a telegraphic despatch in her hand, was in a state almost of collapse upon the sofa. The newcomer looked from one to the other.

"I regret my inevitable intrusion," he began — "Monsieur le Duc, the Marquis' father, has telephoned from Nice."

Mrs. Block banged the end of the sofa with her fist.

"Damn you all — dukes and marquises and the lot of you!" she cried. "Tom will smash you when he comes, and he'll kill me. What a fool I've been!"

"Say, who is this 'Tom,' anyway?" Mr. Billingham demanded.

"My husband!" Mrs. Block declared dramatically.

"Her husband!" the Marquis murmured under his breath with a beatific smile.

Mrs. Block rose to her feet. She was, after all, a woman of force and determination.

"Look here, you two," she confessed, "this is the long and short of it. I'm no widow. My husband's hale and hearty, though he's sixty years old. I've been down here three years, and a lone woman doesn't get the show she ought to. She wants some one attached to her. I guess I lost my head a bit. I wanted a man along, and I chose the simplest way of getting one. Now it's got put in the papers about me and the Marquis, my old man's seen it, and he'll be here to-morrow morning at twelve-thirty. Years ago," she went on, with a livid little shadow of memory blanching her face, "he used to beat me. He'd think nothing of doing it again, and as to any man he's ever run up against — well, he's made short work of him. 'Fighting Tom,' they used to call him. . . . Don't stand there looking like nincompoops, both of you! What are you going to do?"

The Marquis duly interpreted a glance from Mr. Billingham.

"I shall consult with my friend," he said. "You have treated me very badly, madame."

"Following upon your treatment of me," Mr. Billingham added meaningly, "the situation becomes a grave one. With your permission, we will call upon you at half-past ten to-morrow morning."

"Let's have it out now," the lady begged.

Mr. Billingham shook his head.

"At half-past ten," he repeated. "Come along, Marquis!"

Mrs. Block had not the strength to argue. The two men took a dignified leave of her.

At half-past ten on the following morning a very altered Mrs. Block received her two visitors. She was wearing a plainly made gown, her pudgy face was devoid of its artificial colour, her eyebrows appeared to have lost their shape, and nothing but a cascade of jewellery remained of her previous magnificence. She scarcely waited for them to sit down.

"Well?" she demanded eagerly.

Mr. Billingham coughed.

"The Marquis desires to know your wishes, madame," Mr. Billingham announced stiffly.

"What I want him to do is to clear out," the lady declared. "If Tom's seen that bit in the paper about the Marquis and me — which he must have done as he's never left England before in his life — he'll hunt this place until he's found him, and then there'll be trouble. I shall tell him that the whole thing is a bit of newspaper stuff, that I don't know any Marquis, that I haven't any friends here at all."

"I gather that you desire the Marquis to leave Monte Carlo," Mr. Billingham observed.

"This morning," was the prompt assent. "I want him out of the way before Tom starts making enquiries."

"You will understand, I am sure," his friend continued, "that for a man fixed like the Marquis, with a whole heap of social engagements, this is some sacrifice."

"It is intolerable!" the Marquis interposed. "I shall lose my roulette, my rooms are taken for another month — I lose, also, more than I can express," he added, with a little bow.

"You can cut that out," was the blunt retort. "You may or you may not have been in earnest, but I'm not going to believe that you're going to break your heart. Will you go or won't you?"

"I prefer to remain," the Marquis announced coldly. "If your husband desires satisfaction I shall be at his service."

Mrs. Block laughed. It was not exactly a laugh of humour, but it was the first time her features had relaxed.

"Tom's idea of 'satisfaction' would be to knock you into a jelly," she confided — "and he'll do it, too."

"I await the arrival of monsieur," the Marquis repeated haughtily.

"Look here, madame," Mr. Billingham intervened, "I guess we're wasting time. The Marquis is like myself — a man of moderate means. After losing a small fortune, he's struck a vein of luck and he's winning every day at the tables here. His rooms are taken for another month and he'll have to pay for them. If you want him to quit for your convenience, you must talk business about it."

"O-ho!" the lady exclaimed. "So that's the game, is it? I'm beginning to wonder," she added suspiciously, "whether the Marquis isn't another of your kidney."

The Marquis picked up his hat and coat.

"The interview is at an end," he declared. "I find the attitude of madame outrageous."

Mrs. Block sprang up and barred his exit.

"Don't be silly," she enjoined. "Your friend knows what he's talking about. How much do you want to clear out of Monte Carlo before half-past twelve, not show yourself here for at least a week, and deny you ever set eyes on me if Tom finds you out?"

"My friend will arrange such a matter," the Marquis replied icily. "I have no head for figures myself. These moves are very expensive."

"The Marquis will leave by the twelve o'clock train to Nice," Mr. Billingham promised, "for the sum of two thousand pounds."

Mrs. Block looked from one to the other of the two men. There were times when she was a very ugly woman, and this was one of them.

"I believe you two," she began, "are nothing more nor less —— "

Mr. Billingham held out his hand with a warning gesture, and the woman, with an effort, held her tongue. The Marquis threw his card upon the table.

"Present this with my compliments to your husband, madame," he begged. "I shall remain in this afternoon."

The woman leaned over the table, tore up the card savagely, and threw the fragments into the fire. Then she crossed the room, unlocked a drawer and produced a thick wad of mille notes. She counted them out in piles of tens. At a hundred thousand she paused. Mr. Billingham shook his head.

"The exchange to-day," he reminded her dryly. . . .

She flung down another four packets. The Marquis picked them up with well-assumed nonchalance. His fingers trembled a little, however, as he thrust the entire roll into his breast coat pocket.

"I've been a damned fool," the woman confessed, "and I suppose I've got to pay for it."

"Fools always pay," Mr. Billingham murmured, as he picked up his hat and cane. "We have the honour, madame!"

"The deep regret!" the Marquis echoed.

"Go to blazes!" was the lady's valedictory remark.

Madelon and Mr. Billingham that night, being in a festive mood, dined at the Hôtel de Paris. They were still considering the matter of *hors d'œuvres* when a *maître d'hôtel* ushered in some late arrivals. Mr. Billingham glanced up casually, but his eyes remained transfixed. Madelon slightly turned her head. Mrs. Block, in one of her most gorgeous frocks, was sailing through the room. Behind her was a small, ill-made man of about five feet seven, with sandy hair, unpleasant complexion, bushy eyebrows, narrow, suspicious eyes, and a very acquisitive mouth. He was badly dressed and he had the clumsy presence and the assertive manners of a stranger to such places. The *maître d'hôtel*, who had been talking to Madelon, smiled.

"It is the husband of the wealthy lady from Leeds in England," he confided. "He arrived this morning."

"Fighting Tom!" Mr. Billingham gasped.

IV

THE CAFÉ OF TERROR

THE Marquis always talked very bad English when he was angry, and this morning he was very angry indeed. Climbing up narrow and precipitous paths upon a surface of loose stones, pushing his way occasionally through brambles and undergrowth, and looking downwards from heights, which always made him giddy, had been undertakings which had combined to incense him. He was not dressed or built for such mad escapades. The sight of Madelon, bare-headed, and laughing, having the air of one to whom such excursions, instead of being a torture, were a keen pleasure, only irritated him, whereas the final note of exasperation he discovered in the pleasant good temper of Mr. Samuel T. Billingham, their guide and host, who, with a huge cigar in his mouth, was walking with springy steps and unabated cheerfulness up the path which the Marquis had passionately declared to be only fit for goats and idiots.

"I can no further make this absurd promenade," the Marquis announced, sinking on to a heap of stones and dabbing with a scented pocket-handkerchief drops of moisture upon his forehead, which must not be allowed to reach his eyebrows. "It is an absurdity! I have a pain of the stomach, a pain of the knees, a pain of the back. It is not for this I came. Where is the automobile?"

"Poor uncle!" Madelon sympathised. "I had forgotten that you were not used to walking. You should have lived in England as I have done. But the view — you must admit that the view is marvellous!"

The comments of the Marquis upon the view were delivered

in fluent and sacrilegious French. He displayed an acquaintance with the various forms of blasphemy peculiar to his language which moved even Mr. Billingham to wondering admiration. "When I feel better," he concluded, after a moment's electric pause, "I shall apologise. At present I will only say that the view from the window of my *salon,* which takes in the Casino and all that glorious sea, is better worth having."

"Less than a kilometre to go," Mr. Billingham declared. "I reckon we shall strike the main road just beyond that clump of firs, and that's where I told the car to pick us up. Another quarter of an hour, Marquis, and we shall be in St. Félix."

"If one could only drink something!" the latter observed pettishly, as he rose to his feet. "I miss my morning *apéritif.*"

"That's coming to you, sure," Mr. Billingham promised. "I've done this tramp before, and unless I'm mistaken there's a little café where this path joins the cart track."

The prospect was sufficiently encouraging to induce the Marquis to struggle to his feet. They clambered another fifty yards or so up the stony path and found themselves in a rough track which had evidently been made by the carting of timber from the other side of the ravine. A little way along there was a small white-plastered building, to which Mr. Billingham pointed.

"The Café du Forêt!" he exclaimed. "The worst ever, so far as I remember, but a Dubonnet won't poison us."

The Marquis almost smiled.

"A Dubonnet will be acceptable," he admitted. "The place appears poverty-stricken, but if one can secure an unopened bottle —— "

"We'll find that," Mr. Billingham interrupted confidently.

A few minutes' further climb brought them to the café. It was small, dilapidated and uninviting. Nevertheless it proclaimed itself in rudely painted black letters to be a restaurant where *"Vins et Consommations"* were to be obtained. There were three iron tables outside with a couple of chairs at each, but no sign of life. The door stood open and his two companions followed Mr. Billingham inside. There was no one behind the little counter, no one in the rude little compartment with its sanded floor and benches in place of chairs. There were bottles upon the shelves, however, and a tumbler half full of brandy upon the counter. Mr. Billingham raised his voice and the glasses around shook.

"Hullo there!" he shouted.

"Allo, allo!" the Marquis echoed. *"N'y a-t-il personne ici pour nous servir?"*

There was a stolid, unsympathetic lack of response. They waited for a moment, then Mr. Billingham opened the door of the room behind the bar and glanced around. It was a rough-looking kitchen, with a stone floor and a few clumsy articles of furniture. A string of onions, a scraggy piece of meat, and a rabbit hung down from iron hooks in the ceiling. There were pots and dishes upon the table, but no fire or any sign of recent occupation. Mr. Billingham raised his voice again without result, opened still another door, and called up a flight of flimsy stairs —also without result. Then he returned to his companions.

"There is no one about at all," he announced.

"You might try outside," Madelon suggested.

Outside there was no garden but a little clearing, a rudely constructed shed built of pine logs from which the bark had not been stripped, and a lean-to shelter, with a corrugated iron roof, against the wall. Mr. Billingham again, in stentorian tones, invited the presence of the missing innkeeper and again without response. He returned to the bar.

"Deserted!" he exclaimed.

"They were preparing for a *fête* at the small village we passed through last," Madelon remarked. "Perhaps the people have gone there, or the man may work in the woods."

The Marquis smiled. He had been studying the labels upon the bottles.

"At least," he pointed out, "they have left a bottle of Dubonnet. Produce that excellent corkscrew of yours, my friend Billingham. We will serve ourselves and leave the money."

They opened the bottle of Dubonnet which the Marquis had dragged down from the shelf, found some thick wine-glasses, and seated themselves before one of the rude tables outside. Madelon gave a little exclamation of relief as they passed out into the pine-scented sunshine.

"That place gave me the shivers," she declared. "It seemed so very empty, so very silent."

"It's a lonely spot," Mr. Billingham agreed, pouring out the Dubonnet. "They seem to have left off felling the timber round here, and I guess that took the trade away."

"So long as they are absent," the Marquis said, "one owes them gratitude that they left the place open. Never have I tasted Dubonnet with a better flavour. Tell me, my friend Billingham, how much further of this abominable promenade before we reach the automobile?"

"Not more than half a kilometre," Mr. Billingham assured him. "There's a little path which leads straight up to the road from the cart track. There we shall find the automobile. In a few minutes more we shall be in St. Félix. After that — the *déjeuner!*"

The Marquis breathed a little sigh of content and helped himself once more from the bottle. Madelon, who had set her glass down empty, was fidgeting about as though anxious to start.

"Hungry?" Mr. Billingham enquired.

She shook her head.

"I have taken a dislike to this place," she confided. "Am I superstitious, I wonder? I have a terrible feeling about it."

The Marquis was sympathetic but entirely comfortable and not disposed to hurry. He lit a cigarette and leaned back in his chair.

"I understand," he murmured. "A deserted inn on the edge of the forest! There are all the materials here for drama. There was a story I once read —— "

He broke off abruptly and the cigarette fell from his fingers. Mr. Billingham sprang to his feet. Madelon, who had wandered a few yards away from them and turned back towards the house, was standing suddenly rigid, suddenly pale. The cry which had startled them had escaped from her lips. She pointed to the window above the door.

"There was a face there!" she cried. "Some one up in the room!"

Mr. Billingham remained composed.

"Well, I guess that isn't so terrible, after all," he observed. "I dare say there's some one ill there. Who was it—a man or a woman?"

"I do not know," Madelon answered faintly. "It was—just a face!"

"Seems to have given you a shock," Mr. Billingham continued. "Sit down, Miss Madelon, and drink half a glass more of this stuff. Guess I'd better hunt round and see if there's any help wanted."

Madelon—young woman of nerve and courage though she was—staggered into a chair and was utterly unable to raise to her lips the glass which her uncle hastily filled. Mr. Billingham disappeared inside the building. In about five minutes he returned.

"There's only one room upstairs," he announced, "and there ain't a soul in it."

"But I saw some one," Madelon protested.

He strolled a yard or two away and looked back at the window, pausing a moment to relight his cigar which had gone out.

"Well, there's no one there now," he assured her. "There's only one room and not a cupboard for a hiding-place. There are two beds—both look as though they'd been slept in—but there isn't a human being in the shanty. You can take my word for it."

Madelon looked at him steadfastly. She had drunk some of the Dubonnet and she was becoming herself again.

"Do you believe, then," she asked, "that I saw the face of some one who does not exist?"

"I shouldn't say you were the sort who saw spooks," Mr. Billingham admitted. "All I say is, there's no one there now."

"You must surely have realised, my dear Madelon," the Marquis intervened, "whether the face was the face of a man or a woman."

"I should have said that it was the face of a young man," Madelon replied, "but it might have been the face of a girl. There was a mass of black hair. The face itself was smooth. It was the eyes that were horrible."

"You don't say!" Mr. Billingham murmured with tolerant sympathy. "Kind of scared, were they?"

Madelon rose to her feet.

"Please let us go now," she begged. "I cannot talk about it any more. I can only assure you of one thing. Something terrible has happened here. Please, Mr. Billingham!"

"We'll get right along," was the prompt response. "Ten francs will square us for the bottle of Dubonnet, I guess — ten francs and what's left of the bottle. I'll put it underneath the glass — see? Now, we're right! Just a yard or two through the trees and then we'll leave this place behind us."

"I hope," Madelon murmured as they passed swiftly back to the cart track, "that I may be able to forget it."

The Marquis smiled.

"Pooh, pooh, my child!" he exclaimed. "You are too sensitive, too emotional! Material discomforts you scoff at. A fancy sometimes tortures you. Behold, the good news!"

He pointed upwards. At the end of the path was the curling main road and by the side of it the automobile Mr. Billingham had hired for their day's excursion. No vehicle before had ever appealed so greatly to the Marquis.

"We've struck it right after all," Mr. Billingham declared with satisfaction. "Gee, how hot the sun is out here! Lunch on the terrace in twenty minutes, Miss Madelon. Now, let's forget that dirty little shanty and its spook!"

The spook was not so easy to forget. Madelon, with Mr. Billingham as her escort, was on her way that evening from the Casino to Ciro's, when she suddenly gripped her companion's arm.

"Look," she cried, in a tone vibrant with absolute terror. "Look! The boy at that table!"

Mr. Billingham's eyes followed her gesture. The young man was certainly an unusual sight in such surroundings. His clothes, although perfectly new, were clumsily fashioned and of the sort worn on *fête* days by the peasants. His hat was pushed to the back of his head, and, although it was of the sombrero order affected by the mountaineers of the district, it failed to conceal the masses of black hair which gave him almost a grotesque appearance. His complexion was the usual burnt olive of the Provençal labourer. It was again his expression which arrested. His eyes were large and black, without either the vacancy or the humour of the peasant on the holiday. They looked neither at the people who passed, the trees and flowers of the plaza, nor at the bottle of wine which stood half empty by his side. They seemed to be looking at something which, if it existed at all, existed far away.

"That," Madelon said, "was the face I saw at the upstairs window of that place this morning."

Her hand was clutching nervously at his arm. Mr. Billingham patted it gently.

"Say, this boy has got on your nerves some," he declared. "I'll go across and have a talk with him. Sit down and wait for me."

"I think I will for a moment," Madelon acquiesced.

She seated herself on one of the benches by the side of the pavement. Mr. Billingham crossed the road and addressed the boy in hesitating but comprehensible French.

"Do you belong to the inn up near St. Félix?" he enquired. "The young lady and I were there this morning."

The boy stared at his questioner for a moment with parted lips and terrified expression. He made absolutely no reply, however.

"We could not find any one there," Mr. Billingham continued, speaking with laborious care. "We hoped there was nothing wrong."

The boy broke out into a stream of rapid, unintelligible speech, to which Mr. Billingham listened in ever-increasing confusion. He turned round to find Madelon by his side.

"Say, this young goat-herd has got hold of a lingo of his own," he complained. "I don't know as any one but a monkey could tell what he's chattering about. Seems kind of annoyed with me, but I can't get a word of it."

"It is the dialect of the Italians here," Madelon explained. "Let me try."

She spoke to him patiently. The boy only shook his head.

Presently he poured out another glass of wine and drank it. Then he sat quite still, stolid and inattentive. He took no notice of Madelon's questions. He showed no sign of understanding a word she said. In the end she was seized by a sudden revulsion. She tugged at her companion's arm.

"Come away!" she begged. "He will not reply. He pretends not to understand me, though I believe that he does. Let us leave him."

"Guess you're right," Mr. Billingham assented. "He's a crazy loon, if ever there was one, or he wouldn't speak such gibberish. Anyway, it's not our business."

They passed on. The young man looked after them sullenly and helped himself to more wine. Ten minutes later, when Mr. Billingham, obeying an unaccountable impulse, chose a moment when Madelon was talking to some acquaintances and hurried back, the chair was empty. The young man was gone.

"Anyway," Mr. Billingham murmured to himself, struggling against a curious feeling of uneasiness, "it ain't our affair."

Notwithstanding the fact that Mr. Billingham had twice declared that whatever trouble there might be or have been at the little inn on the edge of the forest was not his affair, it was barely ten o'clock in the morning when he left the automobile which he had hired in the Square at Monte Carlo, clambered down the steep path, made his way along the cart track, pushed through the clump of trees and found himself before the café. There was no smoke emerging from the chimney, and Mr. Billingham gave a little start of surprise as he saw on the table, in front of the still open door, the half-consumed bottle of Dubonnet and the ten-franc note under one of the glasses.

"I guess passers-by round here are pretty scarce," he ruminated. "Seems queer that whoever quit the place didn't trouble to lock up. Left in a hurry, perhaps."

Mr. Billingham would doubtless have scorned the suggestion that he talked to himself for the fact of any pleasure he might derive from hearing his own voice, and yet it was without a doubt true that the uneasy feeling of the day before had returned to an even larger extent. He pushed open the door. The half-emptied tumbler was still upon the counter. Some little disarrangement of the bottles upon the shelf, effected by their removal of the bottle of Dubonnet, still existed. He threw open the door leading to the kitchen and called out:

"Hullo there!"

There was no reply. He mounted the stairs with footsteps which he was half-ashamed to admit were reluctant ones. The bedroom was as empty as it had been on the previous day. There was no place to hide anywhere — no other room. As he descended, however, he realised that it was perfectly possible for the owner of the face which Madelon had seen there to have escaped by the back door and reached the wood in the matter of a very few seconds. He returned to the kitchen. Here he noticed for the first time that by the side of the fireplace was a clumsy framework door, which looked as though it might have led into a pantry or cupboard. He moved towards it and raised the latch. Before he threw the door open, he knew. When he closed it again — in the space of a second or two — there were great beads of perspiration upon his forehead. The colour had left his cheeks and the blood seemed to have been drained from his body. He staggered out into the bar, gripped the counter for a moment, saw a bottle of Martell's brandy on the bottom row of the shelf, seized it, made his faltering way outside, knocked off its neck against the top of one of the iron tables, and drank. . . . Mr. Billingham was a strong man and his recovery was prompt. Nevertheless, he was breathing heavily as he hastened up the hill to where his automobile was waiting.

"Drive to the Mairie at St. Félix," he ordered. . . .

Arrived at the Mairie — a small wistaria-covered building on the outskirts of the straggling village of St. Félix — Mr. Billingham was ushered at once by a gendarme into a bare little apartment with whitewashed walls and a row of benches, in which a very formal-looking gentleman with a closely trimmed black beard, very smoothly brushed hair, and gold-rimmed pince-nez, was seated at a table, signing documents. His work for the morning had consisted of adjudicating upon a highly important case of fowl stealing, and he looked with some surprise at his visitor's precipitate entrance. Mr. Billingham's opening statement was in far from lucid English. The magistrate, with a puzzled expression, waved him to a seat.

"*Comment,* Monsieur?" he exclaimed.

Mr. Billingham pulled himself together. His French, though not rapid, was fairly precise, and he had no difficulty in making himself understood.

"A woman has been murdered at a little café at the edge of the forest," he announced.

The magistrate gasped. The gendarme gasped.

"Continue, Monsieur," the former begged.

Mr. Billingham told his story. The magistrate gave him his entire attention. It was a great day, this! A murder! Obviously a murder, in his district! He began to make notes of Mr. Billingham's statement. He was friendly but official. It was quite hopeless for him to conceal the fact that the news had filled him with pleasurable interest. It had been the secret desire of his life to have the handling of such a case.

"I will accompany you to the inn myself at once, Monsieur," he announced, rising to his feet. "You can accommodate a gendarme, perhaps, on the front of your car. . . . Let the Court remain open till my return," he directed a subordinate. "Tell me again your story as we proceed, Monsieur."

Mr. Billingham went through the few facts again. In response to his own enquiries the magistrate gave him certain information.

"The inn," he said, "was kept by a very respectable, good man, of the name of Pierre Anson. He lived there with his wife, the woman who without a doubt is the victim, and his nephew, a young man of whom one hears not too much of good. The wife, it is reported, had savings, — savings of some account — and the nephew knew it. Three days ago news came to Anson of the death of a relative in Marseilles. This I know because he came to me for information as to the burying of the relative and as to his journey. He set off last Monday morning. He was expecting to return to-night. He left alone his wife and this nephew. One fears to reflect what may have happened!"

Mr. Billingham sighed, because he was a kind-hearted man,

and because a vision of that flashing knife of the guillotine is terrible to such. Nevertheless it was his duty.

"Last night," he confided, "the young man, who apparently was the nephew of Pierre Anson, was drinking wine at the Café de Paris in Monte Carlo. He was pointed out to me by the young lady who declared that his was the face she saw at the window."

The magistrate nodded gravely.

"It is a crime," he said, "in effect simple, not uncommon amongst this race of people. When heated with wine and drunk with the desire of pleasure, the shedding of blood is nothing. I, who tell you this, know."

They arrived at their destination. The magistrate and the gendarme made their way to the little room. Mr. Billingham sat outside. He had no soul for horrors. It was an hour before they rejoined him. The magistrate was carrying his notebook in his hand.

"All is clear," he announced. "The savings of the poor woman have disappeared. To-night, or to-morrow at the latest, the young man will be in our hands. Your name and address, if you please, Monsieur. You will attend the Court?"

"Certainly," Mr. Billingham promised.

"The young man," the magistrate continued, "will have had two nights of that wild pleasure of which he has lain awake, here in this place of tranquillity, and dreamed. Afterwards — well — he may escape with the penitentiary. One knows little of his age."

Mr. Billingham looked up at the blank window. The silence which brooded over the place remained unbroken. A gendarme, having closed the door, seated himself outside.

"Pierre Anson will arrive by the night train," the magistrate remarked. "It will be a sad home-coming for him."

"Better," Mr. Billingham rejoined, with a little shiver, "than if he had found the house empty and opened that door, as I did."

The most pathetic sight in the bare, whitewashed little room of the Mairie on the first morning of the examination, was

Pierre Anson, the woodman. The tears streamed down his brown, wrinkled face as the magistrate addressed his first few kindly questions. He had, at one time, as was evident, been a man of great stature and strength. Now he seemed shrunken up, stricken with the horror of his home-coming.

"Your wife had savings, Pierre Anson?" the magistrate asked him.

"She was a thrifty woman," was the tremulous reply. "She had always a stocking."

"Do you know how much was in it?"

"She never told me."

"Did your nephew — the young man between the gendarmes there — the young man whom you trusted alone with your wife — did he know?"

"I cannot tell," Pierre Anson answered. "He was always wanting money."

"You have been to Marseilles to bury a relative — is it not so?"

"Yes, Monsieur."

"You thought it safe to leave this youth, of whose character we hear little that is good, alone with your wife in such a desolate spot?"

"She was his aunt," the man announced, with a little sob. "How would I dream of anything so horrible?"

The magistrate bent over his papers. Mr. Billingham, seated by his side, watched the shaft of sunlight which had found its way through the cobwebbed windows and had fallen upon the boy's face. Madelon, who had also been invited by the magistrate to occupy a chair near him, scribbled something on a piece of paper and passed it to her neighbour. He glanced at it and passed it on to the magistrate, who studied it through his pince-nez with pursed lips. Finally, with a little shrug of the shoulders, he twiddled it between his fingers.

"Where did you stay in Marseilles, Pierre Anson?" he asked suddenly.

The woodman lifted his head and stared uncomprehendingly at his questioner.

"I asked you where you stayed in Marseilles," the magistrate repeated.

Pierre Anson shook his head.

"I do not remember," he said. "It was a small lodging-house down by the quay."

"You do not remember?" the magistrate echoed, in a tone of some surprise. "Is that not strange, Pierre Anson?"

"It was somewhere near where my cousin lay dead," the man answered, a little sullenly. "I could find the place — the name I never knew."

The magistrate's right arm suddenly shot out.

"Or is it that you are lying, Pierre Anson?" he thundered. "Is it that you yourself, before you left home in the small hours of that Tuesday morning, murdered your wife and stole her savings, forced two of the notes on that half-witted youth, persuaded him to buy clothes and go down to Monte Carlo, and went yourself to Nice — your *rendezvous* at Nice — to your *rendezvous* with Lucie Bérard?"

The man half rose to his feet. His eyes seemed suddenly bloodshot. He swayed about as though striving to speak.

"Bring the woman," the magistrate ordered.

Pierre Anson glanced fearfully towards the door. A woman in the care of a gendarme entered. They looked at one another across the room — the man and the woman — and one understood.

"The money of which you robbed your wife, Pierre Anson," the magistrate continued, "was found upon this woman. You have visited her month by month in Nice. You would have thrust the burden of this crime upon your nephew. You yourself are the murderer! Do you confess?"

A cry rang through the Court — not from the man, Pierre .Anson, who was indeed incapable of speech, whose hands were fighting the air, who fought against unconsciousness, but from the boy who stood between the gendarmes. His eyes were fixed upon the woman who had entered the Court Room. His indifference had vanished. His eyes again were filled with fear.

"Mother!" he cried.

"It is I!" she answered.

The boy turned towards the magistrate.

"It was I who killed the woman," he pleaded. "No one else knows anything about it."

"You are a liar and a fool!" the woman declared angrily. "It was he, the bungler there," she added, pointing to Pierre Anson. "And there is the money."

She dashed a bundle of notes upon the floor and stood with folded arms, defiant, the incarnation of an evil spirit. A gendarme touched Pierre Anson upon the shoulder. The proceedings were over.

Afterwards the magistrate entertained his two distinguished guests with a bottle of sweet wine and biscuits in his retiring-room. He was well pleased with the whole business.

"Amongst the lowest classes of our peasants," he explained, "these family dramas are not uncommon. Pierre Anson, as the story goes now, loved both sisters. He married the older one — a widow with money. The rest of the story unfolds itself. Yet Pierre Anson had cunning which few of these peasants possess. He deceived us all. It is to you, Monsieur," he added, turning to Mr. Billingham, "that we owe the clue by means of which we arrived at the truth."

Mr. Billingham shook his head.

"Not to me," he rejoined — "to the young lady."

The magistrate bowed.

"Then might one enquire," he ventured, "what led the young lady to doubt the lad's guilt?"

Madelon was once more serious.

"Something in his eyes," she confided, with a little shudder of reminiscence — "something which was there and something which was not there."

The magistrate raised his glass and bowed first to Madelon, then to Mr. Billingham.

"Something in his eyes," he repeated. "Well, one reads somewhere in a lay commentary upon our laws and the discovery of crime, that the born detective must have an instinct for the truth. Mademoiselle, there is a great vocation open to you."

Madelon smiled. She sipped her wine, but she remained silent.

V

THE ROYAL GAME

"Too bad!" Mr. Billingham murmured sympathetically.

Madelon was almost angry. She leaned across the table towards her companion.

"Speak to him, please," she begged. "It is impossible that we go on like this. It becomes an affair of charity. You dispense the money. Nobody earns anything. He thinks and dreams and talks of nothing but roulette. You wished him to make some enquiries about those people at Nice. He did nothing."

"Well, they've gone now, anyway," her companion remarked.

"Will you speak to him?" she persisted.

"Right away," Mr. Billingham promised. "Here he comes. Now you shall hear for yourself."

"Do not be too easy with him," she enjoined.

"Leave that to me," was the confident reply.

The Marquis drifted in from the Arcade to the glass-sheltered bar. He was happy and spruce. He had a mille's worth of counters in his pocket and the music of the whirling wheel in his ears. He greeted his niece and his friend with gay cordiality.

"A minute or two late, I fear," he apologised. "Let mine be the pleasure. Waiter!"

An approved order was given. The Marquis accepted a chair.

"Mr. Billingham has something to say to you, Uncle," Madelon confided.

"A little matter of business which arises, eh?" the Marquis asked. "Well, I am at your disposal."

"As a matter of fact," Mr. Billingham declared, "neither your niece nor I have had any fortune for the last few weeks, and, to put it bluntly, funds are running low. We think that it is time you bestirred yourself."

"Indeed, yes, Uncle," Madelon intervened. "You spend morning, noon and night at the tables. You make no acquaintances. You take no initiative."

"You being, so to speak," Mr. Billingham went on, "the social bird of the party, we expect you to be more in evidence."

The Marquis gulped down his cocktail.

"You think that I am neglecting our interests — our joint interests?" he demanded, in a hurt tone.

"That idea has occurred to us," Mr. Billingham admitted.

"There is no doubt about it," Madelon said coldly.

The Marquis made signs to the waiter.

"I am," he announced, "in a position to prove that you have misjudged me. I have, in our joint interests, made the acquaintance of two gentlemen who possess the most amazing gifts. They need fresh blood and — er — introductions. I am arranging to provide them with both."

"What may their gifts be?" Mr. Billingham enquired.

"They are expert poker players," the Marquis explained. "Their knowledge of the game is indeed wonderful. Amongst my acquaintances there are several wealthy men to whom the tables are no longer a novelty. A game of cards amuses. I have promised to arrange something, to play myself, to bring you. We are to put up nothing and we are to have a third of the winnings."

Mr. Billingham sighed.

"Are your friends clever enough to put this through?" he asked.

"One of them," the Marquis confided, "was a professional entertainer for some years. His speciality was card tricks. The other learned the game upon an Atlantic liner."

"It is a primitive form of misappropriation, this," Mr. Billingham sighed, "but it depends, of course, upon the measure of skill which your friends possess. Invite them to a rehearsal. Have you pointed me out to them yet?"

"Not yet," the Marquis admitted.

"Bring them along to my sitting-room to-night, after dinner," Mr. Billingham enjoined. "Introduce me as an American tourist upon his travels, one of the jay birds with plenty of the dough.

You may say that I only play a low game, but after a few whiskies and sodas I like to increase the stakes. I'll figure it out myself then if they're to be trusted."

The Marquis looked a little doubtful.

"You will lose your money," he ventured, "and it may not be possible to explain afterwards."

"Guess I'll fix that," Mr. Billingham promised. "Bring your friends along and I'll see what's doing."

When he ascended to his sitting-room that evening after dinner, Mr. Billingham prepared to dispense hospitality on a generous scale. There were two packs of unopened cards upon a green baize table, whiskies and sodas and a box of cigars upon the sideboard, besides a variety of liqueurs. Presently there was a knock at the door and in response to Mr. Billingham's hearty invitation to enter there appeared the Marquis, Madelon, and the Marquis' two friends, whom he introduced as Mr. Conrad Adler and Mr. Blane T. Hackett of St. Louis. Mr. Conrad Adler was a trifle Semitic. He wore a black moustache, curly black hair, and tortoise-shell glasses. Mr. Blane T. Hackett was of a different type — florid, large, and more American than Mr. Billingham himself. His hand-shake was painful, his tone almost vociferous. He eyed the preparations for the evening's entertainment with approval.

"Our friend, Mr. Adler," the Marquis explained, "is in the wine trade. He travels a great deal. Mr. Hackett is like yourself — an American bent on pleasure."

"And very glad to meet a fellow countryman over on this side," Mr. Hackett declared cordially. "You still in business, sir?"

"Only partly," Mr. Billingham confessed. "Linoleum."

"Boots," Mr. Hackett confided — "the Hackett Boot Company, out at St. Louis. I guess I'm like you — get tired of these foreign games. The sight of a couple of decks of cards and a few chips looks good to me. Shall we make it a small game?"

"Fifty francs ante, and a hundred francs rise?" Mr. Billingham suggested. "Will you join us, Marquis?"

"With pleasure," the latter assented.

The four men sat down. Mr. Billingham distributed the chips, and accepted the money. A waiter, who made an unobtrusive appearance, served drinks and passed the cigars. The game proceeded and it was very soon apparent that it was proceeding very contrary to the expectations of Mr. Conrad Adler and his friend. On one occasion, when the former had shown, with a half apologetic air, four eights, having drawn three cards, and Mr. Billingham, with a quiet chuckle, had laid down four knaves, an explosion appeared to be imminent. The game was continued, however, although with the exception of their host the players became more and more silent. At the end of an hour the whole of the chips lay in front of Mr. Billingham. That gentleman paused to light a cigar.

"Seems to me I got all the luck to-night," he remarked. "What do you say, gentlemen,— shall we raise the stakes a bit? The game seems kinder quiet."

Mr. Conrad Adler glanced at his watch.

"I got to go," he mumbled. "I forgot I had an appointment over at the Casino."

There was an expression of pain upon Mr. Hackett's face.

"I'll be getting along too," he announced stiffly. "I don't seem to quite get the hang of this game."

"Eh?" Mr. Billingham ejaculated with ferocious emphasis.

Mr. Hackett opened his mouth and closed it again. His eyes were fixed upon the pile of counters in front of Mr. Billingham's place and the little roll of bills underneath his tumbler.

"Fact of it is," Mr. Hackett confided, "I don't think I know enough about this game for the present company."

"You'll learn," Mr. Billingham assured him cheerfully. "Any day that you feel like a little lesson, make the stakes worth while and I'll show you. Have another cigar before you go."

The two men took their leave, crestfallen, suspicious, and a little vituperative. The Marquis looked at his friend and gasped. Madelon came over and patted him on the shoulder.

"Clever dear!" she murmured.

"Say, that was nothing at all," Mr. Billingham assured her lightly. "Watch me!"

He threw a pack of cards into the air, brought one down

from the ceiling, another from the sleeve of Madelon's dress, and a third from the back of his collar.

"Just a little lesson for you, Marquis," he said. "Now I'm going to let you have it straight. Cardsharping don't come inside our little scheme of life. Do you get that?"

"It really seems," Madelon sighed, "as though with gifts like yours some profitable use should be made of them."

"My dear," Mr. Billingham protested, "cheating at cards is a low-down game. We're out for adventures all right, but we're out to skin the worthless rich and to skin 'em our own way. You take my advice, Marquis, and don't you be seen speaking to that pair of crooks again. They'll get found out the first time they try a serious game with any man who knows his way about."

"But you are so much cleverer than they are," Madelon expostulated. "Couldn't you get hold of some really terrible people and win just a little of their money? I saw the most beautiful chinchilla cape yesterday, and so cheap!"

Mr. Billingham was playing idly with the cards.

"Do you," he asked the Marquis, "happen to know Madame Groosens?"

The Marquis shivered.

"The good God forbid!" he exclaimed.

"That horrible creature!" Madelon cried. "Every one in the club and at the Casino, too, hates her. She claims every one's stakes. She's always trying to bully the croupiers — an unspeakable person!"

"She has no friends," Mr. Billingham remarked, "and therefore to make her acquaintance should be easy. I heard her say that she preferred bridge and poker to all that gambling. Here is your task, Marquis. Make her acquaintance and bring her with two or three absolutely respectable people to a little game of poker. There shall be no cheating, but something might come of it."

"It is a horrible task," the Marquis complained, with a little shiver, "but I must confess that you intrigue me."

"See about it, then," Mr. Billingham enjoined, "and, by the by, you might remember this. Another ten days at the most sees our exchequer dry. I do not know what you have saved out of your share of our little adventures — you have perhaps added to them by your roulette wins — but as a co-operative society we're on the rocks."

The Marquis rose to his feet.

"I will take a stroll through the Club," he observed.

"We will follow," Mr. Billingham agreed. "I feel like a little flutter myself. . . ."

The roulette room of the Club was crowded. Around the louis table people were standing two and three deep. Madelon touched Mr. Billingham on the arm. Almost opposite was the woman of whom they had spoken. They watched her for some moments. She was short and inclined to be fat, expensively dressed and with a profusion of jewellery. Her face was heavy and pallid, her mouth disagreeable, her eyes acquisitive. With her sallow, pendulous cheeks and occasional glimpses of ill-shaped teeth, she was irresistibly reminiscent of a soft and pudgy insect.

"They call her 'the yellow slug,' " Madelon whispered. "Watch her now."

She stood with a plaque in her hand, as though uncertain whether or not to risk it. People on either side of her made their stakes. Still she hesitated. The wheel spun, the number was announced. There was a plaque placed some time previously, almost in front of her upon the table.

"*Un cheval à moi*," she called out shrilly to the croupier.

An Englishwoman seated on the same side of the table protested.

"Madame is mistaken," she exclaimed indignantly. "The plaque was mine."

There was the usual controversy. Madame Groosens ejaculated, shouted, pushed, and finally seized the money. The croupier looked remorseful. The *chef* awaited an appeal. The woman to whom the money belonged shrugged her shoulders.

"It is not worth while," was her only comment.

"Absolute robbery," Madelon murmured, as Madame Groosens thrust the plaques into her gold bag and left the table.

Mr. Billingham nodded.

"I'm glad we saw that," he declared. . . . "Mademoiselle, I take my hat off to your uncle. Behold!"

The Marquis was offering his commiserations. It was most annoying to have one's stake claimed. He was glad that Madame had courage. These people who were not *habituées* threw down their placques right and left and claimed everything.

"Uncle is really doing his best," Madelon whispered.

"He is earning good money," Mr. Billingham assented.

The second poker party in Mr. Billingham's room came off within the next few evenings. It consisted of Mr. Billingham himself, the Marquis, Madame Groosens, and two perfectly respectable acquaintances of the Marquis — Madame de Bernande, a well-known resident of Monte Carlo, and Lord Henerford, whom the Marquis had once met in Paris and who was also a well-known *habitué*. The presence of Madame Groosens appeared to be somewhat of a surprise, and Madame de Bernande's greeting was cool in the extreme. The Marquis, however, who figured as host, exerted all his tact to create a feeling of friendliness.

"Seems deuced odd to be playing poker down here," Lord Henerford remarked. "One does get rather fed up with these other games, though."

"I play poker at my villa once a week," Madame de Bernande announced. "Some of you must join me there one evening. I expect your friend Mr. Billingham plays very well — most Americans do."

"Nothing out of the way, madame," Mr. Billingham assured her. "When I was in business in New York we used to play Saturday nights at the country club and I played coming across on the steamer."

"A risky proceeding," Lord Henerford murmured.

"I guess I can generally size people up," Mr. Billingham declared. "Besides, the gangs who work the steamers are pretty well-known. I wouldn't say they had much chance — on the Southern route, anyway."

The game proceeded without event. The Marquis and Mr. Billingham were excellent joint hosts and they kept the game from flagging. Sandwiches and other forms of refreshment were handed around, and Lord Henerford declared that Mr. Billingham's cigars were the best he had smoked in Monte Carlo. As the evening wore on, Mr. Billingham more than once showed signs of some perturbation. He looked at his cards on several occasions before he threw them in and he paid marked attention to Madame Groosens' play. She, to her intense satisfaction, became in time almost the only winner. A pile of chips and counters was gathered in front of her, by the side of her gold bag. Her little eyes twinkled, her covetous mouth was twisted into a satisfied smile.

Madame de Bernande whispered at last in Madelon's ear: "My dear, what induced your uncle to ask that horrible woman here? She robs every one downstairs and makes life a torment to the croupiers."

"My uncle is very good-natured," Madelon sighed, "but indeed she almost invited herself."

Mr. Billingham was dealing. A very considerable jack-pot had been opened and it was Madame Groosens' turn to take cards.

"Three," she demanded.

Mr. Billingham threw three cards face downwards upon the table. Madame Groosens apparently discarded three and held out her hand to draw the three which had been given her. Suddenly, Madelon, who was standing by the fireplace, dropped a tumbler with a little crash. Everyone started and looked round. There was a moment's pause. Then Mr. Billingham's voice rang out, clear and sharp.

"Madame," he insisted, "don't move! Don't touch your cards!"

His left hand suddenly imprisoned hers.

"Ladies and gentlemen," he announced, "I regret to say that Madame Groosens has been cheating. I have been watching her. This time I am convinced."

The woman was absolutely incapable of speech. She glared at her accuser with an expression of blank and utter amazement. The natural venom of her face, however, destroyed its attempted innocence.

"Don't move!" Mr. Billingham repeated. "I gave you three

cards. Lord Henerford, be so good as to see how many lie in front of Madame."

"Only two," Lord Henerford declared.

"Now lift her reticule."

Lord Henerford did as he was bidden.

"There is another card there," he said producing it.

"That," Mr. Billingham pointed out, "is the third card. Now lift that handkerchief which has been lying on the table by her side all the time."

Lord Henerford obeyed. Underneath the handkerchief another card was concealed.

"Now, Madame, show your hand," Mr. Billingham ordered.

Madame Groosens, still speechless, did as she was told. She held a pair of aces. In obedience to a gesture, Lord Henerford turned up the card under the handkerchief. It was another ace.

"The trick is a simple one," Mr. Billingham explained. "I've seen it done on the steamer more than once. I never expected to see it in company like this. When I gave her three cards, Madame discarded one, but pushed it with her sleeve under the reticule. She was helping herself to the one underneath the handkerchief which had been waiting there for the occasion — the third ace. You see? She would have scooped the pool."

Madame Groosens found words at last. Her abuse was violent, her statements vehement, but both seemed utterly futile. Everyone listened to her coldly.

"If Madame Groosens had not kept that ace underneath her handkerchief, if she had not put it there herself, who else would have been likely to?" Mr. Billingham demanded. "Everyone saw me give three cards upon the table. How did that third card — the one she wanted to get rid of — get underneath her reticule?"

Madame Groosens sprang to her feet and commenced stuffing her winnings into her bag. The Marquis, however, held her wrist.

"Madame," he insisted, "this is a serious affair. You must kindly leave that money where it is." . . .

"You, ladies and gentlemen," Mr. Billingham added, moving towards the bell, "are the best judges of what should be done.

I suggest that I send for the manager of the hotel and a representative of the Casino."

Madame Groosens sat down heavily. She had a sudden and an awful vision of the joy with which this substantiated charge against her would be received. She had a vision of life without Monte Carlo. She shook in every limb.

"It is all a mistake!" she gasped.

"Mistakes of such a nature," the Marquis commented, "do not occur."

"You can take your money," Madame Groosens exclaimed passionately — "take it back. I am innocent, but this shall not be spoken of. You can have your money. I will go!"

Mr. Billingham walked to the door, locked it and returned with the key in his pocket.

"Madame de Bernande," he said, "and you, Lord Henerford, I am an American and I don't quite know how you treat a case like this. I guess I'd be glad of some advice."

"The woman should be punished. She should be exposed," Madame de Bernande declared.

"Without a doubt something should be done," Lord Henerford assented, helping himself to a whisky and soda.

"But I never touched the cards," Madame Groosens protested hysterically. "I took what were given to me."

"I guess you may as well cut that out," Mr. Billingham said shortly. "I am a man who is accustomed to being believed, and I tell you to your face that I have seen you cheat and so have the others."

"There is no possible doubt about it," Madame de Bernande agreed.

Madame Groosens leaned back in the chair, distracted, vicious, impotent. Mr. Billingham took the pile of notes and counters and divided them into heaps. He returned to each an equal portion.

"I guess that leaves us pretty well as we were," he pointed out. "The next thing for us to decide is what ought we to do about this lady."

"Do about me?" she gasped. "You've taken my money. You've lied about me. You've insulted me —— "

"She is always like this," the Marquis interrupted, with an apologetic little gesture. "We have had warning enough below from the croupiers."

"If you think, madame," Mr. Billingham said sternly, "that you're going to get out of this scot-free, you're making a big mistake. I guess you've run up against the wrong crowd this time. How much you've made by cheating people all your life as you tried to cheat us to-night, no one can tell, but some of those dollars you're going to refund. That's a sure thing!"

"This is interesting," the Marquis remarked. "What do you propose?"

"I propose, ladies and gentlemen," Mr. Billingham continued, "that we adopt one of two courses. We either publish an account of what has transpired this evening socially and to the managers of the Casino and the Sporting Club, who, I am inclined to believe, would welcome such information, or we fine Madame a certain sum which shall be entrusted to one of us for distribution amongst certain approved charities."

"I," Madame de Bernande said, "am in favour of reporting Madame to the authorities."

"I, on the other hand," the Marquis intervened, "am not absolutely certain that that would entirely exclude her from the use of the Rooms. I am therefore in favour of making her pay."

"And I, if I have a voice in the matter," Madelon echoed.

"I should make her stump up," Lord Henerford agreed. "Touch 'em through their pockets more readily than in any other way."

"That goes, then," Mr. Billingham decided. "Madame, on receipt of a cheque for two thousand pounds, which I shall devote to certain charities which I have already in my mind, you may leave this room. If you hesitate for more than twenty seconds I shall ring the bell and ask for the Manager."

Madame Groosens hesitated for less than twenty. She wrote the cheque and she left the room, with a venomous backward glance which few of them ever forgot. The little party broke up soon afterwards, leaving Mr. Billingham, the Marquis and Madelon alone. Mr. Billingham, in an enterprising frame of mind, amused himself bringing cards from the chimney, from under the carpet, even fluttering a few down from the ceiling.

"May we ask," Madelon demanded, "to what charities you propose to devote that little cheque?"

Mr. Billingham smiled blandly.

"Charity," he replied, "begins at home!"

"Is poker really a game of skill?" Madelon asked, as she and Mr. Billingham paced the Terrace after dinner a few nights later.

"I shall probably be able to answer that question to-morrow morning," her companion replied, a little grimly. "I have promised to make up a game to-night with some of the New York crowd. I don't much fancy it."

Madelon laughed softly.

"Why, my dear man," she exclaimed, "you can do what you like with them!"

Mr. Billingham shook his head a little sadly.

"In a way we are friends," he explained. "They are fellow club-men. I cannot treat them as I would Mrs. Groosens. So far as any manipulation of the cards is concerned we meet on equal terms."

"Then don't gamble," she begged. "Madame Groosens' two thousand isn't going to last us for ever."

"If I don't gamble," Mr. Billingham objected, "I must lose. Poker's kind of a queer game that way. The man who sits too tight at the stakes this crowd play is bound to get it in the neck."

"Whom are you playing with?" she enquired.

Mr. Billingham inclined his head towards the harbour.

"With Millionaire Frost and his crowd."

"On the yacht?"

Mr. Billingham nodded.

"I've got to get down there in a few minutes," he confided.

"What are you doing?"

"I'm going to the opera after the first act, to Madame de Bernande's box. You can leave me at the door as you pass — and good luck to you! Remember my chinchilla cape, and do not bluff!" . . .

Mr. Billingham looked for a moment or two almost wistfully after Madelon's slim form as she passed into the Casino. Then, with a little sigh, he went on his way down the steps, along the quay, across the drawbridge, to be received with much respect by a smart-looking steward and ushered into the saloon of the famous yacht "The Flying Dutchman." Here four or five men were still sitting over their wine. The host of the party — a thick-set, prosperous-looking New Yorker — waved his hand cordially.

"Glad to see you, Billingham. Take a seat and try my Madeira before we get to business. Shake hands with Senator Curtis — Mr. Billingham. I guess you know the rest of the crowd."

Mr. Billingham accepted the seat, exchanged greetings all round and drank a glass of wine. They were a typical little gathering of New Yorkers — opulent, full of good-nature and friendliness, — and when they moved to the smoke-room and sat down at the poker table everyone was on the best of terms with himself and his neighbour. Only Mr. Billingham was for a moment thoughtful. He had paused to glance through the porthole across the little glittering stretch of water to the flaming lights of the Casino. He pulled himself together, however, with barely an effort, at the rattling of the chips.

"A hundred dollars ante, a thousand dollars rise — how's that?" the host proposed.

"It's steep," Mr. Billingham commented.

"I've seen you play the same game at the Manhattan," one of his acquaintances observed. "And anyway it's no use playing for nuts."

"I'm agreeable to whatever stakes you generally play, gentlemen," Mr. Billingham acquiesced. "I guess it will take three of a kind to get me curious."

"You sit tight and you'll win a wad," Millionaire Frost declared. "We're all fool bluffers here. The Senator's the only man who understands the game and he loses."

The chips were apportioned, the deal commenced, and the game proceeded. Mr. Billingham, playing with the utmost care, managed just to hold his own for the first part of the evening. At half-past eleven his host glanced at the clock.

"We're an early crowd here, Sam," he said. "Twelve o'clock sees us through. What do you say to starting a couple of rounds of jack-pots?"

"I'm agreeable," Mr. Billingham assented readily. "I was kind of set on seeing the folk out of the Opera, anyway."

A round of jack-pots proceeded with varying fortunes. Mr. Billingham saw his stock of chips, notwithstanding the utmost caution, materially reduced, and as each chip represented a hundred or a thousand dollars according to its colour, the fact was not without its significance. The last jack-pot of the game Mr. Billingham himself opened. Every one came in and every one drew three cards, excepting the host, who drew two, and Mr. Billingham, who took one and started the betting with the limit — a thousand dollars. He was seen by every one until it came to the turn of his host, who raised him a thousand dollars. Mr. Billingham without hesitation raised the bid another thousand. The others dropped out. Thenceforward it became a duel. The betting reached ten thousand dollars. Millionaire Frost relit his cigar, studied his cards and looked across at his adversary.

"Say, ain't we wasting our breath like this?" he demanded. "It stands at ten thousand dollars just now. What about the doubling game?"

"I'm agreeable," Mr. Billingham replied without hesitation.

"Twenty thousand dollars, then," Millionaire Frost proposed.

"Forty thousand," Mr. Billingham rejoined.

There was a little chorus of exclamations and chaff.

"Guess you've run up against something, my lad," Senator Curtis observed, with a chuckle. "It's a great game, that doubling game!"

Millionaire Frost studied his cards once more, scratched his head and hesitated. Finally he threw them down on the table.

"I'm letting you have it, Billingham," he announced. "I reckon you've got me. In any case I've quit being inquisitive."

"What did you get, anyway, Frost?" his friend Senator Curtis enquired.

"Only a pair of kings," was the regretful reply. "I kept a kicker and threw two, to put him off, but he wasn't having any. No good seeing him. He drew one card and opened. He must have opened with two pairs, which had me beat, to start with."

"Say, what had you?" the Senator enquired, turning to Mr. Billingham.

The latter hesitated for a single moment.

"I'd have you understand," he explained diffidently, "that this isn't the kind of game I generally play. I picked up the eight, nine, ten, knave of spades and the knave of hearts. I opened the jack-pot, pushed the knave of hearts here to show you my openers," he went on, disclosing it, "and drew for a straight flush."

"And what did you get?" the other demanded.

Mr. Billingham turned his cards face upwards. He had still the eight, nine, ten, knave of spades and the two of hearts.

"Bust!" he pointed out.

They all gazed at the cards open-mouthed. There was a roar of laughter. The Senator leaned across and patted Mr. Billingham on the back.

"You've put one over on the old man," he declared. "Say, Frost, what about it?"

Millionaire Frost laughed good-humouredly.

"A fine bit of play," he pronounced. "We'll have a bottle and a sandwich and drink your health, Mr. Billingham!"

Mr. Billingham was just in time to meet Madelon as she came out of the Opera. She had said good-bye to Madame de Bernande, and she welcomed him with a smile of pleasure.

"I knew Uncle wouldn't be here, although he promised," she said.

"I hurried round," Mr. Billingham confided, "to see how you felt about a bite of supper."

"I should love it," she declared. "But tell me first, please — you didn't bluff?"

"Not exactly what you might call bluffing," Mr. Billingham replied evasively, as he tucked her hand through his arm, and started across the Square.

VI

BLOOD-MONEY

There was something wrong with Mr. Billingham. For two days he had shown a marked lack of interest in his food, his drink, and his gambling. The Spring had laid its relaxing hand upon the hills and the little Principality; the sun had gained in strength, the flowers in the gardens were drooping, there were cracks in the smoothly-shaven lawns, umbrellas at every table in the Café de Paris, and green verdure in place of the snows on the lower slopes of the mountains. Men were wearing flannels and straw hats, and some of the women had even ventured upon muslins. Mr. Billingham, however, seemed slow in responding to these genial signs of the advancing season. For several days he had shown a tendency almost to mope. The climax came when, at half an hour before his usual luncheon-time, he complained of his cocktail at Ciro's.

"*Mais comment,* Monsieur?" the bartender exclaimed. "It is as I have always mixed it day by day for months."

"It tasted flat," Mr. Billingham pronounced — "Flat!"

There was nothing more to be said. The bartender withdrew with a pained look. The Marquis stared first at his friend's frosted glass, then at Mr. Billingham himself.

"My friend," he declared, "it is perhaps the liver. The cocktail is as always. The moment you enter the place Charles braces himself. You have even those much to be treasured drops of absinthe at your disposal."

"It didn't taste good," Mr. Billingham insisted doggedly.

"We will try another," the Marquis suggested. "Charles! In case there should have been any slight discrepancy in the mixing, in case your elbow should have shaken with the angostura, your special attention, if you please."

Charles had scarcely recovered from his hurt, but he obeyed orders. He shook the cocktails himself in front of the two men and poured them out, waiting for the verdict. Mr. Billingham felt that he had perhaps been a little unreasonable.

"I guess the cocktail was all right, Charles," he admitted. "It's myself that's out of sorts."

Charles accepted the *amende* and withdrew. Mr. Billingham leaned forward and gripped his companion by the arm. His eyes were fixed upon two approaching figures.

"Say, Marquis," he demanded, "who the devil's the young man with Madelon?"

The Marquis adjusted his eyeglass and stared at the newcomers. Madelon was wearing a ravishing little gown of lemon-coloured linen, with an adorable little hat. Her companion was a tall, thin young Englishman in grey tweeds, who walked very slowly with the help of a stick.

"That is Captain Bruntingford," the Marquis answered. "Madelon introduced me to him last night."

"Know anything about him?" Mr. Billingham enquired.

"Nothing whatever," was the candid reply.

"Mademoiselle Madelon does, apparently, to judge from the way she's been going round with him the last few days," Mr. Billingham grunted.

The Marquis suddenly understood the cause of his friend's low spirits. Internally he amused himself; externally he remained placid.

"Madelon has, perhaps, an eye to business," her uncle remarked under his breath. "She is scarcely likely to find any other interest in the young man. Be careful! They arrive!"

Madelon entered the little glass-enclosed room with the sunshine streaming through the windows, her eyes laughing, her step light and buoyant. She kissed her hand to Mr. Billingham, installed her companion in a chair and placed his stick by his side.

"Mr. Billingham," she said, "let me introduce you in the best American fashion. Shake hands, if you please, with Captain Bruntingford, late of the British Army. Uncle, you have met Captain Bruntingford. Mr. Billingham, will you order us some of those cocktails with a little froth at the top — or," she added, turning to the young man ——

"I'd like a dry Martini, if I may," he begged.

Mr. Billingham gave the necessary orders. The little party joined forces. Mr. Billingham was prompt in extending an invitation to luncheon, but Madelon shook her head.

"I am lunching with Captain Bruntingford," she answered. "He would be quite polite if we turned it into a *partie carrée,* but he would be very cross with me afterwards. Englishmen need so much humouring."

"Americans can get the needle sometimes," Mr Billingham reminded her.

• "Not wise Americans," she replied — "not really good and kind Americans, who like their friends to be happy and who trust them. Besides, Captain Bruntingford and I have serious matters to discuss."

The cocktails were drunk and approved. Madelon helped her companion out of his chair, gave him his stick, and they departed. Mr. Billingham stared after them gloomily.

"Who the devil is this fellow Bruntingford?" he asked again.

"I expect Madelon will tell you presently," her uncle replied cautiously. "I know nothing about him myself. At the same time ——"

"Well?"

"I do not fancy that Madelon is only amusing herself. She has, what you call, the eye to business, as we, too, upon occasion."

Mr. Billingham found the suggestion consoling. He was able, even, to find some slight interest in his luncheon. Afterwards Madelon unexpectedly joined them. They had the corner table on the terrace and she accepted a chair and some coffee. An older woman might have found the streaming sunshine disconcerting, but the faint violet lines under Madelon's eyes — perhaps a little more readily visible in the flood of light — were, owing to the freshness of her complexion, only intriguing.

"Tell us, my dear," the Marquis invited, "more of your friend, Captain Bruntingford."

Madelon shut her vanity case with a click.

"I like the type," she said, "and he orders the right sort of things to eat. He has just the right tone, too, with head-waiters. In short, I find him quite an agreeable companion."

"Is this sufficient," the Marquis ventured, "to account for the enthusiasm with which you have accepted his recent invitations?"

"Perhaps not altogether," she conceded. "You see, he was wounded in nineteen-fourteen, and afterwards he was attached to the Intelligence Department of the British Army. His section seems to have been broken up since the war and he has gone into partnership with a firm of private detectives."

The Marquis tapped a cigarette upon the tablecloth.

"Indeed," he murmured.

"That sounds kind of interesting," Mr. Billingham observed.

"He is out here," she continued, "on some sort of business for his firm. That is exactly as much as he has confided in me. I am beginning to believe," she went on, with a sigh, "that it is as much as he means to tell me. And I am just a little curious."

Madelon paused for a moment. She was gazing out of the window through the dark green of the gardens, towards the stucco front of the Casino.

"Every afternoon," she proceeded, "he drives himself in a little two-seated car towards La Turbie; always in the same direction, always about the same hour. Another thing about that expedition rather interests me, too. Always, before he starts, he feels in his pocket to be sure that his revolver is there."

"But how observant!" the Marquis murmured.

Madelon shrugged her shoulders.

"The sort of grey tweed lounge suit which he wears," she said, "is not made for carrying things in its pockets if you wish to conceal their shapes. Then, there is one other somewhat singular circumstance. Although he is liberal with his invitations to me for luncheons, dinners, and suppers, he has never once asked me to accompany him in that afternoon drive."

The Marquis smiled faintly.

"A little piqued!" he commented.

"Possibly," Madelon assented. "In any case it has occurred to me that it was my turn to bring something into the bag."

Mr. Billingham smoked serenely. He was feeling a little more content with life.

"There may not be room for us to butt in," he remarked. "He may be just collecting evidence in some divorce case. These detective agencies don't as a rule handle the big jobs."

"Nevertheless, I am intrigued," Madelon persisted. "There is much about Captain Bruntingford that interests me. Sometimes in the middle of a dinner or a luncheon I have seen a shadow pass over his face, and a light in his eyes as though there were something near which he feared. I have see him start when someone has nearly run into us at a corner. I am sure that he is a brave man, yet I am sure that he has been living in fear."

"The remains of shell-shock, perhaps," Mr. Billingham speculated. "Has he taken that little red car out this afternoon?"

Madelon nodded.

"He has taken it out and gone just the same way — upon the route the cars take for La Turbie."

"It's a fine afternoon," Mr. Billingham said. "I'll hire an automobile and treat you to a spin. We'll go up to the Golf Club to tea."

Madelon hesitated, but it was obvious that the idea attracted her.

"I should love to come," she admitted. "Only, if we do happen to meet Captain Bruntingford in his red car, I hope he will not think that we are following him."

"It's an open road," Mr. Billingham reminded her, "and there are plenty of others upon it. We'll get a move on right away and see the sunset from the top."

The little party started within a quarter of an hour. They never reached La Turbie. About halfway up the narrow road which leads into the upper Corniche, just after negotiating a very awkward bend, they came upon an all too common sight in this region of mountainous roads and reckless driving. A little crowd of people were gathered on the edge of the precipitous slope. The remains of a small car lay upside-down, partially concealed by a huge volume of smoke and steam and with little flames bursting from the petrol tank. A few yards away something was stretched upon the ground, covered by a mackintosh sheet. Mr. Billingham touched the driver upon the arm, and by his directions the automobile was brought to an abrupt standstill.

"I shouldn't come on, Miss Madelon," he advised. "Let the chauffeur back with you to the corner. The Marquis and I will see if there is anything to be done."

Madelon was looking straight ahead of her. The colour had left her cheeks, but her voice was quite steady.

"The little red car!" she exclaimed.

Mr. Billingham nodded.

"I thought it might be," he assented. "I'm afraid by the way they've covered the body up there isn't much left of poor Captain Bruntingford."

Madelon half closed her eyes.

"I think perhaps you are right," she murmured. "Please come back to me soon."

The car was reversed slowly to the corner and left in a safe place. From below a large police motor van came tearing up the hill, and from above a doctor's automobile from La Turbie was winding its way to the scene of the disaster. Mr. Billingham and the Marquis joined the little crowd of people. No one seemed to know much of what had happened. The car had struck the low grey stone wall at the side of the road and turned over. The driver was apparently quite dead; his neck must have been broken.

"Better let me see," Mr. Billingham suggested. "I'm not a medical man, but I did a little amateur surgery in the war."

They made way for him and he lifted the waterproof cover. When, a few moments later, he rose from his knees, most of his healthy colour had departed. The doctor from above and a police *commissaire* from below arrived almost together. Mr. Billingham took the Marquis by the arm and led him a little way down the hill. They could see the marks of the car, could see where it had apparently skidded and over-turned. About twenty or thirty paces further on was a small villa, enclosed by a high wall of white plaster. Mr. Billingham looked at it speculatively. Then he looked back at the little group, at the police *commissaire* and the doctor, both bending over the prostrate form. An ambulance which had followed the police car was now drawn up.

"Guess there's nothing else we can do," Mr. Billingham said. "We'll get back to Miss Madelon."

They returned, Mr. Billingham thoughtful and curiously silent. The Marquis answered the enquiry in his niece's eyes with a grave little nod.

"A very serious affair, I am afraid, my dear," he told her kindly. "The car seems to have struck the wall, skidded, and over-turned. Poor fellow! He is quite dead."

"How terrible!" Madelon murmured. "And how strange," she added, a moment later. "I saw him drive once or twice and I thought he was especially skilful. The roads are not slippery. Why should he skid?"

Mr. Billingham came back from his brown study.

"I should say," he remarked, "that it was not exactly a skid. He lost control of the machine."

"But why?" Madelon demanded.

Mr. Billingham pointed to the little pink villa behind the high, plastered wall.

"Because the poor fellow was shot — probably from that villa — on his way up the hill," he announced gravely. "Naturally he lost control of the car and over it went. As a matter of fact his neck was broken as well."

"You mean that he was murdered?" Madelon gasped.

"Not the slightest doubt about it," Mr. Billingham replied. "He was shot well on the left-hand side, and there seems to be no cover anywhere near except from that villa. I heard one of the labourers say that they heard the report of a tyre-burst. As a matter of fact it must have been the report of a rifle."

"Did you tell the *commissaire?*" Madelon asked, as they started off on their homeward journey.

Mr. Billingham shook his head.

"He didn't need any telling," he replied. "Neither he nor the doctor can make any mistake about that. What I am curious about," he went on, "is just this. There's a heap of talk about the way accidents and sudden deaths and motor catastrophes are hushed up in this part of the world. Now we shall be able to judge for ourselves."

A few days later the very suave functionary who presided over the lives and liberties of the Monégasques received a call from Mr. Billingham. He welcomed him with cordiality.

"Official or unofficial?" was his first question.

Mr. Billingham considered the matter.

"Because," the other continued, "officially I can be dumb; unofficially I am able to remember that we are good friends, that you have done us services, that you are not one of these people who go about making trouble unnecessarily."

"My visit is unofficial," Mr. Billingham announced. "I came to ask whether you have formed any conclusions as to how that poor fellow came by his death — the fellow in the little red motorcar."

The police functionary shrugged his shoulders.

"Our roads are dangerous to those not accustomed to them," he declared.

"No one," Mr. Billingham retorted, "can drive a car successfully with a bullet wound in his heart."

The functionary stroked his chin.

"You noticed that, too?" he observed.

"I did," Mr. Billingham replied. "I also noticed that the only very brief report of the accident described it as being due to a skid and Captain Bruntingford's death due to a broken neck."

"His neck certainly was broken," the other remarked — "a sufficient cause of death, I think."

"Have you no curiosity," Mr. Billingham enquired, "as to the bullet wound?"

The other shook his head.

"We are never curious here about these things," he observed. "Besides, what good purpose is served by destroying what is after all an amiable fiction? It is better for the world to believe that this young man died of a broken neck through a motor accident than that he shot himself."

"Shot himself?" Mr. Billingham murmured. "Ah! . . . By the by, was the weapon found?"

"Not to my knowledge," the police functionary admitted. "To tell you the truth, I sent two men up to search, but they were unsuccessful. There were a good many men at work in the fields and on the roads, and I am afraid that anything in the way of firearms is looked upon as a rather desirable acquisition amongst these people."

"I follow you," Mr. Billingham murmured. "You know that I am not a chatterbox. For the moment, nothing more! Oblige me with one piece of information."

"By all means."

"I should like the dossiers of the inmates of the little villa — 'Les Mimosas' it is called — quite close to where the young man met with his accident."

The police functionary looked across at his visitor keenly.

"Why?" he demanded.

Mr. Billingham shrugged his shoulders.

"An idea," he replied.

"They shall be at your hotel within two hours," the other promised. "In the meantime —— "

"We are of one mind," Mr. Billingham declared. "The young man must have friends, probably relations. Let it remain at a broken neck. But be sure I have my dossiers. There is one thing more, too. If any of Captain Bruntingford's business friends should come over from England, will you ask them to favour me with a call?"

"With pleasure," was the ready response.

It was one of the pleasing practices of Mr. Billingham's cleanly life to perform certain acrobatic exercises in his bathroom every morning. He was lying upon his back, pummelling his stomach with both fists and indulging at the same time in deep breathing, when a knock at the door, the next morning, disturbed his praiseworthy efforts at maintaining his physical condition.

"What is it?" he demanded, sitting up.

"A gentleman to see you, sir," was the floor-waiter's reply.

Mr. Billingham reflected for a moment.

"Show the gentleman into the *salon*," he directed, "and leave his card on my tea-tray."

The footsteps outside passed along. Mr. Billingham abandoned further attempts to reduce his girth and jumped into his bath. Five minutes later, with tousled hair and glowing face, he picked up the card which reposed upon his tray.

MR. JAMES H. BERRY.

And underneath, in small type —

Berry and Bruntingford,
Private Inquiry Agency.

Mr. Billingham poured himself out a cup of tea and, with it in his hand, passed through to his *salon*. A small man, with sandy hair and an indifferent complexion, wearing gold-rimmed spectacles and obviously of furtive habits, rose to his feet as he entered.

"Mr. Billingham, sir," he said, "I fear that I have disturbed you too early."

"Don't you worry," was the cheerful reply. "We get up a trifle late here. Monte Carlo isn't New York, or London either, for that matter. Glad to see you, sir."

He shook hands and waved his visitor to a chair.

"You are Captain Bruntingford's partner, I gather," he went on. "Terrible affair! What was the game out here, eh?"

Mr. Berry felt his breath being taken away. He removed his spectacles and polished them.

"I am very much disturbed, Mr. Billingham," he confided. "The news of this accident to Captain Bruntingford was a great shock."

"Accident?" Mr. Billingham repeated.

His visitor nodded gravely.

"He was, I understand, killed in a motor accident."

"I guess not," Mr. Billingham objected. "He was murdered."

The little man jumped almost out of his chair. Then he leaned forward and looked at Mr. Billingham, his hands gripping its sides.

"You don't mean that?" he gasped.

"I surely do," Mr. Billingham replied. "He was shot through the heart. That's how the motor accident happened."

There was no doubt about it that Mr. Berry was not only taken by surprise but that he was deeply moved. He dabbed his forehead with his handkerchief.

"I told Bruntingford," he declared, "that it wasn't our class of business. Too risky and not enough to it! He wouldn't listen to reason. Murdered! Good God! They didn't tell me this at the police station."

"They wouldn't," was the curt rejoinder. "Murders and suicides never happen in Monte Carlo — just accidents, that's all!"

"Well, well, well!" Mr. Berry exclaimed helplessly. "To think they'd go as far as that!"

"Who's 'they'?" Mr. Billingham demanded.

His visitor shivered.

"How much do you know?" he asked.

"Nothing," Mr. Billingham confessed.

"Where do you come in, then?" the other enquired, a little puzzled.

"I don't come in," Mr. Billingham admitted. "I want to. I should like to take on Bruntingford's job — whatever it was. That is, unless you're going to take it on yourself?"

Mr. Berry dabbed his forehead again.

"Take it on myself!" he repeated. "I'd sooner starve first. It ain't my idea of pleasant business, sir, and that's a fact."

"No?" Mr. Billingham murmured sympathetically.

"Give me the makings of a divorce case, or the chance of collecting evidence in a slander job, or even a bit of blackmail, and I'm on the spot," Mr. Berry continued. "When it comes to these big things with desperate people up against one — well, all I say is 'take the job somewhere else.' It's what I told Bruntingford, only he wasn't having any. He'd got used to these tough affairs in the Army."

"Put me wise about this," Mr. Billingham begged. "I'm interested."

Mr. Berry cleared his throat. Somehow or other this powerful pink-and-white-looking man, in his bath robe, still glowing from his exercises, inspired him with confidence. He accepted a cigarette, and Mr. Billingham, after a moment's departure from the room, returned with another cup of tea, helped himself to a cigar, and, crossing his legs, settled down in an easy-chair, with a liberal display of underclothes.

"Bruntingford was after forty thousand pounds," Mr. Berry explained. "I never believed he'd get it, and he didn't. He got something else instead and it's my belief that the next person who goes after that forty thousand will get his the same way."

"What is it?" Mr. Billingham enquired. "Stolen money?"

"Blood-money!" was the hushed reply.

"You've got me guessing," Mr. Billingham confessed.

"Eh?"

"What kind of blood-money?"

Mr. Berry hitched his chair a little closer.

"The Johnny who first came to see Bruntingford," he confided, "was one of them foreign Jews, and he was marked down for trouble right enough. Never came except after dusk, and he was scared stiff if ever there was a footstep on the stairs. Got a cough, he had, too, enough to split him open. I didn't understand a word of their lingo. Bruntingford had to tell me afterwards. It seems the little chap was a Russian — had been in the police, and got into trouble. He bolted from Russia and brought some of the papers from headquarters with him. It was through these he got on to the game. The Russian Government, if there is such a thing, wants that chap Kitilsky who ran things there for a bit after they wiped the Tzar out. He escaped when the Bolshevists took hold, but he's alive still and they want him."

"Why?" Mr. Billingham demanded.

"Got some papers, for one thing," Mr. Berry confided, "and they believe he knows where there's some stolen gold hidden. Anyhow, they want him bad. Ten thousand pounds reward they offered. The little chap, just before he hopped it, got on to the lay. He reckoned Kitilsky was living at a villa somewhere back of Monte Carlo. He daren't leave London himself, though, and daren't claim the reward. He wanted Bruntingford to take hold and see what arrangement he could make. He found most of the money and Bruntingford came out here. Looks as though he had discovered his man if your story's the truth."

"I guess that's so."

There was a moment's silence. Mr. Billingham proffered a cigar, which was promptly accepted.

"You going on with this show?" the latter enquired.

Mr. Berry hesitated. There was a cunning gleam in his eyes.

"I'm none too keen," he confessed. "I'd rather sell my share "

"Your share?"

"The reward."

Mr. Billingham smiled.

"You mean you'd like to get home with a sound skin."

"I was never one of the fighting sort," Mr. Berry admitted apologetically.

"I tell you what I'll do," Mr. Billingham suggested. "I'll look into this matter. I can't say I've got properly the hang of it yet, but I'd kinder like to say a word or two to some one in that villa."

"You're tackling it yourself?" Mr. Berry asked, with a shiver.

"I guess so," Mr. Billingham admitted. "I don't know as I see clearly as to the financial side of it yet, but I'll give you a third of anything I pick up."

"It's a go!" was the eager reply. "I'll stay here for a few days on the chance."

Mr. Berry brought his visit to a close. He looked around the room wonderingly.

"What are you taking this on for?" he demanded. "You seem to have plenty of the stuff already — living here like a prince!"

Mr. Billingham smiled.

"Appearances are sometimes deceptive," he confided, as he showed his guest out. "Besides, there is always the adventure!"

Mr. Billingham, later in the morning, drove up to the Villa des Mimosas in a closed car which he had hired in the Casino Square. He passed the crumpled-up remains of the little red automobile, and descended in a few moments before a huge nail-studded door let into the plastered wall. He pushed down the iron handle with a jerk, but found, as he had expected, that it was fastened on the other side. Rather to his surprise, however, after scarcely a moment's delay a little click was heard and the door was released by means of a catch from within. He stepped into a narrow stretch of garden; uncared for and overgrown with weeds. The front door of the villa had been opened and upon the threshold a woman was standing. Mr. Billingham recognised her at once as an *habituée* of the Casino — a florid-looking woman with too much flesh, too much jewellery, ill-powdered and besmeared with rouge. She was untidily dressed. Her hair was tousled. There was a hole in her black felt slippers. After the somewhat tense sensations of his impending arrival, Mr. Billingham was conscious of a curious sense of something inadequate in the situation. His surprise was increased when the woman addressed him in English.

"Are you the English doctor?" she enquired.

"American," Mr. Billingham replied, with ready presence of mind.

"The same thing," she muttered. "Come in."

She closed the door carefully behind him. Mr. Billingham caught a glimpse of an unkempt-looking man securing the outside gate. The hall of the villa was dirty, ill-kept, and almost devoid of furniture.

The woman paused there. She spoke in a hoarse, husky whisper.

"I don't know that you can do anything," she said. "It's about all up. He wouldn't have a doctor before, though. The only chance is you might be able to keep him going for a week or two."

"Let me see him," Mr. Billingham enjoined.

She opened one of the doors which led out of the hall. Mr. Billingham found himself in what might have once been the *salon* of the villa, but was now a nondescript apartment, containing only a few oddments of furniture, heavy with cigarette smoke, malodorous from the closed windows and reminiscences of past meals. Although it was a brilliantly sunny morning, a pair of shabby curtains were completely drawn — the light in the room was so dim, indeed, that Mr. Billingham nearly blinked. There was heat coming somewhere from a closed stove, and stretched upon a sofa by its side was the emaciated figure of

a man wrapped in a dressing-gown. His throat was so skinny
that its cords seemed to stand out almost singly. His deep sunken
eyes were unnaturally large, brilliant with an uncanny light.
His white face was disfigured by many days' growth of black
and stubbly beard, his fingers were yellow with the stain of
nicotine. By the side of his couch was a small table and a
miniature roulette board. Close to it was the seat from which the
woman had risen. By the side of the roulette board was a strip
of paper and a pencil. The man spoke to the woman in a language of which Mr. Billingham knew nothing, and pointed to
her seat. She replied soothingly. He shook his head and broke
out once more. Then he coughed. She leaned over and patted
his shoulder.

"You had better wait for a moment," she said, turning to Mr.
Billingham. "Every day we do this," she went on, pointing to
the board. "We spin twenty numbers. I take the results down
and go to the Casino and back the same numbers in the same
order. It is the only thing which distracts his thoughts since he
cannot go himself. We have finished seventeen. Will you wait?"

"I will wait," Mr. Billingham agreed.

The woman resumed her seat, threw in the ball and turned
the wheel. The man leaned over, watching it eagerly. He took
note of the number with a little air of satisfaction and muttered
something, whilst the woman scribbled it down in pencil upon
her list. Twice more the operation was repeated. Then the man
leaned back. He spoke a few faint words; apparently in Russian.
The woman appeared to assent and he closed his eyes. She
drew Mr. Billingham a little on one side.

"He wants me to hurry off to the Casino," she explained. "He
says if I do so he will let you examine him."

Mr. Billingham opened his mouth and closed it again. There
were tears streaming down the woman's terrible face; a sob
choked in her throat.

"I am afraid — " Mr. Billingham began.

He stopped short. The door was opened. A man stood there;
corpulent, unprepossessing. He wore only a pair of black trousers
and a flannel shirt. He was the man who had closed the gate
He spoke to the woman; again in that incomprehensible jargon

She listened and turned towards Mr. Billingham. Her face was hardened, her tone was suspicious.

"There is a man here who says that he is the doctor," she announced.

"He is probably right," Mr. Billingham admitted.

"Who are you, then?" she demanded.

"I came to see who fired the shot from this villa which killed Bruntingford," Mr. Billingham declared, keeping his hand near his hip-pocket and his eyes wandering from the woman to the man.

The woman's face had been terrible before, but something of real fury gave it for a moment almost a diabolical expression. Her lips were parted. She remained, however, unexpectedly silent. There was a moan—a low moan but ending in a still more terrible sound—from the man upon the couch.

"The doctor!" Mr. Billingham exclaimed.

She called out something to the servitor. A little dark man with a black bag entered. She pointed to the couch.

"Go out and wait," she ordered Mr. Billingham.

He went into the dirty hall and sat upon a crazy cane chair. The atmosphere of the place stifled him. Presently he withdrew the bolts from the big door and found his way out into the tangled wilderness of garden which still remained beautiful. He wiped the perspiration from his forehead and waited. It was probably half an hour before anything happened. Then the woman came out. She advanced slowly towards him, and Mr. Billingham—who had seldom known fear—was conscious of a strange new sensation in his veins; a feeling that the sun had passed from the heavens and that there was sulphur in the air.

"You came to find out who fired that shot," she said. "I did."

"Why?" he demanded.

"That he should end his days a free man," was the solemn answer. "That has arrived. Are you of the police? I am ready!"

Mr. Billingham shook his head.

"The police do not know," he assured her hoarsely. "What about him?"

"He is dead," she announced. "He died—just then."

Mr. Billingham twirled his hat in his hand. It was so sordid, incomprehensible, amazingly unreal. Through a little clump of olive trees, he saw that the gate remained open.

"My affair here is finished," he said. "I will go."

She nodded.

"Go!" she assented. . . . "You are fortunate," she added, a moment or two later, "that you did not come a few days ago with your question."

"You know, of course, that there was a great reward for information about him?"

"I have known it for years," she admitted. "Nevertheless I kept him hidden. We had always two foes to fight — spies and starvation."

"And now about yourself?" he asked.

She stared at him. Another button of her dress had given way. She seemed more ragged than ever.

"Myself!" she repeated. "What does it matter? He is dead!"

VII

THE SYMBOL IN THE BOOT

MR. BILLINGHAM, attracted always by the unusual, paused in his early morning stroll through the clean streets, the flower-bedecked squares and along the glorious Terrace of Monte Carlo, to regard with some surprise the extraordinary spectacle of a man seated before one of the tables outside the Café de Paris fast asleep. The place was almost deserted, save for the sprinkling of visitors who came to take their early morning *déjeuners* in the sunshine, and Ben Hassim, the swarthy vendor of carpets, who stood patiently in the background, taking apparently no interest whatever in his immediate surroundings, yet with a curious air of watchfulness in his attitude and shining out of his black eyes. The young man who had attracted Mr. Billingham's attention was seated at one of the tables a little removed from the others and was sleeping peacefully and apparently naturally. It was obvious to an *habitué* of the place, however, that so unusual a proceeding would before long evoke interference from the authorities. A waiter had already called the attention of a *maître d'hôtel* to his presence; a gendarme from the Square had halted in his promenade and seemed to be contemplating action. Mr. Billingham approached, leaned over the sleeping man, sniffed the air for a moment and became immediately interested. He summoned the *maître d'hôtel.*

"How long has he been here?" he enquired, indicating the recumbent figure.

"Since the place was opened, Monsieur," the man replied. "It seems probable that he spent a great portion of the night here. It is time he moved on."

Mr. Billingham produced a twenty-franc note.

"Will you let him remain for ten minutes longer?" he begged. "I shall return by then. I am going to the chemist's. The young man is suffering from the effects of some drug."

The twenty-franc note resulted in the usual miracle, and on Mr. Billingham's return, in less than the time he had stated, he found the object of his solicitude still asleep. He poured a little powder into a wineglassful of soda-water and took the young man firmly by the arm.

"You must wake up," he said.

At the second injunction the sleeper opened his eyes and stared around him in a dazed fashion. Mr. Billingham thrust the wineglass into his fingers.

"Drink this," he ordered.

The young man obeyed. Then he blinked several times, stared around him again, and finally looked hard at Mr. Billingham.

"How did I get here, and who are you?" he demanded.

"How you got here is the question we've all been asking," Mr. Billingham replied. "As for me, I'm just an American visitor, staying at the hotel yonder. My name is Billingham."

The young man shook himself. He was a sunburnt, good-looking fellow and had a soldierly air notwithstanding his crumpled clothes, somewhat dishevelled appearance, and the fact, disclosed by the shape of his boots, that one leg was a little longer than the other.

"Well," he declared, "they got me first time. Drugged and robbed, I suppose."

He opened his coat and drew out a pocket-book. A considerable number of mille notes were there, some visiting-cards, and an odd letter or two.

"They've left you some money, at any rate," Mr. Billingham observed.

The young man returned the case to his pocket.

"Yes," he assented. "They haven't touched that. They've taken the packet, though."

He pressed his disabled foot on to the ground for a moment, and leaned once more back in his chair.

"Anything valuable?" Mr. Billingham asked. "Do you want

to get in touch with the police? I'm rather close to the chief here."

The other shook his head.

"The packet," he confided, dropping his voice a little, "is not quite so valuable as the people who stole it imagine. All the same I think I had better be getting along. They'll be after me again as soon as they find out."

He rose to his feet a little unsteadily. There was still rather a drawn look about his face.

"Say, where are you staying?" Mr. Billingham enquired.

"Close by here—at the Robespierre."

"I'll walk down with you if you like," his rescuer suggested. "I'm just out to stroll about."

"It would be very kind of you," was the grateful acknowledgment. "To tell you the truth I'm still feeling a little giddy."

He picked up his rubber-tipped stick and leaned for a moment heavily upon it. Ben Hassim, the vendor of carpets, who had advanced slowly nearer and nearer, salaamed as he accosted them. His white teeth flashed and his smile was as irresistible as ever. Nevertheless, there was a gleam of anxiety in his dark eyes.

"Has the young gentleman been robbed of anything valuable?" he asked anxiously.

"Why should you think that he had?" Mr. Billingham rejoined.

Hassim patiently deposited one of the rugs, which was slipping from his shoulder, upon the back of a chair.

"Because it was I who brought him down here," he confided. "I found him up in Beausoleil. He was on a chair in front of a restaurant—not a good restaurant. I knew that if he stayed there it would be ill for him. I brought him here. I was waiting until he awoke."

The young man's hand went towards his pocket, but Hassim's arresting gesture was full of dignity.

"I desire nothing," he said. "Only I wish to be assured that the gentleman has not been robbed."

The latter thrust the twenty-franc note back into his pocket.

"Curiously enough, I have not," he replied. "Something was taken from my pocket, but it was of no value to anybody. Anything I had with me," he added, looking intently at Hassim, "which is of value, I still possess."

Once more Hassim salaamed. He gathered up his rugs and retreated. They both looked after him curiously.

"That's a quaint fellow," the young man remarked.

"Got something at the back of his mind about you," Mr. Billingham mused, as they walked slowly off together. . . .

"My name is Powell — Leonard Powell," the young man volunteered, after a moment's silence. "I suppose you think that I've been making a night of it?"

"Kinder looks like it," his companion assented.

"Well, I haven't. I'm here on a special errand. I knew I was being watched and I went up to dine at the quietest place I know of — right at the back of the town here. I had half a bottle of wine and a liqueur brandy. The last thing I remember was paying my bill."

"Any ladies about?"

"Not a sign of one," was the emphatic reply.

"Sounds kind of interesting," Mr. Billingham observed, as they neared the hotel. "Sure you don't want me to get you in right with the police?"

The young man shook his head.

"The police couldn't help me," he confided. "If you'd like to come in and have your morning coffee with me, I'll tell you just the little more there is to be told."

Mr. Billingham accepted with alacrity. They made their way into the almost deserted *salon* of the hotel and the young man, after a few minutes' absence for a wash and a change of linen, seated himself at the table opposite his guest. His clothes were well-cut, but a trifle shabby. He was, however, entirely presentable and Mr. Billingham found his original impressions confirmed.

"Read that first," Powell enjoined, producing a newspaper cutting from the *Times*. "I found it in the personal column a fortnight ago."

Mr. Billingham adjusted his glasses and read:—

WANTED: Ex-officer or young man of courage, willing to risk his life in a dangerous enterprise. Adequate remuneration. No hardship, but real danger. Applicant must produce unexceptionable references and be unmarried. — Apply Box B. 771. The Times, E. C. 4.

"I saw this," Mr. Billingham declared, tapping the cutting with his forefinger. "I remember wondering at the time whether it was genuine."

"I should think it is probably genuine enough, judging from last night," the young man observed. "Anyhow, I answered the advertisement. I happen to have a few decent medals and a pretty good record, and I got the job. I was passed through three hands before I came to the principal. I can't tell you his name, but he is the head of the greatest financial and exploration company in the world. The job when I got it seemed almost ludicrously simple. I was to bring a packet here and deliver it safely to the person for whom it was intended."

"Sounds pie to me," Mr. Billingham commented. "Why don't you deliver it and get it off your chest?"

"It isn't quite so simple as that. Even the person who entrusted me with the commission didn't know exactly who would come for the packet. They could only tell me how to recognise him when he did arrive. Meanwhile, as they warned me, there's an ugly crowd around, who would like, apparently, to nobble me and get hold of it, whatever it may be."

Mr. Billingham for the first time felt inclined to doubt his companion's *bona fides*. His story on the face of it was scarcely convincing.

"Do you know what this mysterious packet of yours contains?" he enquired.

"Not an idea," the young man confessed.

"Do you know what sort of person you have to look out for?"

"He isn't an ordinary personage," was the somewhat hesitating reply. "I shall probably know when he is here."

Mr. Billingham coughed. The greatest in the world are not infallible. For once in his life he had arrived at a wrong decision.

"Well," he remarked, as he pushed back his chair and rose, "I wish you luck. I must be getting along."

The young man walked with him to the door. The air was filled with soft sunlight and the faintest of southern breezes stirred the leaves of the trees in the gardens on their left. The hour was still early and there were few people about. A dark-skinned denizen of some southern race was reading a newspaper in the little railed-off space in front of the hotel. Powell glanced towards him with a frown.

"Another of the brutes!" he muttered. "On guard, I suppose. . . . Well, good-morning, sir. Thank you very much for your help."

Mr. Billingham, whose interest in the affair had experienced a slight revival, had a question to ask, but his companion had already left him. Just before he reached the opposite side of the way, he turned around, conscious of an unusual noise. An elderly gentleman of military appearance was knocking the stone balustrade behind which the solitary occupant of the hotel piazza was seated — knocking it with the obvious intention of attracting the dark-skinned foreigner's notice. Mr. Billingham paused on the pretence of lighting a cigarette. He saw the young man who had been reading the newspaper rise to his feet and he heard the exchange of a few sentences in the strangest language to which he had ever listened. After a moment or two, the foreigner, with a curious little bow, resumed his seat, and the elderly gentleman who had accosted him turned towards the gardens. Mr. Billingham, as he passed, beamed at him amiably.

"If I'm not taking a liberty, sir," he said, "I should very much like to know what language that might have been you were talking just now. Don't seem to me that I've ever heard it before."

"I don't suppose you have, sir," was the not ungracious reply. "I don't suppose there's another white man in the place except myself who can speak it. It's the language of a God-forsaken little country right at the back end of Mesopotamia. I had a draft of the natives in a regiment I commanded during the war."

Mr. Billingham fell into step with his companion and signified his interest monosyllabically.

"Gave me quite a start to see that young man seated there

in European clothes," the latter continued. "This place is full, of course, of Anglo-Indians, and there are a few Egyptians, but an Arab of that young man's race very seldom finds his way into civilisation. Damned fine fellows they are, too, most of them!"

"Did he explain his presence here?" Mr. Billingham enquired.

His companion smiled — a smile with which was associated a slight grimace.

"He did not," he admitted. "He seemed rather disturbed at my recognition, but in the politest possible manner he told me to go to the devil. . . . I wish you good-morning, sir. I am due at my barber's." . . .

The Marquis de Félan, Mr. Billingham's friend and confederate, was in high spirits that evening. He had won almost as much in the afternoon on his two favourite numbers as he had lost the evening before, and he insisted upon paying for the dinner with the money which he had previously borrowed from his guest.

"At roulette," he declared didactically, "all that is needed is confidence. I say to myself 'my numbers will arrive — they shall arrive.' I see them arriving and behold they follow one another. But for the unfortunate closing of the tables in the Club at eight o'clock I firmly believe that my winnings this evening would have been enormous."

"You did pretty well as it was, didn't you?" Mr. Billingham asked.

The Marquis hesitated.

"I was on the point of doing well," he confided. "I had re-established myself. A little more capital —— "

"As a matter of fact," Mr. Billingham interrupted, "a little more capital is what we all need. What about you, Miss Madelon?"

Madelon opened her purse and disclosed its contents.

"I am, what you call, nearly on the rocks," she admitted. "I have a hundred-franc note, perhaps two hundred francs' worth of counters, and a five-hundred-franc note at home in my stocking."

"At home," the Marquis repeated disconsolately. "I was rather hoping —— "

"Quite impossible," Madelon pronounced decisively. "My last five hundred francs does not go to the tables. Dear chief," she went on, turning to her neighbour, "the time has arrived for us to act. Is there nobody here we can rob?"

Mr. Billingham shook his head sorrowfully.

"I can think of no one," he confessed, "whom we can rob safely and honestly."

"One might perhaps draw the line a little less rigidly," the Marquis suggested, polishing his eyeglass.

"I'm not out to look for trouble," Mr. Billingham grunted. "No thank you! I guess if you're up a gum tree, Marquis, the croupiers at the Sporting Club have raked in the bits. I myself have not touched that whip-up for charity we worked Mrs. Groosens for. And as for Miss Madelon, you know her position."

Madelon shrugged her shoulders with a little gesture of despair. The Marquis hastened to explain.

"A loan, my dear!" he insisted. "I owe you money. I admit it. All shall be paid. In the meantime, however, our need for capital is somewhat urgent. I am delighted to hear that our friend is in a position to make us a small advance if necessary."

"Mr. Billingham is in a position to do nothing of the sort," Madelon replied. "You have borrowed all my money, Uncle. That must be enough for you. Think of some way of earning it. We will all help. We are an amazing trio — unscrupulous, clever, brave! We are surrounded by pleasure-seekers and fools. There must be some means by which they can be induced to add to our exchequer."

"Guess it's up to you to sound the tocsin, Marquis," Mr. Billingham declared. "You need the money. We don't happen to, just at the moment. Do you get me?"

The Marquis coughed.

"In a partnership like ours," he began, "a certain community of interest as regards —— "

"Cut it out!" Mr. Billingham interrupted brutally. "You've had your share of everything we've done. You've borrowed from your niece, you've borrowed from me. If you can't win, quit it!"

"One needs capital," the Marquis complained. "Besides playing my numbers I have perfected a system which will infallibly bring me in a profit as soon as I get it started."

"Sell it to one of my fellow-countrymen," Mr. Billingham advised. "There are three or four hundred of them landing tomorrow morning. Three or four hundred Americans plumb full of the stuff, with fat pocket-books and large letters of credit!"

The Marquis' eyes glistened wistfully as he toyed with his eyeglass. Suddenly he arrived at an heroic decision.

"I shall go down to the quay," he announced. "I shall offer my services as guide. I will compete with the brawny ruffian from Cooks."

Mr. Billingham smiled incredulously. He said nothing, but the effect of the smile was potent.

"You think that I would not do that?" his *vis-à-vis* demanded.

"I'll match you a mille you don't," was the prompt challenge.

The Marquis hesitated for a moment, gulped and made up his mind.

"Your wager is accepted," he declared. "The money will be mine."

Almost as he spoke the siren of the great incoming steamer rang out its blatant announcement, dwarfing all other noises, audible from Mentone to Beaulieu. Mr. Billingham smiled once more.

"Guess you don't need to worry, Marquis," he observed. "No one will be allowed to land until tomorrow morning. The first tender-full will arrive in the harbour at about nine o'clock, with money oozing out of their finger-nails."

"I shall be there," was the other's valiant pronouncement.

Amongst several hundreds of intrepid transatlantic sight-seers, there stepped from the tender on to the dock at Monaco, the following morning, the illustrious family of the Henry P. Hootermans of Chicago. The family consisted of Mrs. Henry P. Hooterman, a short, squat lady with an immense capacity for speech, pushing in a crowd, and managing her own and everyone else's affairs. She was of dark complexion, sallow, and she wore huge tortoise-shell spectacles. She carried a jewel case, which was somewhat ostentatiously chained to her wrist, and in the other hand an umbrella. She had flat feet which seemed always to take up a little more than their share of room upon the earth, and a voice and mien of authority which had won for her the position of President of the Society of Women Thinkers in her home city. She was accompanied by her daughter, Mamie, who had some claim to good looks and whose eyes were certainly dark and almost beautiful, but whose chances of success in life were considerably handicapped by the maternal environment. There were also a younger daughter, Sadie, still in her early teens, freckled, loquacious and gawky; a lad, who bitterly resented the whole undertaking; and finally Mr. Henry P. Hooterman himself, a tall, thin man, sombrely dressed, of pallid complexion, who had more the appearance of a Methodist minister than the multimillionaire he was reputed to be. This estimable quintette stood upon the landing-stage and looked around them.

"What we need," Mrs. Henry P. Hooterman said firmly, "to give us points about this place, is a Cook's man. Hi, you!" she added, lifting her umbrella and addressing an individual in a gold-laced cap. "Say, are you Cook's or American Express?"

The functionary in question, who happened to be one of the five officers of the standing army of Monaco and ignorant of any of the barbarian tongues, turned coldly away. The boy, looking upwards, espied a familiar sight.

"Say," he exclaimed, "there's a trolley-car up there. I guess if we can make the road we can have a ride round."

"Anyway," his father decided, "we'll be moving along."

It was at this precise moment that the Marquis, who had been talking for a moment to the ship's doctor, with whom he had some slight acquaintance, approached. He raised his hat and addressed Mrs. Henry P. Hooterman in his own language.

"Madame is perhaps in need of some information?" he suggested.

They all looked at him blankly; Mamie in frank admiration.

"Say, ain't they some dressers, Momma!" she exclaimed.

"Isn't he cute!" Sadie echoed.

"Sorry we don't get you," Mr. Hooterman apologised. "We're Americans."

The Marquis removed his hat once more.

"It is for that reason," he explained in English, "that I have ventured to address you. It appeared to me that you might be in need of some information or advice. I am a resident here. My services are at your disposal."

The little party were at once interested.

"Want to show us round, eh?" Mr. Hooterman ventured doubtfully.

"That would give me great pleasure," the Marquis assented. "I might add that I only offer my services occasionally. I believe I have the honour to address Senator Henry P. Hooterman of Chicago."

So far as the countenance of a man whose skin was rather like dried-up leather could express emotion, it was obvious that Mr. Hooterman was pleased. He smiled in wintry fashion.

"You know me," he observed.

"Monte Carlo was apprised of your intended visit," the Marquis rejoined with trenchant grandiloquence. "It was to meet you that I am here. I am not, it is true, a professional guide, but I sometimes occupy that position to people of distinction. My services are at your disposal for the day for the sum of five hundred francs."

"Steep!" Mr. Hooterman commented.

"He talks some!" Mrs. Hooterman agreed.

"I think it would be lovely to be taken round by someone who really knows the place," Miss Mamie cooed.

"That will include your meals and all gratuities?" Mrs. Hooterman enquired.

"It will be inclusive," the Marquis promised. "If you decide to engage me I am at your disposal. Otherwise," he added, glancing across the quay towards another little group.

"Those horrid Smithsons!" Mamie interrupted. "Dad, fix this up, please."

"You are engaged," Mr. Hooterman declared. "Lead on. What shall we do first?" . . .

Many a time in later days the Marquis' tone shook with emotion when he spoke of that morning. It is certain that he carried out his task manfully. He deposited the little company in an automobile and took them to the Casino. He obtained their *cartes d'entrée* in advance of a long line of their fellow-passengers — a fact which immensely impressed the elder members of the family. He explained the game — to the details of which they listened with great earnestness — and at his suggestion Mr. Hooterman changed a note for a hundred dollars into counters, which, with the exception of a small handful which he retained for purposes of instruction, the Marquis distributed amongst his companions.

"Now," he said, "I will show you how the betting is done."

He placed one of the counters on fourteen and one on twentynine. One which Mamie thrust upon him he placed on "red." They all watched breathlessly. The Marquis gave a little start as the ball slipped into its place and the croupier's monotonous voice recited the result.

"*Quatorze, pair, rouge et manque.*"

The Marquis leaned gallantly across, picked up two louis from the "rouge" and handed them to Miss Mamie.

"You have won, Mademoiselle," he announced. "So, it appears, have I."

He accepted thirty-five louis and swept them into his pocket. Mr. Hooterman watched him, fascinated. Mrs. Hooterman nudged her husband. Mamie smiled rapturously.

"Say, did you win all that?" she exclaimed.

"I did," the Marquis acquiesced blandly. "By the by, the original louis belongs to your father. Pray take it and place it where you will upon the table."

He returned the counter and explained further the system of staking. Several more ventures were essayed without result. Then, as it had been necessary to leave the boy and Sadie outside, they quitted the rooms and embarked upon a personally conducted drive to La Turbie and Mentone, winding up outside the Arcade which led to Ciro's. The Marquis, who had been sitting in front, gallantly helped Mrs. Hooterman and Mamie to alight.

"It is, perhaps, the luncheon hour," he ventured.

"Yes, sirree," Mamie assented enthusiastically and with great emphasis.

"You spoke a mouthful, Mr. Guide," Henry junior declared. The Marquis was puzzled, but gathered that his suggestion was favourably received. They made their way along the Arcade until they were met by a *maître d'hôtel* from the restaurant. The season was waning and they were welcome guests. The manager himself ushered them to a table upon the balcony.

"With what can I have the pleasure of serving Monsieur le Marquis?" he enquired, presenting the bill of fare.

One and all, the little party looked up in amazement. The Marquis found them strangely acquiescent in the matter of the luncheon he ordered. They did not even flinch at the idea of cocktails. As soon as the waiter had departed Mamie leaned forward.

"Why did that man with the black tie call you 'Marquis'?" she demanded.

"It happens to be the title which belongs to me," the Marquis explained, dropping his horn-rimmed eyeglass and gazing amiably around. The luncheon he had ordered consisted, curiously enough, of all his favourite dishes and he felt at peace with the world.

"You mean that you are a real Marquis—a nobleman?" Mamie persisted.

"My family has been noble for seven hundred years," the Marquis replied modestly, yet with some dignity. "I am the eleventh Marquis de Félan and I happen to be also a Count of the Holy Roman Empire."

"Say, what are you doing in this guide business, anyway?" Mrs. Hooterman queried, after a moment's awed silence.

The Marquis shrugged his shoulders slightly.

"I am not in the guide business," he declared. "To tell you the truth I have never before undertaken such an enterprise. I happen to be temporarily somewhat embarrassed financially and a friend of mine—a compatriot of yours, by the by—bet me a considerable sum of money that I would not offer my services to a family from your steamer and show them Monte Carlo. I took the liberty," he went on, with a little bow towards Mamie, "of showing some discrimination, and—well, *nous voilà!*"

"Why, did you ever hear anything like this?" Mamie exclaimed.

"Shucks!" her younger sister murmured.

"Say, don't you wear anything if you're a Marquis?" Henry junior asked discontentedly.

"I knew he wasn't an ordinary guide," Mrs. Hooterman confided under her breath to her husband.

"Here, by the by," the Marquis continued, in high good-humour, "comes the gentleman with whom I made the wager and my niece. Permit me," he added, as Mr. Billingham and Madelon paused on their way to a table, "to present my niece and Mr. Billingham — Mr. Henry P. Hooterman and family."

Mr. Hooterman held out his hand and gazed earnestly at his compatriot.

"Linoleum?" he asked.

"You've said it," was the prompt assent.

"Boots," Mr. Hooterman confided.

"I know the plant," Mr. Billingham declared. "The Hooterman, Steadman Plant, Chicago."

"Sit right down, you and the young lady," Mr. Hooterman invited. "We've just heard of that wager of yours. Join us in a bite of luncheon, sir."

Places were laid and a curious but interesting meal was started. Madelon sat between Mamie and her younger sister and enjoyed herself immensely. Mrs. Hooterman told the Marquis all about the Women's Guild and how she became President, and Mr. Billingham discoursed eloquently on financial subjects. They were perhaps half-way through a very excellent repast when Ben Hassim, with half a dozen carpets hung from his shoulders in picturesque fashion, made his smiling and dignified appearance.

"The gentleman would like to take home to New York something wonderful — a carpet fit for a palace?" he enquired, displaying one of his rugs.

"Say, did you ever!" Mrs. Hooterman exclaimed, gazing hard through her tortoise-shell spectacles. "What sort of a foreigner might he be, Marquis?"

"Either an Arab or an Egyptian," the Marquis replied. "He probably comes from somewhere beyond Jaffa."

"He looks quite romantic!" Mamie sighed. "Momma, that's a beautiful blue rug."

"A thousand francs," Ben Hassim declared, smoothing it down — "in your country a thousand dollars. I take it to the steamer for you."

Mrs. Hooterman fell to examining the texture of the carpet, and Mr. Hooterman began to make facetious suggestions as to possible reductions in the price. Suddenly Mamie gave a little exclamation.

"The Prince!" she exclaimed. "Isn't he handsome?"

They all glanced along the terrace. A man, tall, olive-skinned, with the thin aquiline nose and brilliant eyes of an Arab, dressed in robes of flowing white, with a white turban and gold bracelets upon his arms, advanced in leisurely fashion towards one of the empty tables, followed by a servant. The vendor of carpets dropped his wares and performed a strange, genuflectory reverence, to which the other replied only by a slight upraising of his hand. He passed on to the empty table and seated himself with the servant behind his chair.

"Say, do you folks know who that is?" Mr. Billingham enquired with interest.

"He's a Sheik or Prince from somewhere in Mesopotamia," Mamie declared. "He got on the steamer at Jaffa. They said that he had flown from Bagdad in an aeroplane which belonged to the British Government. Isn't he just the most picturesque dear that ever lived?"

Mr. Billingham nodded a little absently. There were other things interesting him just at that moment. In the first place, Leonard Powell, the Englishman who had been occupying a table in a distant corner, had risen to his feet and was gazing across with eager interest at the object of Mamie's admiration. Furthermore, the young foreigner who had been seated outside the Robespierre Hotel earlier in the morning had also made his appearance in the Arcade accompanied by a smaller, coarser and more vicious edition of himself. The two had paused, half-way between the bar and the terrace restaurant, and were talking together eagerly. Their whole attention also seemed concentrated upon the Arab Sheik, who never once glanced in their direction. . . . Then, too, a change had come over Ben Hassim. He had dropped his wares and his eyes were fixed in almost terrified fashion upon the two newcomers. His rugs lay in a little neglected heap upon the floor. He mumbled to himself in some strange dialect. Continually he looked backwards and forwards from the spot where the two had halted to the table where the Arab Prince was seated. The climax of his disquietude arrived when the taller of the former, followed by his unprepossessing companion, began to move forward. Mr. Billingham half unconsciously rose to his feet. He felt the need of freedom in case action was required of him, yet of what might be going to happen he had not the faintest idea. It was Henry junior who first supplied a hint as to the possible course of the proceedings.

"Say, isn't that a dandy dagger!" he exclaimed breathlessly.

Mr. Billingham's eyes followed the direction of the boy's eagerly pointing finger. Ben Hassim had retained one of the rugs upon his arm, and beneath its folds, partially concealed, his right hand was gripping a long, curved knife of wicked-looking blue steel, the hilt of which was of beaten silver, set with precious stones. With the rug still hanging over his arm, he moved stealthily out until he stood almost as though it were his purpose to intercept the two Europeanised Arabians. The manager of the restaurant, conscious of something unusual, hurried up with an angry exclamation. Ben Hassim took no notice. His eyes were fixed upon the advancing figures. Suddenly he began to talk rapidly in French to the manager. The latter appeared at first bewildered and then incredulous. Finally he turned away towards the two young foreigners whom the carpet vendor was indicating now with almost frantic gestures. He bowed, as though welcoming prospective clients.

"You wish for a table on the terrace, sir?" he enquired.

The foremost of the two young men hesitated. Ben Hassim took advantage of his pause to creep round the other tables and emerge upon the Arcade with one rug still hanging over his arm, effectually concealing the knife which only Henry junior and Mr. Billingham had seen. He stood between the table where the Prince was seated and the civilised parody of himself, about whose deliberate approach there had been indeed something almost sinister. The latter, checked in his advance by the manager, was led reluctantly to a table. Ben Hassim turned and with head respectfully bowed commenced to talk to the Prince — to talk in a strange language with many gestures and brandishing of the arms, almost with tears in his eyes. The Prince listened without movement, without any sign of hearing. In the end, however, he rose to his feet, and, screened still by the carpet vendor, turned and entered the indoors portion of the restaurant. Hassim stood in the entrance, breathing heavily, drops of perspiration upon his dusky forehead, agitated yet triumphant. The manager came across to him, frowning.

"There are things here," Hassim said, "which you may not understand — nor even I, wholly. You wish to avoid trouble in this restaurant. Go, then, and bring the Englishman to me who sits at the corner table."

The manager was angry. He had a shrewd idea as to what it was that Hassim held in his hand beneath that rug.

"If there is any brawling here," he threatened, "never again shall you bring your rugs to my clients."

"That will be as Allah directs," was the quiet reply. "Send or seek that Englishman."

The manager, with a shrug of his shoulders, turned away and approached the young Englishman who had risen from his place but had seemed for the last few seconds uncertain how to act. Mr. Billingham, who had been watching his two nearer neighbours, turned to his companions.

"Will you folks just excuse me one moment?" he begged. "I want to say a word to our dusky friend there."

He made his way to the adjoining table, and, uninvited, took the third chair. Neither the young man whom he had seen earlier in the morning, nor his more villainous-looking companion, indulged in any immediate comment upon this very singular behaviour. The former simply looked at the newcomer with expressionless face and eyes from which even enquiry was absent, but the latter's right hand stole promptly underneath the table-cloth and remained out of sight.

"Say, you understand plain English, don't you?" Mr. Billingham asked.

"Naturally," was the calm reply.

"If you don't put your right hand upon the table this second," Mr. Billingham declared, "I'll take you by the scruff of the neck and throw you out, and your gun after you!"

Mr. Billingham's arm was outstretched; a strong, muscular arm. The little Arab with the squinting eyes looked into this intruder's face and decided that it was without doubt the face of a man who meant what he said. He was prompt to obey.

"Now we can talk," Mr. Billingham continued, his eyes straying for a moment to the corner where the Englishman was standing irresolute, leaning upon his stick. "I'm taking a hand in a game I don't quite tumble to, but I guess I'll see it through. You're going to sit here quietly opposite me for another three minutes and let things rip."

"Who are you and why do you interfere?" the taller of the two young Arabs demanded. "What is your interest in this matter?"

"I guess you'd better not be too inquisitive," was the curt reply.

The young man watched with sullen eyes the Englishman, who, with the manager by his side, was now making his way towards the restaurant. He looked back at Mr. Billingham.

"If you knew what was going on there," he said, pointing significantly towards the entrance to the restaurant ——

Mr. Billingham, not wholly, but partially, fell. Ever so slightly he turned his head in the direction indicated. Instantly the younger of the two Arabs, with a movement of incredible swiftness, stooped and half rose again. The sun, which was streaming in through the glass windows, flashed upon his silver-plated pistol. Quick though he was, however, he was not quick enough. With a sudden terrible blow, Mr. Billingham struck and pinned his hand to the table. The pistol clattered harmlessly on to the floor. The young man's eyes glared. There was murder in his face. He dived, sprang to his feet, swayed one way and another. In Mr. Billingham's Herculean grip, however, he was helpless. A couple of waiters hurried forward, followed by the manager. One of them picked up the pistol.

"What is the matter?" the manager demanded.

"Nothing, so long as we don't let him move," Mr. Billingham replied. "There's some trouble going on. I can't get the hang of it, but this little one is the guy who meant mischief."

The Englishman emerged from the restaurant, with a smile of triumph upon his face. He waved his hand to Mr. Billingham. Then, recognising that something unusual had happened, he came over to the table.

"Are you through with your little job?" Mr. Billingham enquired.

"I am," was the prompt reply, "and jolly glad of it, too! . . . Is there anything wrong here?" he added, with a curious glance at Mr. Billingham's companions.

"There might have been if I hadn't taken a chance," Mr. Billingham acquiesced.

"You had better let him go," the taller of the two young Arabs advised, breaking at last his long and impassive silence. "Our task is over. We have failed. The evil has come. The message has been delivered. All that we desire is to depart. I pledge you my word that my brother is now safe. He carries the symbol! He may not be touched!"

Mr. Billingham released his grip, and, in obedience to a sign from the manager, the *vestiaire* brought the two young men their hats and sticks. Very slowly they made their way back down the Arcade and disappeared. Ben Hassim stepped forward from the threshold of the restaurant. Once more he took up his place by the side of his little pile of carpets. Once more that broad and delightful smile illuminated his face.

"It was the great chief of my tribe," he explained. "I had to pay my respects. It is a happy day, this. I will say eight hundred francs. The carpet to you shall be as a thank-offering."

"Delivered down to the steamer?" Mr. Hooterman stipulated.

"You pay me when I bring it," was the dignified response.

"Say, what about that knife?" Henry junior demanded. "Buy that for me, Dad."

"Knife?" Hassim repeated, shaking his head slowly and extending his arms. "I carry no knife. One lives in peace on this side of the blue sea."

Less than a mile from the land, the great steamer lay at anchor, blazing with lights. Twice her siren had made the night hideous. Now, puffing and snorting, the last tender, filled with passengers, had left the harbour. The Marquis, well-content, replaced his hat upon his head, lit a cigarette, and stuffed, with amusement, his five hundred francs into his pocket. Hassim gathered up his rugs one by one, after a final glance into the brown leather pocket-book where eight hundred francs were safely bestowed. It had been a great day for him. Suddenly he felt a hand upon his shoulder. He looked round quickly and perhaps it was some revival of an ancient instinct which sent his right hand down to the folds of his robe. When he recognized Mr. Billingham, however, he shrugged his shoulders and smiled.

"Hassim, my friend," Mr. Billingham begged, "put me wise to what has been happening. Curiosity disturbs my digestion. And let me remind you of this. I, too, had a hand in the game. It was I who found the Englishman recovering from his drugs outside the Café de Paris this morning. Even as I led him away the other came down the hill."

Hassim nodded gravely.

"They come from the land which was once mine," he explained. "He, the Prince, who to-night is in the air — for he flies back from Nice to Jaffa and thence to the valleys where his kingdom lies — and the others, one of whom was his brother."

Mr. Billingham was patient.

"The Englishman brought a letter or something of the sort," he suggested.

Ben Hassim looked around him. They were walking very slowly along the quay. Perhaps the weight of his rugs was great.

"Listen," he said. "Years ago, before the great war, there came to the country where I was born — a great kingdom it was, and is, and ever will be — one of those strange Englishmen who seek for wealth. He stayed nearly a year with the King, the father of the Prince and that other. He paid money which made the Kingdom of my country richer in camels and horses and women and jewellery than any other, and he took in exchange the land where the oil was. But before he left, so that the King might not go back on his bargain, he took with him the secret token, without which no man can be crowned King."

"The secret token?" Mr. Billingham repeated. "I don't get you."

"It is an image of the first king of my country — two thousand years old — beaten in gold," the vendor of carpets continued solemnly. "In it there are emeralds for eyes, rubies for lips, and pearls for teeth, yet so thin is it that a man might carry it in his pocket-book.

"They took it to England, but when they came to sink the wells and the pledge should have been redeemed, the war came. That other — the youngest son of the King — he chose what they call civilisation. He came to England, to school and to college. The Prince remained. Last year the King died."

"Tell me the name of this country," Mr. Billingham begged.

Hassim shook his head.

"Since I left it, I speak of it no longer," he declared. "The King, as I told you, died. That other had become what you see him — a Western creature. He made favour with the Ministers in England. He sought for the throne of his father — the throne which belonged to the Prince — but the Prince, though this is the first time he has ever left his country, was the chosen of the people. He sent to those who owned the token. The land was theirs. The war was over. These English were honest men. The other, he too tried for the token. By arrangement — I know not whose — they sent it here. The other followed him. Because he might not raise his hand against his brother, he brought with him a friend of evil repute. If he could take back the token, the kingship was his. He failed." . . .

The Marquis caught them up. He was in high spirits.

"Madelon waits for us at the Café de Paris," he told Mr. Billingham. "We have supper together and you will pay me a thousand francs. The family of Hooterman were well pleased with me. La belle Mamie has presented me with her photograph, Madame has invited me to Chicago, and Monsieur added a benefice to my fee. If you will give me what you owe me, my friend, I may consider paying for our supper."

They took a little *voiture* and drove up to the Café de Paris. After the strain of the earlier part of the day, they found themselves singularly gay. At the next table, Hassim was stroking one of his beautiful rugs as he displayed it to a little party of new arrivals. The brother of the Prince was dancing with a professional *danseuse*. The Marquis, who was still in high spirits, called for the wine waiter.

"I am appreciating the joy," he explained to his companions, "of leisure and recreation after toil. You others, what have you done? I, on the contrary, have gained — when you, my friend Billingham, have paid me — fifteen hundred francs."

"I," Mr. Billingham protested, "have also been busy. I have saved the life of a Prince."

"And I," Madelon sighed, "have heard all about her Women's Guild from Mrs. Henry P. Hooterman of Chicago."

"I will pay for the wine," the Marquis decided.

VIII

THE SALVATION OF MR. NORTON

EVEN the serious business of losing money gracefully was suspended for a moment or two when Validia, followed by her latest cavalier, emerged from the baccarat room and leaned over the roulette table. All heads were turned. There was a little whisper of half-reluctant admiration. Validia had been the acknowledged beauty of Monte Carlo for several weeks.

"Give me a mille or two," she demanded, turning to her companion with a careless gesture.

He produced a substantial-looking pocket-book, deliberately extracted two mille notes and gave them to her. She passed them a little contemptuously to the croupier.

"*Maximum au zéro et les chevaux,*" she directed. "*La monnaie en plaques.*"

The ball was spun. One of the numbers at the lower end of the table turned up. Validia swept the remaining plaques into her bag and turned away.

"I do not know why I play this game!" she exclaimed angrily. "I always lose. Let us try the other table."

Her cavalier followed her; silent, with an obedience which was a little dog-like and British. Validia walked slowly and there was no one who did not notice her coming and her passing. She was beautiful in the type which pleased most at the moment, with oval face, ivory-tinted complexion and black hair, smooth and glossy, brushed back and ending in almost a chignon. She wore a dress of white silk, with many flounces and with just a suggestion of the crinoline. Her only jewellery was a rope of wonderful pearls. Her total avoidance of all cosmetics, in a season during which even school-girls aimed at making their lips look like lines of scarlet, was in itself an aid to distinction. She walked alluringly. Her dark brown eyes, a little narrow, it is true, but very wonderful, held in them a light which many a man had known to his cost. Her lips were so provocative, at times so inviting, that one failed to notice their wickedness. She had come to Monte Carlo two seasons before in the Russian Ballet, unknown and without particular genius. She had abandoned dancing now and her jewels and toilettes were each month more gorgeous. She had given colour to a report and liked it to be understood that she was secretly married to a somewhat disreputable but wealthy member of a Royal House. She spoke of her secret in the strictest confidence to everyone. It eased somewhat the strain of a position which she herself once naïvely remarked "might be open to misconception."

She approached the farther of the three roulette tables and once more extended her hand to her companion, this time without looking at him. It was a very beautiful hand, with long fingers and exquisitely manicured nails. There was an emerald ring on one of the fingers which was reputed to have belonged to Catherine of Russia.

"A mille," she said.

The man by her side — very English, a little pompous, distinctly middle-class — hesitated.

"You have those plaques," he reminded her.

She turned her head ever so slightly and his fingers went shivering for his pocket-book. He handed her the note which she took without a word of thanks. Again she staked and again she lost. She thrust the plaques which came to her as change into her bag. Then she turned towards the door.

"I think I will drink something," she decided. "You shall take me to the bar, *mon ami*. That man Kretterson is a pig tonight. He will not give up the bank for an hour."

"Why do you like so much to gamble?" he asked. "Why must it be baccarat? They tell me there is no game where you can lose so much."

She laughed quietly and tapped his hand with her little ivory fan.

"I do not often lose," she said.

Madelon, seated with Mr. Billingham in a remote corner of the bar, leaned over suddenly and laid her hand upon his arm.

"My friend," she exclaimed, "I will tell you what it is which makes this place seem so satisfying to us — which makes us loath to leave. Underneath all its tinsel and theatricality there is real life to be seen here — human everyday life."

"I guess we've seen a few strange things this season," Mr. Billingham acquiesced.

"I do not mean the obvious tragedies," Madelon continued. "I do not mean the suicides, the murders, the naked passions. I mean something nearer to our hearts. I will give you an example. . . . You saw the two who just came in?"

"Sure," Mr. Billingham assented. "The woman Validia — the Russian woman — and the pompous English Johnny who follows her like a shadow."

"Now I want you to look at some one else," Madelon went on, dropping her voice a little. "Do you see that middle-aged, badly-dressed woman who has just changed her seat?"

Mr. Billingham nodded.

"Female hayseed type," he observed. "Looks as though she had been dug up from the back woods and dressed in last year's styles from the department store."

Madelon smiled.

"You are really a very observant person," she murmured. "You see her. She is a study in herself. She was probably considered pretty when she was young. She lived in a small town and her father was perhaps a prosperous but unambitious manufacturer. She has gone comfortably through life and her chief troubles have been her domestic servants and the high price of provisions. Just now she has something else in her face. Can you see it?"

"She looks kinder scared," Mr. Billingham suggested.

"She is living in the shadow of a new and terrible fear," Madelon declared. "Something has happened to her of which she has never dreamed. She has jogged comfortably on through life and now suddenly there is a precipice at her feet. She is the wife of the man who is talking to Validia. He has left her alone all the evening. She has just changed her place so as to be out of sight. Look at her sitting there with her hands in her lap and her eyes staring through the wall. She is too rustic even to hide her sorrow."

"Who put you wise to all this?" Mr. Billingham demanded curiously.

"I talked to her yesterday afternoon," Madelon explained. "I could not help it. She looked so lonely. Do you mind if I go and talk to her again now?"

"Why, of course not," Mr. Billingham acquiesced. "Come to look at her closely she does look as though she'd been put through it. I'll try a hand or two at *trente et quarante.*" . . .

Madelon crossed the room and sat down by the woman's side.

"You are not gambling this evening," she remarked pleasantly.

"I do not play these games," the woman confessed, a little timidly. "I don't understand them. At home we play auction bridge sometimes, but I am not fond of cards."

"Where do you live?" Madelon enquired.

"At Exeter, in Devonshire," the woman answered. "My husband is manager of the principal bank there."

"Manager?" Madelon repeated. "I thought he was a banker himself."

The woman shook her head.

"It is a big position," she said, "and my husband is very much esteemed in the city. When we married he was just a clerk in the bank with two hundred a year. He has just got on by being steady and industrious. He has a wonderful head for figures, too."

"This must be a great change for you after an English city," Madelon suggested.

The woman shivered. She was keeping her eyes carefully turned away from the further end of the room.

"It is a horrible place," she declared, with a strange little sob in her throat. "The first day I thought I should like it. The band was playing and the sun was shining and Henry and I took a little carriage and drove out to Cap Martin, and after dinner at the hotel we got our tickets for the Rooms, and I won thirty francs. I thought it was quite a wonderful place that first evening!"

"Tell me," Madelon asked — "that is if you do not think it an impertinent question — is your husband very rich?"

"We are very well off," was the complacent reply. "He gets eight hundred a year now and he has just had a legacy. That is why we are here. We have never been abroad and he had to take his holiday in February, so we came out here for three weeks. Cook's arranged it all for us. I thought that I was going to enjoy it so much and now it all seems terrible."

"You mean because of that woman?" Madelon said kindly.

"I do not know why I talk to you like this," the woman continued, with a note of desperation in her tone, "but there it is! Henry has gone mad. He will not let me speak to him at night. He doesn't sleep. I wake up and find him with his eyes open, muttering to himself. He spends more money every day than our whole hotel bill on flowers for her. If I speak to him he storms. And," she went on confidentially, "if any of the folks from around us were to get to hear of this — any of his big clients or the Bishop — we have all the ecclesiastical business — I can't think what would happen."

"Do you mind my asking you how much this legacy was?" Madelon ventured.

"Ten thousand pounds," the woman confided. "Eight thousand when the duties were paid. We are going to invest it in house property in Exeter, and a little cottage down on the south coast for our summer holidays, but Henry thought he would like to take this trip first."

"How did your husband become acquainted with this woman?" Madelon enquired.

"I don't know," was the helpless reply. "He stood next her one evening whilst she was waiting for a seat at a *chemin de fer* table. If any one had told me," she continued, "that Henry Norton — the Henry I've been married to for twenty-two years — would behave as he is doing, like a stark, raving lunatic, all on account of a half-naked, shameless creature like that, I should have thought that they were crazy. Henry used to go on so at the young girls who wore short skirts in Exeter. He's a church-warden and the Bishop calls him his right-hand man in the city. And now look at him! If any of the directors of the bank were to see him at this moment where should we be?"

"Men are very trying creatures," Madelon agreed soothingly. "Sometimes they break out like this, but it all passes. How long are you staying?"

"For another ten days. . . . How I shall live through them I don't know," Mrs. Norton added, with a little break in her voice. "For a week I have cried myself to sleep and I go and cry in the afternoons, and now I haven't any tears left. I have nothing but just misery. I try to keep away from here, but what can I do? I only fancy things. I sat in the hotel all last night, in the lounge, and read last week's papers. I sat there until one o'clock, and he hadn't come in. Then I went and walked out on the Terrace, where they say people sometimes commit suicide. I never thought of that before, but when one has such a pain ——"

Madelon patted her companion's fat hand for a moment.

"You must not be silly," she enjoined. "Listen. I shall try and help you. There are ways."

"Henry won't stand being interfered with," his wife sighed.

Madelon nodded understandingly.

"I can quite believe that," she said. "When an obstinate, rather narrow-minded man like your husband gets such an obsession he is hard to deal with. But there is always the woman. I shall go and talk to a friend of mine, who is very clever and very fond of helping people in trouble — what you call in English, I think, 'a good sort.'" . . .

Madelon departed with another little nod. On her way out she passed Validia and Mr. Norton, the bank manager from Exeter. Mr. Norton did not appear to be talking much; his attitude was simply one of dogged and deliberate concentration. Validia was gazing at herself in a little mirror. She was looking bored.

"Let us return, my friend, and watch the play," she suggested, putting away her vanity case. "If that hateful man is losing, perhaps he will give me the bank a little earlier. Would you like to be my partner this evening? . . . Well, we shall see!"

She rose to her feet. Her companion immediately followed her example.

"I do not understand the game," he said hesitatingly, "but if you wish it ———— "

He followed at her heels; a little self-conscious, a little vain, only failing to be ridiculous because of his intense earnestness. As they crossed the passage, he leaned towards her.

"Must you gamble to-night?" he asked hoarsely. "Couldn't we go out somewhere — have some supper — talk? I want to talk to you," he went on. "I see nothing of you with all these people. I waited until four o'clock this morning, and then you were too tired."

She laughed and looked at him with one of those sidelong glances which would have been a revelation to any one from Exeter.

"Some time," she whispered, "the caprice will seize me. I will take you by the arm. I shall whisper 'let us go.' Then you will be happy. Just along the passage there — it is not far. You will be glad then that you have waited."

He was a man of imperturbable ways, of stiff and portly demeanour, but little veins stood out upon his forehead and something rose in his throat. Before he could reply they were once more amongst the crowd.

Mr. Kretterson was winning that evening and showed no desire whatever to relinquish the bank. Validia became fretful and irritable. She was ready to welcome any diversion. She received the bow of the Marquis with marked graciousness. She knew all about him — that he was poor but distinguished. Nevertheless, his notice was always pleasant and he might well be the medium to other things.

"Madame has yet not had her chance at the baccarat table?" he enquired.

She made a little grimace.

"That man wearies me," she declared. "He wins and so he persists. After all, why not? I would do the same. The trouble is I desire to play and I do not like to wait for the things which I desire."

"Why not punt against him?" the Marquis suggested.

"It is a winning bank," she replied, "and besides I like the cards myself."

She smiled at him, thinking that although he, too, was elderly, he was indeed a man of great distinction; contrasting him for a moment in her mind with that dumb, stolid Englishman who stood patiently waiting for her notice. And the Marquis, looking at her perfect face, tracing the curve of her smile, appreciating the little glint of red in the liquid brown of her eyes, fancied himself back again in his younger days. She was indeed a very beautiful woman. Then he remembered his mission.

"I wish, madame," he said, "to ask a favour. I wish to present to you my friend Mr. Billingham from New York. Mr. Billingham is one of those giants who have lifted commerce and money-making into a place amongst the fine arts. He has been an admirer of yours for a long time."

No form of introduction could have been more apt. It gave madame great pleasure to make the acquaintance of Mr. Billingham. Her pleasure was enhanced when she found that he spoke quite tolerable French. The three talked together, whilst Mr. Henry Norton stood dumbly in the background. Presently, without a word of excuse to her late companion, Validia pointed to an empty seat and motioned Mr. Billingham to accompany her.

"You have left your friend," he remarked, accepting, however, her invitation.

"Ah, he wearies me!" she murmured. "You need have no fear. He has not a word of French. It wearies me, too, to speak his ugly language. You, Monsieur, speak French so well for an American. You have lived in this country?"

"Only as a pilgrim," was the regretful reply. "We Americans do our best to be patriotic but our law-makers do their best to push us over on this side if we want a little freedom."

"What sort of freedom do you want?" she asked softly.

Mr. Billingham's answering smile was non-committal.

"Madame," he confessed, "the freedom I most desire at this

moment is to talk to you very confidentially — if I might take the liberty on an acquaintance so short."

She leaned a little towards him.

"You intrigue me," she whispered. "What have you to say to me so confidential?"

"I should like to speak," Mr. Billingham confided, "of that fellow who shadows you everywhere."

She laughed; softly at first and then unrestrainedly, her head thrown back, both rows of her brilliant teeth exposed.

"Well," she demanded presently, "what of him?"

"In the first place," Mr. Billingham began, "do you know who he is?"

"A rich English banker," she replied. "He is dull, he is stupid, he is not even generous, except that he is '*fou de moi*.' He wearies me. But what would you have? I make no pretence. I am Validia. Someone must pay that I may live."

Mr. Billingham nodded approvingly.

"Madame," he said, "I admire your frankness. I will imitate it. Your friend is not what you suppose him. He is not a banker at all. He is the local manager in an English country town of a great banking firm at a salary which would not pay for your silk stockings and gloves in the year."

"What does he do here, then?" she asked incredulously.

"He has come into a legacy," Mr. Billingham explained, "and before investing it he has brought his wife here for a short holiday. They have never been abroad before. They have been married twenty-two years. They live in an English Cathedral city in a ten-roomed house with two maid servants. This is his long-talked-of holiday. Of the husband and his madness you know. The wife — she is plain, between forty-five and fifty, and your maid would not wear her dresses. You only need a glance at her to realise her position. She is face to face with a new and terrible sorrow in life."

"You are a very strange person," Validia observed. "Are you in earnest?"

"More or less," Mr. Billingham assented.

"I have deceived myself perhaps in this man's story," she admitted after a moment's reflection. "It is my imperfect knowledge of his language. Besides, he is so stupid that I thought he must be rich. How much is this legacy?"

"Less than eight thousand pounds," Mr. Billingham replied. She yawned.

"It is a disappointment," she confessed. "I am glad that you told me. Still, if he cannot pay much for being foolish, he must pay little. Eight thousand pounds would cover my expenses here and perhaps he can borrow something."

Mr. Billingham sat for a moment in silence. She looked at him curiously. A few yards away Norton stood watching them, waiting for his opportunity to slip into the vacant place if its present occupant should take his departure.

"Is it worth your notice, a small thing like this?" Mr. Billingham asked.

She shrugged her shoulders slightly.

"Why not?" she replied. "If he has no more, then at least I should be rid of him when it was gone. You know who I am and what I am. They say of me, my friends here, that I have one quality. I am truthful. That is all. What I need of men who admire me is money. All that I have to give — and it is much — I will give to the man who can make me feel. That man will not be Mr. Henry Norton — but what would you have? I, even like the others, must live."

Mr. Billingham smiled enigmatically.

"If you were a man," he said, "I should like to do business with you. I like your way of putting the cards upon the table. I shall now show my admiration by following your example. I am one of the few men in the world who have begged for an introduction not to offer their homage, although I am not sure that at the present moment I do not consider you the most beautiful woman in the world."

"It is something," she remarked. "It is perhaps the truth. But I do not attract you, possibly?"

She turned and looked at him — looked at him thoughtfully and with a comprehension which amazed him.

"It is true," she continued. "I do not attract you because you are another of these Saxons who possess the hateful gift of fidelity. You love another woman. Is it not so?"

"Perhaps," he admitted. "In the meanwhile the reason why I asked to be presented to you was to beg you to open the door of that golden cage of yours and let this last captive escape."

She eyed him speculatively.

"He does not wish to escape," she declared. "And besides, why should I do as you ask? What are you offering me? Not even your homage, as you yourself have admitted."

Mr. Billingham was a brave man, but even he was conscious of the peril of the moment. Nevertheless, he braced himself.

"Madame," he confessed, "I have perhaps nothing to offer you. On the other hand there is something, some negative consideration, which I think you might find adequate."

"You talk strangely, Monsieur," she observed.

"It is a difficult subject."

"You need not fear to be frank with me," she told him.

"Let it be so, then. If you do not grant my request I do not think that your nightly games at baccarat will continue."

Whatever she might have been expecting it was not this. Her face showed no surprise nor any anger. She simply seemed suddenly to have become removed into another world. She had become entirely and absolutely aloof.

"I do not understand you," she said presently. "At baccarat I win because I have an instinct for the game. There have been many who have protested to the management against a woman being allowed to take the bank. Yet, you see, I continue! You cannot disturb me!"

"I shall certainly try," he warned her.

She laughed scornfully.

"A challenge!" she exclaimed. "Very well, I accept it! . . . Come here, my good friend, Mr. Norton," she went on in English. "Why do you stand apart? You must meet this gentleman — Mr. Billingham from New York, I think he calls himself. He imagines that to-night I am not to win at baccarat. We shall see! Would you like to take a bank with me?"

"I am not sure that I have enough money with me," was the somewhat hesitating reply.

She frowned and tapped upon the floor impatiently with her foot.

"Of course I will do whatever you wish me to do," he went on hastily. "You know that I do not understand the game."

"They will cash your cheque here," she said. "Get me twenty milles and have more in your pocket. We will see whether we can win. And do not leave me again. I find these others wearisome."

She bade Mr. Billingham a mocking farewell and departed, the man at her side obviously a little bewildered by her sudden graciousness. The Marquis strolled up.

"Any luck?" he enquired.

Mr. Billingham shook his head.

"Not yet," he replied. "We have exchanged long-distance shots. I hoped for terms, but she prefers a fight."

"But I do not see, my friend, what you can do," the Marquis protested.

"I have an idea," Mr. Billingham confided. "When I have an idea of this sort it is not often a mistaken one. I have watched this game for several evenings. We shall see!"

Perhaps because of her beauty and evil reputation, or it may have been from the magnitude of the stakes, or even that the sight of a woman taking a bank at baccarat was in itself an infrequent spectacle, the usual little crowd gathered round the table when Validia took the place which her predecessor had vacated. The first few coups were not productive of any great interest. The bank lost a little and gained a little. Validia sat with the face of a sphinx, drawing her card, announcing her coup with the air of an automaton. Presently, however, the game increased in volume. A wealthy South American, once successfully and once unsuccessfully, had called "banquo." Suddenly there was a little stir. Mr. Kretterson had strolled up and taken the place which had been reserved for him. Every one leaned forward — the gambling was about to begin! He addressed a whispered question to the croupier as to the size of the bank, nodded, and produced a huge packet of bills.

"Fifty milles," he declared.

There was a little hush. Mr. Billingham was amongst the crowd wedged behind his chair and looking over his shoulder.

By his side was a young man — one of the celebrities of the rooms — who out of deference had been allowed a place almost to himself, but of whom Mr. Billingham, perhaps because of his democratic principles, had never once lost sight. Kretterson picked up his cards. He had a king and a queen. He asked for a card, and glanced at it carelessly. It was a nine. Validia toyed with her own cards for a moment, then almost for the first time she raised her head. At the same moment Mr. Billingham leaned forward. Their eyes met. Palpably she hesitated. Mr. Billingham was looking directly at her with his usual good-humoured and friendly smile hovering at the corners of his lips. Apparently, so far as he, at any rate, was concerned, no interchange of glances could have been more harmless or have lacked more completely any ulterior significance. Yet when Validia looked away her fingers were trembling. She glanced at her cards uncertainly and laid them down. She had a king and a six. The croupier began to deal out the winnings.

"What on earth did Validia hesitate for?" some one whispered, behind Mr. Billingham. "She couldn't possibly draw with six, having given the nine."

"Lost her head for a moment, perhaps," some one else commented. "She does make the most extraordinary draws sometimes. Hullo, she's going to quit!"

Validia had risen to her feet with a little gesture of excuse. The croupier announced that Madame was indisposed, and Mr. Kretterson, in response to a universal but unspoken invitation, took the bank. As she passed out, she touched Mr. Billingham on the arm. He followed her to a remote seat in a corner of the bar.

"Order me some brandy," she begged.

Mr. Billingham obeyed in silence. Incidentally he ordered a whisky and soda for himself. In a moment or two Validia spoke.

"How did you know?" she asked, in a low tone.

Mr. Billingham shrugged his shoulders.

"I suppose because I am myself an adventurer," he replied. "I go about the world in search of strange happenings, and I am always watching for them. As a matter of fact there is no game of cards at which I cannot perform miracles myself. I dare not play poker, even with my enemies."

"Still I do not understand," she murmured.

"Simple enough," he continued. "I've watched you take your bank from the background, and once or twice I've stood behind your chair. You are a woman of intelligence. Often I have seen you draw when no woman who knew the game would dream of it. That set me thinking. I looked round the table. There was one person always interested who seldom played; who seemed to prefer to move about and watch the drawer of cards. That person was perhaps the one human being in these rooms whom people would be least likely to suspect of malpractice. A few nights ago I saw! I gave you a warning when I was first introduced to you. You would not take it."

"I never dreamed," she murmured, "that you suspected. I thought you meant that you would complain to the management about a woman taking the bank. Others have done it. They hate women bankers."

"To-night," Mr. Billingham went on, "I stood by the side of your — shall I call him, accomplice? You dared not even look for the sign. It would have been a forlorn hope, in any case, to have drawn to a six, but I think that you would have tried it if I had not stood there."

"Tell me what you propose to do," she begged.

"You will return to that poor fool Norton the twenty milles and all that you have borrowed from him," Mr. Billingham pronounced. "You will simply wash him out completely, and so far as I am concerned the matter passes from my memory."

"You will keep your own counsel?" she asked eagerly.

"Absolutely," he promised. "I am no philanthropist. I am not in the world to protect fools. If you are clever enough to bring this off I am not one of those who would interfere."

She looked at him steadfastly.

"If you were Norton," she said, "I would not let you go."

Mr. Billingham smiled.

"Alas," he sighed, "there is that other reason you were clever enough to divine. Now go and say your farewell to this pseudo-banker of yours. But first — have you any heart at all, I wonder?"

"Not for man or woman," she answered, a little wearily.

"Yet for one moment look across the room," he begged. "There is a plain, middle-aged woman seated there by herself: You see her?"

"I see her," Validia assented. "She is Norton's wife."

Mr. Billingham nodded.

"She is wearing the wrong sort of clothes," he continued, "and she knows it. She is looking plain and commonplace — and she knows it. Somehow or other the truth has come to her; in here, or in the quiet times of the night, when she hasn't been able to sleep. She is suddenly frightened. Everything that meant life to her has gone. She is sitting there because she hasn't the courage to cross through the rooms — sitting there like some creature in pain. You can see all that in her face if you care to look — that commonplace face; eloquent now, perhaps, for the first time since possibly the day of her marriage, or the day her first child was born."

Validia looked across the room incuriously. Her eyes were as hard as ever; her expression unchanged.

"Yes," she said, "I see what you are trying to explain. That means nothing to me, however. I do not understand people who take account of the sufferings of others."

Mr. Billingham was silent for a moment. Then he rose to his feet. She followed suit.

"I will go and keep my bargain," she promised. "On the whole you are an interesting enemy. It is a pity that you are on the other side," she added, with that queer little smile upon her lips which had turned the heads of many men and which two seasons ago had induced the critics to christen her portrait in the *Salon* a modern "Mona Lisa." . . .

Mr. Billingham left her at the door and went in search of Madelon. She made a little grimace as she led him to the bar.

"Here have I been dying for an orangeade," she exclaimed, "and you sitting there with Validia, to the scandal of everybody. Your confessions, if you please!"

He drew her abruptly on one side. Norton, with unseeing eyes and uncertain footsteps, had entered the bar. All the prim stiffness of his deportment, his somewhat awkward self-assertiveness, had gone. He was like a man suddenly made natural by a catastrophe; a little frightened, cowed, stricken into commonsense. He crossed towards the bar, stood there gripping the rail with one hand, called for a drink and finished it at a gulp. His wife leaned forward from her place.

"Henry!" she called out.

He turned and looked at her, almost without recognition. Nevertheless, he made his way to her side. Mr. Billingham whispered in Madelon's ear. Together they approached. Madelon took command of the situation.

"Still not playing?" she said pleasantly to Mrs. Norton. "Let me introduce my friend, Mr. Billingham. This is your husband, is it not?"

Mr. Billingham seemed suddenly possessed by one of those extraordinary fits of geniality which overwhelm any situation. Mrs. Norton's confused surprise and Mr. Norton's stupor were scarcely noticeable.

"Very glad to meet you both, I'm sure," Mr. Billingham declared. "Why, there's the Marquis!" he went on, as the latter looked tentatively in. "Come right along," he invited. "Let me present you — the Marquis de Félan — Mr. and Mrs. Norton. Sit down and join us, Marquis. Waiter! A bottle of Clicquot 1911 — Dry England, mind, not the Brut — some biscuits, and five glasses! You will join us in a glass of wine, Mr. Norton?"

"I thank you very much," was the colourless reply.

"Tell me, you came from Exeter — a banker there," Mr. Billingham continued, producing his cigar-case. "Any connection with the British General Bank?"

"I am the manager of the Exeter Branch, sir," Mr. Norton confided, with a faint return to his old assurance of manner.

"My, is that so?" Mr. Billingham exclaimed. "One of the finest banks going! I congratulate you, sir. Perhaps you know a friend of mine down there — Lord Herrington."

"Lord Herrington is one of my most valued clients," Mr. Norton declared.

"Say, if this isn't a small world!" Mr. Billingham observed, watching the wine being poured out. "That's why I like this place. We men who watch the run of things can come along and rub shoulders with all sorts and be none the worse for it, and then meet our own sort and get all the pleasure imaginable. Say, Mr. Norton, sir, I'm very glad to have met you. Lord Herrington has asked me to stay with him often. We've been associated in more than one financial enterprise on the other side. I guess I may come and look you up at Exeter. Mrs. Norton, your very good health!"

By degrees the situation seemed to become almost normal. Mr. Norton talked about the banking business with increased eloquence, whilst his wife confided to Madelon in an undertone the extraordinary difficulties presented by the servant problem in Exeter. Mr. Billingham glanced at his watch.

"I've had all the gambling I want to-night," he declared. "Let's have a change. There's a Gala Supper at the Carlton. Let's all go. I told them I'd most likely want a table. What do you say, Mrs. Norton? I don't look the figure for it, perhaps, but I'm a useful man at a fox-trot. You dance, of course?"

"We had lessons," Mrs. Norton admitted, looking doubtfully at her husband.

"Anyway, we can watch the fun," her prospective host continued. "Come along, all of you. We'll get an automobile outside. There are one or two questions about banking matters over on your side," he went on, slipping his arm through Mr. Norton's, "I've wanted to ask a man of your experience."

At three o'clock on the following morning, Madelon and Mr. Billingham watched their guests step into a *voiture* outside the Carlton. Mr. Norton handed his wife in amidst a general exchange of good-humoured farewells, and was most impressive in his insistence that no one should forget their luncheon engagement with him on the morrow. He drew the rug over his wife and leaned back by her side, waving his hand with something of his old complacence. Suddenly Mr. Billingham felt Madelon's fingers grasping his arm.

"You are the dearest person in the world," she whispered. "Not only that, but you are the greatest diplomatist. Did you know that he was holding his wife's hand? And did you see him smile at her at the table? If ever a man was trying to assure her that he was sorry and that he had to be forgiven, he was doing it. And her face — why, she was almost good-looking!"

Mr. Billingham watched the approach of the *voiture* which he had summoned.

"I guess that little affair's fixed up all right," he conceded. . . . "I wonder —— "

Suddenly he was silent; thoughtful, almost depressed. Her fingers lingered in his as he handed her into the carriage.

"Sometimes," she whispered — "I wonder too!"

IX

THE STINK WIZARD

THE Marquis was in an evil humour. Neither the sight of that tactfully proffered *apéritif*, nor his niece's ingratiating smile, produced the slightest effect upon him. He had worked himself up into this state and he meant to remain angry.

"Four months ago," he declared, thumping the little table before him with his fist, "you, my friend Billingham, joined company with my niece and myself in a partnership — an unwritten partnership, perhaps, but nevertheless a partnership — which was to be devoted to our mutual gain. I make myself clear?"

"Perfectly," Mr. Billingham assented.

"We embarked upon various enterprises," the Marquis continued, "and met with some success, but lately, what do we do? We rescue a foolish middle-aged man from the clutches of an adventuress. Not one penny comes to our exchequer. We help a young disabled soldier to carry out a delicate mission. Again not a penny! I ask you how long it is to continue? You others may have sources of wealth unknown to me," he went on, casting a suspicious glance at Mr. Billingham. "As for me, I am penniless. I must live as a gentleman needs to live. How am I to do it, I ask you? You, my friend Billingham, tell me that the common funds are exhausted. My niece here has not even a hundred francs to advance. What then, I ask you, is the use of our partnership? You two amuse yourselves whilst I starve."

Mr. Billingham scratched his chin. He seemed disposed to take a lenient view of the other's demeanour.

"There is some sense in what you are saying, Marquis," he admitted. "At the same time, you might remember that your niece and I saved the money we made in one or two little affairs, whereas you —— "

He pointed eloquently towards the Casino. The Marquis sat forward in his chair.

"Listen, then," he interrupted. "I am not a man to accuse a friend of ill-faith. If you assure me that you still maintain your suite at the Hôtel de Paris, your manner of living here, your flowers to my niece, your champagne at our dinners, on the profits of those adventures in which we have been mutually concerned, then you are a very wonderful man. But I will be open. It seems to me that you have been engaged in other enterprises in which we have not been included."

"As to that," Mr. Billingham protested, "you are dead wrong. I may have come into a little bit of my own, but it hasn't been through anything that's happened out here. You're for business again, I take it, Marquis?"

"I have seventeen francs and forty centimes in the world," was the bitter reply.

Mr. Billingham looked at his watch.

"This morning," he announced, "I shall provide luncheon at the Hôtel de Paris. Afterwards you shall both come to my rooms. I will then propound a scheme by means of which some temporary relief may be afforded us."

"Dear, clever man," Madelon murmured. "I have known for two days — since I saw you talking so earnestly with that terrible little Austrian — that something was coming."

"I have an idea," Mr. Billingham acknowledged, "but whether it will result in financial profit or not it is impossible at present to say. I guess we might as well try it out, anyway."

In Mr. Billingham's sitting-room, an hour later, the Marquis and Madelon, on their arrival, found their host indulging in intimate conversation with a black-haired and bespectacled foreigner whom he introduced as Doctor Ludwig Stranz. The Doctor, who spoke English with a very guttural accent, was a man of heavy build and coarse features, untidily dressed and besprinkled with cigar ash. He was cordial but without any grace of manner.

"Friends of Mr. Billingham," he declared, "I make myself glad to know. This is a beastly place. You perhaps haf' gained money."

"I most certainly have not," the Marquis rejoined. "Do I gather that you too are a gambler, Doctor Stranz?"

"I am a scientist," was the verbose reply. "I have discovered many wonderful things in my day, though many of my discoveries have been stolen from me and used to their profits by others. I have been to Paris with an idea of my own — useless! Then I come here. I meet my good friend Mr. Billingham. It was he who once found me money for a little invention of mine."

"That was in the days when I had some," Mr. Billingham explained hastily — "before linoleum went back on me."

"Ah, that was a pity that you lose your money," Doctor Stranz declared. "It is a great invention this of mine now. Even when put to so ridiculous a use —— "

"That will do," Mr. Billingham interrupted abruptly. "We will meet as arranged this afternoon, Doctor Stranz. Better perhaps come five minutes before the time arranged and meet me here. We can go through our plans once more so that there need be no mistake."

"It is so arranged," Doctor Stranz agreed, rising to his feet a little reluctantly. "I go to my lonely breakfast."

It was a hint of which Mr. Billingham took not the slightest notice. They all three watched him depart.

"What an extraordinary man!" Madelon exclaimed.

"He is perhaps concerned with the enterprise you spoke of," the Marquis suggested eagerly.

"He is a necessary part of it," Mr. Billingham assented. "But I warn you there is no certainty about this enterprise. It may come off — it may not. At any rate it is my affair. No one else — though I shall rely upon your help — will be likely to meet with trouble."

"The thought that there is an enterprise to be considered at all," the Marquis declared with satisfaction, "gives to my luncheon an increased appetite. I suggest a descent."

Madelon, who was looking in the mirror, sighed.

"I should like some one to admire my hat," she observed, readjusting it a little.

"Its only fault," Mr. Billingham suggested, "is that it hides too much of your face."

"Its only fault that I can see," the Marquis groaned, "is that it cost too much money."

Madelon made a little grimace.

"Skinflint!" she exclaimed. "I made it myself!"

At four o'clock that afternoon, just as the *Salons de Jeux* of the Sporting Club were opened, one of the liveried footmen attached to the place announced to Monsieur Louchette, the manager, who was seated in his office, a visit from Mr. Billingham and a friend. Mr. Billingham, being a person who during the four months of his sojourn in Monte Carlo had established himself as an *habitué* of some consequence, the manager abandoned his habits of almost papal seclusion and intimated his willingness to receive the two gentlemen. The door was thrown open and they accordingly presented themselves.

"I'd like you," Mr. Billingham said, having shaken hands, "to meet my friend, Doctor Stranz, who has been staying here for a while."

Doctor Stranz bowed and shook hands solemnly. The manager regarded him with some curiosity.

"Ach, what a place!" the former exclaimed.

Monsieur Louchette cleared his throat.

"I trust you have enjoyed your stay here, Doctor," he remarked. "What can I have the pleasure of doing for you, gentlemen?"

"For me nothing," Mr. Billingham replied. "My friend the Doctor, whom I met in New York during the war, just asked me to introduce him. If you gentlemen have business to talk over I guess I'll leave you to it."

The manager looked at Doctor Stranz and disliked him.

"No need for you to leave us, Mr. Billingham," he declared hastily. "What can I do for you, sir?" he added, turning to his companion.

Doctor Stranz sat down ponderously, placing the small black bag which he was carrying with him by his side.

"Sir," he announced, "I haf' met with great misfortunes here. I haf' lost heavily. I haf' lost all my beautiful money."

"Indeed," Monsieur Louchette remarked coldly. "If your business here is simply to tell me this ——"

"It is not," Doctor Stranz interrupted. "I would haf' you know all of the situation. I come here with one hundred thousand francs — money which has been paid me for my marvellous inventions. I am a great inventor. There is no one who has such a brain as mine. I make everything that blow up. With a projectile as big as a pea I could destroy the Palais at Versailles or the Reichstag in Berlin."

"Very wonderful, I am sure," the manager observed a little impatiently, "but you will excuse me if I remark that I am busy."

"Ach, busy!" Doctor Stranz repeated, leaning over and striking the edge of the table before which the other was seated. "You may be busy but you must listen to me. One — more than one hundred thousand francs of my hard-earned money I have lost here. Something must be done for me."

Monsieur Louchette looked at Mr. Billingham as though to ask whether the man were a lunatic. Mr. Billingham shook his head.

"I had not received," he said, "the slightest intimation as to what the Doctor was wanting. He simply asked for an introduction. I am sorry I brought him if he is a nuisance. Perhaps I had better leave you alone."

"Not on any account," the manager begged. "You are sure that the man is sane?" he added, under his breath.

"Sane I am, but insane soon I shall be," the Doctor thundered. "Now I shall show you whether I am a man of sense or not. I will talk to you plainly. I want my money back."

"If you wish us to make an advance to cover your return fare home and reasonable hotel expenses," the manager suggested, drawing a form towards him, "you can make application for a *viatique* which will receive due consideration. You of course understand, however, that you will not be allowed in the rooms again until the amount is repaid."

"I want my money back," Doctor Stranz repeated doggedly. "One hundred and forty thousand francs I want."

"You are wasting my time," Monsieur Louchette declared quietly. "Permit me to wish you good-afternoon."

The official's forefinger strayed towards the bell which stood upon his desk. Doctor Stranz reached out his hand. Something in his expression induced the other to pause.

"I have told you," he said, "that I must have back my one hundred and forty thousand francs. I have not told you what I shall do if you refuse."

"A threat!" the manager exclaimed.

"If you refuse I promise you this," the Doctor continued earnestly. "At eleven o'clock to-night this place will be — is it not so — packed with people. At five minutes past eleven you shall find them in the streets, on the promenade perhaps, the pavements, on the stairway, everywhere — but not in those rooms — not in those rooms, I promise you."

Monsieur Louchette looked towards Mr. Billingham who nodded sympathetically, and, unseen by the Doctor, tapped his forehead. The manager smiled tolerantly.

"Well, well," he said, "I am sorry for you, Doctor Stranz, but you must see that there is no reason why I should return your money any more than anybody else's. There are dozens and scores here every season who lose more than you have done. You must come back next year and hope for better luck."

"Will I haf' back again my one hundred and forty thousand francs?" Doctor Stranz demanded.

"Of course not," was the firm reply. "Your friend Mr. Billingham will explain to you the absurdity of such a suggestion. You will permit me."

This time the manager succeeded in reaching the bell. Doctor Stranz rose stiffly to his feet.

"Perhaps," he announced, "I will visit you again to-morrow morning."

"It will be quite useless," the manager assured him. "I wish you good-afternoon, gentlemen."

A servant entered and held open the door. Mr. Billingham loitered behind.

"Say, I am sorry I brought him in," he apologised. "I had no idea he was luny. He was a bright fellow enough when I knew him. The war again, I suppose."

"Quite all right, Mr. Billingham," the other remarked a little patronisingly. "We are used to strange visitors."

The visit of the mad Austrian had almost passed out of the mind of the manager of the Sporting Club. Nevertheless at a few minutes before eleven he left his office and strolled through the Rooms. Late in the season though it was, they were still crowded, and with a somewhat brilliant gathering. There was an English Duke and an American millionaire playing in maximums at roulette, a noted Greek financier was taking a bank at baccarat, crowds of pretty and well-dressed women and well-known men thronged the place. With a little frown the manager recognised Doctor Stranz seated next to a croupier. He summoned one of his deputies.

"That man's card of admission," he directed, pointing him out, "must be withdrawn. He is a madman and declares he has lost one hundred and forty thousand francs. Doctor Stranz his name is."

"I will see to it at once, sir," the deputy promised.

Eleven o'clock struck. Nothing happened. Suddenly, however, there was a little murmur. The people at the tables raised their heads. The loiterers in the room made for the doors. There was one expression upon every face — an expression of pained and physical distaste, which speedily became loathing. People who had strolled towards the exits commenced to hurry; others from the remote ends of the room pressed behind them. Finally the players at the tables with one accord rose to their feet, some of them clutching at the money in front of them, some of them abandoning it. There seemed to be a faint white mist drifting about the room and becoming thicker every moment, and apparently from it there was emitted the most terrible, stupefying and noxious smell which ever greeted the nostrils of any human being. Every second it became stronger. The manager opened his mouth to give an order, but his lips were powerless. He rushed for the door with the others. In less than sixty seconds the passages leading into the Hôtel de Paris and the stairway — luckily a broad one — leading into the street were packed with a seething mass of shrieking, coughing, half-fainting people. Two of the servants made an heroic effort to open the windows and fell overpowered. The occupants of the bar joined with the waiters in a mad rush down into the back quarters. Here and there a woman fainted. One man, black in the face with coughing, threw himself over the banisters on to the tables below. In an incredibly short space of time not a soul remained in the roulette room, except one. Doctor Stranz, with a respirator over his mouth, strange-looking spectacle, and flaps over his ears, looked around him with a smile half-satanic, half beatific.

"That was good," he said to himself. "Before, it was I who felt sick at heart in these rooms. Now, it is they who feel sick at the stomach!"

At a few minutes after ten o'clock on the following morning, the card of Monsieur Louchette, the manager of the Sporting Club, was brought in to Mr. Billingham, and Monsieur Louchette himself promptly followed. Mr. Billingham welcomed him with a grin.

"Say, that was some trick the Austrian played us!" he observed as he shook hands.

Monsieur Louchette was a man destitute of any sense of humour. For five minutes without ceasing he talked and Mr. Billingham listened in admiration.

"And then some," the latter remarked, when through sheer lack of breath his visitor became silent. "But say, to get down to business, what are you going to do about it?"

"The police search now for the rascal," Monsieur Louchette declared. "He shall be made to pay damages. He shall be imprisoned. Such an outrage has never before been known!"

Mr. Billingham thoughtfully lit a cigarette.

"I don't know how the law goes on this side," he remarked, "but in my country I'm not sure as it's a criminal offence to

make a smell, — even if it could be proved that he did it."
Monsieur Louchette was off again. A smell! It was in such
cold-blooded fashion that his friend Mr. Billingham could allude
to the ghastliness of what had happened? There had been a
soldier there who had declared that never in his worst expe-
riences of the war, when they had been caught without masks,
had anything so hideous crept into their nostrils. There were
ladies lying sick in their rooms in every hotel in Monte Carlo.
The lost property office was beseiged by an endless stream of
men and women who had thrown away everything to escape
from this horror. And Mr. Billingham could call it "a smell"!

"It was nifty," Mr. Billingham admitted, when at last the
manager had once more come to a pause. "I worked once in
a tan-yard when I was a boy and I have been down in the
hold of a Chinese yawl and I know San Francisco pretty well,
but I guess the Doctor had all other smells beaten to a frazzle.
Fortunately," he went on, "my young friend, Mademoiselle de
Félan, and I were near one of the doors, and we got away
slick. If it is a fair question, Monsieur Louchette, what do you
really think you're going to do about the fellow?"

Monsieur Louchette's former eloquence seemed vapid compared to his present expressions. The mad Austrian, it appeared,
was to be drowned in burning oil, guillotined and deported.
In the midst of it all there was a modest knock at the door and
Doctor Stranz was announced.

"I do not intrude, I trust," he said. "I wished for a word
with my friend Mr. Billingham. Ah, it is Monsieur Louchette,
the manager of the Sporting Club. Good-morning Monsieur
Louchette. Are your rooms aired this morning, and what about
my money?"

Monsieur Louchette sprang forward, but Mr. Billingham's
firm arm restrained him. Nothing, however, could check the
torrent of speech which proclaimed his opinion of the newcomer,
his intentions with regard to him, and his certain future. Doctor
Stranz listened with amusement.

"That policeman," he confided, "he has been to see me already,
but what can I do? There was a smell in your rooms last night.

Who knows that I made the smell, and, if I did, what is the law against one who makes a smell? Your policeman he has gone back to consult a judge. I have done nothing. I want my one hundred and forty thousand francs, but I have done nothing. If I get my money and I leave, perhaps there will be no more smells."

"Apart from everything else," Monsieur Louchette found breath to say, "there was money missing last night from the croupier's box near where you were seated."

Doctor Stranz drew himself up with dignity.

"I am a man of great honour," he declared. "I have never stolen from anybody. All that I took with me from the Club last night I won. Why do you not give me back my one hundred and forty thousand francs? Then I think there will be no more smells."

"You rascal!" Monsieur Louchette gasped. "You will never cross the portals of the club again. Your name has a black mark against it for ever. Before the day is out you will be in prison."

"I think not," was the mild reply. "I think no man can go to prison in Monaco for making a smell — if I did. So you keep me out of the Sporting Club, eh? Listen, you give me my one hundred and forty thousand francs and I will leave to-night."

"I will see you in hell first!" Monsieur Louchette thundered.

"What a pity!" Doctor Stranz sighed. "Mind you, I do not say I have done anything, but I tell you this, there is not in the world any chemist so clever as I — not in the whole world, mind. You think once more."

Monsieur Louchette broke partially away from Mr. Billingham, and Doctor Stranz made for the door. On the threshold he looked back.

"You make a mistake — a great mistake!" he called out, departing and slamming the door behind him.

"What do you know about that!" Mr. Billingham exclaimed.

Monsieur Louchette took up his hat.

"I came," he declared, "to ask if you could tell me anything more about this man."

Mr. Billingham shook his head.

"I can tell you that he was in charge of a poison gas factory during the war," he said. "I had a plant in the same city making aeroplane wings. That's how I came across him. 'The Stink Wizard' they called him."

"Do you suppose he has really lost one hundred thousand francs at the tables?" Monsieur Louchette asked abruptly.

Mr. Billingham shrugged his shoulders.

"I am not a heavy player myself," he replied. "I have seen him get through quite a pile, but I kept no tabs on him."

"Anyway," Monsieur Louchette remarked with satisfaction, "he won't get to the Sporting Club to-night."

"I guess there are a good many others who won't either," Mr. Billingham opined.

Mr. Billingham and Madelon dined alone that evening. The latter was a little nervous; Mr. Billingham inclined to be facetious.

"This afternoon," he announced, "I have been to the Law Library up at Monaco with an interpreter. So far as I can see the penalties against a maker of smells are purely nominal."

"There are other things," Madelon reminded him. "I hear Monsieur Louchette complains that a great deal of money was taken."

"Doctor Stranz assures me that he did not take anything with him except what he won," Mr. Billingham declared. "I guess he was telling the truth."

"What did Monsieur Louchette say this morning?" Madelon enquired.

Mr. Billingham grinned.

"If the Doctor had not made a somewhat inopportune arrival in my rooms," he replied, "I'm dead sure that with careful handling, Louchette would have opened his pockets. As it was he lost his temper, but if to-night — well, we shall see! I hear there are twenty-four detectives in the Club and if Doctor Stranz tries to put in an appearance there will be trouble. Fortunately he won't."

"I shall be glad," Madelon sighed, "when he is out of existence altogether."

"Don't say that," Mr. Billingham begged. "He has given a

little colour to a somewhat dull period. Besides which he promises to be an extremely profitable creation."

"Money, always money!" she sighed. "I wonder whether I am getting tired of being an adventuress."

He looked at her a little wistfully.

"There is another world," he said quietly — "a world where pleasure is less of a business, perhaps, and happiness —— "

"You are going to make me sentimental," she interrupted. "Come, we must have our coffee and it is time that we went."

"The first table to the left in the 'Kitchen,'" Mr. Billingham reminded her firmly. "I shall meet you in the gardens — the seat I showed you. You have — everything?"

She nodded.

"Do you not see in how careful a fashion I am carrying my bag?" she asked.

A small crowd of detectives awaited developments in the Sporting Club that evening and a lackey stood by each window. Nothing whatever happened. At half-past eleven, however, the events of the night before were repeated with even more terrifying consequences in both the Casino and the *Salons Privés*. Precautions had been taken here also with regard to the windows, but the spread of the fumes was too rapid and stupefying to allow of more than one or two being opened. The crowds which thronged the two rooms gave even more poignant evidences of terror and panic than the visitors to the Sporting Club on the previous evening. Several croupiers attempted to keep their places but fell forward in a moment or two, overpowered. As a safeguard the various exits to the *Salons Privés* had all been thrown open and from here the flight, although precipitate, was conducted with a certain amount of order. The Marquis, who had been seated next to a croupier at one of the end tables, seemed to have possessed himself of some of the perquisites of the absent Doctor Stranz. At the first symptoms of alarm he slipped a respirator over his mouth, spectacles over his eyes and flaps over his ears. He sat there, watching the scene for a few moments with every appearance of interest. To his amazement, notwithstanding the general exodus, two women, who had been playing on the other side of the table, also remained in their seats, although they gazed around them with many exclamations of astonishment. The Marquis looked at them, then at the wheel which he longed to spin, and the brass box with the mille notes which he longed to investigate. His whole environment was irresistible. He produced from his pocket a hundred franc plaque and four louis, and held them poised in his left hand. With his right forefinger he spun the wheel. The ball sped round in jerky fashion and alighted in number twenty-nine. The Marquis adjusted his eyeglass, to be quite sure that there was no mistake, and promptly deposited his counters upon the number indicated. With painstaking care he counted out from the croupier's well six thousand, three hundred francs, stuffed the amount into his pocket and rose to his feet. One of the women who had been regarding him intently — the fatter and fairer of the two; a woman wearing a dress of bright blue silk and a heavy gold chain around her neck — turned to her companion, who was obviously her daughter, a smaller replica of herself. In her excitement she spoke in German.

"Gretchen," she cried, "where do they all go, these people?"

The daughter sniffed the air for a moment, her fat little nose uplifted.

"I am not sure, but I think they smell something, Mother," she announced, also in German.

The Marquis abandoned his solitary amusement, rose sadly from his place and walked across the room, strewn with evidences of feminine flight, towards the lift.

Whilst Mr. Billingham still slept upon the following morning, there was a knock at his door and Monsieur Louchette was announced. It was a very chastened Monsieur Louchette. He was accompanied on this occasion by another functionary whom Mr. Billingham recognised as one of the principals of the Casino.

"Say, you're bright and early!" Mr. Billingham complained, sitting up in bed and yawning.

"We apologise," Monsieur Louchette said, "but the circumstances may perhaps excuse us. We have searched the place for this man Doctor Stranz. We cannot find him."

"We seek your aid," the other functionary confided.

Mr. Billingham swung out of bed and wrapped himself in a dressing-gown.

"Gentlemen," he explained, "this man is no friend of mine, but he has asked me to respect his confidence as to his whereabouts. What am I to do?"

"We are prepared to make terms," Monsieur Louchette announced.

"In that case," Mr. Billingham replied, "take a seat. Order some coffee if you will and wait whilst I have my bath. Doctor Stranz will be here at nine o'clock."

"Stop!" Monsieur Louchette exclaimed. "Mr. Billingham, you are a well-known citizen of a country we respect, your name and reputation are beyond question. Will you undertake negotiations for us with this abominable person?"

Mr. Billingham considered the matter.

"Why, I should say so," he consented. "What's the great idea?"

"He says that he has lost one hundred and forty thousand francs," Monsieur Louchette continued drearily. "We have that sum here in notes. We will give it to him provided you can extract some guarantee that the proceedings of last night and the night before shall never be repeated by him, or by any one else with his connivance or help."

"It seems a lot of money to part with," Mr. Billingham observed.

"Nevertheless, it is the decision of the Council," Monsieur Louchette replied. "One hundred and forty thousand francs is a great deal of money, but a repetition of the scenes of the last two nights would be utterly and entirely disastrous. If you can arrange this matter for us, Mr. Billingham, the *Société de Bains de Mer* will consider themselves in your debt."

"I guess I can fix it if any one can," Mr. Billingham promised. "Leave the money and come back at half-past ten."

They left the money.

Mr. Billingham had chosen a table that morning on the terrace at the Réserve Restaurant at Beaulieu. A striped umbrella sheltered him and his guests — the Marquis and Madelon —

from the sun. The west breeze across the bay was only a delight. Furthermore, Mr. Billingham had ordered the luncheon with peculiar care. There was caviare — the only pot in the south of France —served with ice and lemon — large caviare, dull, of the colour of olives, procurable only by an epicure of boundless means and boundless influence with those who control the kitchen. Then there was a bouillabaisse, to serve which the *chef* himself had arrived from the kitchen; a chicken which was a speciality of the house; wild strawberries, prepared with red wine; and a cunning mixture of liqueurs. Champagne followed the Chablis, and the brandy was served from a *bidon*. The whole meal was a wonderful effort.

"Never have I eaten better," the Marquis declared, as he selected a cigar.

"A banquet!" Madelon murmured. "And now, please tell us everything."

Mr. Billingham lit his cigar.

"I thought that for this little celebration," he explained, "we were perhaps just as well outside Monte Carlo. However, the news is of the best. The *Société de Bains de Mer* has granted Doctor Stranz a *viatique* of — what do you think?"

"Five thousand francs," the Marquis guessed.

"Don't keep us in suspense," Madelon begged.

"Of one hundred and forty thousand francs," Mr. Billingham announced impressively. "The forty thousand francs I have already parted with."

"For the smells?" Madelon exclaimed.

"Precisely — and to cover Doctor Stranz's losses, which I understand amounted to nearly four milles. If ever I need a friend who can make smells he is at my service. I had hard work to escape from his embraces."

"And the remaining one hundred thousand?" the Marquis gasped.

"The remaining one hundred thousand is for us three," Mr. Billingham declared.

The Marquis' fingers trembled.

"It is incredible!" he murmured.

"It is the adventure of our lives!" Madelon faltered

Mr. Billingham produced three packets of mille notes; one he returned to his own pocket, the other two he handed to his companions.

"Marquis," he said, "I congratulate you. The idea was mine, but a considerable part of the execution was yours and Mademoiselle Madelon's. The organisation certainly never dreamed that the real Doctor Stranz left Monte Carlo twenty-four hours ago, perfectly well content, with my forty thousand francs in his pocket. They believe that he departed at noon to-day with one hundred and forty thousand. However, the result to them is the same and they can afford the money. They paid that the *contretemps* of the last two nights might not happen again. They will have value for their money. Those *contretemps* are finished!"

"We only had six little bottles," Madelon remarked.

"You have now a little over thirty-three thousand francs in your pocket, Marquis," Mr. Billingham concluded. "You will not reproach us any longer, I trust, with those few efforts towards philanthropy which have wasted some of our time. On this occasion we have taken the great lesson to heart that philanthropy begins at home. There is also a little trifle which we have not mentioned — a little trifle to which I believe you helped yourself."

The Marquis coughed.

"I helped myself to nothing that I did not win," he replied. "Incidentally I discovered — the night of the second smell — how to win at roulette."

"Tell us," Madelon begged.

"That might be worth hearing," Mr. Billingham observed.

"Stake your money," the Marquis said impressively, "after the ball has ceased to roll!"

X

CHRISTIAN, THE CONCIERGE

MONTE CARLO, on a moonless night late in May, is not without its sombre effects. Mr. Billingham, loitering on that extension of the Terrace promenade which passes the post-office and reaches to the bottom of the hill, took note of the changed aspects of the place during the last six weeks. The Sporting Club, once gaily illuminated, with blue-liveried servants waiting at the top of the steps to welcome visitors, and rows of automobiles drawn up against the pavement, was closed and dark. The great hotels which lined the hills no longer presented a semicircle of glittering lights. Here and there a few lamps twinkled out from the different villas, but, for the greater part, the hillside had become a chaos of unbroken blackness.

Mr. Billingham, standing with his back to the stone balustrade, smoking thoughtfully and looking landwards, was suddenly aware of a touch upon his arm. He turned abruptly to find Madelon by his side, a black silk cloak thrown over her evening gown. Her approach had been, perhaps purposely, noiseless. She seemed to have crept out of the void.

"Useless!" she laughed. "I came to make discoveries and behold I find you alone and apparently star-gazing."

"Not star-gazing," Mr. Billingham murmured.

"Seriously, I am disappointed," she went on. "I thought there must have been some reason for these mysterious nocturnal strolls of yours."

"There is a reason," Mr. Billingham confided.

"An assignation?"

He shook his head.

"Look carefully," he directed, "exactly where I am pointing and tell me whether you see anything."

She stood by his side and obeyed.

"I see something," she admitted, "which looks like a rapidly-moving glow-worm, appearing and disappearing."

Mr. Billingham nodded.

"I will tell you what it is," he said. "It is someone with an electric torch moving about in a room of an hotel which is closed for the season."

"A caretaker, perhaps," she suggested.

"Perhaps," he assented. "Yet one wonders why a caretaker should be wandering about always in the same room at night-time."

"He may be sleeping there," she observed.

"Then why not use the electric light in an ordinary way?" Mr. Billingham rejoined. "Of course," he went on, "there may be a very simple explanation. There probably is. Yet there are other things which have made me wonder about that light."

"As, for instance?" Madelon demanded.

"The first time I noticed it there was just a little moonlight and I could see that the light came from the fifth window of the third story of the Hôtel d'Angleterre. It was at that hotel, as I dare say you remember, that Seth Dickerson, the American who had been gambling so heavily, committed suicide a week or two ago."

"I remember," Madelon murmured. "They closed the hotel because of it a few days earlier than they meant to."

"Just so," Mr. Billingham agreed. "And the hotel has remained closed ever since. There is no caretaker in it. Whoever is moving about that room with an electric torch is an intruder."

"An empty hotel!" Madelon mused. "It doesn't sound exactly like a happy hunting-ground. And why that particular room? The poor fellow committed suicide because he had lost every penny he possessed at the tables."

Mr. Billingham did not reply. He was watching the faint flashing of the light. Sometimes it disappeared altogether for several minutes. At no time was it more than a glimmer.

"Nevertheless," he said at last, "whoever is moving about that room is searching for something. You see the light is turned in every direction, but never for a moment straight at the window."

"Shall we go up?" she proposed.

Mr. Billingham shook his head.

"Not to-night," he replied. "To-morrow morning I shall call upon the manager of the Royalty Hotel, which belongs to the same people. If you are interested you can come with me."

She thrust her arm through his.

"Meanwhile," she begged, "let us go to the Casino. I am rather uneasy about my uncle. He has borrowed no money for two days and he is becoming mysterious."

The manager of the Royalty Hotel and Mr. Billingham were from the first on the best of terms. Mr. Billingham in a very few words explained his mission.

"That poor chap Dickerson's folk have been writing to me," he said — "the fellow who committed suicide over at the Angleterre, you know."

"That affair is all finished with," the manager exclaimed hastily. "The hotel at first paid for the funeral and all expenses, but the *Société* has now refunded the amount."

"That's all right," Mr. Billingham declared good-humouredly. "Seth Dickerson's people don't want any fuss any more than you do. Theirs is just a sentimental idea. They want me to have a look at the room where he died and send them a few trifling particulars."

"Delighted to do anything we can for you, Mr. Billingham," the manager assured him cordially. "Mr. Dickerson's clothes and effects were all sent to an address in London, as I dare say you know. The loose change on his table was given to the servants. It amounted to less than their weekly tips."

"That's quite all right," Mr. Billingham observed. "Naturally a fellow like Dickerson don't commit suicide while he's got anything left. How can we have a look at the room?"

"Christian, the concierge of the hotel, has the keys," the manager replied. "He is here now helping our own man. I will send for him."

He touched a bell, sent a message, and a few minutes later a tall, remarkably fine-looking man, in the uniform of the hotel, entered the room. He saluted Mr. Billingham, whom he knew slightly, and smiled at the young lady. To all appearance he was the absolute prototype of his class; brimful of knowledge, which he was only too anxious to impart, capable and good-tempered

"This gentleman," the manager explained, "has heard from the relatives of Mr. Dickerson in America. He wants to have a look at the room Mr. Dickerson occupied."

For a single second there was something beyond ordinary interest in the man's face. Mr. Billingham, who had been watching him closely, took note of it.

"There is nothing belonging to Mr. Dickerson left in the room, sir," he pointed out.

"Quite so. I know that," Mr. Billingham intervened. "It's just an idea his people have. Want me to tell them when I get back what sort of a place it was he ended his days in. Silly idea — but folks are silly sometimes."

"You had better take Mr. Billingham and the young lady across," the manager directed.

"Certainly, sir," the man acquiesced. "If you and the young lady will step this way, sir," he continued, turning to Mr. Billingham. "I have the keys in my pocket."

They took leave of the manager and crossed the street towards the Angleterre. The concierge opened the front door of the hotel and they passed into an atmosphere of gloom and silence. There were dust sheets over the mahogany counter and the cushions of the lounge; a faint odour of tea leaves and disinfectants everywhere.

"I shall have to trouble you to come up the stairs, sir," Christian observed. "The lift is not running."

"On which floor was Mr. Dickerson's room?" Mr. Billingham enquired.

"The third, sir," the man replied.

They mounted the stairs in silence. In the corridors the sound of their footsteps awakened faint echoes. Even the stair carpets had been taken up and stood rolled together in corners. The concierge led them unhesitatingly to the door of a room which he unlocked and threw open.

"This was Mr. Dickerson's apartment, sir," he announced. "He shot himself in the easy-chair over there."

It was a bedroom of the plainest possible description; spotlessly clean, bare now of carpet or even rugs, bedstead dismantled —an epitome of dreariness. There was a little dust on the floor and a little rim of dust which Mr. Billingham noticed as the door was opened. He looked around him in some perplexity. "How long has this room been closed up?" he asked.

"About a fortnight, sir."

"And you are sure that this is the room Mr. Dickerson occupied?"

"Quite sure, sir."

"During that fortnight," Mr. Billingham persisted, "has any one entered it at all?"

"Certainly not, sir," was the confident reply. "No one has entered the hotel that I know of."

The man stood, the keys in his hand, patient yet obviously anxious to bring this visitation to a close. Mr. Billingham walked to the window, opened it and stepped out on to the balcony. He looked to the left. There were five windows to be counted. The one through which he had passed was the sixth.

"Have any of these rooms got more than one window?"

"The next door one has, I believe, sir," the man answered, looking a little puzzled. . . . "Is there anything further I can do for you, or the young lady?" he added, after a moment's pause.

Mr. Billingham looked around once more regretfully and sorrowfully.

"Well, I guess not," he decided. "It's a poor room, this. Pretty hard up towards the end, I expect."

The concierge nodded.

"They stripped him clean, sir," he agreed. "It's a way they have down yonder. . . ."

The three descended the stairs almost in silence. Christian led them into the street, and Mr Billingham handed him a twenty franc note.

"I am very much obliged to you, sir," the man said. "You are sure there is nothing more I can do?"

"Nothing at all, thank you," Mr. Billingham assured him. "I will just have a word with your manager. . . ."

They re-entered the Royalty Hotel. Mr. Billingham with Madelon still by his side made his way to the bureau. The manager looked up and nodded.

"Satisfied your curiosity, sir?" he asked.

Mr. Billingham glanced behind him to be sure that the door was closed.

"I guess not," he answered gravely. "I'm afraid there's a little trouble ahead."

The manager's jaw dropped. Like all hotel proprietors he disliked trouble of the sort indicated by his visitor.

"Why, what is wrong?" he demanded.

"In the first place," Mr. Billingham enquired, "what was the number of the room occupied by Seth Dickerson?"

"Number 167," was the prompt reply.

"Precisely. Now your concierge Christian deliberately took us to 168 and showed it to me as the room occupied by Seth Dickerson."

"I cannot imagine how he could have made such a mistake," the manager remarked, with a perplexed frown. "He knows the hotel inside out."

"Oh, he knew all right," Mr. Billingham observed dryly. "Tell me now, have you keys to the hotel yourself, as well as the set Christian has been using?"

The manager opened his drawer.

"Certainly I have."

"And a pass-key to the rooms?"

"I have both."

"Then I want you," Mr. Billingham begged, "to send Christian out of the way for half an hour and to take us across there."

The manager glanced at the clock.

"That is easy," he said. "I will send him down to the station to meet the four-thirty. There is always the chance of a visitor or two. . . . Excuse me!"

He spoke through a tube for a moment, then rose to his feet.

"Of course," he continued, "I have not the least idea what you are driving at, Mr. Billingham, but I am entirely at your disposal. Come along, then!" . . .

They waited for a few minutes until the hotel bus had passed the window, then once more they crossed the road, entered the gloomy-looking building and mounted the stairs to the third floor. This time the manager opened the door of number 167. He had no sooner done so than he himself gave vent to a little exclamation of surprise, and Mr. Billingham, following close behind, whistled softly.

The room — larger than the neighbouring one, with two windows and curved balcony — was in the wildest disorder. The carpet had been rolled back and was lying in an untidy heap upon the floor. The bedclothes had been pulled over the bottom of the bedstead, drawers stood open, an easy-chair had been overturned upon the floor and apparently the whole of its stuffing removed. The manager looked around him in blank amazement. Mr. Billingham was conscious of a feeling of intense satisfaction.

"I'm going to put you wise to something, Monsieur Lavalle," he said. "You see for yourself that someone has made a systematic search of this room. What do you think they wanted? . . . I'll tell you. They wanted the money Seth Dickerson won at the Casino on his last night there."

"Won?" the manager repeated incredulously. "Why, Mr. Dickerson came home a ruined man. That's why he shot himself."

"Dickerson did nothing of the sort," was the confident reply. "That's what put me on the track of this trouble. I happened to know the croupiers at the tables where he played and two of the chefs. Seth Dickerson played at four tables on the night of his death and he brought home with him to this hotel a matter of between sixty and seventy milles. He had no more idea of committing suicide that evening than I have at the present moment."

"Then why did he?" the other demanded.

"He didn't," Mr. Billingham rejoined. "He was murdered."

Monsieur Lavalle had no words. It was Madelon who intervened.

"Murdered!" she gasped. "By whom?"

"By Christian, the concierge," Mr. Billingham pronounced.

There was a moment's breathless silence. In the midst of it

Madelon raised a warning finger. From somewhere outside they seemed to hear the sound of a muffled footstep. Mr. Billingham moved to the door and looked out. There was no one in sight. He closed the door again.

"Listen," he said. "I guess this is mainly conjecture, but I have a sort of knack of putting things together and this is how I build up this little affair. I knew Seth Dickerson. He wasn't much of a man, but he wasn't the sort to use a gun against himself, although I know he kept one handy. I saw him in the Casino the night of his supposed suicide and he couldn't contain himself — told me he had been winning at every table. I asked the croupiers afterwards. They all said the same thing. He had been losing before, but he had been picking it up all the time that night. The long and the short of it is this. Seth Dickerson left the Casino and came back to the hotel with a packet of mille notes in his pocket and as nearly drunk as a man may be and keep on his feet."

"He hadn't forty francs when his things were gone through," the manager objected. "The *Société de Bains de Mer* paid for his funeral."

"Just so," Mr. Billingham agreed, "but nevertheless he brought home sixty milles with him and unless I'm mistaken the sixty milles were at one time or another in this room. I've a friend at Police Headquarters here and although not a word of the proceedings at the inquest crept into the press, I got to know all about it. When Seth Dickerson reached home that night there was only one man up in the hotel. That man was your concierge — a man with whom Dickerson was always too friendly. He invited him up to have a drink. Christian went off to get the bottle of whisky Seth ordered, and brought it up to the room. When he arrived, I'm figuring it out that Seth had hidden the sixty thousand francs or whatever it was. He was just sober enough not to be an utter fool. They sat and drank together, those two, and Seth bragged about his winnings. When he did it, I don't know, but I reckon that your man shot him when he sat in that chair drunk, went through him for the money, failed to find it and got out scared. Or it's likely enough that Seth told him he had hidden it without telling him where.

Anyway when he shot him he expected to get hold of the sixty thousand francs right away. He couldn't find them and he had to clear out. What happened then? The room was closed up for a time, until after the inquest. No searching was done because no one had any idea that there was anything to look for. Your concierge knew, though. You closed the hotel and I don't blame you. Your man didn't want to come in during the day-time, although he had the keys, but for the last two nights he has been ransacking this room."

"How do you know that?" Monsieur Lavalle demanded.

"Because I have a fancy for moonlight strolls," Mr. Billingham explained. "The last two nights, from the promenade down below, I've seen some one hunting round here with an electric torch. It fitted in with my own ideas, so I came to you and asked to be shown this room. Just as I imagined he might, Christian took me to the next room. I could see from below that the room he was searching had two windows, because every now and then the light disappeared."

"There is someone outside," Madelon interrupted suddenly.

They all listened. There was nothing to be heard. The silence of the great empty hotel seemed almost oppressive. Mr. Billingham moved softly to the door and threw it open. He stood there for a moment, listening, his right hand underneath his coat. A peculiar gloom seemed to envelop the place. There was no one in sight, however, no sound to be heard. Yet, curiously enough, Mr. Billingham had the same idea as Madelon. He felt that there was someone near. He closed the door carefully and this time he turned the key in the lock.

"Christian killed Seth Dickerson all right," he declared, "but as yet he hasn't lifted the money."

Monsieur Lavalle took out his handkerchief and dabbed his forehead.

"I do not understand, Mr. Billingham," he said, "how you dare take all this for granted."

"Will you explain to me the lights in this room for the last two nights, then?" Mr. Billingham demanded. "Will you tell me why your concierge, when ordered to show me this room, showed me the adjoining one? Will you tell me what all this disorder means but a systematic search, and by whom? Who else has had access to the place? No, sir, Seth Dickerson never shot himself. He lost his life because he drank like a fool and hobnobbed with a ruffian. The sixty thousand francs for which he was murdered are in this room and I'm laying odds," Mr. Billingham concluded, "that I find them within ten minutes."

"It seems to me that someone has searched the place pretty thoroughly already," Monsieur Lavalle remarked grimly. "They have torn the stuffing out of my chairs and ruined my carpet."

"They have searched," Mr. Billingham admitted, "but they didn't know what I know. Seth Dickerson had been a sailor in his younger days and was just as handy with his needle as any woman. They didn't remember that in the lapel of Seth's coat when he was discovered there was a needle. I'm taking a chance, perhaps," Mr. Billingham added, "but here goes!"

He produced a penknife from his pocket, and, moving to the bed, ripped up one of the pink damask curtains which hung from a movable brass rod at its side. He thrust his hand into the space and a beatific smile parted his lips. Suddenly Madelon pointed to the door. They followed the direction of her finger. There had been no sound, but the handle was slowly moving. The door was pressed inwards until the lock was strained. Mr. Billingham withdrew his left hand from the interior of the doubled curtains upon the bed, whilst his right hand went to his hip pocket. He motioned Madelon over to his side, and pointed at the door.

"Open it," he whispered.

Monsieur Lavalle hesitated. The sight of Mr. Billingham's gleaming revolver, however, reassured him. He turned the key. Almost immediately the door opened. Christian, the concierge, passed across the threshold. He seemed to bring with him something of the ghostly silence of the great closed hotel. He said not a word. He looked from one to the other and it was as though a sudden lunacy had seized him. His cheeks were chalk white, his gracious smile, his portly demeanour, his magnificent self-assurance, were all gone. He was like a person stricken with mortal fear. Nevertheless he did not flinch at the sight of Mr. Billingham's revolver.

"I murdered Mr. Dickerson," he confessed. "He told me he had eighty thousand francs. He was a fool to tell me. I murdered him with his own gun. I knew they would bring it in suicide. I have given myself away looking for the money."

"The money was here all right," Mr. Billingham observed.

Christian looked at him steadfastly, yet incuriously, looked at the notes upon the bed, looked at the ripped-up curtain.

"He put them there when I went for the whisky," he muttered, in a dazed tone. "I thought I had searched the room, too!"

Monsieur Lavalle was standing at the bottom of the bed. He seemed unable to take his eyes off his employee's.

"You must have been mad, Christian," he exclaimed.

"I was mad," was the dreary admission, "but eighty thousand francs seemed a great deal against the life of a man who drank, drank, drank until one could see him passing. I was mad. Now I am not!"

He spoke so coldly and so entirely without any trace of agitation that no one had any idea, until too late, of his purpose. He crossed the room, and stepped out on to the balcony. They saw him silhouetted for a moment against the sky, saw his knee upon the balustrade, saw him go over — a shapeless mass, a gleam of white from his face underneath — and Madelon covered her ears with her hands. The two men stood silent. From somewhere beneath, in that deep gulf of blackness, came the sound, faint but unmistakable, of a dull thud. Mr. Billingham thrust his revolver back in his pocket, and moved anxiously to Madelon's side. From below they could hear the sound of shrieking voices and pattering footsteps along the gravel path.

Mr. Billingham, like the vast majority of his compatriots, thoroughly enjoyed the ministrations of an efficient barber. He was just completing his second session of the day in the chair of his favourite operator — a light, before-dinner shave — when he happened to glance towards the door. Mercifully his attendant had completed his offices with the razor and Mr. Billingham's violent start and sudden leaping to his feet were not accompanied by any disastrous results. With a towel still around his neck he made for the door just in time to confront a tall, thin, very obvious fellow-countryman who was on the point of entering.

"For the love of Mike!" Mr. Billingham exclaimed. "Eli Herd! Say, what are you doing here, anyhow?"

If Mr. Billingham's surprise at recognising his friend had been great, Mr. Eli Herd's amazement amounted to consternation. He was a man of sallow complexion who wore gold-rimmed spectacles and might presumably have been the subject of some nervous affection. He shook hands time after time with Mr. Billingham through sheer incapacity to do anything else.

"Well, well!" he faltered at last, with belated eloquence. "Some meeting, this!"

"Nothing wrong with linoleum, I hope," Mr. Billingham demanded anxiously.

"Booming!" was the reassuring reply.

"Then, darn it all, why don't you look glad to see an old friend?" Mr. Billingham insisted.

The newcomer made manifest efforts to regain some measure of poise.

"Say, Samuel," he begged, "take that towel away from your neck, get your hat and come right along with me."

His friend obeyed and the two men strolled off together.

"Well, what's the good news, anyway?" Mr. Billingham enquired.

Mr. Eli Herd was afflicted with another fit of silence. He shook his head. He had apparently arrived at some mournful resolution.

"Sam," he said, "we will sit down together at one of those little tables outside the Café. You will find — another friend — there. You shall know everything!"

"What the hell is there to know?" Mr. Billingham, who was a little irritable that evening, demanded.

"In three minutes," his companion groaned, "you will understand why my meeting you like this has been something of a shock."

In less than three minutes Mr. Billingham understood perfectly. They crossed the Place in front of the Casino and approached the solitary figure seated underneath one of the striped umbrellas reading a newspaper. At their approach she removed the newspaper for a moment from in front of her face and promptly dropped it. If Mr. Eli Herd had been surprised to see Mr. Billingham the lady was even more so.

"Samuel!" she cried breathlessly.

"Harriet!" Mr. Billingham gasped.

The lady rose to her feet. She was tall, good-looking in a severe way, of Junoesque proportions. She was somewhat severely dressed in the costume of an American lady travelling round the world with a suit-case.

"Say, what are you doing here with Eli?" Mr. Billingham continued.

As usual it was the lady who possessed the courage.

"Eli and I," she announced, "are on our honeymoon."

"My God!" Mr. Billingham exclaimed. "What about me?"

"Our divorce," the lady went on, having now fully recovered her composure, "was pronounced last month. You should have had the papers by this time. In your absence there was no defence to the charges which I was compelled to bring against you."

Mr. Billingham looked helplessly around. A waiter, full of unworthy suspicions, assisted him into a chair.

"Let me get the hang of this," he begged. "You've divorced me and married my lawyer here, Eli Herd."

"Samuel, be calm," she enjoined.

"I'm calm enough," Mr. Billingham assured them, his voice gaining strength at every moment. "Why didn't you let me know about it all?"

"We thought it best to keep the matter to ourselves," the late Mrs. Billingham explained. "Eli said that the divorce would cost us less pronounced in your absence. Our separation, Samuel, as you know, was irretrievable and final. I make no excuses for my action. Eli has looked after my interests in your absence with care and discretion. He is in a position, fortunately, to release me from any financial obligations towards you."

"I've cleaned up a little lately in New York," Mr. Eli Herd confided — "over a million on that Ardington deal, you may have read about."

Mr. Billingham looked around for a waiter. Then his face fell.

"Only one way of celebrating an occasion like this," he sighed, "and alas! that don't go with you folk. Still as hot on prohibition as ever, Harriet?"

Mrs. Eli Herd coughed.

"To tell you the truth, Samuel," she confessed, "although my principles remain unchanged, Eli's health during the last few months —— "

"The doctor has been most insistent," the latter intervened.

"At this time of the day," Mrs. Herd continued graciously, "we have slipped into the habit of taking what I believe is known as a 'champagne cocktail.' "

Mr. Billingham fanned himself with one hand and summoned a waiter with the other. His order was given in such terms that within five minutes the suggested beverage was brought. He promptly raised his glass.

"Well, here's how!" he said, a little weakly — "I mean," he went on, correcting himself, "my best wishes to you both."

"Say, I'm glad you're taking this right, Sam," his friend declared with an air of relief. "It didn't seem to me you'd any kick, but still we didn't reckon upon coming upon you like this before you'd heard the news."

"It might have been more considerate to prepare me," Mr. Billingham remarked, "but we'll forget it."

"I'm sure I shall always wish you every happiness, Samuel," the lady went on, looking thoughtfully at her empty glass. "You and I were wholly unsuited to one another. You must forgive my saying that I looked for more principle and a more serious outlook from a man to whom I gave everything. You, from your point of view, required from me greater tendencies towards frivolity than I was able to indulge in. You took no interest whatever, for instance, in my work for the Women's National Association."

"Or in your campaign for prohibition," Mr. Billingham murmured under his breath as he replenished the lady's glass from the bottle which the waiter, according to instructions, had brought. "My dear," he concluded, "let bygones be bygones. I bear neither of you any ill-will. To-night I am engaged, but during your stay here we must arrange a little dinner. Eli and I, too, must have a talk about business."

Temporary addresses were exchanged. Mr. Billingham bade his friends farewell and made his way over to the Hôtel de Paris, where Madelon, seated at one of the little tables upon the Terrace, was awaiting his arrival. She looked at him curiously as he made his excuses, ordered the cocktails and called for the menu.

"I will forgive you for being late," she said, "but tell me who those strange people were to whom you were talking."

Mr. Billingham sat down.

"One of them," he said, "was my wife."

"Your what?" Madelon exclaimed, with a very queer little note in her tone.

"My wife — was a month ago, I mean," Mr. Billingham explained. "She has just divorced me and married my lawyer. They are on their honeymoon."

"And you didn't know?" Madelon gasped.

"Not an idea," was the emphatic rejoinder. "We parted many years ago. We couldn't hit it off together. She is great on good works and all that sort of thing. And now——"

Mr. Billingham broke off. He was looking across the Square. In the distance he could just see Mr. Eli Herd replenishing his companion's glass from the bottle. Suddenly Mr. Billingham began to laugh. He laughed till the tears stood in his eyes. He laughed till Madelon began to laugh too out of sheer sympathy.

"What a ridiculous story!" she exclaimed. "And a ridiculous situation!"

He wiped the tears from his eyes.

"Talk about adventures!" he murmured. . . . "Why, where is your uncle?"

Madelon shook her head a little sadly.

"He is behaving queerly again," she confided.

"Borrowing money?"

"He didn't ask me for any at luncheon time," she admitted. "He was looking dazed, though, and he scarcely spoke a word. I saw him again later in the afternoon coming out of Wedderburn's, the English solicitor's."

"Can't see how he could touch Wedderburn for anything," Mr. Billingham observed thoughtfully.

"He changed his clothes some time ago," Madelon continued, "so when he does come out he will be ready for dinner — and here he is," she added. "Look at him, on the steps."

Mr. Billingham glanced towards the Marquis who was standing with his hands behind his back, gazing out across the gaily lit Square — lit not only with those tree-shaded electric lights, but with the glamour of the moon which was just showing from behind the hills. He stood for a moment like a man whose thoughts had wandered away. Then with the utmost deliberation he descended the steps and came towards them.

"I bet he's got it stiff," Mr. Billingham sighed. "I don't care. He can have what he wants from me to-night."

"Are you really so happy?" Madelon whispered.

"There's one thing — " he began.

Madelon withdrew her hand — not abruptly, even, perhaps, with some reluctance. A *sommelier* had invited Mr. Billingham's attention to the wine-list, and before he had departed the Marquis had entered, nodded to them both and taken his place. He drank the cocktail which was immediately presented to him, holding it for a moment a little away.

"Forgive me," he begged, as he set down his empty glass, "if my toast is a silent one. You will understand it better, perhaps, when I tell you that I have paid my last visit — my last visit as a gambler, that is to say — to that pleasing but grotesque-looking edifice opposite."

"I thought so," Mr. Billingham groaned.

The Marquis leaned a little forward so that the few words he had to say could be heard by both his companions. His elbows rested lightly upon the table. His elegant finger-tips were pressed together.

"My farewell," he confided, "is not of the nature you imagine. To-day has been for me the wonderful day of which I have always dreamed. I entered the Rooms at eleven o'clock this morning with the scanty remains of a mille note in my pocket. At luncheon time I deposited at the *Crédit Lyonnais* the sum of six hundred and fifty thousand francs. In the middle of the afternoon I handed to my solicitor a further sum of four hundred thousand francs. I have in my pocket — forgive the bulge, which I know is most unsightly — a further two hundred and eighty thousand francs."

Mr. Billingham and Madelon exchanged glances, their expressions instantly betraying one common thought. The Marquis smiled tolerantly. From his waistcoat-pocket he produced a banker's receipt to which was attached a receipt signed by Peter Wedderburn for the sum he had mentioned. From the breast-pocket of his coat he withdrew for an instant an enormous pile of mille notes.

"Systems," he declared, "will never win or even hold their own against the inevitable laws of chance. Inspiration may at times make any man a fortune. The only reason why over there they do not fear inspiration is because there is no man who wins by reason of it, who does not lose by afterwards following a false one. To-day I have been inspired. I started with two modest *en pleins*. I found my numbers at every table. I increased my stakes to maximums. I still won. In the 'kitchen,' before lunch, I had broken every record known. I had had forty-two *en pleins* for my three numbers, three-quarters of which were in maximums. Not only the *en pleins,* mind you, but when I saw this great wave of fortune I let myself go. I heaped on the *carrés* and the *chevaux.* Nothing stopped me. At the first sign of slackening off, however, I buttoned up my pockets. I had been playing for two and a half hours only. I lunched without a word to Madelon. I visited the bank. I returned to the *Cercle Privé* with five milles in my pocket and no more. At twenty minutes past four I had won seventeen maximums on *en pleins* alone with many attendant stakes. I was being followed about so that my progress became almost uncomfortable. For years they will talk of my fortune. The banks were closed, so I saw my friend Mr. Wedderburn, the lawyer and deposited my money with him. Thereupon I changed my ciothes and I returned to the Casino with five milles. I lost four and was preparing to leave. With the last mille I once more strucl that amazing streak of luck. *En plein* followed *en plein.* Fourteen, for instance — on which I had the maximum with all the *carrés* and *chevaux,* the *transversal* and the middle column — turned up fou₁ times following. You could have heard the roa₁ from the centre table in the 'kitchen' outside in the Square. People left off playing at every table to see what was happening. Twenty minutes ago I lost three times following. I smiled. So often I have seen these huge winnings returned to where they came from. I could see it in the faces of the croupiers. I could feel it in the atmosphere. I smiled. I buttoned up my pockets. I lounged outside. I looked around at this beautiful scene. I strolled across here. I dine. Roulette with me is finished."

"This," Mr. Billingham declared solemnly, "is the most amazing evening I have ever known."

The Marquis talked on. He discussed his winnings calmly without the least trace of excitement.

"I have always felt this in my blood," he declared. "It is why I have been so persistent. But I will tell you a strange thing. My great fortune has done this for me. I am no longer a gambler. At the conclusion of our dinner this evening I am telegraphing to Paris to my old friend, General Hernais, who has three times lately begged me to share his apartment and his very pleasant life in Paris. I am in a position now to do so. I regret very much, my friend Billingham," he added, "to break up so our pleasant little companionship, but you will, I know, not blame me. For you, my dear Madelon," he concluded, "I shall make whatever arrangements appeal to you most strongly. I need not say that you will share to the fullest extent in my good fortune."

Madelon squeezed his hand.

"You are a dear, Uncle," she said, a little vaguely. "I cannot tell you how glad I am."

"Confessions and new resolutions seem to be in the fashion," Mr. Billingham observed. "I will make one. You do not know, Marquis, although your niece does, that I have been married all these months of our acquaintance."

The Marquis was evidently disturbed. Mr. Billingham, however, continued without giving him an opportunity for speech.

"My wife," he went on, "has divorced me. We have not lived together for many years. Our temperaments were entirely different. Our marriage was a mistake and my freedom is very welcome — especially as my late wife has found all the happiness she desires with another man. Futhermore, my position as an adventurer has been to a certain extent a fraud. All the things which go with adventures are in my blood and part of my life, but I sold out my business a few months before I came here for a cash sum of over two million dollars and I still have an interest in the firm."

"More than once I suspected it," the Marquis admitted, after a breathless pause. "You had never the appearance of a poor man, my friend Billingham."

Madelon's eyes were fixed upon her plate. For some reason or another Mr. Billingham's confession had seemed to be lacking in interest to her. Presently the Marquis took his departure. Mr. Billingham leaned across the table.

"Madelon," he said, a little hoarsely.

She raised her eyes and looked at him.

"It seems our partnership of three must come to an end," he continued. "Would you — would it be possible — to start a partnership of two?"

The surroundings were very wonderful, even inspiring. The moon now was clear of the hills and the faintest of breezes brought the perfume of the flowers from the gardens, and even of the orange blossoms from beyond, across the Square. The orchestra was playing in the Café. It was all very beautiful, but the most beautiful thing that Mr. Billingham had ever seen in his life was the strange softness in Madelon's eyes and the little quiver of her lips.

"Couldn't we have coffee in your *salon* and then walk along the Terrace and talk about it?" she whispered.

THE END